'Arditti is a literary Hogarth, savaging modern
England on many levels. An astonishingly
intelligent, funny and touching book'
   *The Scotsman*

'Timely, relevant and opportune . . . gripping and
vivid . . . provocative and stimulating. With
scrupulous detail, Michael Arditti describes the
twists and turns in a saga which is a fascinating
blend of legal manoeuvre, personal rancour and
genuine love. A novel of tension and intrigue'
   *Morning Star*

'A passionate case for the homosexual's right to love
and be loved. Arditti is unusually deft in his
manipulation of the way the narrative unfolds'
   *Independent*

'Caustically funny . . . a wonderful and completely
unsentimental evocation of a small girl. Arditti
twists and wrests language like a craftsman'
   *Yorkshire Post*

'Arditti has skilfully crafted a compelling novel and
has created in Leo a charming likeable hero. The
scenes with Leo and Pagan are both funny and
touching'   *Time Out*

'Sardonic wit and keen observation. Emotionally
convincing . . . rich in detail
   *Times Literary Supplement*

'A timely plea for men to be allowed greater
involvement in the upbringing of their children.
The novel raises many uncomfortable questions.
A *Kramer versus Kramer* for the nineties'   *Tatler*

'A compulsive, well-written story that poses
questions about who is best qualified to bring up a
child'
   *Good Housekeeping* (Book of the Month)

# Pagan and Her Parents

Michael Arditti was born in Cheshire
and lives in London. He is also the author
of *The Celibate*.

# Pagan and her Parents

## Michael Arditti

Minerva

**A Minerva Paperback**
PAGAN AND HER PARENTS

First published in Great Britain 1996
by Sinclair-Stevenson
This Minerva edition published 1997
by Mandarin Paperbacks
an imprint of Reed International Books Limited
Michelin House, 81 Fulham Road, London SW3 6RB
and Auckland, Melbourne, Singapore and Toronto
www. minervabooks.com

Copyright © 1996 by Michael Arditti
The author has asserted his moral rights

A CIP catalogue record for this title
is available from the British Library
ISBN 0 7493 9537 0

Typeset in Trump Mediaeval
by Deltatype Ltd, Ellesmere Port, Cheshire
Printed and bound in Great Britain
by Cox & Wyman Ltd, Reading, Berkshire

For my mother

# One

First Affidavit of Leonard Peter Young
on behalf of the Respondent
Sworn the 25th day of March 1992

In the Brighton County Court                    Case No. 7296

In the matter of Pagan Mulliner

And in the matter of the Children's Act 1989


Between

    Muriel Ellen Mulliner &

    Edgar Atkins Mulliner                    APPLICANTS

and

    Leonard Peter Young                    RESPONDENT


I, LEONARD PETER YOUNG, Writer and Broadcaster, of 64 Addison Avenue, London W11, MAKE OATH and say as follows:–

1. I am the respondent in this matter and I have read what purports to be a true copy of the Affidavit sworn by the Applicants on the 12th day of February 1992 and filed herein. I am 37 years old and am the guardian of Pagan Mulliner (herinafter referred to as Pagan).

2. I accept that paragraph 2 of the Applicants' Affidavit is true. I began living with Candida Mulliner in Cambridge in the autumn of 1974 and continued to do so up until her death in November of last year.

3. I accept that paragraph 3 of the Applicants' Affidavit is true.

4. I deny the allegations of inadequacy contained in paragraph 4 of the Applicants' Affidavit and assert that I am fully able to care for Pagan.

5. As to the Applicants' own relationship with Candida, I would

3

say that their account of the matter in paragraph 5 of their Affidavit is distorted and I would give my own account of it as follows:–

a. Candida informed me of her antipathy to the Applicants, her adopted parents, at our first encounter in Italy in the summer of 1973. It is my belief that her obsessive search for her natural parents sprang entirely from this.

b. It is utterly untrue that I alienated Candida from the Applicants. On the contrary, for years I urged a reconciliation and, on several occasions before her death, suggested that she write to them.

c. My own relationship with my parents is an excellent one; I am in regular contact with my mother, who regards Pagan as a granddaughter.

d. The poster in the Maid's Causeway kitchen was Candida's and not mine.

e. I was unaware of the incident said to have occurred on July 30th 1986; but, in view of the Applicants' response to Candida's pregnancy, it is no surprise to learn that she gave orders for her mother to be refused entry to the maternity ward.

6. As to the assertions in paragraph 6 of the Applicants' Affidavit, I would like to comment as follows:–

a. Although my relationship with Candida Mulliner was not a conventional one, it was a perfectly natural one. We enjoyed a loving friendship for over eighteen years, which was the focus of both our lives. It was never exclusive and allowed for the existence of other friendships and other loves.

b. Candida saw sexuality as a means of communication not confinement. She was faithful but not monogamous. She had several lovers at the time of Pagan's conception and resolutely refused to name the father; I sometimes doubt whether she knew.

c. I have never claimed that Pagan was my daughter by birth. To me the issue is immaterial. Fatherhood is in the love, not the blood.

7. As to the assertion in paragraph 7 of the Applicants' Affidavit that they are best equipped to care for Pagan, I would like:–

a. to repeat my paragraph 6c.

b. to refer to Candida Mulliner's express wish in both her sworn statement of 11th September 1988, exhibited to this Affidavit and marked LPY 1, and in her last will and testament, exhibited to this Affidavit and marked LPY 2, in which she asserts that, in the event

4

of her death, the Applicants should have no access to her daughter.

8. I dispute the assertion in paragraph 8 of the Applicants' Affidavit that, as a man, I am unfit to bring up a girl, and ask whether they would have made such a claim in the case of a biological father. I would add that:–

a. I employ a full-time nanny, Susan Redding, who has lived with us since August 1989. Her relationship with both Pagan and myself is excellent. She has declared her intention to continue in the position for the foreseeable future.

b. Pagan is a lively, intelligent girl with many interests. Since last autumn she has been attending school in Cottesmore Gardens, where her form teacher describes her as 'imaginative, eager to learn, happy in herself and with others'. She is developing a wide social circle, both among her schoolmates and the children of our friends. She goes to riding and ballet classes in the neighbourhood and takes leading rein lessons on Saturday mornings in Hyde Park; these would be seriously disrupted were she to move to Hove.

c. She will not lack for female influence. We have many close women friends who have pledged their help and support.

d. She is devoted to her cat, Trouble, to which the Applicant expressed a marked aversion during her visit on January 22nd of this year. Her exact words were 'I don't know why children need pets; dolls are so much cleaner'.

e. If the mother's influence is paramount, how does the Applicant explain the breakdown of her relationship with her own daughter?

9a. As to paragraph 9a of the Applicants' Affidavit, I refute the suggestion that Pagan is in any way miserable. I do however believe that some disturbance in her behaviour is only to be expected after the recent death of her mother. The particular problems on January 22nd were entirely due to her reluctance to see the Applicants.

b. As to Paragraph 9b of the Applicants' Affidavit, I repeat my paragraph 9a and would add that the tension between Pagan and myself noted on January 22nd reflected her fury at my insistence that she meet the Applicants, towards whom she has inherited her mother's hostility.

c. As to Paragraph 9c of the Applicants' Affidavit, I can only suppose that this is a wilful misinterpretation. Pagan was referring to my cooking on a spit, not in spit.

10. I deny the Applicants' assertion that it is not in Pagan's best interests to remain with me. On the contrary, I have been the one constant factor in her life. From the start, I took charge of her when her mother was on photographic assignments abroad; indeed, it was a standing joke among our friends that 'I was left holding the baby'. I have since played a major role in her upbringing and education. I have taken her on several foreign holidays. I have been her father in all but name.

a. During the extended and highly distressing period of her mother's final illness, it was I who cared for her on a daily basis. I ensured that her world stayed secure in the face of her mother's slow decay. I respected Candida's wish to remain at home, both for her own sake and to minimise the disturbance to Pagan. I made sense of her fading senses. I interpreted the basic sentences that she printed out on her screen. More recently, I interpreted her death.

11. I believe that to remove Pagan from my care would cause her incalculable distress and confusion. It would increase her sense of loss after the death of her mother. Besides which, I consider that I am better placed than the Applicants to attend to her emotional, educational and material needs. Despite its pressures, my contract with the BBC allows me considerable latitude; my hours are flexible and my summers free. I would urge therefore that she remain with me. If, however, the Court is to grant residence to the Applicants, I would ask to have regular contact so that I can continue to play a part in her life.

Sworn by the above-named
Leonard Peter Young,

At 12 Field Court,
Grays Inn,
London WC1R 5EN.

This 25th day of March 1992
Before me,

Arthur Ernest Duff.
Solicitor/Commissioner for Oaths

# 1

I know now why coffins seem small; it is because people are so much larger than their bodies. When we walk into a room, we don't just inhabit a space, we change it all around us. And you changed more than a space; you changed my life.

First you changed my name. 'Leonard,' you said dubiously. . . . 'Yes, but my friends call me Lenny.' And you no longer bothered to hide your distaste. 'Leo,' you said triumphantly; 'we'll call you Leo.' And I was as supine as a baby at a christening. Leo: it fitted me; Leo: it flattered me . . . a cross between a pop star and a pope.

They pack you away like a ventriloquist's dummy . . . the same top-heavy torso, the same token legs. I watch the undertaker leaning over you like a children's magician: his black coat a treasure-trove of tricks and props. I wait for him to slide out a saw, to slit open the wood and for you to spring up, head and feet at either end: a confusion, an optical illusion, but alive.

He wills me forward; the lid looms ominously; I know that I am supposed to take my leave. I rage at their earth-bound souls . . . their grave-bound assumptions. I can never take my leave of you; these words are the proof. I gaze inside and search in vain for an identifiable expression – the puckered lip of paradox, the furrowed brow of perversity – your face was only real in the turbulence of emotion; it is not one that I recognise in repose.

They lift the lid and I am seized with panic.

'Not yet!' I bend to adjust a perfectly set hair. I need to rescue your face from a photographic memory, the frozen images of the future; I refuse to become dependent on other men's eyes.

They leave; the house is silent. I yearn for God and the consolations of childhood; but I am lost in an adult black hole. My thoughts are torn between grief and grievance. Ours was a lifelong commitment. I want to grow old with you gratefully, disgracefully, checking each other for signs of senility as we once did for secrets of love. I want us to exit together in a nursing-home blaze, from the flames of the hundred candles on our joint birthday cake. You have no right to die and leave me alone.

But I am not alone; I have Pagan . . . not the consolations of childhood but of one precious child. I have to ease her around your death as I tried to do around your illness . . . a mother who could not hold her close, a mother who could not change her clothes, a mother at the mercy of her mutineering muscles, who could move nothing unaided but her bowels. You were at least spared the foulest indignity and we the cruellest irony of seeing your daughter being trained on the potty while you were forced to wear pads.

She never knew you otherwise. She never saw you armed for an assignment, bags of equipment stretched across your back, so heavy that we supposed that the initial pains in your legs were a direct result of photographer's shoulder, as much of an occupational hazard as housemaid's knee. But then came the numb thumb and the dropped vase and the jerking and the months of misdiagnosis when trapped nerves were superceded by degeneration of the spine and even the false hope of multiple sclerosis; as your chin was collared and your head strapped, which gave you the prospect – and the prospects – of a prisoner in an electric chair.

I scoured the BBC library, borrowed books and burrowed into reports. I re-ran old programmes and lobbied for new. I spoke to experts and ordered equipment until your bedroom resembled a control-room, with every computerised aid that could be operated first with a nod of the head and then with the flick of an eye. I surrounded you with gadgets the way that lovers had showered you with gifts.

And communication became reduced to a few hundred practical phrases that flashed across your screen; the parameters of your life defined by a soft-ware firm in Ohio. And with the same caring cruelty that offers black mastectomy patients white prostheses, they gave you a voice like an overemphatic Swede.

For me that was the hardest loss: that voice, with its assumed huskiness that had become second nature – if I do have bedroom eyes, then you had a bedroom voice – fighting for intelligibility, with vowels white with pain. If I live to be a hundred and I blow out all the candles, alone and afraid, I shall never forget your wail of despair when you first dropped Pagan . . . the world fallen through your fingers and staring up in shock on the floor. And I stood, locked in horror, unable to reassure you or to rescue her.

She was two years old when the sounds began to muffle and you swallowed your words when you could no longer swallow anything else. How she laughed as you were reduced to a diet of baby foods just as she began to eat everything . . . except for pizza, which makes her think of blood.

How much does she understand . . . ? For that matter, how much do I? I see her playing quietly at the foot of your bed, until the telephone rings, and she grabs it and lifts it to your ear and I feel your frustration as she holds it upside down or too far away. I see her wipe away the spittle which pours onto your chin, as though every breath were an epileptic stutter; and I see you torn between rage at your illness and joy in your nurse. I see her bewilderment as your muscles decay and dwindle to the flutter of an eyelid. Then I see her fear, as your emotions veer out of control even more cruelly than your body and you howl with laughter as she comes to you holding a cut finger, until she runs from the room screaming in incomprehension. And that is when I know that you want to die.

Now she stands before me, back from three days staying with Stephanie. I ask if she enjoyed herself.

'I'm not going again. Stephanie has to go to bed when she's not sleepy and her mummy won't even let us talk. Do you think that's when bad dreams come – when you go to bed before you're sleepy?'

'No. They're not that clever.'

'I do. And she kept telling us not to make a noise because it wasn't the right time to play and she wouldn't say why. I think people should say why they say something, don't you?'

My first and only line of defence is breached and a lifetime of euphemism flounders on the floor.

'And she kept looking at me like I was ill or it was the last day of the holidays. I don't want to go back.'

She leaps into the house. Consuela stands in the hall with her best Ash Wednesday face and gathers her into the apron that she says smells of onions and heat. She wriggles free and runs into your bedroom and stares at the whiteness of it all: the sheets and blankets and flowers all removed and the mattress ominously airing on the bed.

'Where's Mummy?' she asks as if I am concealing you . . . as if your illness were just a game and 'let's pretend' has been superceded by hide-and-seek.

I hold her tight and try to explain what has happened. . . . You said that your parents told you that you were adopted at three. I wonder if it were some clumsiness of expression that made you hate them for ever more. I desperately try to find words that will make sense; words that are clear but not cruel. I will my tongue to treacle. We should build up to death: budgies, ponies, grandparents, not mothers . . . mothers are a lesson for book four. What can she know of loss? She has never even known a new nanny. In her world, time is measured in trips and treats and presents, and bereavement was her first day at school.

I weigh my words; but they are crushing her. Death is in her face, her hair, her clothes. She looks at me as if pleading for mercy from a stranger. 'Does it mean I won't ever see Mummy again?'

'Not face to face, no. But she'll always be with us.'

'Where?'

'In our thoughts . . . in our hearts.'

She stands confused. 'But that's nowhere.'

'It's a different way of looking.'

'Does it mean I'll be an orphan?'

I wonder where she has heard the word. 'I know it's hard, darling, but we must think of Mummy. She was so unhappy lying in bed all day. She was in such pain. We must be glad it's been taken away.'

10

'But she said I did that by rubbing her feet.'

'I know.'

'She said.'

'I know.'

'If I rubbed harder. Harder and harder and harder.'

'Would you like a hug?'

She shakes her head and walks into the playroom. She lifts the flap of the Wendy house and steps inside. I stand outside, as isolated as any next-door neighbour. My exclusion frightens me. I feel that she has become a stranger, no longer the baby with basic needs or the infant as predictable as a nursery rhyme, but a growing girl with her own window on the world. I look through the window of the Wendy house; but the opaque plastic merely reflects my own face. I hear her repeating distinctly 'I must be brave; I must be brave'.

Her words are my challenge; her life is my charge. What greater gift can anyone give than a child? What do you want for her? To be herself, to be happy . . . too obvious, too ordinary; or do you want for her what you despised for yourself? To be loved, to be fulfilled, to be famous, to be outrageous? There are so many possibilities. To have so many possibilities; perhaps we should settle for that? If we had only had more time to talk; but it was so hard for you communicating by computer, flicking out words for me to fill out into sentences. And yet your reluctance was more than mechanical. Was it too painful to contemplate giving up Pagan; or did you simply have faith in me?

Why did you choose me? What did you see in me? A good friend, yes; but a good father? If only the two were the same. When you told me you were pregnant, I thought that our life together was ended, convention would take over and you would disappear, if not to Chez Nous, at least to Sans Moi; that the homing or the nesting or the brooding instinct would come into play and I would be left out in the cold. You amazed me by your insistence that nothing should change: that I should be Pagan's father, not in name, no, that would be cheating, but in everything else.

I was flattered then; just as I am frightened now. And it is you who have sown the doubts. Why, when you spent so long trying to trace your natural parents, did you always refuse to identify Pagan's father? If your adopted father was a sham, why should her surrogate one be any less so? I fail to understand why you made it such a secret; we had no secrets – no other secrets – especially about men. Who could be that shameful? I wonder, if I search through your papers, will I come up with an Identikit picture? This one's love letters; that one's recriminations; another one's return to his wife. I have to know, if not for myself then for Pagan. How else can she disprove your equation of fatherhood and fate?

Everything would be so much easier if she were my daughter . . . if we could have made the lie last as long as an erection. I often wonder what would have happened if things had been different that first day; if I had taken my cue from Casanova in his native city. Would we have stayed together all this time? I expected you to make a joke of me . . . I was still living in a world of schoolboys and bikesheds. But it was the others you made fun of, with their flashy, fleshy self-importance. My gaucheness seemed to touch a nerve in you. It was failure which guaranteed my success.

Next year will be our twentieth anniversary . . . will be? would be – no comfort is as cold as a pen's. I planned to take you back, to retrace our steps, to recapture our youth. I see your curled lip: 'Wouldn't it be more fun to capture someone else's?' But your eyes know the answer. Ours was a gilded generation. The gold may have worn thin, like the gilt on the front of the Ca' d'oro, but we can still see its richness in the dazzle of the Venetian sun. We can gaze from the Rialto and smile.

I see you through the mists of memory . . . I see you through the mists of Venice, as we stand in a dimly lit sacristy, peering at an undistinguished Virgin and Child.

'It's not very good, is it?'

I look round, startled by the interruption.

'It's attributed to Rubens.'

'Wishful thinking.'

'Still, what does it matter?' I remember that I am on route to university, where school rules will be subsumed by subjectivity. 'What counts is how you feel.'

'Oh it matters. If you don't know where something comes from, you can never hope to understand it.'

I am troubled by your vehemence.

12

'So, why are you keen on Rubens? The nudes?'

I am thrilled that a girl can ask me such a question.

'Not at all. I find them oppressive: all that too, too solid flesh.' You fail to respond; and the quotation hangs like a fart in the air.

'The patron saint of the fuller figure.'

'Oh no. It wasn't that he found fat women more attractive, simply that the acreage of flesh gave him more scope to experiment with light.'

'Oh dear, my last illusion shattered.'

'You're not fat,' I say, picturing my mother's middle-aged waist-line.

'I know.' You move away to examine some stucco cherubs who appear to be laughing at my unease.

I cannot tell if it marks the end of the conversation. I suddenly need to know you better. 'Are you an artist?' I toss out my greatest compliment.

'God, no.' You explain that you are on a pre-university course in Venice and Florence and that you will be going up to Cambridge in the autumn. I reply that I am on an Easter tour with the Trelawnyd choir and that I will be going up to Cambridge in the autumn. At which you laugh and say that we might have been there for three years and our paths not have crossed, and yet here we meet in Santa Maria Zobenigo. I am struck by the thought that my life will never be as simple again.

We find a café. You smile as I order chocolate cake; I grimace as I remember that savouries are more sophisticated . . . and you are by far the most sophisticated girl that I have ever met. I know that if I don't leave at once, I will be late for the choir; but I want you to see me as an individual and not as part of a group. For the first time I feel an individual . . . for the first time I am being irresponsible; and I wonder if they are the same. Then, when you ask if I want to go back to your *pensione*, as casually as you ordered a *cappuccino*, I say yes.

I never knew that fear could be so exciting; I am usually sick with nerves before I sing. Now here I am, about to attempt my first performance in a new register, and the agony is transmuted into energy. You lead me through overhung streets; Venice seems a city of hidden entrances and dead ends. We emerge at the grand canal and wait for a

13

*vaporetto*. I suggest a gondola; romance makes me feel rich. We step in gingerly and squeeze into the seat. I put my arm behind your shoulders but keep an inch away from the skin. The gondolier is a distraction. As I pluck up the courage to kiss you, he signals approval with his pole.

The light of the room – is it brighter in retrospect? – streams across your skin as you strip off your clothes, while I shrug off mine like a snake's dead skin. As I stare at the crumpled pile, I hear my mother's voice, 'Clothes don't grow on trees', and I suppress the urge to fold them; I see my mother's face and I suppress the urge to scream. I am in Venice to sing, to send postcards and to look at churches. It was foreign frauds that she warned me against, not English sirens. You lure me towards the rocks . . . you plump the pillows. It is half-past three; I am in bed and I am not ill. It is half-past three; I am in bed and I am a man.

'You're wearing your knickers,' you say; and I thrill to the image. Knickers are gym-slips, hockey-sticks and domestic science, filled with the frisson of the fetish; underpants are coarse, functional, stained with shame. And yet, as I fondle your breasts, I am sexually charged but not attracted. My penis curls like a comma, when it should rise in exclamation. It is the illicitness that excites me, which I try to translate into desire.

Sensing my inexperience, you guide me technically, too technically, and I rue the day that I gave up biology in favour of German. I am caught in a confusion of gender far greater than that between masculine and feminine nouns. What use is knowing der, die, dum when I am struck dumb by the lips of a vulva? Is it any wonder that English words are neuter? Am I a neuter or simply cold?

'Relax,' you say; 'let me help you.'

'It's my first time,' I say, in a blatant appeal for sympathy.

'What have you been doing all these years?' . . . I'm only seventeen, I want to reply, but nibble at your nipple to escape the need. I nuzzle in a fold of your flesh before venturing under pressure from your hands and my own expectations into the no-man's land between your legs.

I sniff tentatively and detect a faint aroma of gentleman's relish. The skin is as soft as a baby's but feels slightly chapped. I glimpse myself nose down, tongue out, and an image floods my brain of a hog rooting for truffles. I chuckle, which you take as a sign of pleasure; I am relieved. 'Your first time,' you coo and cradle my head. I know how easily I could play on your maternal instincts; but I am determined to avoid the trap.

My sex is still inert. My brow is wet; my hair is matted. All my blood is rushing to my head, which I will down to my middle. Has this happened to you before? Is it a copulational hazard? I long to ask about your previous experience and turn the coition into conversation. I want the intimacy without the indignity. I want painless, deathless love.

I connect with you, but inadvertently, as though my umbrella were caught in the loop of your coat. I thrust indiscriminately, desperately trying to feel something besides strain. The only naked women I have seen before were playing tennis in the pages of a naturist magazine; their fresh-faced smiles showed no more evidence of emotion than their air-brushed bodies did of sex. My penis pounds like a piston; the repetition is becoming wearing. I worry that I am sweating on your neck.

I have heard that making love is equivalent to playing two sets of tennis; I can well believe it. I have an ache in every muscle and incipient cramp in my back. How long is this supposed to last? Is it a hundred-yard sprint or a marathon? Is a quick spurt a sign of passion, or is a measured pace a sign of power? Please don't hold this against me. I want to see you again, but next time in clothes.

I slip out of you and fall back. You lean over me and kiss me. You seem happy enough and I wonder if I have been worrying unduly. You put your hands between your legs.

'You didn't come,' you say. I know what you mean; although I have never before heard the expression.

'I tried to. It wasn't you,' I say lamely.

'I should think not.' You hand me some grappa which burns my throat.

'I'm afraid men can't fake orgasm.'

'That's a small consolation. They fake almost everything else.'

At another time I would find that witty, but now I am just conscious of the future opening up in front of me like a

15

return to the past. I am a boy again, back in my own skin. I am a snake condemned to slide on my belly. I catch sight of my underpants and yearn to sneak them on.

'I knew it wouldn't work from the moment in the café when you said that your favourite artist was Michelangelo.' I am startled; I imagine Michelangelo to be the most uncontroversial choice, a universal genius like Tolstoy or Bach. But I have yet to learn your theories of 'fag' art. In years to come, 'he likes Michelangelo' will be our coded shorthand, our own 'friend of Dorothy'; the sculptor's marble breasts no more convincing than a drag queen's padded bra. But, for now, *The Agony and the Ecstasy* is showing in a double-bill with *The Wizard of Oz*.

'It has nothing to do with art. It's just that the chemistry wasn't right.'

'It wasn't the chemistry but the biology.'

I don't know . . . I don't want to know what you mean. I put on my pants for protection. I want to go and sing: to lose myself in a madrigal's six-part harmony, not this atonal duet.

'You're not angry with me?' you say, shifting the sheet, making no attempt at modesty. 'I like you so much; I felt at once we could be friends.'

'I'm not queer,' I insist.

'What does it matter?'

'It matters to me.' I'm ready to pull off my pants and prove it to you; my anger is making me hard. 'If you thought that I wasn't interested, why did you suggest it? It was your idea not mine.'

'Because I need a friend. And I somehow knew you were the one. We had to get this over with, or else it would have stood in the way. We'd always be wondering "could we? should we?" There'd be too many barriers between us. And I don't believe in barriers . . . of any sort.'

'I've had girlfriends.'

'You said I was the first.'

'The first in bed. There are other things to do.'

'And we shall do them all. What's the problem? Homosex is far superior to boring old heterosex. Look at Plato; look at the Greeks. . . .' You beguile me with a virile ideal that owes more to Mount Olympus than to Hampstead

16

Heath. 'Are you saying you've never had sex with another man?'

'Yes,' I lie, but honestly . . . it was not a man; it was a mouth.

'I'll introduce you to my friend Robin' . . . a calling card that will be engraved on my heart. I strive to understand why you take such an interest. I thought that women despised men who failed to respond to them sexually; but with you it is quite the opposite . . . an admission of attraction is the quickest route to your scorn.

At first I wonder if you are a lesbian.

'God, no! Women are such cows in every way. Flabby minds and flabby bodies. Udders and underwear. Parturition.'

I wish that I could establish the source of your self-disgust. Mine lies in the white-washed walls of a Methodist chapel; mine lies in the stale stranglehold of a rugby scrum; mine lies in a world of dreary Saturdays and dry Sundays: the petty paternalism of North Wales. But you have the liberty of the South of England. You have poetry and eccentricity and tolerance and travel. I fail to identify the worm in your bud.

Liberty bred liberality. 'I'm such a slut,' you used to say, 'such a slut.' And I never knew whether it was to punish yourself or men or other women. Edward told me, in a confession I never sought, that your favourite ruse was to play dead: to lie motionless – emotionless – while he assaulted you like a soldier with a bayonet. At first he found the power exciting, but then he found it daunting. He felt that he could have killed you and you would have maintained the same distant smile. . . . But you always said that he was a liar; and it suited me to take your word.

However much your sexuality threatened him, it reassured me. I had the intimacy without the intrusion; I was spared the mechanics. My chaste cheeks were suffused with a post-coital glow. We outwitted the world; we wrote our own scenario. You were my public private life; I had no need to confront my own disgust or anyone else's. . . . I think it wise not to speculate as to why you found it equally important, why you desired a love uncompromised by the body, as we lay together on top of the sheets like an effigy on a medieval tomb.

17

But death is no longer set in such serene statuary. And I walk with Pagan up the path to the crematorium. With her chestnut hair swept back in a tortoise-shell band, her black velvet cape hiding a grey check dress, her socks unruffled, her shoes unscuffed, she might be making her way to a party, if it were not for the bunch of weeping lilies in her hand. She grips my hand, and offends me by skipping . . . until I realise that she is skirting the cracks in the stone and the unrealised dangers underneath.

The undertakers meet us on the steps and take us into the chapel, as austere as a prison waiting room – I think of Lewis – as though the absence of religion entails an absence of art. It smells of official disapproval, like the teacher at Pagan's play group: why not give your daughter a Christian name . . . ? Why not give her mother a Christian funeral . . . ? You should be buried in a Temple of Love or a Temple of the Muses, under frescoes of Venus or murals of Mount Parnassus. But the only picture is a Constable landscape, which fails to hide an ancient dust patch; and the sound system stutters with a scratchy recording of Delibes.

Your coffin is on its bier. I look at Pagan. She sits quietly beside me, willing a smell out of the lilies. She refuses to lift her eyes. The seats are filling behind us. I feel the cold breath of condolence on my shoulder; I shake its clammy hand. The doors close and I recognise my cue to move to the lectern. For, in the absence of any cleric, I must guide the proceedings myself. Even the undertakers have disappeared, after showing me where to find the button. I am overwhelmed by the task. I want to disobey orders and declare myself agnostic, to run to another chapel and waylay a vicar. I want to escape the setting and the symbolism. I feel like a medieval cardinal burning a witch.

I take hold of myself and the lectern. I stare into the room and catch sight of friends and colleagues, all trying to register their presence without intruding on my grief. I start to speak but my eyes are transfixed by the button. I lose my thread; I find my notes; I lose my voice. I can only think of the rollers sticking, the curtains catching, the fire going out. I escape into the trivia of public appearances; I declare this supermarket open . . . this life at an end.

Your coffin slides forward with perfect equipoise and

slips behind the curtains. We strain to imagine the other side like condemned schoolboys outside the Headmaster's study. I drag my feet down the steps and return to my seat where Pagan is turning the pages of a book. I am torn between relief and revulsion at her detachment.

'Can we go home now?' she asks.

'Let's just sit here for a minute and think about Mummy.'

'What about her?'

'Anything you want.'

'Her mummy died when she was younger than me.'

'Who told you that?'

'Mummy. That's why she was adopted. Will I be adopted?'

'You have me.'

The service is over; the seats are hard; but no one stirs, as if this minor discomfort were itself a little death. I judge that it is time to lead the way out. We stand in the porch soaking up sympathy. I ask Susan to take Pagan home. I want to spare her the burden of adult inarticulacy; but she insists on staying and grips my hand, the trickle of sweat the only obstacle between us. As Melissa Franklin tells me in ponderous French that I was wrong to let her come, she takes refuge behind my legs.

The last cheek brushed, the last hand shaken, I walk to the office and wait for them to produce your ashes. I am startled by the residue of heat in the box. It is the ultimate indignity: this mockery of warmth. We return to the car; Pagan and Susan sit in the back with you in front beside me . . . the death seat I used to call it as a child. I try not to wonder whether the ashes are all yours; and yet if hospitals can make mistakes with new-born babies. . . . So what do I suggest: some parody of a paternity test? I slam on the breaks at the lights.

We reach home. Consuela is preparing lunch. Laura has declared open house in Hampstead. I can hear your response 'Just like her to push herself forward'; but I was grateful that she took the pressure off me. I have promised to go up there after seeing to Pagan.

'You won't leave me?' she asks, as she toys with Consuela's tortilla. . . . I think that she is growing suspicious at being served so much of her favourite food.

19

'What?'

'You won't go away and leave me like Mummy?'

'Mummy didn't leave you, my darling,' I struggle to explain. 'Mummy would never leave you. She had no choice; she was very ill.'

'Why?' she asks. 'Why? Why?'

And I try to bury her fears in my chest.

'I want Mummy,' she cries, all semblance of bravery lost.

'You mustn't cry,' I say, 'or you'll make me cry too. Then where will we be?' But it is too late and my eyes start to water. She looks at me, aghast, as the voice of authority cracks and its face crumbles.

'Stop it!' she says, smacking my arm as if I were her wetting doll. 'Grown-ups don't cry.'

'It's just that I miss Mummy too.'

'Naughty Leo,' she says and goes on smacking, reassuring me by the force of her hands. 'You mustn't.'

'Silly Leo; I know. I'm here to look after you.'

'And I'm looking after you too. Mummy told me.'

'Really?' I wonder whether you did; and, if so, how her rudimentary reading picked up the phrase on the screen.

'So we'll both have to look after each other,' she says, sharing my hankie; 'and we'll take it in turns to cry.'

# 2

'Look at the pineapples,' Pagan giggles, as we approach the gates which once seemed monumentally disdainful and are now dilapidated and obscure.

'They're hundreds of years old.'

'Older than you?'

'Much older.'

'Older than Miss Jennings?'

'Older than Miss Jennings.'

'Older even than the Queen?'

'Older than anyone who's alive today. They were built about the same time as St Paul's Cathedral. Sir Christopher Wren wanted to put a pineapple on top of that too.'

'Why?'

Why? the thinking child's constant question: the first crack in the parental façade. The reason why is because . . .

'I don't know.'

'You should.'

'I know. When we go home, I'll ask someone.' Was it a recent discovery: the seventeenth-century equivalent of the kiwi fruit? I tease my mind with trivia to keep it on track.

It veers alarmingly at the sight of the gatehouse. This was a dream cottage . . . your dream cottage where, you declare with a mixture of humour and desperation, 'I'll live when you and Robin move into the hall, like a dog curled up at the foot of a bed. We'll stick up a sign Beware of the Spinster.' But the danger now speaks for itself. Stalks shooting up around the walls seem to have sucked the plaster from the brickwork. Rooms are gutted and gutters hang loose. Slabs and slates lie scattered in the garden. The undergrowth has turned into overgrowth. The setting is as abandoned as the dream.

The car jolts and I look guiltily at the dashboard. I fear that my mission will be pre-empted and you will be scattered all over the floor.

'The ground's grumbling,' Pagan exclaims as we trundle over a cattle grid.

'It's to stop cows going out into the road.'

'What about children?'

'They know better.'

'No, what if they fall through it?'

'They couldn't.'

'Or twist their ankles and break their legs and lie there until a car runs them over or a lorry delivering food and squashes them until they're completely flat and dead.'

'Pagan, darling, this is a private road, a quiet place. There's no danger.'

'People should take care when there are children. They're small. They can't see.' Her vehemence is more fitting to a mother than a child. I watch with unease as she squirms in her seatbelt and kicks her heels against the dashboard . . . she has not made the connection. Once again I question my judgement. In Tibet they place a three-year-old child in front of a decomposing corpse; in England they stamp crosses on buns and eat the crucified Christ. I want your death to be part of the cycle of life and the magic of nature. I want to scatter your ashes around her like fairy dust.

'I'm bored.'

'We're almost there,' I say to reassure her . . . and disturb myself by my proximity to the past.

'What are you doing at Easter?' Robin asks, as he nibbles the hairs at the nape of my neck and I spurn his charms for those of George Eliot; 'do you fancy a week at Crierley?'

'What are you doing at Easter?' you ask two hours later, as you sense the confusions in the scattered cushions and the Penguin *Middlemarch* supine on the floor.

'I'm spending a week at Crierley'. . . . And, for a moment, I think that you hate me. To me, it is an ordeal by

22

etiquette. I fear for wrong forks and bad form and flat diphthongs. But, to you, it is the acme of your adolescent dreams.

I persuade Robin to invite you. . . . I can admit it now that all invitations are repaid. He demurs; he has the true lover's tunnel vision. But I stand firm; and we approach the house in a vintage Daimler driven by a veteran chauffeur, whose silvery stateliness matches the car.

'Pineapples,' you say. . . . I feel a frisson.

'Pevsner calls it one of the finest gateways in Herefordshire.' Robin crinkles his nose as he always does when he fears he is being boastful.

You lean back in your seat. 'I never realised the county was so camp.'

We approach the house. It is heavier and flatter than in my memory; the stone that once looked weathered now looks worn. When we came before, all that struck me was the size . . . the colonnade like the British Museum, the Hampton Court chimneys and St Pancras towers. I was blind to the disharmony of the Jacobean manor with its Palladian portico and gothic wings. To you, the mishmash of styles was its attraction: a compendium of history where each generation improved on the one before. But, to me, it seems the most slavish following of fashion . . . less a palimpsest of England than an architectural Vicar of Bray.

We skirt the warren of walls around annexes and outhouses. True to form, Lady Standish has directed me to the back. I undo Pagan's belt and lift her out of the seat. My hands break out in an adolescent sweat. I am nineteen again. I am walking into a stately home with no need of a ticket. Instead, I have a bag packed with a hired dinner suit and my mother's disapproval . . . I have flouted her golden rule: Stick to your own.

'This is Leo,' Robin says; as cramp leaves me tottering at the feet of a formidable woman with her hair pinned in a pepper-and-salt bun and a pearl pendant dangling from each ear.

'You used to have a stuffed lion called Leo as a boy, Robin, do you remember?' She smiles; the lipstick smear on her teeth looks like blood.

'Of course.' His eyes glisten. 'Uncle Ronnie sent him to

me from Kenya. Whatever became of him? I haven't seen him for years.'

'It went mouldy . . . bug-ridden. I had to throw it out.'

'Mother, how could you? I loved Leo. He was my favourite toy.'

'Nonsense; after two days it bored you. It was a mangy old thing, cheap and nasty. I can't think what possessed your uncle to send it to you.' She smiles again; the blood on her teeth has smudged.

'And this is Candida.' Robin presents you with more confidence. 'You met her at school.'

'Of course, the bursar's daughter.' She invests the words with such scorn that I determine to declare my father dead. 'How is your poor father? My heart went out to him, having to spend his life cooped in that stuffy office, coping with blocked drains and pregnant maids.'

'Oh there is a more positive side,' you say with equanimity, 'arranging for favoured boys to complete their education when their parents renege on the fees.'

She smiles again and the blood has vanished. She leads us into the house. 'We'll go in the back way – I hope you don't mind – it's so much cosier.' As Robin giggles, I want to die.

She smiles now and is wearing no lipstick. Her neck is puckered and her distended earlobes emphasise their lack of ornament. Her face is paler and her eyes water; but her bearing is as erect as ever and her bun as perfectly formed . . . it even appears all of a piece now that her hair is completely grey.

'You've changed,' she says, and I am suddenly forced into her perspective.

'It's sixteen years.' I calculated on the speedometer in the car.

'It takes death to bring us together . . . death and Christmas; though to me they're one and the same.' I search for some obscure Catholic theology; she registers my confusion. 'My husband drowned on Christmas Day. Too much festive spirits. He capsized in the lake. We burnt the boat.'

Pagan says nothing but grips my hand tightly. Lady Standish bends to acknowledge her. 'I was sorry to hear about your mother. It's cruel when people we love are wrested from us.' I wonder if she is thinking of Robin. 'I can't say that I liked her and I know she detested me.' Pagan's brow furrows; this is the first time that anyone has discussed you with detachment. I am both offended and relieved.

'She admired you a great deal.'

'She wanted to be me; that's different. She thought she could have done it better; she probably could. You needn't look so surprised. When you reach my advanced age, there's little you don't know.'

'Are you very old?' Pagan asks.

'Me, my dear? I'm older than God.'

Pagan stands pensively. 'Does that mean you're his mother?'

She laughs throatily; 'I don't know. You'll have to ask your . . . what does she call you?'

'Leo,' I say firmly.

'Not Daddy?'

'Leo.'

'Well Leo, would you say I was God's mother?' Her cheeks are suffused with sixteen years of suppressed malice. I think of Robin, his hair burnished in the sunlight, his face burning in my memory. I see him again, for the first time, beneath the dimly lit dome of San Marco, a young god stepped down from the glittering mosaics on the wall. You bring him round at the end of the concert. He congratulates me on the singing, particularly the Weelkes and the Tomkins. I am surprised to find him so well informed. 'Robin's musical,' you laugh; and I discover yet another double meaning. A moment later, he moves to an altar and lights a candle. 'It's for you,' he declares on his return.

'You say nothing,' Lady Standish rebukes me. 'Can it be that you don't remember?'

'On the contrary. I was thinking back to our first meeting. In the nave of St Mark's in Venice. He knelt and lit a candle.'

'To Our Lady?'

'Possibly.'

'He was always devout.' She mistakes my shrug for a shiver. 'You must be cold. Shall we go inside.'

'Will everything be safe in the car? Perhaps I should lock . . . ?'

'Oh don't worry; no one ever comes up here. Besides I don't suppose you have any valuables.' I cannot decide whether she means to be insulting, so I leave you in the glove compartment and make to go into the house.

'Oh no, not that way,' she says with the throaty relish of one determined to make my discomfort equal her humiliation. 'Did you think we still lived in the manor?' And she leads the way to a cream and brown caravan stationed behind a crumbling stone wall. I try to compose my features as we step inside.

'Are you a gypsy?' Pagan asks.

'Oh no, my dear, nothing so romantic. Gypsies have friends and fairs and fortunes. Gypsies have bands and kings and queens. I just have my daughter Lydia. . . . Careful of your head,' she shouts as I crack it, 'the ceilings aren't as high as in Holland Park.'

My confusion is complete as I see the interior. Every inch is crammed with family treasures. Silver frames, jade bowls and ivory boxes sit on toothmug shelves; and Persian rugs cover the floor. Free-standing fans and forlorn feathers droop in corners. A velvet canopy hangs over two box-like beds draped with quilts cut from moth-eaten minks. A large old TV and a bakelite wireless stand on a Sheraton sideboard, which divides the room from the kitchen. Only a set of Regency miniatures seems to scale. Pagan sits on the shell of a giant turtle; I inadvertently stamp on an elephant's foot.

'We'll wait for Lydia before we eat. You're not hungry, are you, my dear?' she asks Pagan, who remembers her manners. 'And I hope you're not cramped.'

'I have a Wendy house.'

'How nice.'

'Leo bought it for my last but one birthday.'

'I'm sure he's very generous.'

I recover my voice, if not my equilibrium. 'Has the house been sold?'

'Oh no, the house can never be sold; it belongs to Robin.' I nod knowingly, although I come from a world of protected tenancies not entailed estates. She corrects me. 'It's nothing legal. I could sell tomorrow if I chose; but I can't betray my son. This house is his inheritance; it's as much a part of him as the smile on his face. . . . You remember the smile on his face?' I nod.

'So what happened?' The Standishes' wealth seemed as secure as England.

'His father happened. His father and his life without loyalty, without morality, without family. His father and his gambling, his father and his drinking, his father and his cars and his boats and his villas.' I wonder whether it is to spare herself or Pagan that she fails to add 'and his women'. 'His father who went through every penny we had, and no one told me until it was too late, until he was dragged from the mud of a drained lake, as foetid in body as in spirit. We were left to sift through the debris; we sold our ancestors to pay his debts . . . portraits for people with Porsches. We tried to make ourselves a commercial proposition – you must know about that – suitable for conferences or courses or a leisure centre. But there was no hope; we're too remote and the costs of reconstruction were too great. So, when parts of the gallery collapsed, Lydia and I simply retreated to the ground floor. Then, when the boilers burst and we couldn't afford to replace them, we moved out here. It's the obvious solution. What more do we need: a prematurely aged woman and a middle-aged girl? We use the old laundry and the buttery and there's no one to turn us off our own land. And when Robin comes back – as one day I know he will – from wherever and whoever has been keeping him from me, he'll rejoice to find that all this has been preserved for him –' . . . I try not to picture the collapsed stairs and rotting timbers . . . 'and that every penny we could save from the rents has been put in his name. Now if you'll excuse me, Lydia or no Lydia, I must see to lunch. Restricted space requires perfect coordination. Thank Heaven I can cook on my precious Baby Belling.'

'She's cooking her baby?' Pagan's pupils dilate in horror.

'No, darling. It's the make of the oven, like Hoover or Frigidaire.'

'Is ours a baby?'

'Ours is big.'

Pagan's whispers bring no response from the kitchen. She picks up a Victorian music box which plaintively plays *There's no place like home.* I put it down promptly. I fear that we will be accused of pocketing the family heirlooms ... guilt comes back so easily, or perhaps it never goes. I catch sight of a picture of Robin at school in his First Eleven flannels. The toss of his head, the tousle of his hair and the sparkle of his smile are heartrending. I see him again in the clarity of your account and the glow of my imagination, as he limbers up to bowl, rubbing the ball against his groin, leaving fine red marks like the pressure of fingertips on a smooth white back ... the thud of fantasy on willow.

No wonder you fell for him as you sat demurely in the pavilion alongside the other staff wives and daughters, the object of bawdy speculation and defensive derision, your presence feeding the frustrations of three hundred hungry adolescents. He alone remained aloof. At first I thought that you must have been attracted by the challenge; now I see that it made him worthy of your respect. He responded to your femininity, not your sexuality; he was the only one uncompromised by desire. You made his romantic ventures into a heroic rebellion, more anarchic than aphrodisiac, a blow for liberty not libido. You were his adolescent alibi ... Candida and Robin, an unlikely but undeniable couple; it was a role that you longed to play for life. But was it him you wanted, or his world?

'This is England,' you say, as you draw back the curtains and gaze out at the newly cut lawn shimmering like shot silk in the breeze. 'I'd know who I was if I lived here. I'd know what I was born to ... what I was born for.' We take in the world of privilege and privacy, where a strategically placed row of beeches ensures that the family are literally lords of all they survey. Even the landscape has been shorn of its confusions, a masterpiece of manipulation, with the perfectly positioned hillock and glade and lake. This is nature as bucolic backdrop, the cosmos refined by cosmetics.

A tear forms in your eye which you make no attempt to hide, for it causes you no embarrassment. This is an England to which you feel you belong by birth and from which you have been exiled by adoption ... this is the place to which you swear you will one day return. Is that why you want to do so now? Dust to dust, if we accept the

28

liturgy . . . memory to memory, if we allow the conceit. For what other reason can there be? You had so many favourite places. You only came here once.

You left such clear instructions and so few explanations. I don't know if it was the pain of communicating or the desire to be deemed a mystery to the end. But I was pledged to do as you wished, even if it were the last place that I would have chosen. So I stored the urn on my awards shelf – camouflaged by company that you would have scorned – and waited for the ground to soften. I had so many romantic notions. I thought of scattering you piecemeal in all six continents. I thought of spilling you in sacred sites, infiltrating you into sacred relics. Then I changed tack and thought of putting you in an egg-timer so that you would remain part of our daily routine; but it seemed inappropriate when you were always so late.

And yet would you have wanted to come back to the view from an overstuffed caravan? Is this England now, as we lift up the blind and look out at an unswept courtyard and an outhouse door swinging on a rusty hinge? Is this still your seigneurial dream as the lords . . . the ladies of the manor are left like beggars in their own backyard, not so much guardians as ghosts?

The heavy smell of stew is becoming oppressive. Pagan is tracing stick-insect portraits of you in the condensation on the glass. She catches my eye and mouths 'I'm hungry'; I smile back that 'it won't be long'. I am about to step outside and clear my head when a scuffle at the door and a stumble through it announces Lydia. She looks around, pulls her balaclava over her ears and giggles. She holds out a bag of sweets upside down. 'For you,' she says to Pagan as the contents scatter over the floor. 'Oh,' she starts to whimper.

'Lydia,' her mother remonstrates, 'what have I told you about sweets before meals?'

'Never mind, I'll pick them up,' I say, as I try to adjust to the thirty-four-year-old woman who has walked in from my youth. I scurry on the floor and am embarrassed by the dust. Lady Standish wrenches off Lydia's balaclava as though she were pulling the vest off a recalcitrant child. Freed of constraint, her hair is surprisingly glossy and the prominent fringe almost hides her bulbous forehead. But nothing can hide the thin lips which are merely a line drawn beneath her nostrils, or the elliptical glasses which make her eyes appear as absent as her mind. She is a visual anomaly, in a pink and white woollen dress, with an absurdly elaborate bow, which looks more suited to a child's tea party. It remains inconceivable that she can be Robin's sister, except in some primitive changeling myth.

Her mother introduces me as an old friend of Robin's. 'Robin,' she repeats with a painless smile, as though they had been playing together only last week. 'Do you like jigsaws?' she asks Pagan.

'No,' she replies.

'What's that? I bought you the one of Beauty and the Beast only last week.'

'That was in the cinema.'

'She does hers every day after lunch. She'll show you.'

'Not now, Lydia, we've not eaten yet. Have you washed your hands?' She holds them up front and back. 'They're filthy.'

Pagan giggles as Lady Standish presses them under a tap. 'But she's a grown-up.'

I shush her with a vehemence that makes me uneasy. It seems unfair to chastise her for a confusion that I once felt myself.

'This is Lydia,' Robin introduces me to a sixteen-year-old girl who is pretending to be ten years younger.

'Can you fly?' she asks me, 'her brother's a bird,' and walks off flapping her arms, distressingly earthbound. Robin makes no comment and continues to show me around the house. Later, I am alone in the trophy room, surrounded by stuffed heads and mangy pelts that make me thankful that my father collects stamps. She approaches and, gesturing to the relevant parts of her body, begins to chant: 'Milk, milk, lemonade; round the corner chocolate's made.' She giggles complicitly. 'Don't tell; promise you won't tell.'

'I promise,' I say, as I am taken back to my nursery school playground and wonder if I am the butt of an elaborate joke. Is she mocking my background? Or, is it a fashionable affectation, like talking Cockney in the twenties, to behave like a six-year-old child? I challenge Robin. 'Is there something wrong with her?'

'She just sees things differently from the rest of us. What's wrong with that? It's only people with conventional minds who don't understand. I might have expected it from you.' He walks away, leaving me alone in the library. I have so much to learn.

'It's Robin's father,' Lady Standish says, as she tries to teach me the rudiments of backgammon. 'My husband,' she adds, as though the relationship were in doubt. 'He drinks.'

'Mama please.'

'No, Robin. These are your friends. They care about you. They'll understand.' I catch a glimpse of a Robin I never suspected and determine never to be ashamed of my family again.

'My husband was a vicious man, a brutal man,' she says with apparent relish; as if distance adds spice, not salt, to the wounds. 'I use the word was, which, while not strictly correct, is appropriate; he is dead to us.' I am chilled by the look of hatred in Robin's eyes. 'I was prepared to accept his cruelty to me, mental and physical. . . .'

'Mama please.'

'This room bears witness. He took a stick to me as I was sitting here. I cracked my head against that pillar. There!' She points so dramatically that I expect to see blood stains and a brass plaque like the Murder of Rizzio. 'After a time his behaviour could no longer be kept secret. My family begged me to leave him; even my friends made their feelings discreetly known. But I couldn't. Marriage is a sacrament and a sacrament is a sacrifice. But, although I could accept my own pain, I could not countenance my son's.'

'He never hit me!'

'My dear, you were five years old. Be thankful you don't remember.'

'Then why remind him?' Your interruption shocks me almost as much as her story; and yet she shows no offence.

'Because of Lydia. She is the daughter of his debauchery. She is the cross I bear. When I would have no more to do with him, when my every feeling had become disgust, he raped me; and it might as well have been with a bottle. His blood was poisoned by alcohol, and so is hers.'

'We can never be certain.'

31

'You've seen the reports; you've seen the evidence. The injuries to her face; the impairment of her mind; the foetal alcohol syndrome: it's all there.'

'It's a lie!'

'How can you deny your own sister? How can you deny your own mother?'

'How can you deny your own husband?'

'That's right; turn on me. Show your friends what a man you are. You're as bad as your father. Worse. What he did to me in passion, you do in cold blood.'

Lady Standish sweeps from the room. Robin unleashes his rage on Rachmaninov and the Bechstein. You stand rapt. I have never understood why you chose the Standishes when there were so many grander families you could have adopted. Of course, it was important that they were Catholics. You may have scorned the theology but you admired the tradition; you were as dismissive of the Reformation as the pre-Raphaelites were of the Renaissance. I resisted the ritual; but the archaism of the practice was precisely what attracted you. In some perverse way, you admired the hypocrisy and liked to picture the clergy as latter-day *Cardinal Pirellis* pouncing on choirboys and pulling the mantillas over middle-aged matrons' eyes.

But then, in a typical switch of mood, you add 'As a gay man, you of all people should deplore Protestantism. It's Protestantism that's led to the supremacy of the nuclear family. For, once you've allowed priests to marry, you've acknowledged that marriage isn't second-best to celibacy; from which it's but a small step to making a moral imperative out of conventional family life.'

'The Vatican is hardly supportive of homosexuality.'

'Or any sexuality. It's just different degrees of sin.'

'If families are such a bad thing, why are you so keen on Robin's?'

'I don't want family life; I want a family history. One with a name and a tradition I can be part of. Ancestors and effigies and escutcheons –'

'With blots?'

'With anything so long as there's blood.'

I try to black out my bedside photograph of Robin's grandmother on her bier.

'Everyone needs to know where they belong.'

32

'You belong to a family of your own.'

'Yes, the way an affiliated company belongs to BP. It's all so arbitrary. My parents went by the book . . . literally; years later I found a dog-eared pamphlet *How to tell your child he's adopted*. It's out-of-print. They told me they'd picked me because I was so pretty. Was that supposed to reassure me? I was convinced that, if I'd been ugly, I'd still be on offer. And what if I lost my looks; would they take me back to exchange for someone prettier?'

'There can't be an easy way to tell a child she's adopted.'

'Because the whole relationship is so false.'

'Would you rather have grown up in an orphanage?'

'I am not an orphan! Somewhere my parents are alive.'

'Alright then, a children's home.'

'Yes. Then at least I'd have known who I was and what I was up against. I'd have seen the truth of being alone. Instead, I was assigned to a fabricated family, people with whom I had nothing in common, not even respect.'

'As a boy, I felt sure I must be adopted. I looked at my parents and thought how could I have come from them? I looked at my father and thought how could I grow into that?'

'But at least your relationship was real. When you said mummy and daddy, it was more than just a form of words. Even now you may fight them, you may disown them, but a part of them is always with you . . . not in abstract memories but in blood.' You extend your argument to the acreage of ancestors. 'Look at them; I expect they loathed one another – they plotted and schemed and connived and fought – but they belong together. The same face in the foreground, the same family background. What runs through it all is blood. But when there's nothing but the thin red ink of an official stamp. . . .'

I cut you off in mid-memory, as I think of Pagan. The perennial doubt nags; if you laid so much importance on blood, why would you never reveal hers? In fifteen years' time will she express the same sentiments? Will she regard me as a mere legal convenience? How could you do it to either of us? I shiver.

'Cold?' Lady Standish asks with evident satisfaction. 'We do our best; but, in the winter, we're rather exposed. Still, at least lunch is hot.'

We hover around the table which, having been set by Lydia, now has to be painstakingly rearranged. Pagan, who enjoys the confusion, refuses to give up her three spoons. There are five places laid on a space barely big enough for two. 'That one is for Robin,' his mother tells me with defiance . . . I think of Prince Albert's pyjamas. Then I remember their family motto: Hope against hope.

We lift our plastic glasses and I hear again the ring of crystal; I pick up my tarnished fork and see again the family crest. I am back in the dining hall where the lustrous glow of the wood complements the richly polished conversation and the row of resident ancestors are spectators, not spectres, at the feast.

'I'm Robin's Aunt Waverley,' an elderly lady with a wiry chin informs me. 'I was named after my grandfather's favourite horse . . . not a racehorse, mind, a carthorse.' She laughs; and I feel as if I am being put through my paces.

I'm Lenny, I want to say; I'm named after my Great-Uncle Len who died of pneumoconiosis. 'I'm Leo,' I hear myself saying; 'I was named after the pope.' Fortunately, both you and Robin are engaged.

'Which one? Not the thirteenth, I hope.' She brays; and I laugh uncertainly. 'Or you and I will never be friends.'

'Where are your people from?' asks a rubicund man, whose introduction was so curt that I am unclear whether he is the local MP or the Master of Foxhounds.

'Denbighshire,' I say, remembering your instruction always to say the county, never the town. 'My father breeds roses and my mother manages our hotel.' I ignore your cough.

'Use your small knife for the butter,' I tell Pagan . . . and only wish that the dinner setting were as simple as the lunch. I am left with a fruit knife for the roast beef; Robin's advice to work from the outside in has gone horribly wrong.

'Robin's told me so much about you.' I am roused from my reverie by an unctuous voice and look up at a face like a sweating cheese. We are sitting in the drawing room drinking coffee; the cream creeping over my spoon puts me in mind of him. I vigorously stir.

'Duncan Treflis. I live next door.' It is some time before I realise that his 'next door' is my mother's 'we never see them since they moved'.

'Leo Young.'

'I know. After the popes.' I am horrified. He was sitting at the other end of the table. Was I shouting or was he snooping on me?

'How do you like life in the country?' He pronounces the word as if it were an intimate part of a woman's anatomy . . . a part that I doubt he has ever been intimate with.

'I like being with Robin.'

'I've known Robin since he was a babe in arms. I dandled him on my knee.' He lowers his voice mockingly. 'To tell the truth, I still do.' I look round for rescue, but you are talking to the carthorse and Robin is nowhere to be seen.

'You have broad shoulders. Such a delicious mix . . . ginger hair and broad shoulders.'

'I played rugby at school.'

'So did I. Until I was banned from the showers.'

Lady Standish joins us. 'I see you've met Leo, Duncan. He and Robin are inseparable. I told Robin when he was grumbling about going up to Trinity that he'd meet so many exciting new people. And he's met Leo.'

'I long to introduce him to Leslie, who'd adore him. They could chatter about music for hours.'

'Is Lesley your wife?' I ask maliciously. He looks disconcerted. I savour my triumph.

'Leslie's my oldest friend. We shared our youth together.' He makes it sound like a *ménage à trois*.

'And Duncan's my dearest friend. I don't know how I'd have managed without him. He's been a second father to Robin. A boy needs a man to look up to.'

'Yours breeds roses.' Treflis emphasises his eavesdropping. 'And his choicest bloom must be his son.' The conventionality of the compliment betrays his contempt.

'Who is he?' I ask you later, as the drawing-room chatter gives way to bedroom confidences.

'He seduced Robin years ago. He was sleeping with him all through school.'

'But that's appalling.'

'Don't be so bourgeois. We're not in Colwyn Bay. They do things differently here. Why, in ancient Greece –'

35

'We're not in ancient Greece either. It's appalling. No wonder Robin's so screwed up. I'm amazed his mother allows him in the house. She must be blind not to have noticed the way he flirts with him.'

'She encourages it. She was the one who pimped for him. She practically threw Robin into his arms.'

'What? Why?'

'Money. Who do you think paid his school fees? Who do you think pays for all this?'

'His father.'

'His father lost everything.'

'There must be trusts.'

'Not a penny. Believe me, my father did the accounts. It's Treflis. And his mother set up everything.' I am sickened. My Christmas card images of mother and child are torn down in a permanent Twelfth Night. 'I admire her for it. No nonsense about loans or mortgages.'

'No, she'll sacrifice flesh and blood for bricks and mortar.'

'They're one and the same; each feeds the other. And she'll protect them both. She's a survivor; so am I. That's why I know I belong.'

She must feel the same. At least she never queried my request to bring you back. 'I don't know if you have any specific place in mind,' she asks as we tramp across a frozen muddy clearing. Pagan enjoys the mixture of squelches and cracks. 'There's a grove of beeches where we buried all the dogs.' I cannot see if she is serious. 'But perhaps that's not ideal.'

'I just thought . . . somewhere romantic.' She looks at me sharply.

'Your friend had the least romantic nature of anyone I've ever met. That's what you never understood.'

What can she mean? We pass the dovecote; I have a strange sense of déjà vu as both you and Pagan ask what it is.

'A dovecote.'

'Where they used to keep doves . . . white pigeons.'

'How charming,' you exclaim. Lady Standish explains its function.

'Not really; it's not a glorified birdbath. You don't just sit back and watch them playing. There's a delicate natural balance: they coo; we cook.'

'How cruel,' you say.

'That's cruel,' Pagan echoes.

'Life is cruel. Slaughter-house or butcher's shop: people should never live too far from their source of food; they begin to think they're civilised. . . . Will this do?' She stands expectantly, as if the precedent makes it appropriate.

'No, I don't think so. It's too enclosed.' We trudge on, muffled and muted, except for Lydia who swings her arms and tries to pull at the branches above her head.

'Stop that, you'll hurt yourself,' her mother warns; and, sure enough, she does.

'She's so silly,' Pagan says as Lydia sits on a stump sobbing.

'Stand up, Lydia; you'll tear your coat. There won't be another. Next winter you'll freeze.' The sobs become wails. 'Right, we're going on. You'll be left behind. . . . You think I'm hard –' she turns to . . . she turns on me; 'you think that I ill-use one child and drove off the other.' I try not to think at all. 'Where is he? How can he hate me this much? It's been so long. He may have a family of his own . . . children. He should bring them here. They'd have space, freedom. No one has walked this way in years.' The breath in front of her freezes. 'You know where he is; you must speak to him. You must tell him I'm old . . . ill. What's to happen to his sister?'

I extricate myself from her clutch. 'I haven't seen or heard from Robin for almost ten years. I live in exile from my past.'

But I see him again, quite unexpectedly, when at the edge of the copse we reach the Temple of Love, an eighteenth-century homage to Athens from the one Lord Standish to resist the pull of Rome. The building is bolted, but its history bursts out; and I spot two young men silhouetted in the moonlight. They are not wearing clothes.

Robin is angry with me for disliking Treflis. 'He's a guest of my mother's. I didn't know he'd be here. It's nothing to do with you.'

'But what's he to do with you? Do you fuck with him?'

'Oh for God's sake!'

'Then you do.'

'So? It's no big deal. I'm sorry to disappoint you but I'm not a virgin.'

'Candida says your mother knows.'

'What?'

'About the two of you. What's more, that she arranged it.'

'Leave my mother out of it.'

'It's sick.'

'You've no idea what she's suffered.'

'I care what you suffer.'

'You know nothing. You have nothing to lose, so you've nothing to lose to keep it. The one trauma in your life was when your voice broke. All the rest is banal.'

'You and me: is that banal?'

'There wouldn't be any you and me without Duncan. There wouldn't be any Venice or Cambridge. Nor would there be any Crierley.'

'It's only a house.'

'A house that's been in my family for four hundred years. A house that's not just where we live but who we are. Its stones are my second skin; its soil is in my blood. I can't be the one to let it go.'

I clutch you to my chest, caught in the crossfire between his pain and your wishes. If only you could hear – not now, but then – would you be so keen to come back?

'Sometimes I hate it so much, I want to raze it to a pile of rubble; but it would be like desecrating a family tomb. It's my heritage; I'm in hock to history.' He laughs . . . or is it history's echo? 'With you, I thought I could break free; with you, I could make my own family.' For an instant he makes me forget his sex. 'But it was a fantasy. If you knew everything I am, you'd hate me.'

'No, I could never hate you.' I run my hand though his hair, over his flesh. 'I love you.' It is the first time that I have said it. I have practised so often and it has always sounded . . . practised. Now I know that it is real. He kisses me, pressing his tongue against my gums so insistently that they ache. Then he lies on a bench and offers himself to me. The cold stone shocks my skin; but the warmth of his insides welcomes me. The sex and the setting combine

38

to confirm your theory; we are no longer English students but Homeric Greeks.

The modern world intrudes with a fate as cruel as any classical deity. Two figures emerge from the trees: Lady Standish and Treflis. We are totally exposed. The moon has no truck with modesty. In its sharp white light, Robin's skin has turned to stone. I try to pull away, but his muscles too have petrified and I am at the mercy of Lady Standish's blows raining down on my back. I try to protect Robin from Treflis who plays the father's part and slaps his upturned face. He makes no protest; but his body emits the most shaming fart as they prise me off and drag him away like two butchers hauling a hunk of meat. I am left choking on my sobs, raw and grimy. I have nowhere to go. I wear his underclothes for extra warmth. I curl up on the bench with his shirt for a pillow and sleep beneath the stars for the first and only time.

I look at Lady Standish, whose face betrays no sign of recognition. 'No, not here,' I say; 'I don't think Candida ever came here. By the lake.'

Lydia shivers. 'She's not allowed to go there.'

'You're alright when you're with someone else,' her mother says; and we walk towards its banks. I try to think of a story for Pagan about your spirit floating in the air; but I simply say that you wanted us to come and remember you here, that this was somewhere you were happy, and that we are going to make a wish with magic dust.

I unscrew the lid of the urn; I tip out some of the ashes. I weigh your life – your after-life – in my hands and feel the softness of death sifting through my fingers. I am surprised; ashes are not hard as in 'sackcloth and . . .' or Cinderella's kitchen grate, but as soft as sun-soaked sand. I feel strangely reassured.

I whirl my arms in a circle and make a private incantation. I am no longer aware of anyone, not even Pagan. My thoughts stream through my head as the ash streams through my fingers . . . I am back with you in the breakfast room, bereft and bedraggled, where Lady Standish makes no mention of what happened – was it all a bad dream? – but informs us with perfect composure that Robin has a touch of flu and has been confined to bed. It is wretched luck but, under the circumstances, she thinks it best that we leave.

'I'm so sorry,' I say to you as we discard the cold kedgeree; 'I ruined everything.'

'No,' you reply quietly; 'it wasn't you.'

'We'll never go back,' I say, as the car deposits us at the station, where the first train to Worcester is cancelled and the second delayed.

'You mustn't say that. Of course we will. We must,' you insist. As indeed we have. And a gust of wind blows the ash in the women's faces. Lady Standish jumps away as if attacked by a swarm of bees, but Lydia tries to catch it, shouting 'snow'. As I take Pagan in my arms, I suspect that it is you trying to puncture the solemnity. And, as we walk back to the car, I trust that you have found a home.

# 3

I have betrayed you. I hardly dare say it, but I have seen your parents. And yet somehow I feel that you know already. As we sit drinking tea, the air is heavy with disapproval . . . although how much of it is yours and how much theirs, I cannot be sure.

Your spirit remains alive, if only in my consciousness. You would dismiss any larger claim as superstition, as grotesque a negation of nature as Mae West's skin; eternal youth or eternal souls are both equally vain. But I feel you in my every moment; you make the past part of the present. I speak to you of it – from it – and I know that I am not speaking to myself. So I pick up my pen . . . my life has become one of paper intimacies. And yet, for you, I fear that it is an endless frustration. 'You used to have such good stories; tell me something I don't already know.'

I think that I would prefer an old-style spirit, a guardian angel or vengeful ghost, someone always at hand with a word of warning; then I might have been better prepared . . . there again, you have warned me against them for nineteen years.

The first indication is an envelope: an indistinct postmark, an unfamiliar hand. It has the copper-plate confidence of a poison-pen letter; and yet it has not been forwarded from the BBC. I turn to the signature: yours sincerely, Muriel Mulliner. My pulse quickens. Pagan laughs; I have sunk my wrist in the marmalade. Then she sees my face.

'Is it a nasty letter?'

'Just a bill. Eat up or we'll be late for school.'

'Good. I hate it. I'm going to run away.'

'And who won a gold star last week?'

'I like it really.'

'I should think so too. Now hurry up and let Susan wipe your face.'

'It's not as sticky as your sleeve.'

'Cheeky monkey.'

We pick up two of her friends, Phoebe and Stephanie; the morning run has changed now that the Sampsons have returned to Washington. I might as well be wearing a peaked hat for all the notice that they take of me. Pagan tells them about our Sunday trip to the zoo. She watched two lemurs very actively mating; I watched the crowd. Some parents withdrew their children instantly as though from an accident; others laughed as the rampant male pushed the recalcitrant female round and round the compound. And I thought what they would say if they came upon two people making delicate love discreetly in the park proper. 'What animals! What beasts!' And we moved on to the reptile house.

'It was yucky,' Pagan says. 'Ginormous snakes, all thick and slimy.'

'Snakes aren't slimy, darling; they're warm and hard.' There is a shocked silence as they register that I have been listening: a breach of etiquette on a Lord Chamberlain scale. Pagan continues in a pointed whisper.

'I hate snakes. When I grow up, I'm going to live in Ireland.'

'Why?'

'Cos there aren't any. A wizard sang a song and they all wriggled into the sea.'

'Are they still there?'

'No, silly. It was in history.'

'They might have babies.'

Pagan ponders. 'It's alright living in Ireland, but not swimming.'

'I expect they put up a notice like when there's a storm.'

'Where my granny lives in Cornwall, when there's a storm, the beach is full of dead fishes,' says Stephanie.

'I 'spect in Ireland there'll be dead snakes,' says Phoebe.

'Urgh,' says Stephanie; 'that'll be worse.'

We arrive at school. All my lingering fears about Pagan's depression disappear with her in the mass of squealing five-year-olds. I chat to Barbara Newsom who persists in her request to interview me for the *Evening Standard*. She wants to know how I am coping on my own with a young girl. I distrust her motives and deflect the offer. I return home and re-read your mother's letter. I know from the start that it will be bad news. She writes that she would like to discuss Pagan's future. There is far too much to say by phone or on paper, so will I be so kind as to arrange to meet her and her husband? They will be glad to come up to London. My first instinct is to refuse. I am Pagan's testamentary guardian; they have never even seen her; there is nothing to discuss. But then I relent. I never understood your grudge against your parents. Besides, it might be useful for Pagan to discover a family that is more than a courtesy one; she asked me last week why all her aunts were only pretend. This is the nearest that she has to blood.

So, against my better judgement, I invite them to tea. I don't know why I spend so long tidying up . . . or rather, I do and I don't like it. I refuse to allow Pagan to play downstairs, which only confirms her in her – in your – prejudice.

'I don't see why I have to see them. They were cruel to my mummy and she hated them.'

'She didn't hate them. It's all very complicated.'

'She did too. And you know it.'

'Wouldn't you like to have grandparents? They live by the seaside. Perhaps we'll go for the day.'

'I want to go to Butlins.'

'And I expect they'll bring you a present. Grandparents always bring presents.'

'You give me presents. You said you'd give me anything I wanted.'

'Now you'll have even more.'

'If you say you're going to do something, you have to do it or else you'll be a liar.'

She snaps at Susan when she tries to change her dress. She doesn't see why she has to put it on; it makes her itch.

But Susan can afford to be stricter; she has references for her role. I am still discovering mine.

The doorbell rings on the stroke of four. It is as if the chimes are synchronised. I am used to a world of fashionable lateness; these are people who run their lives by the clock. Consuela lets them in with an air of dignified disapproval. Pagan and I greet them in the hall. I cannot decide whether it is her hand sweating or mine.

They look so old. I suddenly wonder if the reason for your adoption is that they married late; although I know that in truth they cannot be much more than seventy. But then they are the kind of people who thrive on old age, as if they have been waiting for it all their lives; the respect that they have not earned by any other means, the deference they demand as their due: people to call him 'sir' and stand up for her on buses . . . not, I am sure, that they ever use them, but supposing they should.

'Hello,' your mother says to Pagan. 'I'm Granny.'

'You're old, aren't you?' comes her instant, obsessional reply.

'I suppose I am. Although no well-brought-up child ever mentions a lady's age. Especially since there's nothing she can do.'

'You could buy a bikini.' I apologise for my cough.

Consuela takes their hats and coats and I their hands. We make a tacit agreement on formality. As I say hello, I remember your description of your mother as a woman who enjoys goodbyes. Pagan hangs behind me, outwardly demure, inwardly defiant. I hear my voice growing harsh as I tell her not to be silly; I feel sure that your parents are noting every inflection. I selfishly hope that she will create a good impression because somehow it will reflect on me. This is the first test of my surrogate parenthood, and one that I am determined to pass.

We had a long discussion as to whether she has to kiss them. In the event she holds out a compromise hand. Your father takes it with some amusement. 'Quite the little lady, aren't we?' But your mother bends with conscious condescension. 'Don't you have a kiss for Granny?'

'No,' she replies shortly.

'Pagan . . .' I half-warn, half-remind her.

'Oh, alright,' she says and pecks her on the cheek. Your

44

mother's honour, if not her pride, is satisfied. I pray that she doesn't see the pay-off as Pagan wipes her lips on her sleeve.

'Shall we go upstairs?' I say quickly.

'Haven't you brought any presents?' Pagan asks and turns to me in triumph. 'You said they'd bring me a present.'

'Did he now?' Your mother looks at me sharply. 'That was rash of him.'

'I knew you wouldn't.'

'Little girls who ask don't get.'

'They do too. Leo says I can have anything I ask for. So there.' She sticks out her tongue at her.

'Pagan . . .' I feel events slipping away from me. 'She's nervous,' I explain. Your mother laughs shortly, but her eyes are ice. I make to follow them upstairs and Pagan straps herself into the lift. 'It was for Candida,' I say quickly; 'I keep forgetting to have it removed.'

'You'll lose the use of your legs,' your mother warns her. 'I do ballet.'

'When I was a little girl, I had to walk over a mile every morning to school.'

'Let it rest, Mother.' Your father's epithet surprises me. Is it a pet name, a last point of contact, or something he wants to prove?

'It's not the girl's fault.' She seems primitively anxious not to name her. 'Children take advantage; it's their nature.' She turns to me. 'It seems to me you've let her grow up thoroughly spoilt.'

'I am not spoilt,' Pagan protests with new-learnt precision. 'That would mean I was no good. That would mean like throwing in the dustbin. I am not spoilt. I'm not.' She threatens tears.

'Of course you're not,' I reassure her and reproach your mother. 'Please be careful what you say. She's highly sensitive.'

'Like her mother,' she snorts . . . the first time that she has mentioned you. 'Highly strung.'

Entering the drawing room, your mother stalls at the sight of Trouble. At first I fear that she shares my mother's allergy; but it is a more general aversion. Trouble glares at her, arches his back, flexes his tail and hisses. Pagan picks

45

him up and nuzzles his muzzle. 'Don't put your mouth to the pussy, dear; it's dirty.' I giggle. It must be nerves that are taking me back to the fourth form . . . although, even in the sixth, I thought pussy no more than a synonym for cat.

Trouble stalks out, flashing a curl of contempt at the intruders. Pagan lies on her stomach reading, her heels clicking in the air. Your mother perches primly on the edge of her chair, as if worried what might be lurking between the cushions. Your father leans forward, his arms open, as if waiting for a confidence that never comes. Consuela serves tea. Your mother refuses all food; she has to watch her figure. I start to relax and wish that we could laugh together at her green tweed suit with its velvet panels, stretched like furnishing fabric across her well-upholstered hips. I study her face, which is a pantomime of disapproval as she scans the room, peering through spectacles that she has constantly to adjust.

'They're bisexuals,' she confides. 'I sometimes think they're more trouble than they're worth.'

'Bifocals, Mother,' your father corrects.

'That's what I said,' she retorts sharply. I stir my tea.

We make small talk. I begin to warm to them and feel that I may have taken them too much at your estimation. Your father admires the decor. 'Very tasteful,' he says, in a tone that suggests a 'very tasty' barmaid.

'The taste was Candida's,' I reply; 'she always knew what she wanted.' I remember the first house that we ever shared, in Maid's Causeway, with the poster that you hung in the kitchen, 'Life's a bitch and so's my mother', and the effort it took to convince my mother that shared lodgings did not mean shared sentiments. She had been unhappy enough with my moving out of college and here I was, living not only in sin but in spite. 'One day, she'll be a mother herself,' she said, 'then she'll understand.' Pagan clicks her heels like castanets. Life's a bitch and so's your mother. . . . 'She always had good taste. It was innate.'

Your mother eyes the portrait of you and Pagan above the chiffonier. 'Would you say that photograph was in good taste?'

'I think it's beautiful. It was one of the last Candida ever took. She already found it hard, even with a tripod and an automatic shutter release. Added to which, Pagan found it

46

impossible to keep still. She still does.' Her heels click a fandango in reply.

'With neither of them wearing anything but their birthday suits?'

'What birthday suit?' Pagan looks up. 'It wasn't my birthday.' And I have to suppress my explanation of a woman so prudish that she has to clothe people even when they are naked, like a Mother Superior handing out bathtime smocks.

Your father seems embarrassed, as if nudity is something for other men's daughters. He asks instead about the awards.

'Now they are bad taste, at least according to Candida. I never know whether it's more ostentatious to dismiss them or to put them on display.'

'There are far too many awards.' Your mother asserts her own agenda. 'They should give them to people who really deserve them, who devote their lives to charities, to the community, without any thought of reward. For thirty years I've worked for the St John Ambulance.'

'You deserve a medal, Mother.'

'I've got a medal; but I don't expect to see it on television. I've no wish to be personal, of course; but all you do is ask questions, half of them are written by someone else.'

You should try it, I want to say, as an American actor becomes obstreperous or a British actor obscene, as this week's pop sensation refuses to stray from his press release or last week's turns up stoned, or as the man with the biggest marrow in England and the man with the biggest leek in Wales pick a fight across a crowded couch. You try maintaining your integrity when you are only as big as your last celebrity and even the B-list guest-list has been over-exposed. You try sustaining your ratings through two shows a week thirty weeks a year, while critics carp about seeing the same old faces, of which the samest and oldest is yours. You try keeping your cool as the producer urges you in your earpiece 'to crucify the bastard' and you repeat it in front of five million viewers because you are so keyed up that the words go straight from ear to mouth without stopping off at the brain.

'Actually,' is all I say, 'I do write my own questions and,

47

if you read half the pundits, you'd know that they're pretentious and fawning.'

'We don't read gossip in papers,' your father says.

'We don't watch gossip on television,' your mother says, handing me her cup as though it were a bottle marked 'Drink me'. 'We're very sparing about our viewing ... David Attenborough, Joan Bakewell.'

'Mother likes the *Antiques Roadshow*.'

'I'm afraid we don't watch you.'

'No?'

'But my cleaning woman keeps me in touch.'

The tick of the clock replaces conversation, in a tone that sounds as if each second is ticking off the next. We sit at a loss. I am amazed to see your mother actually twiddling her thumbs. Pagan reaches for another cake.

'My, what an appetite,' your mother says; 'don't you think you've had enough?'

'No, or I wouldn't take one.'

'Don't be rude, darling.'

'She won't eat her supper.'

'Oh, we won't be eating until much later.' I explain, to my instant regret. 'It's Consuela's night off, so I'm in the hot seat.'

'We're having chicken cooked in spit.'

'On a spit, on a spit, darling.' I laugh. 'She enjoys the theatricality. It's a major disappointment that Pancake Tuesday isn't once a week.' I laugh again, alone.

'Children shouldn't eat after six o'clock. It's bad for the digestion.'

'I don't have digestion. So there!' She sticks out a caky tongue at her.

'Now stop it, Pagan. She's nervous ... showing off.'

'Like mother like daughter,' your father says.

'If I were your mother, you wouldn't behave like this.'

'Well you're not.'

'I'm your granny. It's the next best thing.'

'No, it's not; Leo is. Grannies are wolves in disguise.'

'What?'

'No, it's the other way round, darling; wolves are grannies. Little Red Riding Hood,' I inform them. 'Her favourite story' ... You taught her well.

We sit in silence, until your father asks: 'Do you enjoy school, young lady?'

'It's alright.'

'Do you play games?'

'No, we work. I was in a play at Christmas.'

'A nativity play?' Your mother finds a redeeming feature.

'It was about a garden. I was a bee with a yellow bottom.'

'It's a multi-faith school,' I explain.

'It's a Christian country.'

'It serves several embassies.'

'Do you know the Lord's Prayer, dear?'

'What?'

'Your mummy knew the Lord's Prayer when she was much younger than you. She said it on her knees every night.'

'Why her knees?'

'So God would listen.'

'My mummy didn't believe in God. She used to cry. I expect it was because her knees hurt. Why were you so horrid to her?'

'What? Have you told her that?'

'I've told her nothing. I just tried to support Candida.'

'She was such a gentle, accommodating little girl. Everybody loved her. But then she changed. Do you remember, Father?'

'No.'

'She felt you never understood her; you never even tried.' Is this true? Am I misrepresenting you? 'She told me how you constantly expected gratitude for taking her in like a waif in a melodrama. You told her that she'd never given you a moment's pleasure, as if she were a package holiday ruined by rain. She went to see you when she was pregnant with Pagan. You know what you said.'

'It's not true! She was a born liar.'

'That's when you gave up on her. That's when your husband truly said "like mother like daughter". Get rid of it, you told her. It!' I point to Pagan.

'Lies, lies, lies,' your mother says triumphantly. 'I would never have said it; I abhor abortion.'

'Not abortion, adoption. That's what you told her. Although in her experience it was almost the same.'

'How can you spout such filth in front of a child?'

'Because I know what Candida felt. I know how much she detested the thought of adoption. If she'd given up Pagan, it would have been for the dead.'

Pagan herself approaches me, her feet curling inward, pained by so much vehemence in her name.

'We tried to build bridges –'

'I went to the hospital when the child was born –'

'But she shunned us. We only learnt about the illness from her brother.'

'She had her reasons.'

'You can't conceive how it feels to be barred from your own granddaughter. I thought of hiding across the road like a private detective.'

'We've never so much as seen a picture of her.'

'There was a photo-spread in *Marie Claire*.' I bite my tongue.

'She's not a model; she's our own flesh and blood.' I gasp; does she have any idea what she is saying?

'Easy now, Mother,' your father moves beside her, patting her hand clumsily, like a reluctant actor in a village hall. 'We came here in good faith. You have no right to upset her. If only for the child's sake.' I fail to see the connection but appreciate the need for calm.

'I can show you some pictures of me and Mummy.' Pagan seems to connect their loss with her own, as she proposes to fetch the book that we are writing . . . for our own eyes only, don't worry. It is one of Deborah's aids for bereaved children. I haven't mentioned it before because I know what you think of her theories. But, by putting together our reminiscences, we put back together our lives.

'You're honoured,' I tell them as she leaves the room. 'She hasn't shown it to anyone; she says it's just for us.'

'We're not anyone; we're family,' your mother replies.

'I don't see that there's any need to be so hostile,' your father says, 'even if you do resent us.' I am taken aback. 'No doubt you people think it clever to mock genuine feelings. The family means nothing to you. I've seen you on television with your smiles and your eyebrows.' I thought that they never watched. 'Our friends say it's an act, but we know better. Not content with turning our daughter against us, you're now trying to do the same with our granddaughter.'

'Now wait a minute, if there were any turning, it was the other way round. I went to a grammar school, remember; I didn't have the advantage of public school alienation. I loved my parents; I still do. When I met Candida, I'd have described myself as a happy person. You could hear it when I sang. But she changed that. According to her, the only people who had happy childhoods were amnesiacs.'

'Typical.'

'She filled me with discontent as though it were philosophical speculation. You might say that I was easily influenced; I'd say I was insecure. But, for years, I believed that happiness meant superficiality and was as shameful as wearing white socks.'

'And with that attitude you propose to bring up a child?'

'It was her attitude, not mine. It must have come from somewhere.'

'How I wish we'd never told her she was adopted. We didn't have to; she need never have known. But you . . .' your mother turns on your father; 'for some reason you couldn't wait.'

'It was the book. You read the book.'

'Until then she was like everyone else's daughter: a carefree, ordinary little girl. But she was ours. Then it all changed. At five years old she became difficult. She made everything as secretive as her origins. I had to stop reading her fairy tales when I heard her telling a friend that I wasn't her real mummy; I'd stolen her like a witch. She became a nuisance at school; her teachers complained. She was bullying other children, and worse. And all because of what it said in a book. Don't talk to me about books. And, as she grew up, it got harder. We were never good enough. After all, if parents could choose their children, why shouldn't children choose their parents? You'd have thought she were the Grand Duchess Anastasia! Normal girls dream of marrying princes; she dreamt of regaining her throne.'

I begin to feel sorry for her with the sentimentality which you insist is a direct result of my sexuality, when Pagan returns, clasping the album in one hand and Susan in the other. As I effect introductions, your father questions her with all the expertise of thirty years of hiring matrons. Your mother seems more concerned with domestic arrangements; and I am convinced that she suspects us of conducting an affair. My mind – or rather hers – is full of lurid images: the consumptive wife coughing her last in white satin, while the would-be widower brutally seduces the downstairs maid. Has she no idea of our relationship? At least she can entertain no illusions about Pagan ... as if illegitimacy were not punishment enough, you had to hit her with an unknown father.

'What sort of man would take on another man's child?' she asks of me disparagingly.

'A man like your husband,' you reply.

'There's no comparison,' she says.

'There's no comparison,' you rush to reassure me. And, as I look at the trim little man with his broken-veined cheeks, handlebar moustache, honorary old-school tie and regimental blazer, his shoulders shaking from the strain of maintaining his military bearing, I trust that you are right. And yet, as he deflects my glance, I detect a fellow-furtiveness and feel sure that he takes secret Scandinavian lessons or keeps a cache of pornography underneath the seed-trays in his potting shed.

Pagan thrusts the album on your mother's knee and slowly turns the pages. 'We're writing this book for us ... Leo and me. That's my writing, look. I started doing each letter in a different colour. It took too long. It's the story of Mummy's life and we're going to have it printed in case of thieves' .... I mention desktop publishing. 'Leo does most of the writing; but sometimes I help. And I do most of the remembering. Except from before I was born.' She has lost her earlier reticence. 'This is the beginning, when Mummy was a little girl.' Your mother gasps.

'You've cut us out,' she shrieks at me. 'These were taken at Giant's Causeway; I remember the row over that skirt. But you've put her in the middle of strangers. You've cut us out of Candida's childhood, just as you want to cut us out of hers.'

'These are my pictures,' Pagan insists and clasps the album protectively.

'Tell him, Father. You took them. Your camera was never out of your hand. It was your skill she inherited.'

'Observed perhaps, not inherited.' My distinction sounds cruel. I explain that they are experiments: a technique of your own devising: an imaginary autobiography from your exhibition, The Camera Never Lies.

'It's all lies. Everything in this book, in this house, in your life is a lie.'

'I'm sorry; it was thoughtless. I should have realised you wouldn't understand.'

'Isn't it Mummy?' Pagan's brow furrows.

'No, not at all. We were with her. Your grandpa, me, your Uncle William. We were on holiday in Northern Ireland. These people are from magazines. . . . She's replaced us with people from magazines!'

'That's the point. It's not deception but dreams. A touch of the Côte d'Azur in County Antrim.'

'What sort of life can it be when she cuts out her own parents?'

'She wanted to be her own parent just as she wanted to be Pagan's . . . I think that may be why she never named the father, so that there would be no one to gainsay her. She chose to reinvent herself with her camera; it gave her authenticity. She longed for flesh and blood but felt that yours was fake and anaemic; so she went the other way and recreated herself in prints.' I trust that I am not setting up another false image.

'And you plan to publish this?'

'Privately.' I try to reassure them without disappointing Pagan. 'A handful of copies. For a few friends. Pagan's mother has died. We have to find a way to accept it. Have you never heard of grief?'

'You're filling our granddaughter's head with lies.'

Pagan starts to cry. 'It's not lies; it's my mummy's stories. I tell Leo and he writes them down.' She slams the album shut. 'I'm not going to show you any more.'

Susan takes Pagan's hand. 'Perhaps I should take her upstairs; she's a little fractious.'

'Yes,' your father concurs. 'It would make things easier. We have some serious business to discuss.' I wonder if he means to ask for money. 'I think it would be best. Little pitchers have big ears.'

'I'm not a picture,' Pagan protests; 'I'm a person.'

Susan tells her about old-fashioned words; and I agree to your father's request. I promise – and warn – that I will only spare a few minutes. As I watch Pagan being led out, I am seized by a sense of betrayal.

Your mother turns to me, pressing her curls into her cheeks as though to keep her face in place. 'The last thing we want is to make an enemy of you.' I am confused by the change of tack. 'Father and I are truly grateful for all that you've done. It can't have been easy with Candida so ill for so long. You might have thought she'd have come to her parents; but no, we only even heard by chance . . . well, that's water under the bridge. She preferred to call on a stranger.'

'I was her closest friend.'

'But you weren't family. We've imposed on your good nature long enough.'

'I wouldn't say that; I can think of pleasanter ways of spending an afternoon, but . . .'

'I mean over the last six years.'

I don't . . . I don't want to understand.

'You've done very well for yourself,' your father chips in, as though they are working to formula, the good and bad policemen . . . which of them has the more dangerous smile? 'We never thought much of you when we came to Cambridge; always tagging along with Candida and the Standish boy. Half the time you seemed afraid to open your mouth' . . . Not for the words that might have come out but the vowels. 'And yet you've turned the shyness into an asset. You put your guests at their ease; you make them feel at home.'

'You make the viewer feel at home.'

'The viewer is at home.'

'You make him feel as if you're at home with him. I admire that; it can't come easily. It must take a lot of research, a lot of rehearsal.'

'It's under control.'

'And your documentaries: we read that you prefer them to your show.'

'Egotism, I'm afraid; they're my baby.'

'Last year's *Musical Christmas* was a classic.'

'We filmed in seventeen countries.' I refuse to lower my guard.

'So that's how they spend our licence fee. Only joking, old man. How long did it take to make?'

'Nine months on and off.'

'It can't leave much time for anything else.'

'I can stagger my schedules. If I go abroad, I'll take Pagan.'

'What about school?'

'In the holidays. I want her to have an informed view of the world. I didn't leave England until I was seventeen.'

'It doesn't seem to have held you back.'

'Let me assure you that Pagan is my number one priority. If there's ever any conflict . . .'

'But you shouldn't be in that position,' your mother returns to the fray. 'You're a young man, a single man' . . . . How I wish that you had agreed to marry me. I was never sure if you felt that the institution was second-rate and we would be bowing to the bourgeois or that the ideal was sacred and we would be making it a sham. It would have been a true marriage of convenience . . . not ours but Pagan's. I fear that your scruples may cost her dear.

'You might want to marry.'

'I have quite enough with Pagan.'

'You must admit it's an odd set-up: a grown man and a young girl.'

'We didn't plan on Candida dying.'

'What experience do you have of bringing up a child?'

'What experience does anyone have? You learn as you go along.'

'Trial and error?'

'No, trial and success. It's only three months since Candida died. Pagan had difficulties at first; we both did. It's just that I didn't start pulling my friends' hair at lunch or tearing the pages out of schoolbooks or wetting my pants. But I found ways of helping her accept it . . . that book for one, as we sit and talk and write and paste and remember. Then she has her ballet and her riding and her piano.'

'She doesn't get that from Candida' . . . All this emphasis on blood is a kind of butchery.

'No, she gets it from me.'

'That's all to the good, but, as she grows up, there'll be problems you can't handle. Girl problems –' he corrects himself; 'girl's problems.'

'There's Susan. They're devoted to each other.'

'She's a young woman; she'll want to marry.'

'Not necessarily.'

'I was a school bursar for more than thirty years; there's very little I don't know about young women.'

'Really?' I raise my eyebrows and remember his strictures.

'As employees. They're never reliable.'

'That's insulting.'

'They're all full of good intentions; but at the first whiff of man. . . .'

'There are other nannies.'

'She needs stability: the security of a family; not a succession of second-best.'

'We are a family, she and I: a one-parent –'

'Non-parent –'

'Family.'

'What about lavatories?' your mother interjects. I am lost. 'When you're out and about. She's a young girl with a weak bladder, as you've just admitted. When she needs to pay a visit, what will you do?'

'I'll find a lavatory. I don't understand.' I don't; I really don't.

'And then? You can hardly go into the ladies or take her into the gents.'

'I'll ask someone to take her in; I'll wait outside.'

'With the world as it is, you'll allow her to go into a public lavatory with a perfect stranger?'

'While you lurk outside.'

'I can't believe you're reducing her whole upbringing to a question of lavatories.'

'It has to be faced.'

'So I'll make her carry a whistle. What else would you suggest?'

'Us.'

'What?'

'We've thought it over very carefully –'

'We haven't reached our decision lightly.'

'And Father and I think it would be best if she came to live with us.'

'You think! What gives you the right to think? Candida entrusted Pagan to me. It's in her will: black and white, signed and sealed, legal and binding. I've lived with her all her life; you're passers-by.'

'Whose fault is that? We begged to see her.'

'I've let you see her, against my better judgement, against Candida's express desire. I only hope that she'll forgive me.' Please forgive me. Put not your trust in parents: I should have heeded your advice.

'She may not have been of sound mind; what with illness eating away at her brain.'

'She may not have been of sound muscles, but there was nothing wrong with her mind.'

'That's where you're mistaken. The rot set in very young. I'm her mother, I should know.'

'That's not what she would have said.'

'Why? Because she was adopted? She made it sound like abducted. We took her in; we gave her a home. We may not have been up to her standards; we may not have been rich –'

'She said that you told her her real parents were too poor to look after her. She was always terrified that you'd lose all your money and send her away.'

'From the way that she talked, you'd have thought she'd have been glad.'

'For better or worse, it was still her home.'

'It's our own fault. We were warned against her. Bad blood: it always comes out in the end.'

'You never understood her; you gave her no space. You adopted a daughter; you should have bought a doll.'

'Every word you speak convinces me you are quite unfit to bring up a young girl.'

'I intend to bring up Pagan.'

'That name: it pains me every time I hear it.'

'Easy, Mother.'

'There's a simple solution; don't stay. I'd hate to cause you distress.'

'May we at least say goodbye to our granddaughter?'

'Of course. I'll fetch her.' I bound up the stairs, two at a time, to stress my energy and defiance. I shake my head free of static. Pagan is playing with Raisa and Gorby and wants me to send them on another adventure. I promise one before dinner in return for a quick goodbye to her grandparents, with the coda that she will never have to see them again.

'Can I take the bears?'

'Just as long as you don't tell them their names.' I remember how you accused me of indoctrinating your daughter with Soviet propaganda. Your parents would probably name me as the fifth man.

'Of course not, silly. Names are special. They might try to steal them.'

We go down to the hall. Your parents are standing by the door; your father's face as grey as his mackintosh, your mother's as buttoned up as her coat. 'It's made us so happy to meet you,' she tells Pagan. 'Grandpa and I have been waiting for so long.'

'We look forward to seeing you again soon.'

'But you said . . .' Pagan turns to me in anguish. I mime a sh-sh.

'Perhaps you'd like to stay with us in the Easter holidays?'

'We're going away in the holidays, aren't we, Daddy?'

'Yes.' I blush.

'She calls you Daddy?' Your mother's buttons burst.

'She knows that she's not supposed to.' It feels like taking advantage. She is hardly spoilt for choice. If you were the only girl in the world . . . how could I tell loneliness from love?

'Where are you taking her?'

'It's under discussion. I fancy Corsica; she fancies Butlins.' I catch the grimace on your mother's face. 'She saw a programme on TV and thought that it looked fun.'

'It's fun for grown-ups too. They have lots of little houses and ladies in red coats who walk around at night. So you could go out and leave me.'

'But I don't want to leave you.'

'All grown-ups want to leave children,' she says, and her eyes suffuse with sadness. Is she thinking of you?

'Grandpa and I don't want to leave you; we want to see more of you. We live in a little house by the seaside.'

'Bigger than Butlins,' he adds.

'You could come and stay with us.'

'Does your house have a name?' Pagan asks.

'Yes –'

'So does mine.'

'Really? What's that?'

'Home.'

The kiss freezes on your mother's lips as Pagan stands defiantly behind me.

'Don't think we'll leave it at this; you'll hear from us again.' The effect of her exit is marred when her handbag slips open and spills its contents on the step. She and your father rescue them, while Pagan and I stand aloof.

'I disliked you on first meeting,' he tells me. 'And I see that my instinct was right. Don't worry,' he turns to Pagan, 'your grandparents won't let you down.'

I close the door. The air is suddenly still. Pagan starts to cry. To diffuse the tension, I fetch an air-freshener from the loo and spray the hall like an exorcist. Pagan grabs it from me and runs up to the drawing room, squirting and giggling and shouting 'all gone'. The synthetic scent of woodland pine dispels every trace of malevolence.

'Story, story,' she shouts, flinging herself on the sofa.

'I'm tired,' I insist, knowing that my reluctance is as predictable a prelude as 'Are you sitting comfortably?'

'You promised.'

'Very well.' She buries her head in my lap.

'It was a sweltering summer's day, so Raisa and Gorby decided to give a tea party for their forest friends. She wanted to make some orange juice, but there were no oranges in any of the shops. "Oh dear," she said. "How can I make orange juice without any oranges? I know; I'll ask my friend Andropov." '

'That's a silly name.'

'Are you telling this story, or am I?'

'You, you!'

'So she left a note for Gorby –'

'But a bit me. Like when we do a drawing. You do the lines and I do the colours.'

'So I get the difficult part?'

'Go on!'

'Andropov worked in a marmalade factory.'

'Was he all sticky?'

59

'Yes, all his paws and his fur and his whiskers.' I tickle her.

'Stop it,' she reproaches me. 'You're spoiling the story.'

' "Do you have any oranges you can lend me?" she asked.'

'You won't make me, will you?' she asks.

'Make you what?'

'Go and stay with *them*.' She juts out her lip in scorn like a labret.

'Don't worry. I promised Mummy that I'd look after you. And we must always keep our promises.'

'Not if we have our fingers crossed.'

I spread mine out for inspection; she clasps them and nestles against my knees.

' "What sort of oranges?" he asked. "There are Seville oranges and sour oranges and blood oranges –" '

'Urgh. . . . Ow!' She jumps up as a red spot appears on her leg almost on cue. She looks at it in confusion. I find the cause. It's your mother's St John Ambulance badge; she must have dropped it. *For the faith, for the service of mankind.* I fling it at the grate.

# 4

I advocate a change in the postal system. From now on, no mail is to be delivered before noon; so postmen can spend longer in bed and the rest of us enjoy a few hours' grace. Even a fool's paradise is a paradise of sorts.

Your parents have applied for a residence order for Pagan. I tear open the envelope to find a form as impersonal as a tax demand. . . . There is a child's life at stake! They had to fill in the relevant boxes. Self-employment; capital allowance; cars and car fuel. . . . *The full name of the child is . . . the child is a . . . the child was born on the . . .* Expenses for which you wish to claim; expenses from work abroad; pensions. . . . *The child lives with . . . the child is also cared for by . . . the carer is the child's . . .* Mother's friend: they make me sound so marginal. You and Pagan are my family; you are where I come from and where I come back to. You are my home.

*I am . . . the child; the child's mother or father; a guardian of the child; a person with parental responsibility (see part 4 of the form); none of the above. . . .* That's true. I am the one with parental responsibility; I am Pagan's testamentary guardian. So put a big tick in box five. . . . I am the child's grandmother; I am the child's grandfather. . . . Leave to make the application has been given by the Brighton County Court on the 27th February 1992.

I demand a rebate – a retake – a retraction. I am standing behind police lines watching my house explode. I want to remake my programme on IRA victims. It gained our lowest ever ratings. Bring back Sylvester Stallone! One of the men had seen his daughter murdered and yet he forgave her killers; he was a saint. But I should rake up rancour like the ashes they have made of my heart. Bring back Albert Pierrepoint . . . ! We are making this application because it is our belief that Pagan will be best served by a traditional family structure with two loving grandparents, rather than the ad hoc arrangement occasioned by her mother's death.

They state their case in an affidavit . . . flat vowels may be erased, but not flat words. They interpret Pagan's antagonism towards them as a symptom of general maladjustment. They view the two nude portraits in the hall as the decor of a bordello. And they seize on a five-year-old's verbal confusion about my cooking on a spit to make me sound like the wicked sister in the Grimm fairy tale, the demon expectorator with a mouthful of toads. It would be laughable if it were not so threatening. I can rebut their argument point by point, but I fear for the overall tenor . . . spit sticks.

As I leave Pagan at school, I feel an aching sense of loss. I tell myself that it is my morbid imagination, when I know that it is a premonition. How did such fatuity ever become fate? I wish that I understood the nature of time; I am locked in the past with Isaac Newton. And yet, if all life exists in a permanent present, then the future is a definite force and the psychic as reliable as the historian. My brain consigns the truth to the pit of my stomach. I feel sick.

I repress the urge to drive to Brighton and, instead, pick up the phone. I am prepared to be conciliatory. If this is your parents' idea of revenge, it has worked. I am amply repaid for any hurt to their pride. Your father feigns a diplomatic deafness. I elocute in icy fury; they have no right to punish Pagan in their vendetta against me. He disclaims any such intention and says, with a deal of satisfaction, that they have been instructed not to speak to me. Any further communication should be addressed to their solicitors. The details are on the form.

I ring Max Barrowman. He is all affability and advice. But then he has his daughter's picture propped on his desk like a talisman; no witch or ogre threatens to steal her away. If the guardianship is as watertight as he says, why are they allowed to bring the case? Surely one should be brought against them for wasting the Court's time? But he mutters some cant about 'the best interests of the child'. In any case, the next step is the Directions Hearing in Brighton on March 21st, which will allow for the application to be answered. There is no point in fretting until then.

I fret; I sweat. I wake up in the greyness of the night with a tropical sheen on my skin. How can I ever give her up? I may be over-anxious, but ideas are insidious. I love her so much. At first I just loved the thought of her. I always wanted a child; my favourite services were baptisms. I even wondered whether you and I might revisit Venice . . . but I was afraid that you would feel compromised. Besides, I knew that I was never parental material. My son-of-the-soil stock might serve to spite your mother, but not to father your child.

I fantasise. Since you never named the father, I am as likely a candidate as any. Perhaps I was drunk one night and, when putting me to bed, you were overcome by passion, to which I responded as though in a dream: a delayed adolescence at thirty. Or, to adapt the lavatory-seat theory of sexuality – that convenient receptacle of all our misadventures – while using the shared facilities I let drop some sperm which swiftly impregnated you. It might be the equivalent of swimming the Channel blindfold, but the possibility remains. So I may be Pagan's father; who is to say without a blood test? I destroy my own case; there is more to fatherhood than blood.

You, of course, disagree. Your own parents supply the argument. They never loved you; you and William were part of their domestic ideal: the furniture of mortgage-land. You filled the void like an old lady's budgie. Until your vocabulary grew. Clever Joey . . . silly bitch! Cover the cage . . . go to your room; I won't have language in this house! The peace was shattered and the ideal exposed. And yet you admit that it was not their fault; all love is selfish . . . you wave away my protest. . . . The love of child for parent is self-protection, the love of parent for child self-preservation. And, in the constant clash of wills that constitutes family life, nature provides symbols to prevent complete carnage: her father's nose, her mother's chin . . . fleshy intimations of immortality. But, with adoptive parents, such symbols do not exist; blood is lacking and bloodshed takes its place.

I hope that I state your case fairly; one of my great fears is of misrepresenting you, even to myself, now that you are no longer here to set me right. The truth is that you did not believe in idealism. All love was suspect; even a saint's was just deferred self-interest. And it was impossible to argue without sounding either sentimental or naive. Cynicism has all the smart words on its side; idealism uses a nursery school dictionary. And you studied quickly to disguise your childhood pain. But it is not universal; I know because of what I feel for Pagan. I love her as much as if she were my own . . . more; I love her with a love uncompromised by personal pride or proprietary instinct. I am not listening for my voice or looking for my mother's colouring. I love her for what she is herself.

I admit that I also love her as your daughter; but that is a bonus. In the past months, I have scanned her face for your expression like an explorer with an incomplete map. I delight in her idiosyncracies, while taking heart in their association. It may be heresy, but she reminds me of you far more than any photograph. When she smiles, your face flushes; when she rubs her ankle, you cross your legs.

There are other resemblances, as I discover at the opening of your memorial exhibition. Helena has filled the gallery with nearly two hundred of your photographs; and I have invited a similar number of guests. We arrive far too early; so, to calm my nerves and to prevent Pagan gorging all the canapés, I take her next door to inspect the opposition. 'Where are the pictures?' she asks in an audible whisper. The only exhibit is *Wall Street*, in which a pin-striped artist paces up and down a paper-strewn compound. While the adult visitors strive for meaning, she strips off his new clothes.

'What are you making?'

'I'm making a statement.'

'You're making a mess.'

I remove her and return to your retrospective, where there are enough pictures to satisfy the youngest critic. It is a shock to see so much of your life laid out, and in the confines of one room. I look at the early Soho portraits and wonder how many of those women are still alive. I try not to recognise their faces; I try not to remember their stories; I rename Brewer Street Acacia Avenue as I invest us with post-Cambridge careers that would placate even your parents. But the women are more real. They may be stripped of glamour but never of dignity. The straining dress over padded hips, the caked make-up over pitted skin, the smudged lipstick over rotten teeth are never the whole story. The light with which you suffuse their features is no mere trick of the trade . . . you had a very different trade; the sexual sympathy shines through.

'What is it you do?' There is a lull in the dining-room chatter.

'I photograph brothels.'

'Nice work if you can get it.'

'I did. I was on the game myself. For fun, I took pictures of some of the other girls. One of my punters worked for the *Criterion*. He arranged my first commission. Now, there's barely a red light from Berlin to Bangkok that hasn't been filtered through my lens.' Conversation chokes. Your eyes meet mine in triumph . . . the truth is dangerous, Leo; you must only admit it when you can be sure that it won't be believed. Our hostess wipes her mouth and turns to her husband.

'Ask a silly question, darling . . .' He slaps his forehead.

'I know; I'd be hopeless on *What's My Line?*' You break the tension with a titter.

'So, are you on the *Criterion* staff?'

'No, freelance. I go with anyone who'll pay me.' All lingering doubts are dispelled by the obvious metaphor. Regular small talk is resumed.

'Candida's just been invited to join the Magnum Agency. She's had spreads in dozens of magazines. Not only prostitutes.'

'Leo's afraid it might rub off on me . . . my darkroom a private backroom. But they remain my trademark. I am to tarts what Cezanne was to apples.'

'She's just come back from Manila.'

'Are any of your pictures for sale?'

'Oh yes. Prurience pays.'

The scene fades into inconsequentiality; and I look

again at the Filipino girl standing next to her one-eyed pimp, his proprietorial hand emphasising his missing fingers, her inane grin her abject youth. What strikes me most is the lack of prurience. This is no tourist tut-tutting, no pictorial equivalent of fish on Friday and sins of the flesh the rest of week. As the couple stare boldly at the camera, gazes drop and certainties shift. Who will throw the first stone? He who threw the first coin? One man's transgression is another's transaction. I know; thanks to you, I was there.

His missing fingers haunt me. Just as you offer no easy morality, you allow no painless pleasure. This is sex on the knife-edge, a dance to the music of mutilation, blood streaming down the legs as it rushes to the brain. These are pictures from a war-zone . . . ravaged faces in a rictus of horror. Where I once saw documents of others' desperation, I now see only your own.

'Who are those ladies?' Pagan points to a pair of bleary-eyed, bloated Spaniards.

'Actresses,' I reply, and recall an earlier excuse in a Soho strip joint. 'She's just doing it to get her Equity card.'

'Let's look at those,' I say, 'they're in colour.' And I rush her away from the backstreets of Barcelona, just as I brush aside our own Soho nights.

Question: when is a call-girl not a prostitute?

I give up; when is a call-girl not a prostitute?

When she's my best friend.

The faces change; the gaps in the teeth narrow; the pores close. The clever call-girl reinvents herself as actress, aristocrat and magnate's mistress; and you match her progress with your own. Film stars guying their fame, countesses clinging to the wreckage, tycoons glorying in excess: no wonder they all clamoured for your treatment. You made their profligacy heroic, their vulgarity ironic, their frivolity wit. People were your forte; which is strange, since you never seemed to like them that much. Or did the camera contain them? I think of the Africans who feared that it would steal their souls. You had no truck with souls; but you did control their image. You were the eyes of the eighties. . . . In the decade of the morally myopic, the one-eyed woman is queen.

Lights flash, as my own image is captured for the

morning papers. I raise a glass of champagne to their breakfast orange juice: a buck's fizz uniting the new two nations, celebrity and crowd. I exchange a few words with a journalist and picture the inevitable captions: *TV's Leo pays tribute to Candida's candid camera . . . Lonely Leo says life will never be the same.* And, as I sell my soul for a few squares of newsprint, I realise that the Africans were right.

Much to her annoyance, I remove Pagan from the line of fire. She has kissed enough cheeks and eaten too many 'alcoholic cherries', so I send her home with Susan and turn my attention to our friends. The Cambridge contingent is so strong that, for a moment, I find myself back at the Freshers' Squash . . . belts are tightened, the Guccis become Levis, and the gallery dissolves into the Corn Exchange, filled with posters enticing us to every kind of activity. The Cambridge Stamp Collecting Society catches my eye . . . and sticks in my mind; it seems such a contradiction in terms. Stamps are for simple-minded men like George V and my father, not the intellectual élite to which I aspire. I find it disturbing; you find it intriguing. 'We must join at once,' you say, 'and make it chic.'

My old insecurities erupt like acne. You have no idea how alien your Cambridge is to me. I would be happier downing a pint of Abbot at the Baron of Beef with the choirmen; but I am flattered into restaurants with you and Robin and your 'chic' friends. You don't know how often I fail to order what I want because I am afraid of mispronouncing it . . . or worse.

'Don't let's go to *Don Pasquale* tonight.'

'I thought you liked Italian food.'

Half the time I am not even sure what it means and play safe with spaghetti. Or else I try to attract your attention by dropping my napkin (née serviette). 'Psst, what's zucchini?'

'Courgettes.'

I sit up, none the wiser. What are courgettes?

It is another world from the meat and two veg of my mother's guest-house where 'c' stood for cabbage, cauliflower or carrot, not calabash, chicory or courgette. Forget the social whirl; I am in a social maze where everyone seems to be related, so much so that I wonder whether cousin might be a courtesy title like esquire. And, even when I learn to put names to faces, it is impossible to put them to college lists because they all have nicknames that have been given to them by nannies – and stuck. I didn't have a nanny; I had a nan. I loved her with the one uncompromised emotion of my life. Until I met you and it was compromised by language. Now I cover my embarrassment – and the word – with a cough.

You move through the maze as though each dead end were an opening. I used to think it was that you were well connected; I know now it is that you are well read. Mix two parts Sally Bowles and three parts Becky Sharp with a dash of Zuleika Dobson; and there you have her – you – Candida Mulliner. I am never sure how carefully the ingredients are calculated; but the effect is intoxicating. Cambridge laps you up like an exotic cocktail. And yet the discerning palate picks out the strong taste of bitters underneath.

'Dear heart' ... a hand strokes my spine; I turn to confront Imogen. 'Don't look at me,' she squeals coquettishly; 'I'm a fearful mess.' I try hard not to nod, as I take in the bird's-nest hair, the face that is the visual equivalent of a giggle and the Cupid's-bow lips which look more like a pantomime pout. She cloys me in an embrace. We discuss life (hers), death (yours), and the universe. Her thesis is now twelve years overdue, but she blames that on Morgan le Fay. 'She's afraid of my research, and so she does all in her power to thwart me. She's placed a hex on my love-life. Why else would so many men vanish into thin air?' My self-control is as great as her self-deception. 'I speak as one witch of another.' Girth aside, she seems scarcely to have changed since she cornered me on the Bridge of Sighs after the John's May Ball.

'Don't you like me?'

'I like you like a sister.'

She rips open her dress and bares her bust to the dawn. 'Does you sister have breasts like these?'

My hands reach to screen her décolletage from the gallery's gaze and the embarrassment from my memory. She seizes my fluttering fingers and presses them to her lips. 'I worry about you, Leo. You're letting life pass you by.'

'I lead a very full life.'

'Not a sexual life. No, allow me to speak. You mustn't neglect it. You're a very sensual man.'

'I don't have a sister.'

'What?'

'Nothing.'

'You have deep, dark forces welling inside you; they need release. Are you afraid of your orgasms?'

'Imogen, you're spilling wine on your dress.'

'Always so practical. But there's darkness in you; there's danger. I can tell.'

'I don't have a sex life. I know that defines me as somewhat more deviant than a serial killer, but I have all the love I need in Pagan.'

'What are you trying to hide?'

'I'm a boringly transparent person.'

'This is me, Imogen. I know you of old.'

I'll try to explain . . . to you, not to her. I see myself in Pagan's eyes and I feel a glow. I catch myself in the unexpected mirrors of chance encounters and I am repulsed. You know that sex is not important to me. That is why you trusted me with Pagan. 'The thing about Leo,' I hear you say, 'is that he isn't interested in women, men or dogs.' I will not let your confidence be misplaced.

'Find yourself a boy,' she is saying. 'Better still, find two.'

'What's that?' Trust Duncan Mossop to sniff out any sexual snippet. But then he is acting true to form and even to physiognomy . . . with his sharp eyes, aquiline nose and pallid complexion, he looks more than ever like Sherlock Holmes.

'I was just telling Leo to find an amenable boy.'

'It would hardly go down well at the Beeb: Aunty's favourite nephew doing the dirties. Besides, I always thought you were above all that. I remember Candida telling me you weren't interested in boys, girls or dogs.'

'That was you?'

'It made me feel a bit iffy. I mean I'm there with Mrs Pat: anything that doesn't scare the horses. But dogs . . . Though that was Candida all over: putting ideas in your head. From then on, every time I saw a borzoi . . . '

The coincidence is unnerving. I am confused; he must have mentioned it first. Or is it a sign? I connect everything

69

with the Brighton hearing. I have grown as superstitious as a widow with her only son at sea.

Anecdotes abound, as everyone tries to pull rank in intimacy, basking in reflected aphorisms . . . she made her wittiest riposte/played her most outrageous trick/dealt her most devastating blow when she was with me. Duncan describes how you took a white stick to the Henry Moore exhibition, 'so that she could fondle the sculpture, and was only found out when she began to take photographs. Even then, for a few moments, the guard believed that her camera had been specially adapted for the blind.'

Brian ffoulkes tells of an invitation to the Ritz in the days when it was as remote as Rio. 'She insisted that I ordered the most expensive dishes and, as I became increasingly uneasy, explained that she had no intention of paying. "Drink up," she urged, as I turned the colour of my Chartreuse, and then threw the remains of her dessert at me. Screaming insults, she chased me onto the street and halfway across St James's. No one followed. The only expense was removing the *crème brûlée* from my suit.'

In the ensuing laughter, my own rings somewhat hollow. I am disconcerted to discover so many unknown stories about you. Are they true? They sound in character; but the outlines of your character are covered in myth. Legends accumulate like lichen; I am left scratching the surface. Why did you never stage such stunts with me? Did you think me too stuffy? Or am I too poor an actor to carry them off?

Duty draws me to Edward and Melissa, both so tall and trim and tanned, like founder members of an exclusive gym. Carefully dressed-down in matching designer denim, they stand examining your Palestinian camps. 'It's a magnificent display,' he says; 'she was a genuine artist.'

'A talented craftswoman, I grant' . . . she grants; 'their composition is striking. But they remain arid.'

'Well they are set in the desert.'

'Don't try to be clever, Edward; you know very well what I mean. Candida the humanitarian just doesn't ring true. She slips on the role along with her flak jacket. There's no engagement.'

'Well I admire them.'

'You respond to them; you're in the same game. They are

to art what your columns are to literature.' I look the other way, into the void. 'I never feel she cares about people. Except the whores. She showed real sympathy with whores. Otherwise she never gives herself.'

'As I recall, she gave herself quite liberally.' He grins at me complicitly. Her glare checks him and sets my mind racing. I resent their conscripting my memories in their private warfare. I have reached a consensus with the past that is now threatening to explode. They dig up old bones – the relics of youthful folly – which I have long since buried . . . which you have long since buried. They scatter them over the well-kept lawns on which we have walked for years. They turn my garden of remembrance into a field of contention. They have no right; they forget the meaning of 'friend'.

Melissa runs her hand through her mop of greying hair – its mass strangely at odds with its colour – and claims to be missing you, which, considering how little she liked you, I find somewhat bizarre. But perhaps your case is proved . . . 'Even old friends are expendable, but no one can replace the enemies we make in our youth.'

I am back there now in conversation – in Clare Gardens. We are rehearsing *As You Like It*. Melissa is giving her Rosalind, Edward his Orlando and you your Celia. I am Amiens, on account of the songs. Only Robin is missing. Having failed in his bid for an all-male production, in which to recapture the magic – and the wardrobe – of his schoolboy Imogen, he has rejected Silvius in a sulk. We explore the scene. Julius is frustrated by the chastity of expression; he is adamant that it is a play about passion, not pastoral, and proposes an exercise where we form a line according to the last time that we had sex. I make for the safety of the middle; even though honesty requires the rear. But that is occupied by Isabel Leaver, who tearfully declares herself a virgin. Julius takes her in his arms . . . did he learn how to hug in California? 'That's great,' he tells her; 'that's really something special. You're a truly beautiful woman. Any man would be glad to have you. I myself would be honoured. . . . ' At which point she shrieks and runs off through the bushes. Julius deputes the props mistress to follow her and turns to us.

'That's it; that's the kind of emotional honesty I want.

This is a play about losing your virginity. It hits you here and here.' He gestures anatomically. 'It's a rite of spring. Blood, sweat, sperm.'

'And comedy?' someone asks.

'Sure. Sex is funny. It's the funniest thing in the world'. . . . Is that where I have been going wrong? 'Two bodies squealing and squelching in absurd positions: it's pure slapstick. But, if we're to bring out the humour, we have to be honest . . . OK?'

He walks down the line as if inspecting troops. You, needless to say, are at the head. You see me ranked between Stuart Coley-Brown and Phil Sharman and smile at my self-assessment. My knees knock like a classroom cheat's. I expect exposure; but Julius begins to speak.

'Now, one by one, we're going to say when we last had sex, what we did, how it felt and what it meant.' There are murmurs of mutiny. 'Trust me. Only this way can we strip off our inhibitions and reach to the heart of the play. You want to be actors; you are actors. . . . ' No, I am not; I am a choral scholar. I am a novice when it comes to acting, let alone sex. 'You have to be true to Shakespeare; you have to be true to each other; and, dare I say it, you have to be true to me. I love you all; don't betray me.'

My mind blanks as I try to think up a story that will titillate but not humiliate and worry that, if the production fails, it will be the direct result of my mendacity. I wish I had stuck to the choir and blame you for coercing me. Even climbing the tower on Ascension Day is less frightening than this. My attention returns to Julius.

'Candida, you've assumed pride of place. Let's see if it's merited.'

'It's the only thing about her that is.' Melissa's off-stage whisper whirrs in the wind.

'When was the last time you had sex?'

'About half an hour before rehearsal.'

Melissa snorts. If the point of the exercise is to bind the ensemble, it is going sadly awry.

'Tell us about it.'

'If only I could. It was just an after-lunch quickie. Not even wham-bam, more flop-plop. I wasn't in the mood, but a friend came round – that's the trouble with being in King's; one's so central – and, well, *tendresse oblige*.'

72

'No wonder you're known as the college bicycle.' Melissa has left Rosalind way behind.

'Oh, last week, it was the college tandem.' This creates a genuine frisson; Julius is delighted. Is it a passing cloud or does Edward turn grey?

'Tell us more.' Julius squats by your side . . . a calf-crippling position which he feels duty-bound to maintain.

'First, you tell me something,' you target Melissa, who stands beside Edward in all the misplaced confidence of confirmed coupledom. 'When did you last have sex?'

'Saturday, if you must know. We don't all feel the need to go at it every hour of the day and night.'

'And you, Edward?'

'Saturday, I just said. I think I can speak for us both.'

'But Melissa dear, you weren't on the tandem.'

'What?'

'Edward, I fear you've not been honest.' Your tone mocks everyone: him, Melissa, Julius, even yourself. 'How can you hope to reach the heart of Orlando if you're not honest about your own? You've spent months trying to worm your way into my knickers. Then you come round last week with Brendan Hislop and practically rape me.'

'This is pathetic,' Melissa sneers.

'Oh no, apart from the odd puncture, it was the Tour de France.'

Melissa breaks out of the line in which we stand like a Sunday school crocodile. 'Is this true?' she challenges Edward, who squirms, searching desperately for support that is not forthcoming. 'We went round. Brendan . . . we were drunk. Fooling around. It was late. Fooling . . . just fooling.'

You sigh. 'And I suppose last week at Newmarket was fooling too?'

'What?'

'Candida told me she'd never been to the races.'

'You whore!' She strides up to you. . . . A voice from the future rings in my ear: 'Except the whores. She showed real sympathy with whores'. . . . She grabs your wrist; I prepare to assert my best-friend status.

'You're sick. You can't bear the idea of two people in love. Like a spoilt child, you want to destroy everything you can't have.'

'Oh I had it. And I'm not the only one. Ask Clare Lennox, Leonora Jardine, Hilary Parker.' Melissa responds with a scream that is more Medea than Rosalind. Julius intervenes.

'OK, cut. That was fabulous. Now the important thing is to use these emotions: pain, jealousy, resentment, power. Let them inform your performance. There's far more to love than sentiment.'

'And there's far more to life than theatre. You think I mean to share the stage with her . . . with him.' It is the first time that I have seen Melissa look vulnerable; Lucinda Dodd understudies Celia and leads her away. Julius appears perplexed.

'You don't understand. That was a breakthrough. We must build on it now. Act Three Scene Two. Orlando, Corin, Touchstone, Rosalind and Celia.' But the lovers have left the glade: the actors have left the garden. Edward approaches indignantly.

'Thanks a bunch. You landed me right in the faeces.'

'Don't worry, you'll come out on top; you always do.'

'Will she ever forgive you?' I inject a note of practicality.

'Oh yes. She'll threaten boiling oil but let me off with bread and water. It's par for the course.'

'You're wrong. You're not just in the shit; you are one.'

'Why else did you want me?'

Your reply is lost in the breeze from the backs . . . and the mists of memory. Edward is right about Melissa, who packs her bags for Girton and then tells the taxi to wait. After all, she knows his weaknesses; and it would be punishing him twice over to leave him in your clutches. But she won't trust you with him or herself with you. She refuses to play Rosalind if you remain as Celia; and Julius, weighing your respective parts – not, I assure you, your talents – substitutes Lucinda. You insist that it is a relief; you have had your fill of Cambridge theatricals. But I worry. Gazing into a dressing-room mirror is the acceptable face of fantasy; when that is removed, there are more dangerous ones to explore.

Rosalind is reconciled to Orlando and scores a triumph. She refuses to let any private grief cast a shadow over Arden just as she refuses to miss a performance on the night that her mother dies. No doubt her professionalism impresses the London agent in the audience. You sit sportingly in the front row and bravo her solo call. But you stay silent at Edward's. The loss is too painful. I misjudged his appeal. I thought that it was the subterfuge that attracted you, not the man . . . unless they were one and the same and his callousness fed your cynicism. And you misjudged his maturity. He needed the reassurance of Melissa's reactions. Naughtiness is no fun without a nurse.

The chance for revenge comes at their wedding. Your scarlet dress fills me with foreboding as we drive to Suffolk and enter the church directly behind the bride.

'Which side?' asks an etiolated usher.

'Oh the groom's, definitely,' you say with such a knowing laugh that I give thanks for the soaring chords of the Charpentier *Te Deum* and the focus of attention on the nave. Two hours later, you are at his side less publicly when Melissa's nanny – the real thing, no self-revealing diminutive – discovers you indulging a very unbibliographic passion in the library.

'We share a taste for fine bindings,' you protest as Melissa's father orders us from the house. 'It was just a final fling,' you insist to me in the car.

'It was their wedding day!'

'I know; I bought them a toaster.'

'That hardly gives you *droit de seigneur*. They made a vow.'

'I see. So it's God I've offended?'

'It has nothing to do with religion; it's basic decency.'

'I suppose that's the trouble. I have none.'

'That's nothing to be proud of.'

'I can't help it. I'm just a slut. It's in my blood.'

'Don't start that. Morality isn't genetic. We're talking about the Candida cunt not the Hapsburg chin.'

You twiddle the radio; I accelerate to distort the sound.

'Melissa was right: I'm no good; I destroy everything I can lay my hands on. So take care. One day I'll even destroy you.'

'You're talking nonsense. You made me. Think what I was like when I met you; my bluffer's guide to life tucked neatly inside my *Companion Guide to Venice*. My only distinction was my voice. I'd have probably wound up in the Mike Sammes Singers.'

'Oh darling, you're so sweet.' You lean over and kiss me. 'Who needs men when I have you?'

'Thank you'. . . . And for a long time I did. I thought that we had something deeper than the ordinary; now I wonder if it were not just more oblique. Seeing all these people with their little bits of you makes me question our intimacy. They turn a portrait into a patchwork. Even Edward casts his doubts. I remember an uneasy lunchtime in the French pub when he described how you liked to play dead in bed. Your fantasy was that he was breaking into your coffin. You were cold and crystalline: the ultimate taboo. Why? Was it the lure of self-destruction? Or was there a more sinister attraction? I will never know.

What do any two people ever know of each other? I look at Melissa examining the exhibits and Edward standing two paces behind, less like a consort than an irreverent footman, and ponder on their relationship. She no longer conceals her contempt for him. It is as though she cannot understand how, of all the men in the world, he was the one she fell in love with. Now nothing remains of that love but their children. . . . 'All sons,' she asserts with a peasant pride. Indeed, half the time she treats Edward as if he were one of them. 'I'm surrounded by boys,' she simpers, rewriting *Oedipus* as *Peter Pan*. No wonder Edward resists his parental role.

'You've been on my conscience for weeks,' she tells me. 'But life has been somewhat fraught.'

'Really?'

'A succession of family crises.'

'Dougall and drugs.'

'Edward, you promised! It was never proved. Besides, is your nose clean?'

'Well I never stuffed coke up it at fifteen.'

'Too busy sniffing around elsewhere.'

'Not as successfully as your darling second son. I've spent the last week trying to placate homicidal Belgians. Sweeney's thirteen-year-old girlfriend is on the pill.'

'She explained; she has very heavy periods.'

'I suppose that's why her father's applying for a posting in Dar es Salaam.'

'It's no joke. If you'd shown more interest in them when they were younger, none of this might have happened. As it was, I had to be both mother and father. It never works.'

'Doesn't it?' I think of myself.

'Children need two parents: one to remonstrate, one to reassure.'

'If you wanted a neo-Victorian husband, you should have married your father.'

'I'd make do with just a husband.'

'Family life, Leo: it's no joke. You're well out of it.'

'I have Pagan.'

'Of course, I forgot. But that's different.'

'Why? I'm her guardian.'

'Yes, I know. But it's always different, isn't it? Other people's children.'

'Why? Why is it different?'

'Whoa there! All I meant was that the stakes aren't so high.'

'In this case they couldn't be higher.' Am I becoming paranoid? I suspect them of being emissaries from your parents, sent to change my mind. But I cannot recall if they ever met, in Cambridge or after, and my memory resists all attempts at manipulation.

'Actually,' Melissa intervenes, 'we wanted to talk to you about Pagan.'

'Oh yes?'

'I'm not sure that this is the time, but I suppose it's as good as any. Laura says you mean to keep her.'

'You talk as though she were a stray puppy! Of course I shall keep her. She's my life.'

'Have you thought – of course you've thought – but have you really thought what you're doing? Looking after a child isn't easy.'

'You managed.'

'But there were two of us.' She flicks ash over her skirt and her inconsistencies. 'You have a life of your own. You can't sacrifice it for Pagan. On the contrary, you need someone who'll do as much for you'. . . . Not another! What do they all want: to fix me up or file me away?

'Like you and Edward?'

'Well, I don't suppose it'll be quite like that. After all, we've been together eighteen years. We have something very special. It's hardly the same for you. Besides,' she adds quickly, 'you wouldn't want to ape heterosexual marriage. We must seem awfully staid.'

'I'm sure that you have your moments.'

'You can't devote all of your life to children. As a mother, I know. They grow up and you resent them for it, while they resent you for making them feel guilty. I know that you think it's your duty; but you also have a duty to yourself. Now's the perfect opportunity. To tell the truth, I never thought it was healthy your living with Candida for so long.'

'Why when people say "to tell the truth" is the truth they tell always unpleasant?'

'Everyone could see that she was using you. You were the perfect partner, providing the comfort of the double mortgage without the pressure of the double bed. But it can't have been the same for you. Of course, it may have fulfilled some deep-seated masochism.'

'Melissa . . .'

'No, Edward, we're Leo's friends. If we can't be honest with him, who can?'

'That's it, Melissa; the secret's out. Actually, she used to wear thigh-length PVC boots with six-inch stiletto heels, and spurs on Sundays, and I wore a red-satin jockstrap. Then she stood over me with a whip while I scrubbed the house from top to bottom.'

'Really . . . ? Oh God, am I losing my ear for irony?'

'The short answer's yes.'

'There are people like that.'

'I know, I've read your novels. . . . Candida and I were friends. You remember: Plato, E. M. Forster, the Famous Five. We loved each other.'

'You used each other.'

'Have a canapé, precious. Have two.'

'No, Edward. We've talked about it often enough. And we aren't alone.'

'I didn't know you cared. . . .' Now I know that they don't.

'Of course it was an excellent front. I used to think that it was to hide from the tabloids; now I suspect it was to hide from yourself.'

'Put me in a story, Melissa – all names changed to

protect the inadequate – and then I'll be able to see for myself.'

'But you can't hide behind Pagan the way you hid behind Candida. She's not even your own child.'

'It's not so long ago that you were going to adopt a Romanian baby; would you have loved it any less than your own?'

'Of course. I have to be honest. We'd never have shown it. We'd have given him everything: Hampstead, Southwold, us. But I can't pretend it would have been like a child I'd carried.' I start to see your objections to your mother. 'Why did Candida never say who the father was? It was pure amateur dramatics; a mystery in a played-out genre. I suppose she'd got all the mileage she could from her own origins – no one's interested in your parents when you're thirty – so she had to muddy things for her daughter instead. She always had to be different; she couldn't even give birth like the rest of us. She had to be the most miraculous mother since Mary. And, since virginity would have defeated even her, she decided to throw a veil over the father.'

'Maybe she genuinely didn't know,' Edward suggests.

'That's something a woman always knows. It was sheer attention-seeking. Hey Mummy, look at me; my baby has no daddy. Aren't I the wickedest girl in the world?'

'Maybe Edward knows better than either of us.'

'Why? What's that supposed to mean?'

'What I said.'

'There was nothing between them but some stupid student stunts. We were children.'

'That's alright then.'

'Why does everyone picture Edward as a latterday Don Juan? I wish!'

'Don't make such a fuss! I'm married to you, aren't I? Candida's dead.'

I recall how you met in secret for years after he married and calculate as desperately as a teenager late with her period. Could it be Edward? I discounted him years ago. Now I mentally transpose Pagan and Dougall . . . no; Rory . . . no; Sweeney . . . well, there is a likeness about the mouth. This is absurd. What a sentimental view of family resemblance! I don't look anything like my father and I know . . . at least I assume . . . it couldn't possibly . . . Is nothing sacred? Or at least sure?

'What's the matter?' Melissa asks. 'You have a wild look in your eyes.'

'It's nothing. I was just speculating on Pagan's father.'

She examines the room as if it were the hall of a country house thriller.

'Pagan's the one who'll suffer. Children can be so cruel . . . to themselves as much as to each other. When her friends stop taunting her, then she'll start on herself.'

'I'll be here to prevent it.'

'And what will you do if one day her father does turn up?'

'You're plotting again.'

'If he claims her, he'd have a powerful case. And children are fickle, always ready to throw up the tried and tested for the thrill of the new. I'm under no illusions about ours; they'd ditch us at the first opportunity. You can't close your eyes to these things.'

If she only knew; mine are propped open with matchsticks, bloodshot testaments to sleepless nights. Her words echo in my head as I drive down to the coast. Instead of support from my friends, all I gain is confusion. And I can no longer even be sure of myself. Is she right? I rack my motives. Am I hiding from the implications of my sexuality? Am I so afraid of rejection that I take the easiest option? Why do I rate a bedtime kiss from Pagan above a night of torrid passion? I switch on the windscreen wipers; but the raindrops are tears.

Self-doubt becomes self-dramatisation, a process heightened by the backdrop of Brighton. I make my way through the web of winding streets, as ramshackle as theatre wings, that leads to the footlit flamboyance of the Front. I aim for the Court with the aid of Max's map. To ask directions risks recognition. I search for a building that combines the majesty of the law with the raffishness of a town that exists on the edge of it. I sigh with relief, and then disbelief, as I see the signs.

It is a squat, unimpressive building, like a polytechnic that has lost its funding. The brutality of the architecture fails to inspire hope. I have to remind myself that I am not on trial. Max meets me and tells me again that I did not need to come. I know full well that it is just a preliminary hearing to allow for the filing of affidavits and that ten minutes in court scarcely justify a two-hour drive, but I want the Judge to appreciate how important the case is to me. I even fantasise that he may be a fan. As it is, he addresses all his remarks to Counsel and barely looks at me.

Your parents are even more determined to ignore me. They abort my every glance. I delight in any discomfort I can cause. I sense a calculated air of grievance about their appearance; although it may just be the faded formality of their clothes. Your mother's floral print dress and your father's cavalry twill are designed to define them as the backbone of England. My concern is with the heart.

I listen to Counsel's statements. Max has engaged Rebecca Colestone whom he rates as the finest QC in the Family Division; but today she has sent her junior, whose name I fail to catch. He is disconcertingly young, less like a qualified lawyer than a student performing in a Footlights sketch, an impression heightened by the lack of a wig and gown . . . the decor may be authentic but where are the props? I must stop these theatrical analogies. This is real; it is happening to me. I suspect that it is his youth which makes me uneasy. I just wish that he would show less interest in my career and more in my case.

The Judge makes an order for myself and any witnesses to file affidavits within twenty-eight days. I immediately resolve to marshal my forces with as impressive a list of signatures as a protest letter to *The Times*. But Max and the revue artist advise against it and say that the only statements necessary are from Susan, Dr Bradshaw, Miss Lister and, perhaps, my mother. The Judge also rules that the case is to be heard on the first open day after two months. My disgust at the delay doubles when officials tell us that this will not be before the end of June.

My real resentment is reserved for the Welfare Officer's report. It is not that I subscribe to some superior notion that welfare officers, like toilets and the dole, are for other people. I was once another person myself; I can still feel the humiliation when they examined my head for lice at school. But, in such an open-and-shut case as this, it seems a shocking waste of resources. And I am worried about the effect on Pagan. I have taken great care that she should

81

have no hint of the threat hanging over us. Now I must bang another nail in the coffin of childhood, alongside the dangers of sweet-offering strangers and drivers proposing lifts.

Her legs go limp and her eyes water; and I realise that, despite the colloquialism, children are the hardest people to kid. I sit her on my lap and explain in my best ice-cream voice that, when they came to tea, her grandparents did not like the way that I was looking after her and so they are sending someone – a sort of teacher – to check.

'Miss Lister's my teacher.'

'She'll just ask a few questions. It won't last long. And if it makes Granny and Grandpa happy.'

'I don't want them to be happy. I hate them.'

'Then you must say so to the lady.' I abandon all pretence of objectivity. 'You must tell her everything.'

'They're old,' she repeats, 'they're old.'

'It's very important that you say how much you want to stay with me.'

'If they send me away, I'll run away like Tom in *The Babies*.' You were right; Kingsley is not suitable reading for a five-year-old. 'Or *101 Dalmatians*.' There again, I am beginning to wonder what is.

'You mustn't worry; it'll all be fine, so long as you say everything – absolutely everything – to the lady. Then she'll say it all for you and in big, long words.'

At supper she is subdued; but she rallies as she slips on her pyjamas, using the two-legs-in-one-hole trick to re-run the school sack race. She lies back and falls asleep during one of Gorby's and Raisa's more involved adventures, somewhat to my own chagrin since I am keen to see how it ends. Then, at half-past midnight, my doorknob turns slowly as she appears, clutching a teddy, teetering on the brink of defiance.

'You should be in bed, miss.'

'I had a bad dream; it was horrid. It was all about Mummy and she had a face like a doll.' I pat the mattress and she runs towards me. 'She had eyes like buttons and they didn't look at me.'

'It's all over; don't think of it.' Her hot heart pounds against my chest.

'Dreams are so nasty. Why do we have to have them?'

'It's like clearing up your room when there's mess on the floor. All the mess gets brushed into dreams, so that in the morning it will be neat and tidy.'

'I wish we didn't have dreams. I wish we didn't have sleep at all.'

'Then think how tired we'd be.'

'I'm going to learn to sleep with my eyes open.'

'Come on, I'll take you back to bed.'

'Can't I sleep in your bed?'

'You know you're not supposed to.'

'Please . . . I'll only take a teeny much room. I'm still small.'

'Well alright. Just this once.' She jumps in. 'I don't remember saying anything about teddy.' She clutches him to her chest, too tired to play games. I switch off the light; she absorbs my warmth and falls asleep. The kicks to my thigh attest to her restlessness; but, after a while, I doze, only to wake to feel something hot and sticky on my leg. She has wet the bed. I hear you complain that women always have to sleep in the damp patch and hate myself for making the connection. Then I am knocked in the groin as she twists and turns, shouting 'fast forward'. I know that I am tired, but 'fast forward' . . . ? 'Fast forward . . . fast forward.' Of course. Has video culture even invaded our dreams?

I shake her gently out of her nightmare and lull her back to sleep before she opens her eyes. I carry her to her room and fetch her clean pyjamas, reassured by the soapy freshness of the smell. Too exhausted to attend to my sheets, I opt for your room. The bed is cold and unfamiliar and sleep is hard. In the morning, I apologise to Consuela for the extra work and explain that Pagan was disrupted. She says nothing but rips off the soiled sheet, screws it tight, and, holding it at arm's length, feeds it to the machine.

From her look of disgust, more profound than any I have known since my mother discovered my teenage copy of Health and Efficiency, I sense that she does not believe me. Does she think that I am using Pagan as an excuse for my own incontinence? It is almost funny. But the smile freezes on my lips, as the thought flicks through my mind, that she may suspect something infinitely worse.

83

# 5

I keep my memories under lock and key; they would be prime evidence in your parents' case against me . . . since November my only confidant has been death. And yet I fail to keep them under control; the past shows no more respect in retrospect. Memory is the mockery of the well-ordered mind.

I escape from your parents to mine. The hearing has now been postponed for a month and I make my annual pilgrimage home. My mother opens the door as the car pulls up. Her timing as always is perfect. I strain to see the shiver of a curtain or the shadow of a face pressed to the glass; but it must be second sight. 'I have eyes in the back of my head,' she used to tell me, as my misdeeds spilled out like contraband chocolates on the floor. And I believed her. Although her image backfired when, in an end-of-term painting of 'my mother', I opted for a spider-like alien with four popping eyes and three pairs of pincer-like hands. The teacher asked her in to discuss it. They decided that I should give up art.

'It's good of you to come,' she says, wiping her hands on her apron in a show of anticipation and disturbance. 'I know how busy you are.'

'Never too busy to see my old mum.' I sound like a travelling salesman.

'Let me look at you.' She looks with her hands. 'You're skin and bone.'

'I'm twelve and a half stone.'

'You don't take care of yourself. You need someone to take care of you.'

'I have Consuela.'

'That's not what I mean; and well you know it.'

'Mother, please, I'm not yet through the door.'

We stand by a balustrade of peeling stucco. Gleneagles guest-house: the name seems so nebulous. A No Vacancies sign in my mother's classiest curlicue hangs in the porch. She won a prize for calligraphy at fourteen and has written the chapel notices ever since. Some of the elders took it amiss. The loop on her 'p's was suspiciously flamboyant, not to mention the tail of her 'q's. Where would it end: smells, bells and priests in chasubles? I could have reassured them. One whiff of Gleneagles and its airless, cheerless sobriety would have shown that she was sound.

She offers her cheek – she never kisses me – it is surprisingly soft. She turns to Pagan. 'How's my little girl then . . . not so little any more.'

'I've grown two inches since Christmas.'

'You're lucky; at my age, you start to shrink.'

'Are you very old?'

'Not too old to give you a big hug.' She lifts Pagan and extends the kiss that she has kept from me. Pagan responds with reassuring enthusiasm.

'I've put you in number three and Pagan in number four.'

'Next door.'

'Not number six?' – the Hawaii of guest rooms, added when I finally moved to London and the Egon Schiele posters were replaced by Van Gogh Sunflowers and the bean-bag by a chintzy chair. And yet I still like to use it, prompted more by fantasy than nostalgia: that I might wake up again as a boy of seventeen.

'Not after last time. I left it empty for two weeks.'

'I thought I'd explained: I had a work-crisis.'

'I'm not blaming you . . . simply stating a fact.'

'You've no need for guests,' I say, 'I make plenty of money.'

'That's nice for you.'

'You deserve a break. Let people look after you for a change.'

'I wouldn't know what to do if I wasn't working.'

'That's what's so sad.'

I still expect to see the headline: *Shame of TV's Leo. Mother forced to take in guests while star lives in luxury*. . . . Oh, it is too ridiculous. I want to help her, and not out of duty but gratitude; and yet she spurns every offer. It is not her independence that she refuses to give up but her right of disapproval.

We go through to the morning room where my father sits watching cartoons. The incongruity puzzles Pagan, for whom second childhood poses a threat to the first. She clambers on the pouffe to examine the metal plate in his head. 'Pagan . . .' I warn. But you have made her fearless of illness; its accoutrements are an adventure. He does not lift his eyes from the screen.

'It's the boy, Bill,' my mother says. 'It's Len come to see you.' He looks up; his gaze glazes; his dentures dribble. A bulge of belly through an open button makes me fear for the future.

'How are you, Dad?' I feel nothing for this man; I must feel nothing, or else I will feel too much.

'Cats. . . .' It is a poor child's *Tom and Jerry*: the mindless viewing of a man who used only to like westerns.

'He hated cartoons,' I say to my mother.

'Then tell them to change the schedules. I'm sure a word in high places. . . . It makes no difference as long as it's colour. I always have to check it's in colour. He's disturbed by black and white.'

I attempt communication. 'Dad, it's Lenny. Don't you have anything to say to me?'

'Cats.'

'He seems so much worse.'

'No. You just blot it out. But don't fret; it would make no difference if you came up every week; he forgets. Any case, he sees you twice a week on the screen.'

'It's hardly the same.'

'Oh, it is to him. He talks to you in his way. You're as real to him there as you are now. He's lost all sense of touch.'

'What happens now, when the programme's off air till September?'

'I tell him you're on holiday. I show him a postcard. I keep them all in a box.'

My eyes mist. So my work is of some value. What would

she have done if I had joined the Westminster Abbey choir: held up a record sleeve? That's Len, third from the left on the back row? He could hardly talk back to a chorus.

She thinks otherwise. Her every word bears the assumption that I have wasted my life. 'You had a God-given voice' . . . in which case, why did He stop there? What about my brain and the rest of my anatomy? 'When I think of all I had to do to get you to Bangor twice a week, not to mention Mr Llewellyn's lessons.'

'Yes, every sacrifice is in order as long as it's not compromised by ambition: "God's are the gifts and God's is the glory." I remember one birthday when you gave me the parable of the talents inscribed on a scroll.'

'I copied it myself.'

'Other mothers knit socks.'

'You lacked for nothing. I even paid for that trip to Venice. More's the pity.' She looks at Pagan. 'Your father wasn't interested.'

'As you never ceased to inform me.'

' "What are you doing it for?" he'd ask; "he'll only get above himself . . . and us." Well I'm saying nothing.'

'Any other mother would be proud of what I've done.'

'It's not that I'm not proud, son; it's that you shouldn't be.'

'Don't worry, there's no danger of that.'

My public persona has other uses than a paternal sedative. On Saturday, I open the chapel jumble sale and, on Sunday, an Abbeyfield Home garden fête. They ask me to be a sideshow. I presume that they want me to sell kisses. When they propose that I be pelted with soggy sponges, I decline.

Pagan is delighted when I win her a goldfish, with a fluke flick of the wrist that is conveniently caught by the *North Wales Weekly News*. From my mother's frown, you would think that it were riddled with some kind of mad-fish disease. I fear that she may even enforce the 'no pets' rule, but she lets it pass.

'Mind you feed it now,' she tells Pagan, 'or it'll die.'

'Of course I will. At home, I have a cat.'

'I know. That's why I can't come and stay. It gives me asthma.'

'It's all in your mind, Mother.'

'And on my chest.'

'I've told you. If you come, we'll board it out for a few days.'

'It wouldn't be fair on the poor creature. Besides, any chance it had, it would make for home. Cats always do. That's why you have to put butter on their paws.'

'Butter?' Pagan sounds incredulous.

'Unlike people, they don't forget where their home is.'

'I'm here now, Mother.'

'Did I mention any names? Your Uncle Lenny –'

'She calls me Leo.'

'And your mother had a cat when they were at university. It was called Dog, which they thought was amusing. They didn't feed it so it died.'

'You didn't?' Pagan's eyes narrow. An animal rights activist is born.

'It's a long story. We went for a fortnight to Cornwall and there was no one to see to the cat. So Mummy had the idea of sending it a kipper every day through the mail. Dog would be able to smell it and tear the envelope open for its meal. It must have worked because when we came home, the hall was a mass of little bones and scraps of paper. But then the letters were stopped. A sorter at the Post Office was Italian – oh, this is very complicated – and, in Italy, there's a gang of nasty men who, if they don't like you, send you a fish. Which means that you have to be very careful. He found a rip in the envelope and smelt a rat –'

'Do rats smell like kippers?'

'No . . . no, it's a phrase – like "something fishy". So he told the police and they kept all the remaining kippers as evidence. In the meantime, Dog died.'

'Poor thing! I hope no one ever sends me a fish.'

'Of course they won't.'

'That's not a story for a child, Lenny. You'll give her bad dreams.'

'You used to tell me that bad dreams came from my own wickedness.'

'I expect I had my reasons.'

'Why do you call him Lenny when his name's Leo?'

'It's the name he was christened.'

'What's christened?'

'It was Lenny a long time ago but your mummy changed it.'

'Why?'

'I think she wanted me to be more like her.'

'Will I have to change my name?'

'No, you'll always be Pagan.'

I am beginning to think that I have a permanent smut on my nose. The incessant 'is it? . . . it can't be . . . it is too . . . my friend says you're the spitting image . . . only taller, smaller, fatter, thinner, greyer' is so much more intrusive here than in London. I am buying groceries for my mother when an old dear exclaims 'you wouldn't think he'd have to eat food'. So it comes as a considerable relief to escape. I persuade my mother to leave my father in the formidable hands of Mrs Coombes and join us for a picnic on the Great Orme. She makes a daisy chain for Pagan and teaches her the names of the different flowers. I like to watch them together; I am not sure whether it prompts a memory or a desire.

She plumps herself beside me as Pagan wanders off to pick buttercups. 'She's a lovely little girl. It makes me sad.'

'Don't worry, Mum. No one's going to take her away from me.'

'No, not that. Not that at all. That I don't have any grandchildren of my own.'

'What's the difference? You can see her whenever you like. You have pictures of her all over the house.'

'That's because you send them. She doesn't call me Granny.'

'It's just a word.'

'Words count. You were the one who said so. "Don't call it a lounge in company." '

'That was years ago.' I blush.

'You're so good with her. You ought to have a daughter of your own.'

'I'm thirty-seven, Mother.'

'I know how old you are. I was there. Three days in labour. You ripped me apart; my insides were like offal.'

'Please!'

'The midwife said she'd never seen a woman suffer like me.'

'So I must make someone else suffer to make it up to you?'

'It's different now . . . with everything that's available. Mothers today don't know they're born. "You have a beautiful son," the midwife said. "Don't show me," I said. "Not yet, or I may never forgive him." '

'She obviously didn't listen.'

' "Not after what he's put me through." You tore me apart then; but you didn't know what you were doing. You do now.'

'Perhaps we should go back to the car. It's turning cold.'

'There are so many pretty girls on television.' I place my index finger and thumb around my navel and concentrate on my breathing. 'I don't want to speak ill of the dead and I know you were very close; but I can't help feeling Candida wasn't right for you.'

'Please don't, Mother.'

'Oh, I know she was good company – very lively. But she held you back. You were always a part of her life rather the other way round. And then when she became ill. . . .' She leaves her real resentment unexpressed. You are the daughter-in-law she never had. She blames you for my disaffection. If it were not for you, I would be singing canticles in a cathedral choir, my heart as pure as my music. It may sound absurd – and insulting – but it suits her to condemn you rather than to confront me. And you gave her ample opportunity from the start.

'Candida, that's an unusual name.'

'It never ceases to amaze me that my parents named me after a disease.'

'What sort of disease?'

'It's a yeast infection – of the throat and the vagina.'

My eyes drop; my spirits sink. Pagan runs into my reverie.

'What sort of a bird is that?'

'A thrush.'

'What are you saying, Lenny? It's a chaffinch.'

'I'm sorry; I was thinking of candida.'

'I'm sure she was never interested in birds.'

Silence descends, both on the Great Orme and in Maid's Causeway, where I am preparing to take my mother to choral evensong.

'Is your friend coming?'

'Not me,' you say wilfully. 'At school we were asked to name mankind's greatest invention. The official answer was the wheel. I said God.'

My mother chokes; I slap her back and imagine that it is yours. . . . My mother coughs; I pass her a tumbler of water.

'I'm sure half the things she said were for effect. Like the time she told me she was named after a venereal disease.'

I start. The coincidence is as unnerving as the confusion.

'I don't think she ever said that, Mother.'

'You must remember. It was when I came to visit you in Cambridge. The house with the poster.'

'Life's a bitch and so's my – ?'

'That's just what I mean. Things like that upset people.'

'Although if you'd met her mother. . . .'

'It was the same when she came here with her boy-friend.'

'He wasn't her boyfriend.'

'You were in tears.'

'Best to forget it.'

'That's easier said than done.'

'I know'. . . . I know. I can try not to remember, but all the goodwill in the world cannot make me forget.

A cloud crosses the sky and hangs over my memory. It is the Easter vacation. After four wet days, the rain has stopped, but the air retains the dampness like a sponge. My mother is expecting two new guests: a Miss Rubens and a Mr Dorothy. The names sound comic but authentic; in Colwyn Bay, no pseudonym would be so overt. But then you are the mistress of the double bluff. 'Surprise, surprise!' The taxi disgorges you and Robin. . . . When the Marquis de Sade threw a party, he called it a surprise.

'Why do you have to humiliate me?' I confront you in the lobby.

'Don't be ridiculous, darling; we couldn't bear to be parted from you a moment longer.'

'You must go back first thing tomorrow. No, this evening. There's a train around six.'

'But we've paid a deposit.' You wave the receipt.

'Don't you realise; we're short-staffed. I have to help out in the dining room.'

'Better and better,' Robin says. 'I've always had a thing about waiters.'

I storm out, shame and frustration mingled with fury. I am appalled that you should identify me with the coy conventionality of my mother's guest-house, where Mr and Mrs Elwes have stayed every Easter for nine years with their two, now four, children, still call me lad and remember when I had spots. In an effort to contain the damage, I tamper with the TV, so that, at least, you will be spared the room with its Rocky Mountains mural; but the repairman soon discovers the twisted wires. And nothing I do can hide the sauce served in plastic tomatoes, the Fred Basset draught excluder and the flamenco dolls. My home life, which was a treasury of mundane eccentricities, is exposed as a seaside joke.

You are surprised by the vehemence of my reaction. To you, it is quite natural to want to see someone in his own home; it is the only way to understand him . . . but then you treat character as a mixture of genealogy and interior decoration. It is so reductive. I insist that we can make ourselves. I am the perfect example as I elocute my way out of the lower-middle class. 'Oh yes,' you agree; 'but you will always be in reaction against it; you can take a man out of his background but never the background out of the man.'

'I beg to differ.' We begin to dispute. 'I believe we are what we are because of what we believe.'

'And I believe we believe what we believe because of what we are.'

'If all you say were true, there'd be no human progress. We'd still be living in caves.'

'We are. They just have better plumbing.'

You would have an easy convert in my mother: a woman who considers 'know your place' to be a more important lesson than 'know yourself'. She refuses to cancel your booking and insists that I continue to help out. I determine on dignity and strive for an outer expression of inner calm. My resolve is sorely shaken at dinner when Robin addresses the entire room on the etymology of Welsh rarebit, the pleasures of home cooking and the virtues of friendly staff. I smile steelily and imagine myself an exiled archduke, the tables turned, waiting on tables in Paris. My

White Russian blood boils when he pinches my bottom; and I inadvertently ladle trifle into his lap . . . which he scrapes off with a seraphic grin.

Honour is satisfied the next day, when I serve your early morning tea heavily salted and polish his brown brogues an indelible black. We agree to call a truce. But my humiliation is complete when you meet my father. For a moment, I wonder if I can pass him off as an odd-job man, some ex-inmate whom we employ for bed, board and beer money. But that would be to reckon without my mother: 'First they beat his brains out; now you cut out his heart.' How can I disown him when she stands by him . . . she still lies beside him, her only feather-bedding a plastic sheet? I am spared the full horror; she nurses it, dresses it and wipes it clean.

At times, I am drawn closer. He has a turn in the bath; and she calls me to help. His blubbery body slips through my fingers, as he shakes and splashes and froths. It is the first time that I have seen him naked; it feels like a post-mortem. I strive to get a grip on my revulsion and his chest; both slip out of control. 'He's your father,' my mother says. Does she think that I don't know? You used to say how hard it was not knowing your natural mother, not just the absence of pictures from the past but of any kind of blueprint for the future . . . this will be me in ten, twenty, thirty years' time. But, believe me, ignorance is a blessing. As I catch sight of his flaccid penis floundering in the murky water, I grab the basin and vomit.

'He's your father,' my mother says. I know; but even before the accident. . . . 'Never call it an accident,' she says, 'it was a vicious, brutal assault.' I know; but even before the vicious, brutal assault we barely communicated. We shared the same blood; but that was all. He never hid his disappointment in me, and I responded with a show of disdain. He saw my intelligence as a threat. 'What good are brains?' he would ask. 'Brains never made anyone happy.' He might find an answer now that his own have been bludgeoned away. He refused to come to Cambridge. To him, choral scholar was a contradiction in terms. The finest singers in the world were the ones he grew up with, the male voice choirs from the mines and the quarries, men who worked with their hands and sang with their hearts.

'He's your father,' my mother says. Yes, I admit, at the moment of production; although even that I find hard to credit. It is not just the lack of passion, but the logistics: the who did what to whom of a schoolboy limerick . . . sex with her must rank as a form of *lèse-majesté*. Do you remember a therapy exercise when I had to picture my parents naked? What I never told you was that all I could see was an empty bed. . . . Is there a temperance equivalent of a drunken fumble? Whatever else was going through his mind, there was no thought of me. And there have been precious few since. Fatherhood does not lie in blood and still less in a piece of gristle: a momentary spurt of enthusiasm and nearly four decades of indifference. The so-called paternity test should be banned; it is a virility test, nothing more. Paternity lies in life-long love. I am a far better father than him.

'He's your father,' my mother says. Yes, words are important. There is no clumsier transition in the English language than that from daddy to father: the one too infantile, the other too funereally formal . . . with dad popping up like a poor relation in-between. Nothing better illustrates the uneasy relationship at the heart of our family lives. The only words that cause equal embarrassment are those for genitals . . . the connection is made again.

'This is my father,' I say, opting for the conventional definition; I am eighteen years old. He is picking snails from a line of lettuces. 'Little buggers,' he says, 'we'd be alright in France.'

'That's right, Dad; foreigners and their funny food. You're better off in a North Wales guest-house, where the sauce is left on the table and you can see what you eat . . . even when you can't taste it.'

Irony is lost on him; but then so is conversation. I attempt to introduce you, but he is back in his weevilly world. As he bends to crush a beetle, his metal plate gleams in the austere April sun to strangely beatific effect. We escape down the promenade towards St Trillo's, where you question me about his injury. I respond with a reverie of revenge.

'Ever since he left school, he worked as a park-keeper. Out all winds and weathers, but he didn't mind. He enjoyed the company: the children in the playground, the old men on the bowling green, the women with dogs. There was one old lady who used to sit for hours painting flowers. You'll find some of her efforts in Gleneagles. When she died, she left him £2000. My mother wanted him to buy me a gramophone, but he put it all towards a shelter for the park. There was a plaque; the council has promised to replace it. . . .' My voice falters as I see a side of him that I prefer to ignore. 'It's also the favourite haunt of local homosexuals.'

'Wherever two or three bushes are gathered together. . . .'

'That's blasphemy, Candida.' Robin is offended and intrigued. 'Did you frequent it?'

'Frequently,' I lie, determined on a change of image. 'On my way back from choir practice in Rhyl, I used to stop off in his precious park and trample over the shrubs. The darkness added danger to the desire. One night I spent ten minutes making unrequited advances to a birch tree; George III was certified for less. How I loved it when he came home in the evenings and complained of the debris he had to clear – the tissues and handkerchieves and torn pages of magazines – and I'd imagine that some of that was me: the tissue he spiked into his basket was caked in me. It was my seed; it was his.'

'How primitive.'

'How perverse.'

'Then, one night two years ago, I was busy in the bushes with two builders from Abergele; we had our trousers by our knees and our faces in similar positions. A torch was suddenly turned on us. "Caught you, you filthy buggers"; it was my father fighting his one-man campaign to eradicate vice. I covered my face; but, for a moment, I'm sure he saw it. Then one of the men picked up a fallen branch and thwacked him about the head so hard that I thought he'd kill him, while the other kicked him violently in the balls. "Run," they shouted to me, as they shinned over the fence to their motorbikes; but I was in shock. I stared at my father with the blood oozing over his hair into the darkness and, as the beam of the torch skimmed the surface, I saw worms – that is, ants – caught in the flow. It was only when I tried to move that I realised my trousers were down; I tripped and skewered my groin on a rose-bush.' I improvise on a birth-mark. 'You've both seen the scar.'

'What about your father: did you help him?'

'I couldn't think straight; I was terrified. I pictured my mother, my friends, Oscar Wilde, Ronnie Kray. I had to run. I planned to disguise my voice and ring the police with descriptions; but it wasn't their faces I remembered. In the end, no one was charged. The only fingerprints on the torch were mine.'

'They never suspected . . . ?'

'No. The surgeons said that, if they'd operated on him straight away, they might have saved some of his mind . . . today is a good day. I have no one but myself to blame; for years, I longed for his death and this is my punishment. . . . And the subject of my next essay will be Tragedy is Dead.'

As we walk down the cliff wall to the beach, you are silent. I sense that my stature has grown in your eyes. I am not just a coastal bumpkin; I have a trauma to equal yours, a classic mix of sex, violence and family passions . . . Oedipus at Old Colwyn. I stifle a laugh for fear that I will shock you, as I skip the last three steps.

Our feet drag in the sea-heavy sand. You scratch weird hieroglyphics with an umbrella-frame, salvaged from driftwood, that resembles a prop from a symbolist play. Robin takes my arm with a sympathetic squeeze. 'Fathers are bloody,' he says. The pun threatens hysteria; but I furrow my finger-nails into my palms and regain control. Is pain with our parents the link that binds us? You and I can rely on the minutiae of friendship; but it may explain Robin's passion for me if, instead of falling for an average mind and an imperfect body, he has recognised another damaged soul.

Without you, I would never have met him. 'From Cupid to gooseberry in four short steps,' you said later, when we were at the all-embracing stage. I retained a residue of unease; I knew what you felt for him. But I also knew that it was a lost cause. To my certain knowledge, Robin slept with only one woman, regaling us with his horror the following day.

'I had to pretend I was with a man.'

'No doubt,' you snorted, 'so did she.'

And yet his reluctance did not deter you. You rejected anyone whose idea of Heaven lay between your thighs; in your personal cosmography, it was more the Devil's gateway. Abraham's bosom was not yours. You laughed at our friends' white weddings, while longing for a *mariage blanc*. But then you despised your sexuality almost as much as you despaired of your sex.

Instead, you made for the middle ground. With gay men, you could maintain your innocence ... or, rather, your illusions. Homosexuality was heroic, like a bout of wrestling on a Greek vase; it was more a trial of strength than a sentimental tussle. The world called it deviance, you defiance. You lambasted David and his friends' insistence that it was natural; its glory lay in its perversity. It was man-made and man-centred and stood at the heart of man's greatest achievement: the sublime perversity of art.

I tried to recognise myself in that picture, but it was so hard. Robin was the closest I came, not just to the Greek ideal but to any ideal at all. And the reality was much more Mykonos than Troy. I never went into details – you were strangely prudish about details – but he made love more to himself than to me. At the time, I failed to realise – I was deducing from Hollywood heterosexuality . . . my feelings at two removes – but he would never let me touch his penis. He would touch mine and more, much more. He would linger and lick and kiss and suck – if ecstasy frustrates memory, frustration turns it pornographic – he would do everything for my pleasure; but, when it came to his own, he would lie on his belly and rub himself up and down on the sheet. I tried to intercept, but he would push me away. Then, just as he came, he would grab hold of my arm, as if to sustain him in his agony rather than share in his bliss.

He wanted me to fuck him. He would place himself on top of me until I felt violated by the strength of his desire. He would engineer me into him until my will melted like wax in the heat of his bowels. He would sit astride me and plead. And I was forced to reject him when, in fact, I was

97

rejecting the violence coursing through my body and bursting to a head. I could never engage in an act of such self-assertion nor of such wilful self-annihilation. I longed for him – he was the love of my life – and I let him go.

I search for him now in the haze of sea from the parlour window. Where is he? Is he still alive? Why have none of us heard from him for so many years? I yearn to see him again and talk about you. He is the only one who will understand, who will corroborate, who will correct.

'A penny for them,' my mother says.

'I was thinking about inflation.'

Switching my glance to my car, I see a bird attack the mirror. I sense the impact and watch it fly off, winged and wounded. It circles three times before swooping back in revenge on its reflection. It scratches its own eyes and pecks at its own heart, its battered beak oozing blood. Feathers fly in a phantom fight, the deception as disturbing as the violence. It falls on the bonnet, rights itself and hovers unsteadily. I anticipate a further bout and run out with a paper bag to cover the glass. The bird falters into flight, its left wing hanging like a torn sleeve. Then, just as I turn up the steps, it hurls itself at the other mirror. It lies inert on the ground. I decapitate it with my father's spade.

Pagan cries. 'It's God's will,' my mother says approvingly. 'It's Robin,' I think and wonder why. Is it some sort of bird association, even though it is clearly a starling; or is it the self-destruction that has shadowed his life? I see him now at a Cambridge party, staring at a wall of mirrors and raising his glass in a toast. I join him, and he asks me, in all seriousness, if I know the name of the stunningly beautiful man opposite. I laugh and presume that he is joking; but he is drunk. 'Why won't you introduce me?' he asks. 'Are you afraid of a rival?' If so, it is the only one who can hurt me. When I tell him that the rival is his own reflection, he totters towards it, spits in its face and cries.

Why wouldn't he let me touch him? I feel the lack like the throb of an ancient wound. My thoughts coalesce into patterns: Robin rocks himself and you play dead, while Edward and I look on, perplexed and excluded. Did you both feel a secret shame for your bodies? Was that another spiritual bond? Your sexuality always appeared so grown-up, while mine was still in nappies. As I was experimenting with 'da-da', you were dispensing *bon mots*. 'Virginity,' you declared, 'is the one virtue which, when lost, can never be recovered.' And I laughed, as expected. But was your levity a mask for anguish? Did my admiration blind me to the pain?

However hard you tried, you never escaped your mother's values. When Pagan was born in a membrane of green mucus, you claimed that it was the embodiment of your own vice. No matter that she was three weeks overdue; no matter that the muck soon washed off. 'Sins don't wash off,' you insisted. I watched, riven with pain and embarrassment, as you refused to hold her in case you did her harm or even to look at her in case you cast the evil eye. You covered your breasts for fear that she should imbibe your wickedness ... the deadliest infections came from mother's milk.

'She's suffering from post-natal depression,' the consultant diagnosed. But I knew that that was only half of it. Like post-coital *tristesse*, what mattered was what went before.

You put the pain behind you in the mother and baby unit. 'They always say that loving your baby is the most natural thing in the world; it isn't, but it is the best.' And yet, when I asked if you were planning to have a second, you were adamant both that you would not want a family with more than one father and that you would never see Pagan's again. I confirmed my surrogate status with my daily visits; one nurse even called me Mr Mulliner. Sister said that I was perfect therapy for several of the women, who showed no interest in their babies and made their first efforts for me. You laughed and said that it was like a royal visit. What next? The King's Evil cured by a chat show smile?

Your own cure was far more substantive. But it was me whom you wanted as witness; you refused entry to your mother. So how dare my mother suggest that she should be trusted with Pagan now? She seizes the moment when I seem most ineffectual, emerging from bath-duty, my dripping sleeves the testament to my disciplinary defeat.

'Look at you! I don't know. You're as wet as she is.'

'Susan usually sees to Pagan's baths. I'm much more the

rub-down-with-a-towel, snug-as-a-bug-in-a-rug man later.'

'It's no job for a man.'

'Most fathers bath their children these days; it's not the 1950s.'

'She isn't your child.'

'So what should I do? Put her in an orphanage and make a documentary about Dr Barnardo's?'

'I think you should think again about her grandparents' offer.'

'I didn't hear that.'

'They may not have gone about it the right way. But that's because they care for Pagan.'

'Logic has never been your strong point.'

'A grandmother is the best of both worlds: a mother who's learnt from experience.'

'You haven't met Muriel Mulliner.'

'I know how she must feel, to be deprived of her grandchild.'

Anger blinds me to the snare.

'How? You don't have one.'

'Exactly.... Besides, it isn't healthy.'

'What do you mean?'

'The way you were kissing this afternoon; it frightened me.'

I tell you this so that you don't think that I am keeping anything from you. It transpires that she saw Pagan and me playing this afternoon ... a game that she calls 'slug sandwich', where she darts her tongue at yours – mine – and then whisks it away. You must remember; you used to play yourself, until your mouth lost all sensation and I became the surrogate mother-tongue. So you can vouch for its innocence. It is simply a test of endurance, enabling her to relish her revulsion ... like dipping her toes in a mossy stream, the texture midway between silk and slime.

I am furious with my mother and her sordid imaginings. Do you recall the priest who was convicted of smuggling sex films in a consignment of bibles? She does that every day of her life. Where will it end? Must I think twice before stroking a dog? I decide against asking her for an affidavit. Whatever she says on paper may be overturned in court. Besides we have more than enough expert witnesses: from the school and doctor and ballet mistress, not to mention Susan, whose glowing testimonial moved me to tears.

Max suggests that I bring Pagan with me to Brighton . . . just to prepare for every contingency; the word feels viscous on my flesh. She is furious that she cannot accompany me to court and tell them how much she hates her grandparents – when all this is over, I shall have to amend her vocabulary – but there have been some compensations. Last night her tooth fell out and I swapped it for a pound coin; I was too preoccupied to remember the previous rate. She was thrilled. 'London fairies are mean. I want all my teeth to come out at the seaside . . . though it must hurt their wings more when they fly.'

This morning, while Susan and I are otherwise engaged, she is going to the pier with Max's assistant, Gemma, who has promised to take her on the ghost train. 'Is it scary?' she asks. . . . 'Not if you hold Gemma's hand.' Susan takes mine as we approach the court and a prospect that scares us both. We sit in the waiting room cum corridor among the peeling plastic chairs chewing-gummed to the floor and a family of restless East Europeans who take the opportunity to beg. I respond over-generously and wonder whether I am bribing fate or tempting it. We make desultory conversation, until Max calls me into the interview room. Susan gives me such a loving squeeze that tears spring more readily to my eyes than from the most bone-cracking wrestler's grip.

The air in the interview room is a foul mixture of stale sweat and tobacco, so foetid that, unlike the ashtrays, it cannot be cleaned overnight. I gulp and speculate on the reasons for such agitation. Max affects not to notice. He adopts a courtside manner to put me at my ease and then talks privately to Rebecca at a pitch designed to unnerve me. I feel like a problem pupil whose teacher is addressing his mother over his head. Turning to the wall, I read a poster from a pressure group for paternal rights. 'Missing your child? Contact Families Need Fathers.' It is clearly a sign . . . but of what?

We are summoned into court. I may not endorse traditional values, but the decor offends me as much as the New English Bible. It is not the majesty of the law that I miss, so much as the history. It is all stripped pine walls and green and yellow carpets, as if humanising the judicial process were merely a matter of soft furnishings. Even on those terms it misfires. The vast metallic crest behind the Judge's chair is far more oppressive than a straightforward sword and scales.

With row upon row of padded green seats, my second shock is to see the room so empty: just your parents, their solicitor and barrister, Rebecca, her junior, Max, the Welfare Officer and me. I am accustomed to House Full signs outside the Greenwood Theatre and crowds queuing from lunchtime on the day that we record a show. For a moment I forget that we are in a closed court and wonder if my popularity is slipping. Then I catch myself and laugh. Max sobers me with a look as we rise for the Judge. He bows to the Court, which bows back, although I am convinced that your mother curtsies. I look at him, Judge Flower – the most unlikely personification – and try to prejudge his reactions; but he sits in stone-carved silence, the inscrutable face of the law.

Counsel for your parents opens. I am uneasy when the Judge then describes the whole hearing as 'your case', for fear that he extend his proprietorial rights to Pagan. The procedures are frustrating and the procedural moves even more so. The real issues seem to disappear beneath the formalities and point-scoring; which might be reassuring if I had something to hide. I am sickened by the general toadying to the Judge. Even Rebecca is party to it, preceding every remark with somesuch tag as 'May I thank Your Honour for the time you've given us', as though he were giving it for free. Nevertheless, as the morning progresses, I feel confident that events are moving our way.

Your parents enter the witness box, ladies first naturally. I worry that their two-head one-voice act might give them an undue advantage, but their manner gives them away. Sugaring their tones and buttering their smiles in an attempt at sweetness and light merely makes her seem saccharine and him slippery. Their Counsel establishes that what they are offering is a Christian home and family values; mine, while careful to denigrate neither, demolishes their case. She stresses their age and a medical history in which every varicose vein becomes a major disability . . . and did you know that your father has a replacement hip? She gently confronts them with their own mortality and the possibility that one – or both – of them might die and Pagan be orphaned again. She paints a picture of her boisterousness which, however much I appreciate, I have to say that I fail to recognise. And yet, seeing your parents' discomfort, I would be happy for her to fill the house with frenzied five-year-olds every day of the week. She questions them on your own relationship – I wonder why they have not asked William to testify – and demonstrates that their real source of resentment is not me but you; which hardly bodes well for your daughter.

Although I say so myself, I make a far better showing. I swear on the Bible in order to convince the Judge of my good faith and to prove that, despite your mother's insinuations, there is nothing sinister in the name Pagan. My experience leaves me exposed. Answering questions in court is very different to asking them on TV; I even miss the autocue crackling in my ear. I am used to thinking on my feet, but standing in the witness box is daunting. It has the same effect on me as seeing a nun: all my past offences flash before my eyes. As your parents' Counsel probes, I lose heart and think of the many reasons why I am not equipped to care for Pagan. Now, hold on . . . ! Hold on to the ledge, take a deep breath and smile.

As I reply to Rebecca's re-examination, I begin to relax. My testament is my territory; I feel secure. I repeat my assurance that, if and when I marry, I shall be choosing a mother for Pagan as much as a wife for myself. Nevertheless, the primary issue is my own fitness as a father. And the consensus is undeniable, not only in the affidavits but in the Welfare Officer's report. I am amazed at her perspicacity. She sets out your parents' fears and confronts each in turn. Her style may be impenetrable – 'She interacts with her peer group in an appropriate way . . . she has attained her normal percentiles' – but her conclusions are clear. Pagan's home situation, schooling and everyday care are all excellent; she has an estimable quality of life. And at its heart is her devotion to me.

Devotion is the Welfare Officer's word, not mine, and it sits strangely in the numbered paragraphs of socio-speak that constitute her report, a throwback to different values, from an age when Pagan and I were not threatened. She writes that it is apparent that we enjoy an exceptionally loving relationship, which the child affirms without prejudice or prompting. Were she to be removed from my care, it would be immensely disruptive and could well affect her entire emotional development. Rebecca, whose experience of such reports is unrivalled, says that it rates as one of the most positive that she has ever read. While most hover on the fence, this leaps straight off and into our camp.

There is a postscript . . . to my account, not hers. I must beware of underestimating Pagan's perception. The reality of Crierley was not lost on her; when I said abracadabra, she heard ashes to ashes. 'There is one bad thing Leo did,' she said in response to questioning. 'He threw my mummy away like dust.'

After a break for lunch and Counsel's final speeches, the Judge declares that he will state his findings straightaway. I waver between gratitude that the suspense will end and fear of snap decisions. As his tombstone teeth fix in a sinister smile, I am already establishing grounds for appeal. He announces that he will 'maintain the status quo'. . . . What's that? My brain has turned to sludge and my legs to jelly. . . . He lays great stress on the principles of psychological parenting. . . . I think – I think that's me. . . . 'One does not have to be a natural parent to be the best person to bring up a child'. . . . May I thank Your Honour for the time you've given us. . . . 'One does not have to be a parent at all.'

He makes an Order dismissing your parents' application and declaring that Pagan shall continue to reside with me. I have instructed Rebecca not to apply for costs; I can afford to be magnanimous . . . if I had only known. The true cost comes in his Order that Pagan is to 'have contact with her grandparents on a monthly basis'. I want to protest, not on my behalf but on hers. I pass notes to Rebecca and Max, who studiously ignore them; suddenly, we are lucky to have done this well. The Court rises and Counsel retire to work out the practical arrangements. But who collects her and who brings her back are to me far less important than whether she wants to go.

I decide to say nothing to Pagan; I refuse to sour the fruits of victory. Tomorrow we return to London and the rest of our lives; tonight we celebrate. As we sit in the candied dining room of the Grand Hotel, I order champagne and, for the first time, a glass for her.

'You won't put water in like wine?'

'Unfortunately, I can't; it would lose its fizz.'

She drinks three half-glasses – 'I like it' – and grows a little tipsy. Bedtime beckons. We take her upstairs and Susan asks if she can walk in a straight line.

'Why?'

'It's a test of whether you're drunk.'

'I am not drunk,' she insists, affronted, and falls headlong into a sofa.

'Well you're certainly tiddly,' I say, and she smothers the word in giggles.

'So am I,' Susan says, as she disengages her charge from the cushions.

'And me,' I add from the respectability of the door.

'If her grandparents could see us now . . . ' Susan says. And I suddenly feel sober.

# Two

Second Affidavit of Leonard Peter Young
on behalf of the Respondent
Sworn the 30th day of November 1992

In the Brighton County Court                    Case No. 7296

In the matter of Pagan Mulliner

And in the matter of the Children's Act 1989

Between

      Muriel Ellen Mulliner &

      Edgar Atkins Mulliner                    APPLICANTS

and

      Leonard Peter Young                    RESPONDENT

I, LEONARD PETER YOUNG, Writer and Broadcaster of 64 Addison Avenue, London W11, MAKE OATH and say as follows:–

1. I make this Affidavit further to my Affidavit sworn in these proceedings on the 25th day of March 1992 and in response to the various Affidavits so far filed by the other parties.

2. Before addressing myself to the above matters, I would like to acquaint the Court with what has occurred in the period between my first Affidavit and the present:–

a. On the 17th day of July 1992, I appeared with my legal representatives before His Honour Judge Flower, who rejected the Applicants' petition and ordered that the above-named minor, Pagan Mulliner (hereinafter referred to as Pagan), should remain with me.

b. Since the granting of the residence order:–
i. Pagan has celebrated her sixth birthday.
ii. Pagan has completed her first year at primary school and commenced her second.
iii. Pagan and I have taken a three-week holiday in Umbria.

iv. Pagan has continued to discover and develop her interests:–

a. Her riding instructor has promised that, if she maintains regular attendance, she can take part in the *Own a pony for a week* scheme next year.

b. She has been cast as a rabbit in the school production of *Toad of Toad Hall*.

c. She has started to learn the flute.

v. Pagan has visited her grandparents every other weekend.

c. Almost a year to the day since her mother's death, Pagan's progress remains a source of considerable encouragement to everyone concerned with her education and welfare and a particular joy to myself.

3. By an application dated the 3rd day of November 1992, the Applicants have again sought a Residence Order in respect of Pagan. I have now read what purports to be a true copy of their Affidavit in support of the said application; and I would like to comment on the matters contained therein.

4. With reference to paragraph 3 of the Applicants' Affidavit, it is not right to say that I have attempted to destroy their relationship with Pagan or to 'turn her against them' in any way. On the contrary, I have always considered it my duty to reconcile Pagan to her grandparents, particularly in view of her manifest distress at the approach of every weekend visit.

5. As to the incidents referred to in paragraph 4 of the Applicants' Affidavit, I would say that the Applicants' account of these matters is distorted; and I would give my own account of them as follows:–

a. The delay referred to as occurring on September 18th was the result of a school visit to the Polka Theatre in Wimbledon, about which the Applicants were fully informed.

b. The delay referred to as occurring on October 2nd was the result of Pagan being violently sick on the A23 and my having to stop at the Handcross Happy Eater café in order to clean her and change her clothes.

c. As to the delay referred to as occurring on October 15th, I believe that this took place on October 16th. I deny the Applicants' allegation that it was deliberate and would state that:–

i. Owing to a tailback in Tooting, the journey out of London took two and a half hours.

ii. In view of Pagan's constant complaints of hunger, I decided to stop for a meal. On trying to telephone the Applicants, I found that I had left my address book at home. I contacted my housekeeper;

but her limited English, together with static on the carphone, made communication impossible.

iii. Shortly after the meal, Pagan was violently sick; and I had to stop once more at the Handcross Happy Eater café in order to clean her and change her clothes. The waitresses were very helpful and, when they asked me to pose for a photograph, I felt unable to refuse ... I did not foresee that 'one quick picture' would become a roll. Further delay occurred while they made Pagan a milkshake to settle her stomach.

iv. Ten minutes later, Pagan was again violently sick; and I had to stop at a service station in order to clean her and change her clothes.

v. Pagan's inadequate wardrobe for the weekend was entirely due to the two above-mentioned changes, with which the Applicants showed very little sympathy.

d. As to paragraph 4d of the Applicants' Affidavit, I deny that the tiredness observed in Pagan on October 30th and 31st was due to my laxity over bedtimes and would state that it was the consequence of my giving her two Kwells on the evening of the 30th in order to avoid any further bouts of sickness, such as those described above, and the unpleasantness which ensued.

6. As to paragraph 5 of the Applicants' Affidavit, I would state that leave was given in the Order of the 17th day of July 1992 for me to take Pagan out of the Jurisdiction between the 3rd and the 25th of August.

7. As to paragraph 6 of the Applicants' Affidavit, I can only say that I find this paragraph very difficult to understand.

8. As to paragraph 7 of the Applicants' Affidavit, I would state that Raisa and Gorby are the names of two small teddy bears and that any other suggestion is risible. I would add that I consider the Applicants' destruction of these toys to be indefensible.

9. As to paragraph 8 of the Applicants' Affidavit, I deeply resent this attempt to blacken Candida Mulliner's name. I would like to ask whether they pursue a similar line with their granddaughter; if so, her aversion to them is easy to comprehend. I offer my own account as follows:–

a. Candida's final year at Cambridge was marred by poor health, which left her particularly ill-equipped for the transition to post-graduate life.

b. She worked briefly as a cleaner for various friends before pursuing her theatrical ambitions. Faced with the closed shop of

111

Equity entrance, she found that the one way in was by exotic dancing. In the course of this, she met Roger Forbes-Martin who was researching his study of Soho. On learning that she had befriended many of his subjects, he asked her to take the photographs; it was their success that launched her internationally renowned career.

10. As to paragraph 9 of the Applicants' Affidavit, far from being an indication of immorality, an address in Soho was almost a guarantee of respectability. The 'working girls' all made the journey from North and South London every day.

11. As to paragraph 10 of the Applicants' Affidavit, I utterly refute the suggestion that I was living off Candida in Soho and outline my own post-Cambridge career as follows:–

a. After teaching for fifteen months at St Bride's Preparatory School in Market Drayton, I moved to London. While trying to break into broadcasting, I earned my living by offering singing lessons.

b. Through Roger Forbes-Martin, I met Rodger Standing, then the producer of Radio Four's This Morning show, who heard some of my old Cambridge revue songs and asked me to contribute to the programme. This led to numerous radio appearances, including a regular spot on *Light Waves*. From there, I moved to television to present the Arts magazine, Addendum. Since then, I have worked continuously for the BBC; in the last seven years, as host of my own twice-weekly chat show.

c. For the past nine years, I have written a fortnightly column for the Criterion.

12. With reference to the Affidavit of Jennifer Knatchpole, sworn on the 20th day of November 1992, I have little comment to make, save that I have never been on friendly terms with the deponent and her Affidavit reflects this. I should add that:–

a. Candida Mulliner had a passionate affair with the deponent's husband immediately prior to their engagement. The deponent has always blamed her for the souring of her marriage.

b. Candida's announcement that she had herpes was an act of revenge on Guy Knatchpole for proposing that, despite his engagement, they should continue the affair; it had no basis in fact.

c. The deponent clearly considers that my intimacy with Candida makes me guilty by association.

112

13. With reference to the Affidavit of Lewis Kelly, sworn on the 24th day of November 1992, I would like to state that I have never enjoyed a good relationship with the deponent. I met him and, to my lasting regret, introduced him to Candida Mulliner in Wormwood Scrubs, where he was serving a life-sentence for murder. He was involved in a drama project which we were featuring on *Light Waves*. Candida subsequently visited him in prison and lived with him on his release. His violent and abusive behaviour was such that she soon left him.

a. As to paragraph 3 of the deponent's Affidavit, if this is true, how does he explain his agent's repeated requests that he appear on my show?

b. As to paragraph 5 of the deponent's Affidavit, far from there being any possibility that Pagan is his daughter, after one particularly violent incident, Candida chose to have an abortion rather than to bear his child.

14. I turn to the Applicants' allegations of my homosexuality, which appear to constitute the sole reason for their return to this Court. I would state as follows:–

a. I deny any suggestion that I am homosexual. Over the past twenty years, I have had several well-documented affairs with women.

b. Candida Mulliner and I lived together at Cambridge and for most of the ensuing seventeen years. For an account of our relationship, I respectfully refer the Court to my Affidavit of the 25th day of March 1992.

c. With reference to paragraph 6 of the Affidavit of Lewis Kelly, not only was there no homosexual scandal attached to my departure from St Bride's, but my dismissal occurred when Candida and I were discovered in bed during her visit to the school . . . as a simple inquiry to the headmaster will confirm.

d. With reference to paragraphs 7 and 8 of the Affidavit of Lewis Kelly, I fail to see what relation such insinuations have either to me or to this hearing.

e. With reference to paragraph 9 of the Affidavit of Lewis Kelly, I would state that the deponent was always jealous of my intimacy with Candida. His very limited concept of friendship was threatened by our relationship. For all his subsequent success, his prison prejudices have remained intact.

f. With reference to paragraph 6 of the Affidavit of Jennifer

113

Knatchpole, I was under the misapprehension that the party was to be in fancy dress.

g. With reference to paragraph 7 of the Affidavit of Jennifer Knatchpole, I repeat my paragraph 14b.

15. I maintain that the Applicants have produced no substantive evidence to suggest that Pagan Mulliner should be removed from my care. I would ask the Court to confirm its Order of the 17th day of July 1992 and rule that the above-named minor should remain with me.

Sworn by the above-named
Leonard Peter Young,

At 12 Field Court,
Grays Inn,
London WCIR 5EN.

This 17th day of November 1992
Before me,

Arthur Ernest Duff.
Solicitor/Commissioner for Oaths

Third Affidavit of Leonard Peter Young
on behalf of the Respondent
Sworn the 12th day of January 1993

<u>In the Brighton County Court</u>                    <u>Case No. 7296</u>

In the matter of Pagan Mulliner

And in the matter of the Children's Act 1989

Between

       Muriel Ellen Mulliner &

       Edgar Atkins Mulliner                    APPLICANTS

and

       Leonard Peter Young                    RESPONDENT


I, LEONARD PETER YOUNG, Writer and Broadcaster of 64 Addison Avenue, London W11, MAKE OATH and say as follows:–

1. I am the respondent in this matter. I have read what purports to be a true copy of the third Affidavit of the Applicants sworn on the 22nd day of December 1992 and of the second Affidavit of Lewis Kelly sworn on the 18th day of December 1992 and of the exhibit thereto.

2. I respectfully refer this Honourable Court to my Affidavit sworn on the 30th day of November 1992, to which I would like to add the following:–

3. I accept that paragraph 2 of the Applicants' Affidavit is true.

4. I accept that paragraph 3a of the Applicants' Affidavit is true.

5. I utterly refute the allegations contained in paragraph 3b of the Applicants' Affidavit and would say as follows:–

a. The so-called 'revelations' in the *Nation* of 13th December 1992 are nearly a decade old. David Sunning was a researcher on the BBC Arts programme *Addendum*, with whom I enjoyed a brief relationship. His bitterness at my decision to end it has festered to this day.

b. I have had no contact with David Sunning since January 1985 . . . eighteen months before Pagan was born. The relationship has had no bearing on my subsequent life nor on my ability to care for Pagan.

c. I deny that I attempted to mislead the Court in my Affidavit sworn on the 20th day of November 1992 and would state that the relationship was of so little significance that it had slipped my mind.

6. I turn now to the second Affidavit of Lewis Kelly and to Candida Mulliner's letter to the deponent of 3rd July 1981, exhibit LK1, and would comment as follows:–

7. With reference to paragraph 3 of the Affidavit, it is untrue that Candida Mulliner and I never slept together. While our primary relationship may not have been sexual, we were physically very intimate from the first afternoon that we met. The problem, as she put it, was that the 'chemistry' was wrong.

8. With reference to paragraph 4 of the Affidavit, the insinuations are distasteful. In both cases, the deponent is deliberately misunderstanding information that he has half-heard from Candida Mulliner about mishaps in which I was loosely involved.

9. With reference to paragraph 5 of the Affidavit and to Candida Mulliner's letter, exhibit LK1, I would state as follows:–

a. Candida was writing to the deponent in Wormwood Scrubs where he still had two years to serve of a fourteen-year sentence for murder. She wanted to sustain him by planning their life together on his release. In order to assure him that she was unattached, she made out that her discovery in my bed at St Bride's was a mere device to engineer my dismissal from the school.

b. In view of the deponent's history of violence, Candida claimed that our relationship was platonic in order to protect me.

116

10. I would conclude by saying that, in the circles in which Candida Mulliner and I moved in the early 1980s, it was fashionable to dabble in bisexuality, and I do not deny that I followed the trend; I do, however, strenuously deny that it amounted to anything more. I have now been celibate for the past eight years. I would therefore ask the Court to confirm its Order that Pagan Mulliner remain with me.

Sworn by the above-named
Leonard Peter Young,

At 12 Field Court,
Grays Inn,
London WC1R 5EN.

This 12th day of January 1993
Before me,

Arthur Ernest Duff.
Solicitor/Commissioner for Oaths

Fourth Affidavit of Leonard Peter Young
on behalf of the Respondent
Sworn the 14th day of February 1993

In the Brighton County Court          <u>Case No. 7296</u>

In the matter of Pagan Mulliner

And in the matter of the Children's Act 1989

Between

         Muriel Ellen Mulliner &

         Edgar Atkins Mulliner          **APPLICANTS**

and

         Leonard Peter Young          **RESPONDENT**

I, LEONARD PETER YOUNG, Writer and Broadcaster of 64 Addison Avenue, London W11, MAKE OATH and say as follows:–

1. I am the respondent in this matter. I make this Affidavit further to my previous Affidavit in these proceedings of the 12th day of January 1993.

2. Increasing speculation about my sexuality in certain sections of the press has culminated in the front-page article in the *Nation* today, the 14th of February 1993. While I regard such intrusions into my privacy as beneath contempt, I consider it necessary to comment on a matter which may be felt to bear on these proceedings.

3. The burden of the afore-mentioned article, that I have intermittently used the Streetwise escort agency, is correct. The transactions were anonymous, brief and clinical; I have not allowed them to impinge on any other aspect of my life, least of all my guardianship of Pagan.

4.  The reference to eight years of celibacy in paragraph 10 of my Affidavit of the 12th day of January 1993 was primarily metaphorical.

5.  No prostitute has visited my house at any time, let alone when Pagan was present.

6.  I very much regret that this matter has been raised. With the large number of adult influences available to Pagan, I feel sure that my sexuality will have no injurious effect on her development. Research has shown that the children of homosexual parents are no more likely to grow up homosexual than those of heterosexuals. Far from my causing her harm, I believe that my awareness of my own nature makes me more sensitive to hers.

7.  I have profound doubts about the Applicants' ability to care for Pagan, based both on the evidence of the past few months and on Candida Mulliner's account of her childhood. I am convinced that the Applicants have no genuine fears for Pagan's well-being but rather that they desire to sever all contact between us; to which end, they are prepared to countenance any calumny.

8.  It is clear that the *Nation*'s report constitutes a deliberate attempt to blacken my character and to bring outside influence to bear on the decisions of this Court. I trust that such tactics will fail and that the Court will confirm its earlier Order that Pagan Mulliner should remain with me.

Sworn this 14th day of February 1993
at The Grand Hotel, King's Road, Brighton
In the County of Sussex

Before me,

Neil Morley-Macmillan.
A Solicitor empowered to administer oaths

# 1

Do you mind if I give Pagan a guardian angel? I am afraid that you may regard it as another betrayal. But, as Raisa's and Gorby's fate has shown, teddy bears are no longer enough. She needs something that she can keep on her shoulder not on her pillow, something that she can call on – something that she can cling to – when I am not at hand. What is the alternative? A Fairy Godmother of Christmas Tree tweeness, who will go up in smoke at the panto-mime? She is hardly in line for a patron saint.

She needs one for her visits to Hove, which do not become any easier. Her baleful eyes remind me of Texas when I used to drive him to kennels, and she is equally hard to convince of my good faith. She demands to stop every few miles to pee or to vomit. Last weekend, I gave her two Kwells before we set off; and, ever since, I have had a sickening sense of myself as a white slaver. If only I had insisted on your parents fetching her and my bringing her home . . . at least I would be less implicated in her pain.

She tells me very little about the weekend routine; it is as though any detail will detract from the general horror. Her constant complaint is of boredom. They make such a to-do about having her and then give her nothing to do once she is there. Even the television is permanently tuned to your father's weekend sport. 'It's not fair,' she grumbles, 'in the day-time programmes should be for children and in the night-time for grown-ups.'

I remonstrate with your mother, who replies that, when

she was her age, young girls were able to entertain themselves ('they didn't always need to be doing') and adds that, far from neglecting her, she is teaching her to cook and your father teaching her to swim. But the pleasures of rolling pastry are lost in a world of bake but don't touch, and her poolside euphoria deflates as fast as the water-wings which your father refuses to let her wear.

'I don't like it. He says there's nothing scary, cos he's holding me tight. But, even when he's holding me tight, I don't like it. When he's holding me tight, I don't like it more. And his body's soggy. And he holds me too tight. And I slip and drink all the water. And I tell him what you said about naughty boys doing pee in it. "Not in Brighton," he said; "only in London." But I say phooey.'

I say far more, as they bring her home and accuse me of filling her head with nonsense. They produce a list of complaints, as if they are co-parents. I stand firm.

'At school we used to call it urinated water.'

'I take it then you went to a state school?'

'That's it; there's no more to be said.'

'You said it, sir, not me.'

It seems to me that I have far more cause for complaint. I am tucking up Pagan in bed when she asks me what dying is like.

'Why do you want to know?'

'Tell me.'

'Like going to sleep on the bounciest mattress, your head full of the sweetest dreams. But I can't say for sure, since no one has ever come back to tell the tale.'

'What about Lazarus?'

'What do you know about him?'

'She told me.'

'Who's she? The cat's mother?'

'Why do you call her that? She hates cats.' She shouts for Trouble. 'Do you think Mummy may come back too?'

'I don't think so, darling. That's just a story which happened a very long time ago. Besides, Mummy's never really gone away: not when we talk about her and think about her and write our book.'

'It's not the same.'

'No, I know. But it's the next best thing. And sometimes that's all we can have.'

122

The next day we are walking down Kensington High Street when she is sure that she sees you. 'Mummy,' she shouts and runs into Barkers Arcade. She hurls herself at several shoppers. 'You're not my mummy, you're not,' she shrieks and stands lost in confusion and tears. As I reach her, I am met with looks first of mistrust and then of recognition. One woman holds out a tissue and a pen in the same hand. I decline both and seek sanctuary in St Mary Abbots, where a secluded pew gives Pagan a chance to recover. She insists that she saw you. I explain that it is a trick of her mind which, for a moment, has forgotten that you are dead. But even as I speak to her – and even more as I speak to you – I betray myself. Who is to say that you are not as real to her as you are to me? I see you; I hear you; I feel you; I just cannot touch you. Since when has touch been the test of truth?

I offer her words not of comfort but of convention; and yet perhaps that is for the best. Do we want her to grow up with second sight or sixth sense? That may suit a twin or a genius, but, for the rest of us, the price is too high. We have to survive in the workaday world, which is run by politicians not poets. So I shall never again say that a dream is more real to me than waking, or a dead friend than the living, but simply that it – that you – are more vivid. She is too young to believe in ghosts.

I wipe her eyes and cloud her vision. 'No, you didn't see Mummy, darling. You saw someone whom you thought looked like her, that's all.'

'I can't see what she looks like. I'm scared.' She sobs.

'I'll take you home and we'll go through the photographs.'

'It's not the same.'

'I know.'

On our next trip to Hove, I ask your mother to avoid any mention of death or religion, as it only confuses her. 'I see,' she says. 'Now you have the right to censor our conversation. I must have missed that in the judgement.'

'It's for her sake,' I say, 'not mine.'

The following week, Pagan is even more taciturn, finally revealing that your parents accused her of betraying them and made her promise never again to repeat anything that happened there. I insist that there are some promises that she is allowed to break and that she must never keep anything from me or else the secrets will grow between us like the thorns that surrounded Sleeping Beauty's palace. Then I call her my Sleeping Beauty and blow on her eyes.

I only discover that she has met William when she lets slip that she has a new uncle and that he has a 'pram just like Mummy's'.

'He asked me to kiss him, but I asked if he was going to die like Mummy. And she –'

'Who?'

'You know . . . said that was a wicked thing to say and I should say sorry. But he said he didn't mind and it was just his legs. And I asked when would they be better and he said never and I said I bet they could and I told him about your programme with the man who stood up when they put wires in his dead legs. And he said you mustn't believe everything on television and I said "I know that, silly". But I do when it's you.'

She likes William, who played ping-pong with her in the dining room, until your mother spotted the scuff-marks on the parquet. 'She said he should have known and he just drove away. Then she said "guess who'll have to clean it up", so I said "Grandpa", which made her cross; but she said to guess.'

All my fears of her disaffection vanish in her open hostility to your parents. When they bring her home, she rushes upstairs so quickly that I have to force her down to say goodbye.

'She's just showing off,' your father says.

'She never did before,' I lie.

I try to maintain good relations, like an ex-wife hiding her hurt for the sake of the children. So I accept their weak tea on Fridays and bring out my whisky on Sundays. At which point, your mother always reminds your father that he is driving; as if her security rests less in his sobriety than in the familiarity of the phrase.

Last Friday, I noted an addition to their sideboard: a photograph of your parents with Pagan.

'William took it,' she explains to me.

'Uncle William, dear,' your mother says, from the foot of the family tree.

'You're smiling,' I say, almost in accusation.

'I couldn't help it. He said "Say Primula", that's like cream-cheese. And I said your favourite cream-cheese –'

'That's enough,' your mother says with unexpected vehemence and stares at me in disgust.

'He said how if he was photographed from his tummy, no one would know about his legs,' she continues defiantly. Your mother looks sour; such talk is taboo. I have never understood what led them to adopt William. If they picked you because you were pretty, how did they explain him? Or did they fail to discover the truth until it was too late . . . your father's dreams of his opening for England shattered by his refusal to crawl; your mother's Home Sweet Home harmony destroyed by the squeak of his chair?

'There's no shame in being adopted,' your father told you, following his rule-book. 'It means that we chose you above all the others; we wanted you even more.'

'You must never tell people you're adopted,' your mother told you, ironing her towels. 'It has nothing to do with anyone but us.'

These days, concealment is harder. With the dearth of healthy white babies, hopes are as handicapped as the children; desperation has to face every disadvantage. No wonder she is so keen on traditional family values: the stigma attached to illegitimacy was a life-line to her. Am I being cynical? Believe me, in the light of your parents' behaviour, I have every right.

They have made another application for Pagan. Max assumes that they must have new evidence. Why have they said nothing to me? I thought that their middle-class code specified being good losers. And yet they compete for Pagan like a challenge cup. At least she will be spared any upset. She likes the Welfare Officer, whom she calls the Doll's House Lady on account of their games. I am the one who will have to suffer the strain of another hearing, although Max assures me that it will be painless. Having rejected your parents once, the Judge is bound to be on our side.

I doubt that he will look kindly on their having sold their story to the *Sunday Sentinel*, a paper whose initials give a fair indication of its social stance. In 'their own words' and a mass of editorialising, they share their sorrow on being deprived of their only grandchild; in bewildered tones, they describe your estrangement, which they see as a typical teenage rebellion, and claim that their sole crime was to love you too much. They seem to believe – on what grounds I cannot say – that the weakness of their case lay in your adoption and that, had they been natural parents, the ruling would have been reversed.

Illustrating the article is William's picture of the proud – but desolate – grandparents with Pagan, whose face has been blacked out in a manner that I find both symbolic and sinister. The risk of identifying her is the reason for not naming me, a somewhat superfluous gesture given the clues liberally scattered about the text . . . I suggest that they offer a prize to the first four million readers who work it out. Publication is carefully timed, between the hearing and the new application, to leave us no redress. Technicality is now nine tenths of the law.

It is the perfect story for a paper that espouses family values while luridly exposing anyone who flouts them. Even the word bachelor seems to be less a description than a charge. Equally cynical is its depiction of your parents as little people at the mercy of those with power, on a par with elderly victims of muggers – as long as they are black – and council neglect – as long as it is Left. Your father's war record is so lauded as to qualify him for the Errol Flynn Single Combat Medal, while the eulogy to your mother's ambulance work would honour Edith Cavell.

I now face a more direct attack. I am working at home after a fractious day at Television Centre, when Consuela informs me that there is a socialist at the door. From her note of disdain, I assume that it is someone canvassing for the SWP, which must be an uphill struggle in W11. Old sympathies stir, and I go down to see her. She turns out to be a social worker; Consuela having subscribed to popular prejudice in good faith. From her smart clothes and sophisticated manner, it is clear, however, that she is a long way from any Leftie-and-lentils stereotype. She flashes her identification and tells me that she has come to talk about Pagan. I am affronted and remind her that it is customary to make an appointment. She insists that she has already spoken to Susan, which surprises me as it is quite unlike her to forget. She assures me that her inquiry will only take a few minutes, and so I invite her upstairs. From her reluctance to reveal anything further, I presume that your parents have lodged another complaint.

'May I offer you a drink?'

'Just water.'

'Evian or Badois?'

'Plain Thames will do me.'

I exit to the kitchen and, on my return, I am amazed to find her leafing through a file. She puts it down without the least trace of embarrassment. I hand her the glass, which she takes to the couch, where she sits, crossing her legs and picking the cushion. She produces a tape-recorder, which seems unduly formal after her predecessor's notes. As she tests my voice-level, I joke that I might as well be back at work, which fails to raise a smile. She seizes on my suggestion that she look at the holiday snaps of Spoleto, only to skip the pictures of Pagan and linger over me. She presses me for details of domestic arrangements. I conceal my annoyance; it is as well to settle matters once and for all.

She suddenly changes tack and asks if I have seen your parents' interview in the *Sunday Sentinel*. When I tell her that I never read the tabloids, she produces a copy and asks if I would like to comment.

'No, I would not. And I'd like to know what it has to do with Pagan.'

'My superiors are very concerned about her moral welfare.'

I am appalled and demand names, which she claims not to be at liberty to divulge. She then proceeds to display a frightening intimacy with our lives. After hinting at your affairs with Edward and Peter Cruikshank, she questions me about David, stating that their records show that he lived here for nearly two years in 1983 and 1984. I do not think to ask how . . . he was on no register; he paid no rent. So I stutter my explanation.

'He was a researcher at the BBC on a short-term contract. When it ran out, both Candida Mulliner and I employed him as a secretary.'

'Come, Mr Young, you'll have to do better than that. Ms Mulliner was based in the States during most of that period, taking photographs for *Vanity Fair*. Meanwhile you were alone here with the youth.'

'He was twenty-three when I met him, only five years younger than me.' I am over-defensive and scared. 'He had a self-contained flat in the basement.'

'With easy access to the rest of the house?'

'He came and went like everyone else.'

'Mr Young . . . Leo; let's drop the pretence. I think we know one another.' But I do not know her at all until she reintroduces herself a few moments later. 'Louise Sable, the *Nation*.'

'Then you're not a social worker?' I am aghast.

'Hardly. My editor thought that it was the simplest way to gain access. I said that you'd talk of your own accord. After all, we work for the same organisation.'

'A columnist for the *Criterion* has nothing in common with a journalist for the *Nation*. I can't believe . . . Isn't there a law against this?'

'I hardly think you're in any position to invoke the law.' My head pounds. 'We've been investigating you for months. Ever since the custody case.'

'How . . . what do you know? It was a closed court . . . a private hearing.'

'There are always people prepared to talk. You're a very familiar face, Leo. You'd have to go far further than Brighton to go to ground.'

'I am not Ernest Simpson avoiding the press in Ipswich! Brighton happens to be Pagan's grandparents' home town.'

'We have a file as thick as this on you.' Her fingers open a dismaying distance. 'The *Sentinel* has given the Mulliners' story. The *Nation* would like yours.'

'What is this? Competition or coercion? If you think you can scare me, you've got the wrong man. You force your way into my house –'

'You invited me in.'

'You showed me forged identification.'

'Did I? Take a look.' She mockingly holds up a gym membership card. I was blind to the small print.

'Do you have no scruples?'

'I'm just a journalist doing her job.'

'Are professional ethics the only ones left?'

'You're doing yourself no good.'

'Just leave. Go on, out. Before I call the police.' I brook no argument and bundle her down the stairs. When a waiting photographer shoots me pushing her through the front door, my patience snaps. 'I shall go to Print House tomorrow. I'll speak to your editor. Your job is on the line.'

'Come on, it was his idea.'

'Then you've both made a big mistake. I'm an old friend of Brian Derwent. I'll apply to him. You'll regret coming here with your threats.'

I am conscious of my raised voice and look for ruffled curtains; but the only reaction comes from inside where Pagan appears on the stairs, a strand of hair in her eyes and her cot comfort-blanket clutched to her chest.

'Why are you shouting?'

'What are you doing out of bed?'

'I heard you shouting.'

'It must have been a dream. Come on, I'll take you back upstairs.'

'Why were you shouting in my dream?'

'I don't know.' I wish that I did or that, at least, I had your ability to lie, whatever the occasion, even at the woozy breakfast when she overheard our inquest on the night before.

'He wanted fellatio. I told him that I never put anything in my mouth that Nanny wouldn't approve of.'

'What's fellatio?'

'It's a cream-cheese to which your Uncle Leo is particularly partial.' I am not sure which impressed me more, the explanation or the speed.

I determine to discover the truth the next morning and drive to Vauxhall to confront Derwent. I meet my first obstacle at the car-park where, having forgotten my pass, I am refused entry. The attendant admits that he knows my face; he admits that he knows my show; but I am no one without identification. The horns hooting behind me threaten to drown the voice of reason. 'If I am not me, who am I? Someone so desperate for a space that he resorts to impersonation? Perhaps one of the impressionists who does me on TV?' As he ponders the possibility, exasperation magnifies my mannerisms to the point where it might well be true.

He rings for authorisation with vengeful slowness. The

barriers grudgingly rise. I enter the building and submit to the body search and security checks that attest more to Charles Mitchell's self-importance than to any actual threat. As I appear on the monitors, the receptionist cracks her usual joke about my being on TV. I make my usual riposte about a fee. *Sic transit spontaneity*. From the pungent perfume, I assume that she has overdosed in cologne, until she explains that Mitchell has had a scented air system fitted after his wife read about the benefits in New York. 'Pity he can't deodorise his papers' prose-style,' I suggest. She laughs tentatively, while the grim-faced guard grunts and rubs a faded tattoo.

I take the lift to the *Criterion* floor. Babel meets bedlam, as the prejudices of the nation are shaped in open-plan chaos. News bulletins blast, phones ring, editors shout, and integrity lies buried in the archives. This is the architecture not of efficiency but of paranoia. Partitions threaten the party-line; walls are dangerous; closed doors foster open minds.

'Fierce column,' Freddie Leaver calls to me with studied coolness. At twenty-eight he has been appointed Culture Editor after some controversial articles in *Smash Hits*. His arrival has been designed less to appeal to youth than to flatter the management into thinking that they do. So he peppers his speech with enough buzz words to be hip but too few to be intimidating.

'Actually, the column was cut. I found it almost incomprehensible. It's in my contract: no changes are to be made without my approval.'

'Last-minute ad, mate. You know the score. Monster column, cooking ideas, major feedback.'

'Don't you find it ironic that a piece about slipshod speech should display the very traits that I deplored?'

His eyes narrow. 'Think of Shakespeare, mate. Do you think he complained? Burbage comes along. H.M. is making a rare visitation to Bankside in the p.m. Wants to see the Hamlet gig. Trouble is two hours max. Do you think he said sorry bro, no go. Did he fuck! Snip, snip went the scissors. Out went the ghost and Ophelia. But do you suppose anyone cared?'

'How about Shakespeare?'

'That's what I like about you, Leo. Always stick to your

guns. Catch you on the flip side.' And, with a tap on my shoulder that feels like a stab in the back, he shimmies away.

I sit outside Brian Derwent's office soaking up his secretary's shrugged smile. As my stomach flutters, I remind myself that I am thirty-seven years old. The trouble is that my memory is a good ten years younger. It turns me ... he turns me from the successful television host into the tyro radio performer. I am once again waiting in the Caprice for my first dinner with you both. I go down to the loo in anticipation. As I wash my hands, I drench my flies. I dab them frantically, futilely, but break off at the sound of steps. He takes me in instantly. 'What's up? Pissed yourself?' he asks cheerily and then himself proceeds to piss, more forcefully than anyone I have ever heard. I hurry back to the table and, when you introduce us, he smacks a proprietorial kiss on your cheek and says that we have already met.

I assert my prior claim: 'I certainly feel that we have. Candida has told me so much about you.' He looks startled.

'Not everything, I hope?' You both laugh flatly.

'I can't believe that there's much more.' How I would love to prick his complacency by revealing that I know every detail of his sagging, sallow flesh and missing toes and the way that he calls his penis Derek. And yet, as he glances between us, it is clear that for the first time he appreciates the extent of our intimacy and it frightens him. I have seen him naked, albeit at one remove, which is a privilege granted to few men. Women are different; they can be bought or bought off, betrayed or bedded. But men – even gay men – are a threat.

He reassures himself by scratching his balls and feeling his wallet; he asserts himself by ordering a bottle of champagne. As he urges me, superfluously, to choose whatever I want, I feel his hostility spicing every dish. I debate whether to have the *agneau aux haricots* but decide against it. 'Flageolets bring flatulence,' I say to impress him and fail.

He considers me closely. 'I like to call a fart a fart.'

'When Brian farts, people listen.'

'There's nothing half-arsed about me.'

131

I am grateful that at dinner, at least, he restricts himself to belching.

'Better out than in,' he says.

'In China, it's considered perfect etiquette,' you add.

'You should have saved money and taken us to the local Chinese.' I narrowly avoid yelping as you kick me. He looks at me sharply and then laughs.

'That's funny. And brave. I like you. I know you don't like me, but why should you? And why should I care? Tell me a bit about yourself.'

I tell him about the radio, which is a mistake, as to him broadcasting is synonymous with television. You add that I want to write and that they should give me a column on the *Criterion*. You sing my praise (and my prose) so loudly that I abandon hope. I am amazed when he suggests that, if I ring him next week, he will arrange an appointment with the Editor. You look triumphant. I try to thank him, but he dismisses it as a matter of no importance. And it is clear that any exertion is not because he believes in me, or even cares for you, but to prove his power. . . . He is fully clothed again and I am no longer a threat.

Your attempts to engage my complicity only emphasise my exclusion, as you flirt and flatter through the meal.

'I don't know what Brian sees in me.'

'You titillate my fancy.'

'You mean you fancy my tits.' I am amazed. Is his coarseness contagious? I blow my nose and concentrate on my food. I try to like him; I want to like him . . . at least I have wanted to meet him ever since you came back from your first *Criterion* party and told me how he singled you out among the stuffed shirts and canapés and lavished praise on your South African portfolio . . . Johannesburg matrons with mudpacks on their faces set against Soweto mothers with mud-caked packs on their backs hold an obvious appeal for him. Your photographs, his morality, their system, all neatly black and white.

'He wouldn't leave me alone. It was outrageous. Eventually, his wife came up.'

'And that rang no alarm bells?'

'No more than it did for him. He insisted on seeing me later. So he sent her home to Reigate while he put the paper – and me – to bed. He took me up to his office. He spent so long jiggling the key in the lock that I thought he was drunk until I realised it was a come-on.' I am more depressed by your amusement than his technique. 'Once inside, he was like a mad dog.'

'All slavering chops?'

'He ripped off my dress with his teeth.'

'Your *Caroline Charles*?'

'He said he'd buy me another . . . three, four. To him, money is no object.'

'But you presumably are.'

'Am I telling this story or are you?'

You were then . . . you are now . . . but I need to refresh my memory.

'He didn't even take off his trousers but simply unbuttoned his flies.' I picture him standing at a urinal. 'We made love on the boardroom table. I've never felt so much power.'

It seems to me that you have never been so helpless, as you report the brutality with which he scoops up your breasts in his hands and then swats you with leather-bound blotters, before slipping them beneath you to absorb the damp. You take such pleasure in the way that he separates your body from your personality that I think back to Edward and our conversation in the French pub. A flicker of unease runs through me: is feeling disembodied another way of playing dead? At least you are alive to the comedy of his penis, describing it rearing its ugly head, fat and apoplectic, before withdrawing, soft and apologetic, as he rolls off you and almost onto the floor. 'Thank you,' he says as you pull him back. 'Now I know that I can trust you. A great many people would be only too glad to see me fall.'

He assaults a recalcitrant fibre of meat with a tooth pick. 'Cartier,' you mouth; I am unimpressed. I appreciate his appeal to Mitchell; his Cockney barrow-boyishness is itself a statement of intent. 'I'm here to upset the apple-cart,' he declares and sets the pin-stripes shaking in their brogues. But it is a denial of all that we hold dear. When I mention Covent Garden, he snorts; 'I haven't been since the Jubilee Gala. It was my silver wedding; my wife enjoyed it. I don't believe in suffering for art.'

'Brian regards art as a con-trick devised by liberals to disguise their own futility.'

'A highly successful one, I grant. They create a market for something that no one needs and a mystique that intimidates everyone. But not me. I'm proud to stand with the Philistines. They were a noble nation who've had an unfair press.'

'You can change that.'

'In time, Candy'. . . . I choke on the contraction. 'When we've sorted out the rest of them, then we'll see to the artists.'

Is power really such an aphrodisiac? Does it signify so much that he can sit beside – and unseat – prime ministers? Or is it the duplicity that attracts you? 'He calls me his bit on the side,' is a strange boast from one who has always insisted on standing stage-centre. It is almost as though you believe that is where you belong. You indulge his taste for low-life; from dog-fights in Essex barns, where the blood that spurts onto your skirt stirs his in a nearby lay-by, to bare-knuckle fights in West End hotels, where men from his past spill their guts to thrill men from his present. Meanwhile, Westminster and Ascot and Charles Mitchell's yacht are reserved for his wife.

'Sheila must know nothing,' he tells you. 'She is the mother of my son. If it ever comes to a choice, there won't be one.' You find his loyalty touching. 'There may have been other women – I'm a busy man – but I go home to her at the end of the day . . . or at least the weekend. That's what family values mean.'

His words disturb me as you report them . . . they disturb me still more as I sit at table and watch you play a part for which you are twenty years too old. As he rolls an oyster around his throat and you brush your lips with buttered asparagus, food becomes foreplay. I feel less like a guest than a voyeur. Then, when we reach the dessert course and he feeds you *bavarois* from his spoon, your napkin becomes a bib; I half-expect a wheedling plea of 'one for Daddy'. The implications make me so queasy that I push away my plate.

I wish that I could push away the memory; but the aftertaste – the ten-years-after taste – sticks in my throat. I need a drink. Ignoring the secretary's strained smile, I walk through the No Entry door which I know from – your – experience leads to his private loo. As I cup my hands, the taps prove to be as wayward as before, first spluttering, and then spurting over my thighs. I refuse to panic and pick up a copy of the *Nation* – a most inappropriate fig-leaf – and exit with it pressed to my crotch. The office door is now open and I sidle in like a character in a farce. Brian greets me expansively. I realise that I am holding the paper in my right hand and have to lower my guard to meet his grip. He sees the stain but makes no comment. He has aged.

He waves me to a chair, which stands uncomfortably close to his desk; but the distance must be deliberate for the feet are fixed. He leans back, and I find myself craning forward to compensate. A faint fading in the print of his shirt is evident when he crosses his arms behind his head. He no longer makes any attempt to disguise his girth, appearing to regard it as a badge of office, the embodiment of the weight on his mind. I picture him making jokes about his corporation at his club. The hair that he lacks on his head seems to sprout from his ears, and he looks like a bloated pub landlord. I wait to be offered a drink.

He scratches an armpit and congratulates me on my recent columns. I express surprise that he reads them. He pulls himself up and lunges across the desk. I shut my eyes and feel his breath on my cheeks. I wait for him to lock horns.

'Believe me, Leo, I read every word in all four of our titles. And ninety per cent of our competitors. So to those who say that the *Criterion* is too big –' he pats his paunch – 'I say do you know how long it takes me cover to cover? Forty-two minutes. I did a speed-reading course five years ago. I read *Bleak House* and *Hard Times* last Bank Holiday Monday. Sheila said that, if I took a week off, I could go on *Mastermind*. But I can't afford the time. I leave that to blokes like you.'

'I had no idea.'

'And your plea for proper English struck a chord.'

'Sarah was worried that it might offend the "it's what you say not the way you say it" brigade.'

'Balls. It's what we expect from you. A little overblown perhaps, a little flowery. But if it's good enough for . . . how many viewers?'

135

'On average, around five million.'

'Then it's good enough for us. And it fits our agenda. More discipline at home, in school and in the work-place. Flout the rules of grammar and, next thing, you'll be mugging old ladies, fathering illegitimate children and off your head on crack.'

'I don't think that that was my point at all, Brian.'

'I'm quite sure it wasn't; but it is ours.' He smiles and I feel my integrity run dry.

'But you didn't come here to argue ideology, or did you?' He leans back and the armpit print is now thick with sweat. I explain about the journalist's visit. He stands and moves behind me; I summon all my self-control not to turn round. He hovers over me and, while his words are all reassurance, his body is all threat. He dismisses the file as a formality, the basis for a profile or an obituary . . . I expect that they have access to my medical records. Do they know something that I do not?

I refuse to be deflected and repeat my fears about the intrusion, particularly after the *Sunday Sentinel* story.

'Well of course I read that. . . .' How many minutes does he allow for the *Sentinel*? 'I saw that it was about you and Candy. To speak frankly, I was hurt, Leo, that, if you had a story, you didn't come to us first.'

'But I didn't . . . don't have a story; that's just it. I'm asking for it to be spiked.'

He looks at me with an air of disappointment. 'Be fair, Leo; you'd be the first to cry foul if I challenged an editor's independence. And rightly so. Charles Mitchell has always said that he gives his editors complete control, whatever the Trots and their friends in the media might make out; and, as his Chief Executive, I back him all the way.'

'But this isn't a story of any interest.'

'Then it's quite simple; it won't run.'

'I'm trying to bring up a little girl, Candida's little girl; it isn't easy. And something like this won't help.' For an agonising moment, I wonder if Pagan might be his daughter . . . dates dissolve as in an exam. Then I remember your views on heredity; Bow Bells ring reassuringly in my ears.

'I must say that the *Sentinel* story put the parents' case very powerfully.'

'Grandparents' case! And it has already been answered in court. Why air it again in the press?'

'With kids divorcing their parents and child-molesters set free, when judges are so out-of-touch, where else can people look for justice?'

'I cannot understand how you can employ someone on one paper and attack him in another.'

'They serve quite different markets; that's what freedom of choice means.' He picks up the phone and tells his secretary to place his call to Tokyo; he flicks through a file. I stand, aware that we have resolved nothing. He looks up as if surprised to find me still there. 'Good to see you, Leo. Drop by any time. We must have lunch, at this rate sometime in 1995.' His laughter sounds more self-satisfied than self-mocking. 'I shouldn't worry. You have no idea how many stories are researched, written, even put on the system, and yet never run.'

'Then why not kill it now? I can't believe that the channels don't exist. If there were a story about your private life. . . .'

He looks up sharply. 'What story?'

'If, just if.'

'There is no story. I don't have a private life. I'm stuck here all the hours God sends. Do you know I now have a bed in the office?' I see him unbuttoning his flies as he spreads you out on the boardroom table . . . 'It's not that I'm old-fashioned; I've just been caught too often in the zip.'

I begin to laugh. I check myself. 'How's Sheila?' I ask; but, instead of easing the tension, I increase it.

'What are you implying?'

'Nothing. I was just wondering. It must be years –'

'Is that meant as a threat?'

'She's your wife; I thought it polite to inquire.'

'She's my wife, yes. This summer we celebrated our ruby wedding.'

'I saw the pictures in the *Nation*.'

'Forty years and never an angry word.'

'They don't speak,' I hear you saying. 'He locks her up in Reigate behind a Beware of the Dog sign with an electric bark.'

'That's what this country needs,' he says, 'stability. Kids

137

today have no sense of responsibility. Have a bonk and do a bunk; that's their attitude. Bonk and bunk!' He savours a future headline. 'The *Nation* is launching a campaign. Instead of calling next year the Year of the Dwarf or the Disabled or some other hardluck group, they should call it the Year of the Family; then we can all take heart. . . . Yes, Sheila's fine, thank you. Never better.'

I long to assert the Family of Man but fear that he would smell a perversion.

'I was sorry that you weren't able to come to Candida's exhibition. It would have meant a lot to her.' Would it? Or is my attitude as sentimental as his? 'You meant a lot to her; she told me.' Does he wonder what else you may have told me? Does he care? 'Publish and be damned' comes cheap when you control the country's largest newspaper group.

'I'd have liked to, but it was my sister-in-law's fiftieth birthday. A family affair.'

He knows that I know and he knows what I know and he is signalling that it is of no value. I gave her up, he is saying; I am clean. And yet, if his son's motorbike hadn't skidded and if you hadn't fallen ill . . . there are too many 'if's; the past is complex enough without revision. For Brian, it leaves a future without hope. Young Brian was his only son; now he has only daughters. 'Who will carry on my name?' he asks, and rejects his daughter's double-barrelled compromise. He has never done anything by halves.

Your attempts to console him fail. He becomes impotent from the day of the accident. As grief and guilt mingle in his mind, he blames you for destroying both his son and his manhood, refusing to see or even to speak to you again.

'I'm in despair,' you say; and you say it so lightly that I know that it must be true.

And, as I walk out backwards, not from deference but self-defence, I study his face and cringe at its cruelty. 'He's so ruthless,' you once said admiringly; 'he'd feed you to the sharks if he thought that the water looked better red.'

'Don't worry, Leo,' he calls; 'I'm sure you've no need.'

And I sense something stir beneath the waves.

# 2

I am boycotting Brighton. In March, I was determined to show willing; now I stand aloof. The hearing is a travesty, which I refuse to acknowledge. I try to banish it from my mind; but it sneaks back into my imagination, as my office becomes an ante-room where the secretaries are clerks, the messengers ushers, and Judge Flower glares at me from the wall. I am granted a temporary reprieve over lunch in order to propose a toast to Bridget Newscombe, who is taking early retirement from Music and Arts. I brave-face my way through the aperitifs; but my composure cracks on being seated next to Ginny Lawson, who rails against the BBC's switch from Reithian ethics to Birtian economics. As she alliterates into our costive, cost-effective corporation, I push aside my plate and console myself with the Chablis.

'You must eat,' she insists.

'I'm on a diet.'

'Then should you be drinking?'

'It isn't weight that I'm trying to lose but memories.' By the end of the meal, I am so on edge that I mangle my speech, losing the thread and pulling the punch-line of several jokes.

I return to work and try to assess Vicky's colour-coded guest-lists for prospective programmes, but my own prospects are too black. At four thirty, Max rings from Brighton, but, after a short preamble, the line goes dead. He rings again. This time there is no preamble, only pips. I pace around the office which starts to feel sinisterly small, fuelling my resentment of an organisation that undervalues me. The telephone rings again; I fly at it, upsetting the cone of water which is balanced precariously on the inkwell. It is the switchboard asking if I will be personally responsible for a reversed-charge call from Brighton. I hiss my assent. As the colours on Vicky's sodden chart start to run, Edward Heath seeps into Vera Lynn.

Max is connected and launches a bitter tirade on the inadequacies of British Telecom and the BBC switchboard. I steer him unceremoniously back into court, and he assures me that the Directions Hearing went without a hitch. As before, the Judge has allowed us three weeks to file affidavits, while making an Interim Order for Pagan to remain with me. Although your parents were in court, they raised no objection. Max was surprised. I am suspicious. I yearn to share the benefit of your experience; is their reticence a sign of weakness or of a willingness to wait?

At least we know their new evidence. They have sniffed out my sexuality, while yours has been dug from the grave and dragged through the gutter . . . I keep picturing Oliver Cromwell's corpse disinterred in disgrace and displayed at Tyburn. History is not always a help. The resurrectionists are Jenny Knatchpole and Lewis Kelly, an extraordinary combination in themselves, let alone in collaboration with your parents; I fail to see how they made contact, let alone common cause. The retired major, the minister's wife and the murderer form a trio straight out of Agatha Christie. Their affidavits present such a picture of your unfitness as a mother that I am amazed that Pagan was not wrenched from your arms at birth. She could have been put up for adoption and your parents could have applied; in which case, this whole ordeal would have been avoided. Not that any adoption society would have considered them; they are too old.

A social worker in Nottingham has caused an outcry by refusing a foster-child to a couple on the grounds that they are too fat. The tabloids have lambasted another example of red talk and red tape: the Nanny State discriminating against parents. They ignore the fact that, with a combined weight of fifty-two stone, they might not have the stamina for a six-year-old and that the six-year-old might be mercilessly mocked at school. No, they are a happily married couple and so have a God-given right to a child.

Homosexuality tilts the scales the other way. Reading your parents' affidavit – the actual words, not between the lines – their case is clear; every breath that I take is tainted by my sexual preference. I am no longer a person but a pathology: an abnormality in their eyes and an abomination in God's. I betrayed myself when I ordered your mother to stop telling Pagan about Jesus's miracles . . . as I recall, I made the specific request that she stop confusing her about Lazarus. My revulsion from the Scriptures is as marked as a mystery-play Satan tortured by the name of Christ.

Their affidavit is a testament to my inadequacy. They show no compunction about vilifying you in order to hit at me. They have discovered the flat in Brewer Street and the club in Meard Street; and, from the tenor of their remarks, I was not just living with you but off you. Let me introduce myself; Leo Young, parasite and pimp. The absurdity of the idea is concealed by the formality of the language. The legal terminology gives it authority, while the numbered paragraphs present established facts. What is worse, they imply that, if they leave her in my hands, Pagan will go the same way. 'She is encouraged to mix with undesirables.' Who are they? Actors, writers, television executives? 'She stays up until all hours and tells us that, at a recent party, the respondent allowed her to come downstairs in her pyjamas and say goodnight to the guests, several of whom she kissed.' Just what are they trying to suggest?

The murkiness of middle-class morality is frightening. They, of course, level similar charges at me. They write that I adopt a cynical attitude to Pagan's development and take no care of her personal hygiene or toilet training . . . if my image of you were not ashen-faced already, it would be now. I know exactly the reference, I can quote you chapter and verse; or does that sound too biblical? Pagan told me that, when she wet her bed one Friday, your mother pressed her nose to the sheets in a primitive aversion therapy. She consoled her by saying – oh my darling, why did you never tell me? – that she had done the same to you. When Saturday brought no improvement, she was smacked for being wilful. On Sunday, she came home and her sheets were bone-dry. Terrified of your parents' injunction, she made me promise to say nothing; any adult conversation sounds to her a form of collusion. So I used the Welfare Officer as an intermediary. Heaven knows what construction they have put on her words!

'Who has a personality without being a person and a lifestyle without a life?' might not head any list of the world's great riddles but, as a description of yours truly, it has a piquant truth. According to your parents, it is my lifestyle that puts Pagan at risk. I appear to be simultaneously working late, painting the town and filling the house with people. I neglect her by at once sending her off to classes, dragging her round to my friends and dumping her on hers. I both treat her too much like an adult (inappropriate activities, meal-times, bedtimes and consultation) and baby her (lack of discipline, overindulgence). How I manage to reconcile such contradictions defeats me, but no doubt my master the Devil shows the way.

The animals come in two by two ... your parents' attitudes are antediluvian. This is 1992; homosexuals can police the streets but are barred from nurseries. For heterosexuals, the only qualification for parenthood is puberty; for homosexuals, pre-pubescents must be kept at bay. Your parents and their friends and newspapers decry the teenage pregnancies and single mothers who, to them, lie behind every evil from the budget deficit to the rise in crime; and yet they still locate fatherhood in the genitals. Parentage requires no more than a drunken fumble, so long as the right organs are used; but anyone who turns them – dare I say it? – arsy-versy is ruled out of court. . . . No, not court, that is just a figure of speech. Court is where sanity will prevail; court is where integrity will be acknowledged; court is where justice will be done.

Until then, your parents prefer to take the word – or rather, affidavit – of a convicted murderer: Lewis Patrick Perjury Kelly. . . . 'I was crossing my fingers, Ma, so it don't count.'

I hear you raise your voice in his defence; at least I do ten years ago. He has hit you and I remind you of his history; whereupon you cry foul prejudice. 'Can people never change? So much for your so-called liberalism.'

142

'Liberalism isn't blindness; it means seeing every angle, not closing your eyes.'

'The past is dead and buried. After fourteen years, he's earned a fresh start.'

'The past is dead and buried; there are fourteen years of weeds on the grave.'

'Since when have you joined the hanging, shooting, flogging brigade?'

'I quite agree that his previous convictions shouldn't be mentioned in court ... although, if you showed those bruises, I'm sure you'd have a case. But you're not sentencing him, you're living with him, and you can't ignore the violence in his blood.'

'But you don't hold with blood; according to you, we're all free agents.'

'His blood, *his*; not his South London criminal genes. He's a strong man ... and not just with his fists. Anyone with the strength of mind to land a place at the Drama Centre six months after leaving jail should be able to defeat his background. We are not our parents' prisoners.'

I shake myself by the hand; so often my youthful sentiments sound callow; these hold true. I look again at Lewis's affidavit. I never thought to come across him again, except at the Variety Club and BBC parties, where he conceals his hostility behind a practised smile. He now has the perfect excuse to vent his resentment. I little imagined that an evening at Wormwood Scrubs would have such lifelong repercussions. I should have taken Struan's advice – and Struan – instead of you. And yet it was through you that I gained the job on *Light Waves*; so the responsibility – and the memory – runs full circle.

We are walking through the suburban slough of East Acton on a dull November day, heavy with dankness and gloom. We reach the prison precincts and an incongruous group of playgoers, all anxious to pretend that Wormwood Scrubs is as familiar a venue as Stratford or the Old Vic. Disdainful guards take our names and herd us through the gates. We negotiate a network of electronic doors, to be greeted by an affable young man with his ear pressed to a walkie-talkie. He apologises for the delay with a winning smile. You decide that he must be kept on permanent front-line duty, buttering up the public, while the old guard are beating up the inmates inside.

I try to reply; but my lips are frozen. I fight for breath as my imagination runs riot. This is no innocent invitation, but a deliberate ploy. Some young man has lied to me about his age and to the police about my behaviour. They have struck a secret deal with my producers to avoid any scandal touching the BBC. I am to be incarcerated without a trial. . . . Look, the walls are closing in; or is it just that the doors are closing . . . ? Even you are implicated; there is no one I can trust. At any moment, the guards will drag me away. I will be segregated with the sex offenders and assaulted in the showers. My tea will be poisoned with piss and my food gritted with broken glass. My family and friends will disown me. . . . I am the prisoner of my paranoia; my guilt has found the perfect home.

'Wake up,' you say, 'you look miles away.'

'I feel that I'm here for life.'

We process through the prison proper and a confusion of brutal brick buildings. Mayhem breaks out in a cell-block. Arms squeeze through grilles and bang on tin-plates, followed by piercing shrieks of 'they're killing us' and 'get me out of here'. The young guard genially explains that the show has already begun; the entire cast deserves Oscars. Unconvinced, I think back to the painful day I spent locked in a Cambridge cage on behalf of Amnesty. A harsh shout warns me away from the walls, just in time to avoid a parcel of shit that explodes at my feet. A corduroy man asks if I was at the Roundhouse when the Brazilians pelted the stalls with offal. I shake my head.   Howling dogs begin a running commentary on our visit.

'Are they adequately fed?' demands a tweedy lady.

'Yes, ma'am,' the guard replies. 'We let them loose every night in the punishment block.' He looks hurt when she takes him at his word.

We are led into a very makeshift theatre and told that, owing to a lunch-time disturbance, the planned performance in the main hall has been cancelled and the play is to be presented in private before the governor and guests. The director courts sympathy by listing his complaints. While the men themselves could not have worked harder, a number of hostile guards have sabotaged rehearsals from

144

the start, withdrawing privileges, imposing duties . . . indeed, he has no doubt that they were behind the trouble at lunch. Added to which, two of Sergeant Musgrave's gang were transferred, without warning, to Parkhurst, leaving him five days to train professionals in their place.

Against all the odds, the play begins and, against all expectations, it triumphs. We are both impressed by the flinty intensity of the actor playing Musgrave and by the magnificent musculature of Attercliffe, whose shoulders and chest suggest hours of sweaty sit-ups in his cell. The applause is thunderous, and, for the first time in the evening, it succeeds in drowning out the dogs. The actors disappear and the governor tells us that they will be allowed back for a fifteen-minute discussion. They return, to a new round of cheers, slapped backs, slipped cigarettes and a kissing ovation from several women.

'*Nostalgie de la boue*?' I ask.

'They wouldn't say *boue* to a goose.'

The only two who do not re-emerge are Musgrave and Attercliffe . . . no other identification is permissible by law. We each devise explanations which reveal our particular bias. I feel sure that Musgrave is a professional who does not wish to outshine the prisoners, while you insist that Attercliffe is considered too dangerous for social contact; his every movement containing the threat of GBH. In the event, we are both mistaken; Attercliffe is a last-minute replacement whose abs, pecs and lats are the product of days at the gym and nights at the disco; and Musgrave is Lewis, serving a life-sentence for murder, who is too overwhelmed by his reception to return.

He is finally coaxed out of hiding and kissed on both cheeks by an opportunistic young director fresh from Sloane Square. He flinches in fury; and it is only when he raises his fists that we see that his wrist is handcuffed. Your face is a palimpsest registering excitement, compassion and lust in swift succession. 'Simon Smith and his amazing dancing bear,' you breathe, before walking slowly towards him, assuming potency with every step. I watch, powerless to prevent a meeting that I know will prove fateful. Is it second sight or déjà vu . . . ? If time is standing still for you, it is spinning for me in all directions. I desperately search for a diversion that will send the prisoners back to their cells.

It is too late. It is not that his face relaxes – his skin is too taut on the bone – but his body acknowledges yours in such a way as to suggest a future. I fail to read your lips, but your intentions are clear. You beckon me over and I mumble my practised plaudits. I am taken aback as he makes no attempt to interrupt or to deflect the flow; and yet I see that it is not from the usual actor's vanity – the 'that's enough about me, so what did you think of my performance?' egotism – but from a desperate desire to learn. We are joined by two middle-aged women who twitter and touch him; but his eyes remain fixed on you. I note how slowly he speaks, which I attribute to years in solitary confinement, until I realise that it signals the regard in which he holds words.

The governor calls for silence and congratulates everyone involved in the project, not least, if he may so, himself for resisting the sceptics both in the Home Office and on his staff. He praises the vision of the director and the dedication of the men, which is all the more remarkable considering that there are several who have never set foot inside a theatre. The play has given them a rare sense of achievement, endorsed by the generous response of such a distinguished audience; indeed, his emphasis suggests that the real achievement lies more in the audience's indulgence than in the actors' skill. He concludes to loud applause. Lewis alone remains silent; until his guard yanks his hand with such a resounding smack that I fear for their return to the cells.

'Right, say your goodbyes now, lads, please.' The head warder shatters the illusion more cruelly than the most insensitive stage-manager.

'Got any smokes?' Lewis asks, as the prison regime takes over.

'I'm sorry, I don't. . . .' I stammer.

'You should still know to bring some to a nick.'

'Come on, lad,' the guard pulls him away. You grab him back.

'Thank you so much for a wonderful performance. I shall never forget it,' you say, clasping his hand for just a moment too long. Suddenly, the prisoners are gone and we are back in the Barbican buffet, scoring points and comparing productions. Intimacy dissolves as we wait impatiently for our escort. We are ushered out of the gates to a final blast of the canine chorus and retrace the dismal trek to the tube. There, we discover Attercliffe, or rather Peter, sitting on the platform. His distressed leather jacket and faded jeans emphasise his ersatz toughness, more YMCA than GBH. We introduce ourselves and you press him for details of Lewis. He knows very few, having only been involved with the group for five days.

'I had my mind full of a part which I last played at drama school. The most I could hope was to remember the lines and not trip over the furniture.'

'No one would know. You had real presence. I shan't forget that look of horror when you realised you'd killed Sparky.'

'Really? At least someone noticed. Those guys are so undisciplined; you never know how they'll come out with a line. Talk about Best Supporting Performance. I had to carry the play.'

We suppress a smile. As we rattle back from East Acton to the West End, we make an equivalent journey from Lewis's untutored passion to Peter's professional pride. Having elicited that he will be returning next week for a second performance, you persuade him to take a letter to Lewis. I add that we should send him some cigarettes; it was stupid not to have thought.

'Don't worry, it wasn't like turning up empty-handed to Melissa's dinner party. Besides, as he left, I slipped him a gram of cocaine.'

'What?' We both look aghast.

'I had it in my bag. It seemed only fair. His need was greater than mine.'

'We might have been kept there ourselves.' I check the carriage to make sure that no one has heard.

'That might have had its compensations. You know: new kid on the block.'

'New head more like.'

'Or new meat,' Peter grins.

I find that I am sweating; dogs are howling at my heels. You avoid further discussion by feigning sleep. Peter leaves us at Tottenham Court Road to go clubbing.

'Why didn't you go with him? He could hardly have made it any plainer.'

'How would he know I was gay?'

'Oh please.'

'Well, how do you know that he fancied me?'

'Short of undoing your flies and fellating you between Marble Arch and Bond Street, what more could he do? Why do you think he gave you his number?'

'That was so you could give him your letter.'

'You can't really be that naive. You complain that no one's interested in you, but what do you expect when you always push them away?'

'Anyway, there was something thuggish about him.'

'Is, not was. Don't use the past tense so dismissively.'

'He's probably into whips and chains and things.'

'So? Live dangerously.'

'I leave that to you.'

My words rebound on me as you and Lewis become increasingly involved. My request to interview him for *Light Waves* is refused, while yours to photograph prison life for the *Criterion* magazine is granted. I am bemused by the distinction, until you explain that Brian Derwent is not a governor of the BBC.

'He went straight to James Merfield and won his backing. In return, he agreed to ease off on some story about MI5.'

'But that's dreadful.'

'That's life. Arm-twisting, back-scratching, horse-trading are second nature to Brian. I just hope he thinks that the pictures measure up.'

A ten-page spread says that he does. The images are as exciting as they are unexpected. In place of grizzled figures in grainy monochrome, all hand-rolled cigarettes and death's-head tattoos, are the radiant friars of a Renaissance fresco. The light comes courtesy of Fra Angelico and the cells belong to St Dominic or St Jerome. It is as if you find in them – and, in particular, in Lewis – a liberation. He shows a sensitivity that I never anticipated . . . and am never to see again.

He declares that, on his release, he will use the portraits to make up a portfolio. As you continue to visit him, first in the Scrubs and then in Leyhill, you discuss his future.

He is determined to act, despite many reservations, not least about the prevalence of 'poofs' in the profession.

'Charming.'

'You can't blame him. If you'd been born into his family, you'd say the same.'

'I thought that Catholics were supposed to believe in free will.'

'He's lapsed.'

You encourage him to apply to the Drama Centre, where the intensity of his acting and the notoriety of his past combine to create a lycanthropic legend. You introduce him to Melissa who is wrestling with the book that will take her from indifferent ingénue to hottest young novelist of her generation. She, in turn, introduces him to various directors. Although you insist that her motives are self-serving, you cannot argue with their success when, six months after leaving the school, he is offered a lead at Stratford.

'East, not on Avon, but then you have to start somewhere,' Melissa smiles blithely. 'As you, of all people, should know.'

You bite your tongue. For three years, you smart under the obligation. When, however, she puts a thinly disguised version of your affair with Lewis at the heart of her second novel, you consider the debt erased.

'I despise her. She stores up gossip like a housemaid . . . and writes like one too. Less *romans-à-clef* than *à-key-hole.*' You take your revenge in her bed – or rather by the side of it when, renewing your acquaintance with Edward, you leave your knickers prominently discarded. But revenge is as risky as love. Marriage has toughened Melissa, who sends them to Lewis with the simple message: 'I believe that these belong to you.' At first, he is outraged by the imputation; later, he takes out his rage on you.

Throughout his career, he has been desperate to avoid any breath of scandal . . . read every profile, watch every chat show except mine, and you will find the same story: a man who made a fatal mistake in his youth but who paid the price and now asks only to put the past behind him. The wisest decision he ever made was to forestall the tabloids when he landed the part in the soap. And yet the conversion is unconvincing. He can boogie and floozie his

149

nights away in clubs; he can jog around Queen's Park for an hour the next morning; but he still cannot curb his temper. . . . What do you consider your greatest asset as an actor, Mr Kelly? Your fists?

His first present for any prospective girlfriend should be a pair of dark glasses. . . . I hear you saying – if only you could speak to me – that I do not understand women. I disagree. I need think back no further than last Tuesday's show and Magdalena Dorsa's story of the night that her husband accused her of sleeping with Picasso.

'He slit my throat from 'ere to 'ere.' She removes her choker to reveal the scar.

'And you didn't leave him?'

She looks at me with a blend of contempt and pity. 'Only a man could ask this question. Why should I leave him? I was enslaved for him. Such passion! Such fury! Such pride!' The studio audience roars its applause.

Are your black eyes similar signs of affection . . . no more than love-bites writ large? You insist that I know nothing about him; but I know what he does to you. Why do you allow yourself to be abused? Why do you encourage it? Does it spring from a childhood sense that you are intrinsically wicked . . . a naughty little girl who deserves to be smacked by Daddy? Or have you been seduced by the adolescent sophistry that sadism is a more sophisticated form of love; which provides another opportunity to look down on Mr and Mrs Average, with their twin-bedded Teasmade sex? I fail to see how a blow to the face can ever be construed as a blow for freedom. . . . You smile and tell me that passion spells SOS pain.

'He's the first man who has ever given me an orgasm.' I am taken aback; our sex talk has always focused on foreplay. I assume that inducing an orgasm is as mechanical as setting the sprinkler-system on a lawn. 'I'm amazed; I never thought that it mattered so much. I feel so grateful to him . . . unutterably grateful. Once you've experienced that power of physical pleasure, it's possible to forgive everything else.' I suddenly feel cold. 'That's why I've decided to move in with him.'

I slip into automatic. 'I suppose I shouldn't see it so much as losing a sister as gaining a brother-in-law.'

'I wish you'd try to like him.'

'He hates me. He's the most homophobic actor in captivity. No pun intended.'

'It still applies. Fourteen years in prison leave their mark.'

'He's not there now! And I'm sorry but I don't see him as some pathetic inadequate gang-raped by the tobacco barons. Quite the opposite. I bet no one picked up the soap when he was in the showers.'

'Who's being homophobic now?'

'The truth is that he feels threatened by me. He sees women as good for one thing and one thing only; he cannot understand a man who wants something else. It confuses his compartmentalised mind. What was it he told you? "Every time I meet him, I think you've discussed what I was like the night before." '

'Not any more.'

'I see.'

'I won't be disloyal.'

'That's the curse of divided loyalties.'

So you leave me and move in with him; and I learn about loneliness. I explore the power of physical pleasure for myself; but, despite the groiny excitement, I am left with morning-after blues more acute than any hangover. There is a remedy for a hangover – some concoction of raw eggs and Worcester sauce – but the only cure for solitude is people . . . and the men I meet seem to consider one-night stands too long an emotional commitment. I yearn for an intimacy that is not measured in inches. I despair of finding it until, several months later, you leave Lewis and return to me. He has failed an audition and relieved his frustration by punching you in the stomach . . . your pain is too painful to recall. What he does not know is that you are carrying – were carrying – his child.

I feel sure that he holds me to blame for your departure and, for the past eight years, has been harbouring hopes of revenge. It was fanciful to propose a conspiracy; he may just have read your parents' interview in the *Sunday Sentinel* and resented the fact that I was the one with the daughter, not him. His affidavit makes wretched reading. Didn't I warn you to keep him away from Soho? . . . I'm sorry; 'I told you so' is a particularly futile response to a memory. I understand your motives – or, at least, I trust my interpretation – but, for all that you may have wanted to identify with him and show that you were not the clean-living, middle-class girl that he may have imagined, you left him feeling betrayed.

I would have thought that you, of all people, would have recognised the importance of illusions. In confessing your past, you allowed him to throw it back – literally – in your face. Now he hopes to do the same to me. But, unlike you, I have no need for dark glasses; unlike you, I can raise my guard. His charges are mere innuendo; your parents are building their case on mud. I am supremely confident. What judge will accept the hearsay evidence of a murderer (I have changed my mind on the matter of previous convictions) . . . or have the Courts become an extension of the prison hierarchy, where murderers are respected while sex-offenders – and my sexuality is in itself an offence to them – are reviled?

I sweep the paper off my desk with a show of scorn which is wasted without an audience; although I am grateful that there is no one to see me, five minutes later, stooping to scoop it up off the floor. I turn to Jenny Knatchpole's affidavit, which is more worrying because less expected. Apart from the odd glimpse of her accompanying Guy to an official function or standing by him when his secretary went public, I have not seen her in – it must be – twelve years . . . your barbed definition of a housewife as someone who falls in love with a man and ends up married to his house holds doubly true of the House of Commons. Still, I am sure that she consoles herself in the country, rescuing sheepdogs and counting sheep.

The sheepdogs are not respondent's licence; they figured prominently in a colour-spread in the *Criterion* supplement. Guy Knatchpole, rising star of the Tory right, invites you into his lovely home and his lovely wife . . . oops, sorry, cock-up on the computer. It was part of that glamorous lifestyle series in which they wanted to feature me . . . at least they did until they came to research. Your health was failing and we were converting the house. In place of envy-inducing elegance, they found grab-rails and stair-lifts and pulleys and consoles; the commode was functional rather than decorative. Two weeks later, I received a letter of regret. They had decided against using any more television personalities ... especially those whose accessories set the wrong tone.

Guy's and Jenny's, on the other hand, set the tone impeccably. The furniture was solid and the decor muted. The lilies lilted at the perfect angle. Even the sweet-wrappers matched the bowl. It was a far cry from the flat in Fulham which you once cleaned for him, where bachelor squalor met public-school indolence in week-old take-aways mouldering in the kitchen and matted socks scattered around the bed. I opposed the whole enterprise. You had a Cambridge degree – albeit an aegrotat – and a brilliant – or, at any rate, an incisive – mind; both of which you were wasting. But you saw it differently. 'If I had nothing else, I agree I would be pitiful ... a young drudge with no future but buses, babies, and varicose veins. But, for me, it's an adventure. And it's one I get paid for: I have to eat.'

'But there are so many other things you could do.'

'Such as? I have a degree in English. That fits me for nothing but teaching; which I willingly leave to you. My only talent is for being myself, so I need to marry someone rich enough to provide a suitable setting. I have one foot in the door already.'

'Carrying a mop and bucket?'

'It's a start.'

It is Robin who introduces Guy ... another cousin. With that expert genealogy which appears to compensate for your own unknown genes, you inform me that he belongs to the senior branch of the family, superior in every way to Robin, who is beginning to tax even your patience with his antics. Guy hires you for one day a week – 'I told him to call me Mrs Thursday' – and prevails on two of his colleagues to take up Monday and Wednesday afternoons. They suggest someone else, a woman ... I think ... yes, it may sound extraordinary but I am sure that it is Rebecca, a feminist lawyer who practises in the Family Division. I wonder if she remembers ... but how can she when you refused to consider her? 'I make it my rule only to clean for men. Women are slave-drivers; they know what they could do themselves. Whereas men regard it as their birthright to have someone clear up after them; they're grateful just to have it taken off their hands.'

You make as marked an impression on Guy as on his flat. He compliments you on your work. You simper: 'I aim to give satisfaction to all my gentlemen' . . . Cambridge has furnished the vocabulary if nothing else. He takes you at your word. It is as though having an affair with a cleaner meets a long-repressed need . . . I must resist the temptation to play Freud. For the first time in his life, he is rebelling; you are long hair, free love, Kathmandu and Glastonbury all rolled into one. But, as he and I both know and you refuse to recognise, it cannot last.

'He's so boring,' I say, after another dreary dinner where he has droned on about steam engines.

'You have a basic clash of personalities.'

'Precisely. I have one and he doesn't.'

'You wouldn't say that if you were interested in old railways.'

'Come on; that's like saying someone speaks excellent Esperanto.' Nevertheless, you agree to accompany him to a convention in Halifax to celebrate the reopening of five miles of disused track. You spend the weekend sitting in the hotel foyer, taking tea with the wives and girlfriends, while the boys go off to play chug-chug . . . the sexes staying as segregated as in a school-yard. Even that fails to deter you. 'After a few hours, the boredom becomes transcendent. It's very Zen.'

'Bullshit.'

'Just think; once we're married, he can have the nursery laid out as a model railway. He can play with the children.' I am taken aback. This is the first time that I have heard you express a desire for children. In the past, the fantasy has always ended with 'Reader, I married him'; I see now that there is a sequel.

'Won't Guy be child enough?'

'I intend to have a large family. Don't you find there's an air of the National Portrait Gallery about him? He needs a wife and children by his side.'

'Do men like Guy marry their cleaners? You're not exactly the seventies equivalent of a chorus girl. It's one thing when the Duchess of Loamshire kicked up her legs at Drury Lane; quite another when she's scrubbing the loo.'

'I don't clean for him any more . . . at least not professionally.'

'You mean that's something else he gets for free?'

'You're so predictable'. . . . That may be true; but so, I am afraid, is he.

He invites you to *Madame Butterfly* at Covent Garden. Robin sneers at the choice . . . 'Puccini's about his level.' I suggest that he may be preparing you for when he does a Pinkerton. Robin replies that he is not so intelligent; you that he is not so sly. And yet why else is he so frugal with his friends? He surely cannot expect you to fall for the guff about your finding them stuffy? Nor, despite your repeated requests, has he taken you to Northumberland; and your excuses for his excuses sound increasingly lame. But, when his mother and sister come to town on a shopping trip ('Although London isn't the same since they closed Marshall and Snelgrove'), your exclusion from the official programme is harder to explain.

'You don't have to tell them I'm your cleaner. I went to Cambridge. I've stayed at Crierley.'

I avoid Robin's glance and my memory.

'It's not the cleaning that's a problem, not really. It's you.' Your silence forces him to fill it. 'You're just not their sort of person. Believe me, the loss is entirely theirs; but they wouldn't see the joke.'

I have to restrain my basic instincts, which are reassuringly red-blooded, while you pour coffee with a sangfroid that would put any country-house hostess to shame.

'Take this flat. If I told my mother that you were living in Soho, she'd think you were either a Bohemian or a tart.'

'Why?' you ask. 'She's not a man.'

Robin laughs. 'You don't know Aunt Jessie.' And, despite renewed pleading, you never do. Her visit lasts a week, at the end of which you and Guy resume your former routine . . . although you admit that your cleaning is somewhat more perfunctory, sweeping the dust under the carpet rather than into the bin. Then one morning, over breakfast in his flat – he is nothing if not territorial – he announces his engagement. He does not even have the grace to wait until you are out of your pyjamas, or rather his pyjamas, since you wear the top and he the bottom. He tells you – you tell me – that he is to marry Jenny Dacre. I am doubly shocked. She is the girl whom Lady Standish picked out for Robin; she is the one for whom I stepped

155

aside . . . if *One Fine Day* is to be your theme song, *This Nearly Was Mine* should be mine.

You are so shaken that you start spreading butter very thinly over his *Daily Mail*. You press him for details, not because they make any sense, but from fear that, if he stops talking, you will collapse. He describes how they were introduced by Robin six months ago and fell in love. 'You made love to me last night,' you counter. He blushes like a public schoolboy caught with one of the maids.

I reconstruct the scene through the sobs, silences and static of a long-distance line to Shropshire. I picture the knife aimlessly spreading . . . the deceptive harmony of the shared pyjamas.

'There's no need for us to stop seeing each other,' he says. One look at your face convinces him of his error. 'That is if you still want to clean for me. You don't have to give up your job. We could return to the old arrangement . . . at a new rate.'

'And, after all, a good cleaner is hard to find. One who knows all your little ways, who doesn't mix the socks with the knickers, the cleavers with the carving-knives.'

'It's just a thought. I don't want you to lose out.'

'Oh believe me, I'm losing nothing.'

'You're a realist. You must have known that this couldn't last for ever. . . . Do you know you're buttering the leader page of the *Daily Mail*?'

'Of course. Why? Do you think that I'm crazed with grief?' And you tear it into strips and stuff it in your mouth.

At which point, I stop picturing and wonder whether some of the details may have been added a day later for my benefit. From a hundred and fifty miles away, it is impossible to judge.

There are no such problems the following month when I come down to London for the Easter break and you persuade me to gatecrash the official engagement party. The only people I know are the Standishes. Lydia is dressed as if for the *Good Ship Lollipop*, with ribbons in her hair, frills on her sleeves, and knee-length white socks. The intention may be protective, but the effect is cruel. Her equine Aunt Waverley coos over her. 'You'll be the next, my dear,' she insists, with all the complacency of her class. Lydia grins; Lady Standish grimaces. She stands poker-backed, her bosom and hands encrusted with jewels. 'All fakes,' Robin whispers. 'That's why she keeps to the shadows. They're first-rate reproductions of her old pieces; but the secret's out when they catch the light.' He moves to greet his mother, who barely acknowledges him. He turns away as she holds out her hand to me.

'This should have been Robin's.' I cannot tell whether she is referring to the engagement or to the flat.

'He preferred to play Cupid.' He seems to have passed her on as casually as he recommended you as a cleaner.

'That is not the role for which I intended him. Disappointment is a disease, Leo; people can die of it.'

'People can die of anything if they so choose.'

'I understand that you are teaching.'

'Yes, music. At St Bride's, a small prep school in Shropshire.'

'I feel sure that you have found your niche.'

'Do you?'

'Robin writes film reviews for a puerile magazine.'

'It's very popular.'

'None of my friends read it. They say that it's obscene.'

'With respect, it's aimed at a younger generation.'

'But a boy with his talents. There's nothing he couldn't do. Duncan Treflis – do you remember? – has offered him a job in the bank. I try to talk to him but he won't listen. Perhaps he will listen to you?' Her insensitivity astounds me.

'I rarely see him; he no longer trusts me. He called me a moral coward.'

'Yes, yes, of course,' she says quickly. 'That was all a long time ago; you were children.'

'It was last year.'

'He treats his family like strangers. He never visits Crierley and, when he does, I feel ashamed. I had to beg him to come here tonight; and he is wearing that shirt to spite me. Never love anyone, Leo; if you do, it will break your heart.' I glance significantly at Robin. She has the grace to look away.

If disappointment is a disease, it is contagious. As Lady Standish sighs, I feel a surge of emptiness inside. But, before I can ponder further, I am roused by a roar from the dining room. Jenny is shrieking. I know, without pause for

157

reflection, that you are involved. This is confirmed, as you dart into the room, with Jenny pursuing you. Her hair is unpinned, her cheeks raw, her features so distorted that she might have had a stroke. She is bent double, lunging at you, dragging Guy and her mother in her wake, as they attempt to restrain her.

'I don't know why she's reacting like this,' you announce to the assembled company. 'You'd think she'd thank me. I simply warned her to be careful in bed on account of my herpes. The number of times we've made love, it would be a miracle if he'd escaped.'

Jenny continues to scream, while a musty dowager booms to her daughter. 'What did she say she had?'

'Herpes, Mother,' the daughter drawls.

'What's that?'

'A venereal disease, which ruins your lips and plays hell with your sex life. There's no cure.' The ensuing silence is registered even by Jenny. I cannot be alone in wondering where such a homely, Home Counties girl completed her education.

Guy moves towards you. 'I'd like to kill you,' he says coldly.

'Don't worry, you already have.'

You turn to go. I follow, worried that I am suggesting not just complicity but a common infection. Robin breaks from the elderly colonel with whom he has been flirting and moves towards us, only to be intercepted by his mother's imperious 'remember you are family, Robin'; at which he wavers, shrugs and stays. We run the gauntlet of affronted aunts and reach the front door, where the butler hands us our coats. While I grab mine, you coolly turn your back and wait for him to help you into the sleeves. Then, with a bazaar-opening wave, you leave. We take the lift into the cold. You stay silent until we are halfway across Cadogan Square, where you look back and shout 'revenge is sweet'.

I wonder if Jenny is saying the same, albeit less publicly, as she strides across the Chilterns, exercising the dogs. What else is her affidavit but retaliation for a sixteen-year-long hurt? She claims, with all the authority of one who has bred thirty puppies, that you were incapable of bringing up a child; as indeed has been shown by your leaving Pagan to me. Her specific charges are that you harassed Guy – which I shall have no difficulty rebutting – and did irreparable damage to Robin, which exercises me more, especially since she cites his disappearance as proof. I long to find him and persuade him to testify . . . I long to find him, full stop. Should I place an advertisement in the *Criterion*: Would R.P.St-J.S. please contact L.P.Y., from whom he will learn something to his advantage? I doubt that he would recognise the initials, let alone reply.

Where is he? How has he vanished so completely from all our lives? Has he been spirited away by the Special Branch and fitted with a new identity? Or is he lost in the aftermath of an accident, searching for his name? I sift the evidence of our last encounter. He is walking down Wardour Street in the company of two Junoesque transsexuals, like a schoolboy in the care of a pair of raffish aunts. They are going to see a film. I insist on my greater need to see him. He consents with a reluctance that robs me of my past. His friends depart in a flurry of costume-kisses, and he leads me off to a nearby bar. It is low-lit, low-life and loathsome, and, to my dismay, he seems to feel at home.

There are no clues in our conversation . . . indeed, there is precious little conversation. My questions – then and now – lead nowhere, as we sit in a strangers' silence, his wandering eyes fixing on me only when I charge him with wasting his life.

'You really are your mother's son.' If nothing else, he still knows how to hurt me.

'And you're not, I suppose? "Hey Mummy, look at me, hanging out with my friends, the transvestites." '

'They're transsexuals.'

'What's the difference?'

'A hell of a lot, especially to them.'

'I mean to you, Robin . . . to us.'

'There is no "us", thanks to you.'

'To people like us.'

'They're people like me. You've no idea. I've found myself here. They're more like me than any of you ever were.'

'No. You're wrong. You may choose to read your life as a tabloid headline. "Shock! Horror! Peer's son in Soho vice

159

den." But it isn't a real shock or horror; it's simply a shame. Just as it was for Candida. Thank God, she broke out.'

'I can't take photographs.'

'You can do so much more. It may amuse you to picture generations of your ancestors turning in their graves . . . or rather on their tombs, but it's just the rebellion of someone who believes that decadence is having green nails. To quote Candida, however hard you try, you'll always be an upper-class man.'

'That's where you're quite wrong.' He stands. 'Goodbye, Leo. Be happy. We won't meet again.'

I dismiss his threat as the thud of a first act curtain. But the interval has lasted ten years. I put down Jenny's affidavit and turn to drafting my own. I wish that I had more on my side than right. I have to convince the Court that the herpes was a ploy and that you were as innocent a victim of Guy's libido as Jenny . . . more so, for Cadogan Square leads me as directly to Brewer Street as if they intersected; and I am fairly certain that it was after Guy's engagement that you plunged headlong into Soho life. And yet 'fairly' is not enough; I need to be sure. As of now, we have a pox-ridden prostitute who has left her child to a cross-dressing homosexual, pitched against a retired war-hero-turned-bursar and his angel-of-mercy wife. The Army, the Public Schools, the Ambulance Service, Parliament . . . I can fight them all; I will fight them all, as long as I can substantiate my facts.

I remember when the past was a book: a history book. *Life in Elizabethan England* . . . *The Struggle for the Constitution* . . . even *The Whig Interpretation of History* . . . were all based on solid facts. Now the genre has shifted. The past has been rewritten as a thriller: *The Mystery of the Unknown Father* . . . *The Mystery of the Disappearing Friend*. The text-books have been pulped and recycled as popular fiction. I have to restock my library; I have to take stock of your life.

The one person who may be able to help is your mother – no, your real mother . . . natural mother . . . biological mother; that's better (any other adjective reflects on Pagan's relationship to me). It must have been at about the time of Guy's engagement that you found her. Let me see; we leave Cambridge in 1975 and, a year later, they alter the law to allow adopted children access to their birth records. You amaze me by ignoring it. I thought that you would be the first in line, queuing all night outside the Registrar General's Office. Here is the end of your quest ... the answer to all your questions. At last, you can escape from the uncertainty that confounds you and claim not just your birth records but your birth-right.

Am I wrong to encourage you? Would it be safer to maintain the fantasy? In my more self-scourging moments, I accuse myself of morbid curiosity, and yet how can I remain indifferent when I feel sure that not knowing is ruining your life? Your theories are so absurdly romantic. How often have I heard you claim, with complete conviction, to be the product of a doomed romance between an impetuous younger son and his mother's maid or a chatelaine and her under-gardener? I fail to understand how you can make a plot that you would reject in the slushiest novel into the corner-stone of your life.

Of course, if you dislodge it, the entire edifice may crumble. You foresee the danger far more clearly than I. You agonise over application, sending for a form, only to destroy it, and then sending for another with the excuse that the first was lost in the post. You ask my advice and, when I urge you to fill it in without delay, accuse me of never allowing you to think for yourself. I resolve to say nothing more, whereupon you accuse me of indifference. Then, one morning, I find a bottle of champagne in the fridge. I ask if it is somebody's birthday. 'In a way,' you say, 'it's mine', and add that we will be celebrating later. Without a word to me, you have sent back the form to Merseyside. Last week, you received a reply stating that your birth records have been despatched to Westminster Social Services. You have an appointment to see a social worker this afternoon.

I take your hands, which are like ice. 'How are you feeling?'

'Scared. No, Californian.' You laugh. 'What was that phrase Imogen came back with? "Today is the first day of the rest of my life." '

When you return, your mood is electric. You are so full of loathing for the Social Worker that, at first, I fear that the information has been withheld.

'She reminded me of Muriel. She had the same margarine voice . . . you know, vowels that spread straight from the fridge. She began by explaining that she disapproved of the new law. She'd been an adoption officer in the fifties and remembered promising the mothers complete anonymity. She claimed that a young woman today – I felt as though I were on *Panorama* – could have no idea of the slur that illegitimacy used to carry. She insisted that I consider my mother's feelings. I said that I'd considered little else for twenty years. It's the most important relationship of my life; does she think I mean to screw it up like all the rest?'

'There may be some children who are less well prepared.'

'I'm not a child!'

'In the adopted sense.'

'She hid behind this huge file, smugly holding my past – no, my future – in her hands. I had to sit on my hands to stop myself lashing out. I kept reminding myself that I was required by law to see her. She was determined to drag it out . . . again like Muriel, who used to read my school report so slowly that she made me feel bad even when it was good. Bitches! She asked if I appreciated that my mother might have died; a surprising number of the women had. "I see," I said, "then the wages of sin really is death." And, for a moment, I thought that she might reject me. But my patience paid off, and she handed me these.' You hold up two slips of paper.

'What are they?' I ask.

'It's all she gave me. The bitch took great delight in telling me how little information she'd been sent. But it's enough. This gives me the details on my birth certificate, and this authorises me to apply to Peterborough Crown Court for the name of the adoption agency.'

'Peterborough?'

'That's where I was born. Look.'

'But this is for a Joan Davies.'

'*Voilà*. That's the name on my birth certificate. Tomorrow, I shall go to St Catherine's House for my own copy. Then I intend to frame it. You remember how your mother wanted to frame your degree certificate?'

'And you remember what I said?'

'But now I understand. It may only be a piece of paper, but it authenticates my life.'

Joan Davies . . . Joan . . . I try to see you as Joan, but it jars. Names come attached to so much baggage; who expects a Sid to compose a symphony or a Constance to conduct a bus? You rechristened me, but I find the reverse so much harder. Candida is whimsical and witty; Joan is sensible and severe. You are the quintessential Candida. I know that your parents picked the name for its purity – thereby reprieving you from a lifetime of Prudence – and yet, whether in reaction or defiance, you have made it your own. But Joan Davies . . . Joan . . . the exuberance of your personality is mocked by the monosyllable . . . Still, we can always pretend that they named you after the Pope.

'Joan Davies,' you say slowly. 'Mother's name: Linda. Father's a blank. My father a blank. That says it all.'

'They may have had something to hide.'

'Yes, if he were the Earl of Peterborough and she were one of his tenants.'

'Why not put "Father's name: Jasper" and have done with it? Candida, darling, it may just be that he was married or else that she may not have known.'

'A woman always knows the father of her child'. . . . I feel a pang for Pagan. . . . 'Besides, Joan Davies is far too nondescript to be genuine; it's the hotel register John Smith.'

I move a few steps away from the font. . . . 'Then how can you hope to find her?'

'There's an address.'

'From twenty-two years ago.'

'So? Not everyone's a nomad. Some people live in communities; they die in the houses where they were born. Did you know there are still people living in South London who have never been north of the river? What if her family was like that? And, if not, there may be neighbours. I'll knock on every door in the street . . . in the town, if need be. I'll hire a balloon and scatter leaflets. I'll plaster posters on billboards'. . . . The Candida is eclipsing the Joan again. . . . 'I'm sure someone will remember: a single woman with a child. Small-town people – small-minded people. I'll find a way.'

I wish that I could offer more than moral support, but I

am off again to St Bride's. We keep in regular contact and I chart your progress like a boy with victory flags. At times, I sense that you are close to despair, as you spend days in St Catherine's House, poring over the Marriage records, buckling under the weight of coupledom. But persistence pays when you discover that, in 1960, your mother married a bank-clerk called Saxon ... Sancton ... Sacristan ... I have an image of something archaic. A search through Births adds two daughters and a 1965 address in Huntingdon; which a trip to the District Council offices, and a trawl through the Electoral Registers, updates to 1971. Then the trail goes blank.

I forget how you proceed – perhaps I never knew – but I think that an estate agent comes into it, along with a neighbour who has kept in Christmas card contact since they moved to Stamford, where Sexton – of course – has been made assistant manager of Barclays Bank. Then, one evening, I am summoned from choir practice to receive an urgent phone call from my sister. I may not have a sister, but you, at last, have the address. The line crackles with excitement as you announce your plan to spring a surprise visit. You charge me with treachery when I side with the Social Worker's 'write first, meet later' approach.

You are as reluctant to brook any delay as your mother is to agree to a meeting; and yet, in time, her resistance wears thin. I am as nervous as you. On the appointed day, I neglect my work and watch the clock like the idlest schoolboy. Unable to bear the suspense, I stand in the staff phone-booth with a sweaty store of 10ps. I can tell at once, in spite of your chirpy, chin-up voice, that the encounter was a disaster. I am loath to add to the pain, but I have to know what happened. You provide a brief report in exchange for a promise never to mention it again. My suspicions are confirmed. Far from clasping you to her bosom, your mother never so much as took your hand. She resented the revived memories and refused to discuss either her past or present life. She did, however, tell you the one thing that you most needed – and dreaded – to hear. She is a sales assistant at Boots; in Peterborough, she worked as a telephonist, while your father packed meat.

'You mean in an abattoir?'

'No, there's not even any blood in it. He worked in a deep

freeze.' Your laughter chills me. 'She hasn't seen or heard from him in over twenty years. He did a runner as soon as he found she was pregnant. She was living with her father. . . .' Your voice falters. 'So there was never any question of her keeping me. But she claims to have made sure that I went to a good home. "How?" I asked. "By giving you to the Church of England Children's Society instead of the council," she said. She stipulated that they be church-goers. "Big deal!" I said. "Have you never heard of the Pharisees?" She took me to mean some series with Susan Hampshire on TV.'

'What? Oh, she must have been thinking of *The Pallisers*.'

'Who cares? It's all so trivial. . . . She hasn't told her husband or her new daughters anything about me. I feel like a cheap hotel room full of soiled sheets and stale air. She was terrified that I'd cause trouble; and I suddenly felt so powerful. Our positions were reversed; she'd given me up and now I could give her away. But why? I felt nothing for her. I wanted nothing from her. And the thing I cared about least was that I couldn't call her Mother. The word caught like a bone in my throat.'

My concern on the phone is magnified when I return at half-term and find you standing on a tatty, tinselly stage, gyrating in a g-string. You wear a curly blonde wig, fuchsia false nails and glossy red lipstick which smears on my cheeks. Soho, from being an eccentric address for someone who could not afford Chelsea and refused to compromise with Camden, has become a way of life. Snatched conversations with the girls, in the alleyways where they work and in the shops where you buy cigarettes, have solicited you more successfully than any of their men.

'I don't understand what's come over you.'

'Joan Davies.'

'She died, at five days old, when you became Candida Mulliner.'

'And I've been carrying her around ever since. She's not some role that I can discard at the cast party. She's me. There again, she's no one: the product of a telephone call to a frozen-food factory. I hope that you're all enjoying a good laugh.'

'I'm not laughing.'

'Why not? I deserve it. I thought I was special, that I'd find my parents and come into my kingdom. I built castles in the air when it should have been semi-detacheds . . . I warn you, if you give me one of your homilies about everyone being special, I'll scream.'

'I wasn't going to. . . . ' I bite my tongue.

'But I'm so bloody ordinary. That's the worst fate of all. I could live with poverty or tragedy or terminal illness, but ordinariness . . . I'd rather die.'

'I find it comforting.'

'I was so naive. I didn't imagine that God was just – I'm not that naive – but I did think that he was sporting. I couldn't believe that anyone would be given the intensity of my desire without the chance to fulfil it. I knew that I didn't have any particular talent or creativity, so I invested all my hopes in my story. I'd fulfil myself not by being myself – that's far too easy – but by becoming myself; and, for that, I had to be someone worth becoming. Now I'm paying for my presumption. Who am I? Joan Davies: a non-person; Candida Mulliner: a nonentity; so why not Sylvie Labelle, thrusting her pelvis into her customers' cocktails? At least I made her up myself.'

I may be obtuse, but I fail to see how your trip to Stamford leads quite so directly to the dressing room of The Pigalle. I feel that the equation of disillusion and self-abasement requires an extra 'x' factor that you have yet to reveal. But, before I can ask, you are summoned on stage by Dom, the Maltese 'stage-manager' . . . or so he is termed for tax purposes and court appearances. You throw off your wrap and stand in a crimson and black satin corset that puts me in mind less of the *Folies Bergère* than a Feydeau farce. I sit and pour myself a large glass of your whisky, while Patti and Velma, the speciality double act, slip through the curtain, their bitterness tempered by the knowledge that they have paraded their passion in front of an unsuspecting, all-male audience.

Patti shakes; Velma comforts her. Dom rushes in and pulls them apart. 'We have none of that here. This club is clean, clean clean,' he repeats, while they spit out a very different adjective. My presence is ignored; after two days, I am already part of the furniture . . . as scuffed and soiled as the rest. Even Dom regards me with indifference, calling me Professor with all the irony of one who has graduated *summa cum laude* from the University of Life.

He scurries out. The music starts. From the intermittent whoops, sporadic shouts and occasional words of encouragement, I know that you are performing and try to fit the action to the applause. But the flimsy cotton curtain falls like an iron screen across my imagination. . . . Now it falls again, across my memory, as, by some involuntary impulse, I prevent myself from delving deeper and leave you locked in an eternal bump and grind.

And yet, as I turn again to my affidavit, I know that I must trust to my instincts. There is nothing arbitrary about memory; I simply have to learn its language. I feel sure that it is trying to tell me something . . . are you trying to tell me something? If so, should I consult a fortune-teller or a medium? I intend to find your mother. I need to establish the connection between Stamford and Soho. If you can play private detective, so can I.

# 3

'Knock knock!'

'Who's there?'

'Franz Kafka.'

'Franz who?'

'No, that's all wrong; you should say Franz Kafka who?'

'I'm sorry . . . Franz Kafka who?'

But my mind blanks and my vision blurs. I look down at the floor and I find that I am naked. I am only saved from the jeers of the audience by the sound of a telephone. . . . Franz Kafka who? Who's Franz Kafka? I am torn from a nightmare fantasy to confront the reality: not the pounding on the door at three in the morning but the ringing of the telephone at six.

A measured voice asks if I would like to comment on the story in today's *Nation*. I flick the lamp switch; the filament flashes. I fling my head back on the pillow and try not to swear. What comment? What story? It is ten past six by the luminous hands of my Mickey Mouse clock . . . your gift seems prophetic as I am plunged into a Mickey Mouse world. While sleep makes a last attempt to reclaim me, my informant explains that the *Nation* has published a piece on my sexuality and suggests that she read it to me. I agree, even though the words run into each other like paint and my throbbing bladder forces my attention onto my groin. When I catch the name David Sunning, I realise that it is serious. What is the gay equivalent of Kiss and Tell? Suck and Spit?

'No comment,' I insist ... I sound like a politician. ... 'No comment.' I have always wanted to say it, even though I know that my silence leaves more space for them to fill. I drag myself out of bed and to the lavatory, where I barely register that I am peeing blood. I creep downstairs in fear that my early rising will license Pagan's. The telephone rings and I disconnect it. I throw on some clothes, but any thought of slipping out for the paper disappears when I see three shadowy figures huddled by the gate. I start to cry, vast sobs that heave my chest like push-ups. My entire body strains with grief, which transmutes into laughter. I feel an inexplicable sense of liberation ... until I think of Pagan, my mother, your mother and the BBC.

I take a shower. My limbs are so uncoordinated that I wonder if I may be in shock. I return to the bedroom dressed only in a hand-towel. I approach the window and fall to the floor at the thought of photographers with telescopic lenses perched in trees. As I crawl to the wardrobe for my underwear, Pagan enters for her Sunday morning cuddle and the chance to snuggle in the warmth at the bottom of my bed. She is at first confused and then delighted by the opportunity to play horses so early in the day. She bounces from the bed onto my back. 'Ooh, you're all wet.' She squirms and abandons the race in disgust.

The problem of fetching today's paper without featuring on tomorrow's front page is solved when Susan asks Consuela to buy one on her way home from mass. 'Is not a good paper,' she replies, which hardly squares with her relish for the royal scandals in Spanish magazines. At eleven thirty, I wonder whether, having read the paper, she has decided never to return. Then the bell rings; and it is clear that she has simply forgotten her key. Susan counsels caution and calls out before opening the door. There is no reply. My own request in rudimentary Spanish is greeted by stirrings in the letter-box and a reporter from the *Standard*, asking me first for a quote and then for a break.

I resist the disconcertingly powerful urge to grab an umbrella and poke it in his face. Susan kneels by the door and shouts back that no one will be saying anything, even if they wait from now until the January sales. She looks up, stunned by her vehemence. Pagan starts to cry. The fun of creeping through the house bent double has palled; she cannot understand why we will not open the door. Susan takes her upstairs for a special-treat chocolate-and-banana sandwich. I cut insulating tape into strips and stick it over the letter-box, until the threat feels as muted as a muzzled dog.

Consuela returns with the paper and the sinister news that she had to walk as far as Bayswater, because 'every shop I go to is sold'. It seems that the whole of London wants to witness my disgrace. But, to my relief, I see that the front page is an exclusive about the Prince of Wales and his mistress. Thank God for the Order of Precedence! Then I catch a caption underneath, *TV's Leo's gay lover speaks out. Turn to Pages Six, Seven and Eight.* Three pages! What on earth can they have to say that fills three pages? I fumble to find out. Meanwhile Consuela, who sees only the headlines, promises that 'after lunch I show you beautiful pictures of Princess Diana with the Queen of Spain'.

I reach the pertinent pages. The headline reads *Double Life of Chat Show Host*. I suppose that I should be grateful that it is not Secret Shame. There are two small photographs, one of me in black tie and one of David wearing a Queer As Fuck tee-shirt, or rather Queer As * * * *, since the word has been blacked out. Above them is an old snapshot, taken by you, of the two of us in Suffolk. I am in shirt-sleeves and he is in shorts. I look so happy that it hurts. I cannot remember feeling so happy; I must not remember feeling so happy. I can still hear you shouting 'closer, closer', as if you were pushing us into each other's arms and not just into the frame. 'Right now, look at the birdie and say sleaze.'

The article is surprisingly unsleazy. It is the fact, not the content, of it that is painful. He describes how we met on *Addendum* . . . although his mention of my helping him to a permanent contract has an unfortunate ring of 'for services rendered', when he was, unquestionably, our best researcher. He declares that we fell in love . . . I envy his certainty. It would be some comfort to know that I was able to experience – and to inspire – passion. For once, it is not my memory that I cannot trust, but my emotions . . .

170

or, rather, my recollected emotions, so perhaps the distinction is false. How much of what I felt came from me and how much from books? Was I responding to him or to Gabriel Oak and George Emerson? I fear that I have made literature not just a reference but a reality and my feelings as fictional as theirs.

David knows no such doubts. To him the problem is simply my timidity, for which read hypocrisy ... I read another line and find it spelt out. He calls my sexuality an open secret and claims that the verbal and physical mannerisms that comedians love to mock and critics to castigate are obvious defence mechanisms. How sad that he should have grown so glib. He complains that, for over a year, I would not let him live with me and that, when I finally relented, I put him in the basement and kept him apart from my friends. You would think that he were Mrs Rochester in her attic ... no, no more books! But then that may be appropriate since he felt – or at least Ms Sable makes him feel – 'less like a person than a fact of life that Leo refused to acknowledge'.

He states that he was compelled to speak by the three articles that I wrote in the *Criterion* detailing my response to your death and describing how we lived together and loved each other for seventeen years. That is no lie, believe me ... well, I know that you do; it is the words that are equivocal, not the feelings. Ours was a love that had neither rules nor models, a love that at once defined our parameters and gave us space, a love more select than the love of families, more reasoned than the love of lovers and more intense than the love of friends. And yet, to David, it was a fantasy. He cannot accept such unselfish love ... or rather, he considers it self-interest. He asserts that we simply served each other's purpose: that I needed you in order to hide – and to hide from – my sexuality and that you used me in order to ... I won't repeat what he says about you.

Might he be right? I am mad even to think of it. And yet, once planted, the thought grows. Was our relationship based, not on a false premise, but on a false perception? I followed your romances as intently as if I were one of the reporters clustered in the Christmas crispness outside the gate ... Susan tells me that they now number nine. I noted

171

the all-embracing excitement and then the extended despair. I saw you slip into promiscuity, despite your denial – 'I'm not promiscuous, just easily bored' – and trembled at the violence of your contempt for the men you bedded . . . and sofaed and carpeted and floored. It was almost as though you could not decide whom you despised more: the men for the predictability of their desires or yourself for pandering to them. 'I'm such a slut,' you said. 'How can anyone be such a slut? I'm all bad inside.'

I was determined to show that there was one man who wanted more from you than your body, one who responded to you as a person. With us, there would be no sexual subterfuge, no erotic bargaining. We would defy conventional society and deny conventional wisdom. Our intimacy would be all the closer for bypassing bed; our table talk would say more than any pillow talk. . . . And yet was I rationalising from your neuroses? Was I seduced not by your passion but by your pain? I was turning away from sex not on the grounds of my own experience, but of yours. I am beginning to feel like the man who built his house on stilts.

You made it clear, after all, that I was not enough for you. 'I want a lover,' you said, whether as a birthday present, Christmas wish or New Year's resolution. 'Although I know that it's a lost cause. Love must be blind, or why is no one in love with me?'

'Won't I do?'

'Oh darling, you know you will – you do.' And you rubbed my nose the way that Pagan rubs Trouble's. 'But it's the difference between being ravaged by a tiger and cuddled by a pussy cat. Although, in my case, it would have to be a sabre-toothed tiger. If the man for me ever existed, he's extinct.'

I put my fingers in my ears, but I cannot muffle my memory. I simply jolt it forward a year or so.

'Sex destroys things,' I am saying to David, with all the spurious authority of one who has picked up the pieces. 'Friendship binds them together.'

'Is that you talking or Ms Mulliner?'

'I can think for myself; I've a mind of my own.'

'I don't doubt. What worries me more is whether you have a cock.' It stirs, as if to make its presence felt; he feels

172

it. I blush and he grins. 'Sex can be so many things. Exciting . . . exotic . . . loving . . . funny . . . expansive . . . expensive.' He makes a different part of my body glow with each adjective. 'Let me prove it to you.' It is an invitation that I find hard to resist, and yet a lesson that I find impossible to learn. 'Relax a little. If only you could stop thinking.'

If only I could stop remembering . . . but each word that I read reverberates. I wish that you had made more of an effort to like him; I am sure that he felt as threatened by you as Lewis did by me. But then perhaps you felt as threatened by him as I did by Lewis; which makes us square. I don't think that he ever forgave you for the 'be quiet, little boy' gibe at Duncan's party. I was afraid that he would hand me an ultimatum on the way home, but he was scared of the reply. Now he has his revenge, or at any rate his recognition. Ms Sable devotes two paragraphs to his politics. Perhaps that was the pay-off? I hope that they did pay him. And it may be seeing his photograph, but I find it impossible to blame him. My resentment is reserved for Brian Derwent and the *Nation*. What possible interest can the story serve except the most prurient? The details are too old to pass as news. I am afraid that it must have some connection with Pagan. Conspiracy theories may be the last resort of the disenfranchised, but the coincidence is too neat.

Max rings from the National Film Theatre where he is attending an all-day Anton Walbrook tribute. He insists that I do nothing, unless the reporters intrude; in which case, I call the police.

'Say nothing, end of story . . . as, indeed, it will be.'

'What if they make something up?'

'Then we sue.'

He seems to be spoiling for a fight – or, as you would say, a fee – a prospect which fills me with foreboding. Our conversation is curtailed as he is called to *The Life and Death of Colonel Blimp* and I to lunch; after which Susan and I prepare to take Pagan to Stephanie's party. We warn her about the reporters.

'Why do they want to take photographs?' she asks.

'Because we're important,' Susan replies.

'Like the Queen?'

I allow Susan three minutes to warm up the engine and then follow. I yearn for a house with two gates. The front door slams like a starting pistol and the press pack leaps into action. Despite my qualms, I regret not requesting police protection. Pagan is bewildered and clasps my hand. I lead her through the crowd, ignoring all entreaties, gritting my teeth to the microphones and glazing my eyes to the cameras. As we jostle our way to the car, one importunate hack almost traps Pagan's fingers in the door. Susan steps on the accelerator, and he barely escapes with his life.

After a short stop for breath (me), a cuddle (Pagan) and a cigarette (Susan), we reach Stephanie's, where Pagan at first shows me off and then disowns me . . . when I see her next, she has a zebra mask painted on her face and a braid in her hair. Stephanie's mother, whose name I can never remember, and, after two years of child-connections, find it impossible to ask, presses me to join a grown-up gathering in the 'den'. To my surprise, I agree. Her husband, whose name – Stephen – I learn on introduction, sees me glance at the pile of newspapers. He picks up the *Nation*. 'I read this the way my daughters read *Bunty*.' The subtext and the support are clear.

'It's the only way that we can see how the other half live,' claims a sedentary man in a rugby shirt with POLO printed across his paunch. I bridle; does he mean the other half or the other ten per cent?

'And love?' I inquire.

'Oh no. I don't think the *Nation* knows much about love.'

I return home, fortified by their kindness and Stephen's Glenfiddich, to be greeted by a batch of messages that almost reconciles me to the answer-machine. Ismene's assurance that 'today's front page is tomorrow's fish and chip paper' is followed by Keith's insistence that such poisonous pieces explain the EEC ban on using them to wrap food. Imogen declares that she is cancelling her order for the paper; 'which is a real blow because, at my age, how else can I get my kicks? But it's one thing when it's naughty vicars, quite another when it's naughty friends' . . . pause for giggles . . . 'It's so awful. I never mean what I say – that is say what I mean – on machines.' The final and

174

most heartening call comes from Kaye Blake, the new Head of Music and Arts, who wonders whether I may have misinterpreted her remarks on revamping the show's image. 'Never mind, Auntie is shaken but not stirred.'

I can no longer put off ringing my mother. The whisky has blurred my responses, so it may be fanciful to identify an edge to her voice. We embark on the usual round of small talk: my father, my job, her health, her guests, Pagan. I despair of communication. I finally broach the subject of the paper.

'I never read newspapers on a Sunday. It's the Lord's day, not one for idling.'

'Still, someone may bring it to your notice.'

'Someone already has. And I'll tell you exactly what I told her: I never believe what they write about anyone else, so why should I believe it of you? What about all the decent people? The men who love God and their wives and children: when does anyone write about them?'

'Every week in your local paper. I can still see the headline: *Well-loved caretaker retires.*'

'I don't wish to continue with this.'

'But we must. It's not the way that I'd have chosen, God knows –'

'God knows everything, Leonard; He doesn't need you to remind Him.'

'I'm sorry, Mother. It's just that I want to explain.'

'I said "no". I've always prided myself on my fairness. Do you remember when they asked me to judge the Choral Society competition after Mr Elves had his heart-attack on the platform?'

'I do.'

'I treated you no different from all the rest. As I watched you sing, I put a box over your head.'

'I know . . . universally acknowledged as the best voice in the society and you didn't place me.'

'I'm putting a box over your head again now.'

I fail to follow her logic, just as I fail to discuss David. Grandchildren apart, I think that she would have liked me to grow up a castrato. She is only sixty-three . . . too young to be set in her ways, let alone in her ways of thinking; but then she was set in those at thirty. I concede defeat and take refuge in Christmas. She tells me that there are presents in the post for Susan, whom she has never met, Pagan and me. She thanks me for my cheque, chides my extravagance, and insists that she already has more than she needs.

Pagan's present, a crystal kaleidoscope, is a great success; mine, an argyle sweater, is not . . . it is bad enough having red hair without picking it up in the pattern. And why are the clothes that she buys me always two sizes too big? Do I still need room for growth? Nevertheless, it is Pagan's pleasure which is paramount. She decides that she likes Christmas even more than birthdays because, at Christmas, everyone is given presents so everyone feels happy, not just her. I fear that she has reached an age where magic gives way to materialism. She draws up two lists of presents, one for Father Christmas and one for me . . . 'just in case he isn't real'. And, when I hold up her bulging pillow-case as proof of his existence, she looks at the labels, thinks for a moment and declares that 'I half-believe in Father Christmas because he gave me half my presents'.

One present which comes very clearly labelled is a Barbie doll, complete with wedding outfit, from your parents. The only cloud of the day looms when I insist that she ring and thank them. I hear your mother assuring her that she will have a proper 'family' Christmas next weekend and Pagan asking how it can be proper if it is late. Afterwards, she tells me that she wants to give the doll to the poor children.

'I don't think that's a very good idea.'

'You always say that if I don't play with my toys, you're going to give them away. And those are toys I like.'

'You may like this when you're older.'

'I won't. I'll never like it. It's soppy. Yuck!' She illustrates her distaste by holding Barbie by the feet and hitting her head against the wall.

Susan has gone to Hampshire to spend the holiday with her parents and Geoffrey, so Pagan and I are left with Consuela, who divides her time between telephoning her family in Santiago, visiting her friends in Shepherd's Bush, and declaring that I am 'the most gracious patron'; because of me, her children can stay at school.

'Doesn't Consuela want to see Licia and Roberto?' Pagan asks.

'Of course she does. But, when their daddy died, she had to come here to find work.'

'You should give her some pounds.'

'I did.'

'Lots and lots.'

'I did. But she'd rather save everything for them. She'll see them in the summer.'

'Does Licia miss her mummy?'

'She has lots of other people who love her . . . her granny and her brother and her uncles.'

'I miss my mummy.'

'I know.'

'Do you think that there's Christmas in Heaven . . . ? Why are you crying?'

'I'm not . . . it's just my contact lens.'

'Yuck! Do you remember when we put sparkle over Mummy's screen and holly on her bed and middle-toes over the top, so everyone had to kiss her?'

'Yes. I do.' The ghost of Christmas Past returns to haunt me. It leads me from 'Santa's Soho Grotto' to the foot of Pagan's cot. I wipe my eyes. This second year without you is so much harder. Twelve months ago, we were feeling our way around your absence; I was being brave for Pagan's sake and she was being grown-up for mine. The evidence of you was everywhere . . . even on the cards which I retrieved from Consuela's safe-keeping. They consoled me far more than all the letters of condolence; they seemed to confirm your presence . . . not to put back the clock but to stand outside time. Now, you are addressed only in error. Last year's ralliers-round have become this year's mustn't-intruders. . . . Would Christmas in Heaven be a permanent season or a contradiction in terms?

We spend the evening with Edward and Melissa, who invite us for mulled wine and mince pies.

'It's only family,' Melissa insists to overcome my reluctance, 'so it's quite informal.'

'It's only family,' Edward echoes, as he takes our coats, 'so thank God you've come.'

Resentments smoulder, as the boys cast aching glances at the television and Melissa murderous ones at Edward.

177

She breaks her own no-presents rule with a pre-publication copy of *The Madwoman of Muswell Hill* . . . 'because you need cheering up'.

'Has she told you about her next?' Edward asks. 'A scorching saga of necrophilia, entitled *Under the Sod*.'

'You must be confusing it with the story of our marriage.'

'If you two mean to fight, I'm going to bed,' Rory warns them.

'This isn't fighting,' his father counters; 'it's weighing in.'

The evening simmers on. I feel as though we have arrived not so much in the second act of a play as in the third part of a trilogy; the setting may be English drawing room, but the emotions are Greek. I wait for the climax. It comes sooner than I expect, when Dougall, who is handing round the mulled wine, whispers that I should watch his grandmother since he has slipped a tab of Ecstasy into her mug. I am appalled and fail to see why he has confided in me. I plot an accident . . . but it is too late. After half an hour in which I studiously avoid Dougall's gaze, Mrs Frobisher bursts into a fit of giggles. Edward, who views her less as a person than as a premonition, rants that she has ruined his joke; Melissa accuses him of intolerance; Dougall winks at me. His grandmother is unconcerned, laughing wildly, and running her fingers through her hair.

'Switch the lights down a little, will you, dear?' she asks Sweeney.

Melissa jibs at criticism: 'Mummy, anything less and we'll be plunged into darkness.'

'Everything's so bright; it's hurting my eyes.'

'Perhaps she's seeing God?' Dougall suggests, as his grandmother scratches her head.

'Do you think she's had some sort of stroke?' Melissa asks Edward.

'More likely pissed.'

'On two mugs of mulled wine?'

'Remember your cousin Cynthia's wedding.'

'Come here, dear,' Mrs Frobisher calls to Pagan, who recoils. 'Will you run your fingers through my hair? It gives the most delicious tingle.' Pagan looks to me for rescue; I

178

mouth 'go on' and mime scratching. She reluctantly responds.

'I can feel it all the way down my spine. Harder, dear, harder.' Dougall sways with suppressed laughter.

'Do you think we should ring the doctor?' Melissa asks Edward.

'It's Christmas Day, for Christ's sake! Would you want to be called out to some drunken old trout?'

I agree with Edward and glare at Dougall. 'I'm sure sleep's the answer.'

'Harder, dear, harder.' Pagan takes her at her word, as Mrs Frobisher squeals with delight. 'This is ecstasy.' Dougall bangs his face with a cushion.

'I think that's enough now,' I say, as Pagan scratches so hard that Mrs Frobisher's wig slides over her forehead.

Pagan and Melissa both scream. Dougall runs from the room, clasping a darkening patch on his groin, while his brothers look blank. Mrs Frobisher, seemingly oblivious to her exposed scalp, scratches for herself. 'Sheer Heaven! I'm all a-tingle.'

I pick up Pagan for a reassuring hug.

'Her hair came off,' she sobs.

'It's just a wig. Like in the pantomime.'

'She's got no hair – like a man. Why?'

'I'll explain later.'

'Only men have no hair, not ladies. . . .' As Melissa and Edward argue over the relative faults of their relations, we gather our gifts and leave.

Susan returns on New Year's Eve, as Geoffrey has to rejoin his submarine or 'go back to the zoo' as he puts it, which, given the lack of showers and ventilation, seems to be no idle phrase. I am invited to spend the evening with the Savages and find myself alone among seven couples. Tristan whispers that there were originally meant to be six, until Deborah, who is going through a 'spiritual' phase, all soya beans and birth signs, realised that that would make thirteen at table. Catastrophe looms when the Chubbs' au-pair runs off with Priscilla's nephew and they ring to cancel. Deborah at once declares that, on account of her bruised coccyx, she intends to stand.

She hovers over the meal, casting a shadow which I attempt to dispel with a succession of stories. I fear that I am turning into the Court Jester of David's accusation. 'Relax,' I tell myself, 'you're among friends.' And yet, in a world of seven couples and me, I never feel justified by friendship alone. I cannot shrug off the sense of being tolerated, 'the pet poof', in David's phrase . . . no, that is going too far. Nevertheless, I am convinced that they like me not on account of what I am, but in spite of it, and find my sexuality acceptable only because it remains academic (where David might describe a holiday in Ibiza or a night at a disco, I discuss a poem by Rimbaud or an essay by Freud); furthermore, in the unlikely event of its becoming practical, I can always be relied on to excise any emotion and fashion an amusing anecdote. . . . The thing that we love best about you, Leo, is the way you can laugh at yourself.

As dinner drags on, I feel increasingly lonely. I may refrain from ramming my sexuality down their throats (cue laughter), but no one shows the same consideration for me. After a stream of in-jokes about in-laws, Penny launches her familiar attack on the size of Fergus's penis and Jessica tipsily asks to judge for herself; at which he unzips. Matty seeks advice on maternity bras and breast pumps, adding that 'this must be very boring for you, Leo'. 'Not at all,' I reply, as my left leg goes to sleep. Edward and Tristan debate whether watching Matty give birth will turn Tim off sex, while Joan and Melissa lambast the insensitivity of men. By the time that we reach the nanny course, I am ready to scream.

Suddenly, it is midnight and harmony is restored . . . apart from a raucous rendition of *Auld Lang Syne*, during which Edward kisses Lucinda so tenderly that I foresee the plot of Melissa's next book.

The new year begins in earnest for me on the fourth of January, when Max returns to his office and faxes me a copy of Lewis's second affidavit. My assertion of heterosexuality, which was lamed by the *Nation* article, is now completely crippled. I even used our discovery in bed at St Bride's to illustrate our intimacy. How was I to know that you had written to Lewis in prison with the full story? You were always such a reluctant correspondent. *Pace* my mother and God, I am sure that you considered mankind's greatest invention to be the telephone. Why did you have to fall for the one man who was unable to receive calls?

Why did he have to keep your letters? It is so unlike you, so unlike him, so unjust.

I pick up your letter of November 3rd 1982, which is attached to his affidavit . . . 'I only wish I could spring you from the Scrubs as easily as I sprung Leo from his prep school'. . . . It is not an occasion that I choose to remember. I know that I should never have invited you to St Bride's; but I thought that, if you saw my production of *Curlew River*, you would at least acknowledge the creative side of my work. I may not be singing Don Ottavio at the ENO, but neither am I merely teaching scales and playing hymns. And yet you remain unconvinced. You are angry that I have failed to justify your faith in me. You accuse me of selling myself short.

'You might as well change your name back to Lenny.'

'It's too late; it's on their books.'

'When we first met, all you wanted to do was sing. You had your life mapped out. The only question was whether it would be in opera or oratorio, Covent Garden or St Paul's.'

'People change.'

'No, things happen to divert them.'

'Well then, let me introduce you to the diversions: you . . . Robin . . . Duncan Treflis.'

'Duncan Treflis?'

'I really loved my time at John's . . . the services and the records and the feasts and the tours. I don't think I've ever told you how, after the Tallis programme at the Sainte Chapelle, I met a man who introduced himself as belonging to one of the oldest Protestant families in France. He offered to take me round the private apartments in Versailles, to which he had some historic right of access. As we went, I addressed him formally as Monsieur le Comte. He stopped and said quietly "You do not call me Monsieur le Comte; that is what my butler calls me. You call me simply Comte; you are my equal." '

'And then he buggered you in the boudoir?'

'For Christ's sake, Candida!'

'Why else are you telling me?'

'Because I felt so elated. This was the aristocracy of art . . . the democracy of talent. *Liberté, égalité, fraternité* . . . even in the heart of Versailles. I'd entertained him; now he

181

wanted to do as much for me. But it was an exception. I discovered the rule back in London, when Duncan Treflis invited me to his box at Covent Garden.'

'Not the private apartments at Hampton Court?'

'They might as well have been. He introduced me to his friend Leslie Meacham. "Ah, the Methodist," he lisped, as if it were a title, like *The Huguenots*, and rubbed my hand. Not that he has any love of music. His interest is focused on the foyers . . . the louche young men lounging in the Crush Bar or fingering their genitals in the gents. He wanders the corridors as if he were kerb-crawling. Robin says that's why they have such long intervals. Then they can consummate during the second act.'

'Typical Robin!'

'I was there. I saw. . . . It was *La Traviata*, appropriately enough. After pushing Meacham's hand off my thigh for the umpteenth time during *Un di felice*, I finally lost patience and yanked back his fingers. He gave such a yelp that even the singers looked up. In the interval, he left us in the bar and returned with a barely articulate youth, with powdered cheeks and breath that smelt like syrup of figs, who, when the conversation turned to the modern art exhibition at the Hayward, announced that he didn't like modern paintings; "I prefer originals." And those two evil men, who'd mocked me for confusing Bauhaus and Balthus, laughed as if he were Oscar Wilde. Then, during the second act, Meacham fellated him at the back of the box.'

'I don't believe it.'

'While Violetta was giving up the life of a tart, Meacham's new friend was pursuing it. He and Treflis had swapped seats. And Robin didn't bat an eyelid; he says that it happens all the time . . . and, on ballet nights, it's worse.'

'So forget the boxes, play to the gallery.'

'Then I'd be playing to their ghosts. Treflis claimed that, until recently, the amphitheatre was a brothel for Guardsmen. There was a rail at the back and you placed yourself in front or behind, depending on whether you wanted to service them or wanted them to service you.'

'So that's why they wear those cloaks. . . .'

'I expect you think I'm being prissy. Robin reproached me for putting on airs. But I could never be part of it, either on stage or off. Now I know the double meaning of "musical", and it repels me.'

'So what about plan b, and a place on the Deputies List for St Paul's?'

'How can I put my heart – my soul – into sacred music when I don't believe in God? Is my whole life to be a pretence? I could audition for the Gothic Voices or the BBC Singers, but what would be the point? I'm far happier teaching the boys the joy . . . the power . . . the discipline of singing; although I would never encourage any of them to make it his life.'

'I won't let you settle for such mediocrity. You forget that I grew up in a school like this . . . my father has been a bursar for nearly twenty years. I saw the disappointment that grew like moss on the masters' faces: men who exude failure like the stale smell of boiled cabbage. I picture you, twenty years from now, in some musty common room, your only intellectual challenge the *Criterion* crossword, your only intimacy supervising the fifth-form showers. I see you shrivel into a collection of mannerisms, desperately trying to keep the boys amused.'

I hear you across almost twenty years, and I look at myself. What am I but a collection of mannerisms desperately trying to keep the viewers amused? Only now I exude the clotted-cream smell of success. Pagan used to call the television the turn-on; I prefer a different preposition. Switch me on, switch me off, play me back, wind me forward; I am the Petroushka of the remote control. Or should that be the Pinocchio? I have always read the lying puppet with the nose that grows as a metaphor for masturbation. In which case, it would be doubly appropriate. . . . At least, at St Bride's, I was someone whom I could respect.

'It's time to say goodbye to *Goodbye Mr Chips*.'

'I'm happy here. I enjoy the routines and the rituals . . . knowing whose chair not to sit on, which newspaper not to open, that, every Tuesday, it's roly-poly pudding and, every second Saturday, we show a film.'

'It's called becoming institutionalised. You'll be booking into hospital for unnecessary operations next.'

'Whereas your life is so thrilling, thrusting your tits in the faces of tired businessmen?'

'If I didn't, then they'd be thrusting their cocks some-where else.'

'No, I won't buy that. You said that they were all middle-aged tax inspectors and businessmen from Birmingham, celebrating their first night without their wives in fifteen years . . . hardly prime sex-fiend material.'

'You've no idea. You talk of Duncan Treflis or Leslie Meacham and their squalid liaisons, but that's nothing compared to the foulness of so-called respectable men, with their need to dominate and degrade and abuse.'

'A place like The Pigalle is bound to distort your perspective.'

'Which came first: the place or the perspective? I've seen what those men are like, and that's why I have to be there, at the hub of it, in control of it, thrusting not just my tits but my fanny in their faces . . . and more, oh yes, much more. "Is there anyone who'd care for a private encoun-ter?" But it makes me strong. Once I've experienced every humiliation, nothing will ever be able to hurt me again.'

'I know that Guy hurt you –'

'You can't think that it's because of Guy?'

'But there are other men.'

'Yes, there's you.'

'Not just gay men; that's too easy for both of us.'

'You're the only man I can trust – the one person I can talk to. That's why I can't bear you to be so far away.'

'I'll be back in London in July . . . well, August. Geoffrey Lindley has invited me to spend the first two weeks of the holiday on a walking tour of northern Greece.'

'A walking tour?'

'He teaches Latin, so he should know his way around.'

'You said Greece.'

'He'd teach Greek too in a smarter school.'

'It's perverse.'

Looking back, I realise that anyone who could take revenge on one lover by inserting a notice of his engage-ment to his secretary in *The Times* and an announcement of his death in the *Telegraph* on the same day, and punish another by scribbling 'Small Penis' under Distinguishing Marks in his passport, would have no difficulty in extricat-ing me from both my teaching and holiday commitments. But, at the time, the hypothetical herpes had been my only

184

experience of your schemes. So, when the Headmaster and his wife invited me to dinner after the final performance of *Curlew River*, it was in all innocence that I asked if I might bring you.

Mrs Headmaster, which as you soon find is her favoured mode of address ('it saves confusion'), serves her speciality, Creamed Finnan Haddie.

'I always enjoy your haddie,' simpers Cynthia Singleton, who, for convenience, I call Mrs Maths. Mrs Headmaster glowers, as if this says less about her skill than her repertoire.

'Are you also a singer?' Mrs Maths asks to divert attention.

'I'm a stripper,' you say, casting off your cover as though it were your clothes. Mr Maths splutters a mouthful of peas across the table. The younger guests, Mr and Mrs Nature Study, and the man of the world, Mr Gym, suspect the *double entendre* of a situation comedy. Are you a paint-stripper, or even an asset-stripper? I find the situation increasingly uncomic, as you turn to Geoffrey Lindley. 'You know, an ecdysiast . . . someone who sheds her skin.'

'I most certainly do not know,' he protests.

'I'm sorry. I understood that you were a classicist.'

'Candida, please.' I am the voice of sweet reason and the undertone of blind fury. 'People who don't know you may not appreciate your sense of humour; it's an acquired taste.'

'It's easy to acquire. £20 an hour basic. £10 more for fetishists.'

'I'm never quite sure what a fetishist is,' Mrs Maths cuts in on cue.

'In my experience,' you say slowly, 'it's someone who's more aroused by my underwear than by me.'

I rush to fill the silence. 'What Candida hasn't explained is that she wants to be an actress. After Cambridge – we were up at Cambridge together – she needed an Equity card; and stripping – that's to say, exotic dancing – was the only way.' The bombshell has dropped but the building is still standing. These are words to hide behind . . . Cambridge, actress, equity.

185

'It's so hard for young people today with all the unemployment,' says Mrs Nature Study, who prides herself on being a liberal.

'Nonsense, Julia!' Her husband has his eye on a House. 'It's the fault of the closed shop.'

Mr Gym boldly asks for the name of the club . . . gym masters are never given Houses. Mrs Headmaster decides that it is time for dessert and replaces the fish plates with a treacle tart. 'I always enjoy your treacle tarts,' says Mrs Maths. 'How do you make them so sticky?' Mr Gym looks at you and guffaws.

Mr Maths comes to the rescue. 'I gather that you and Young are preparing for a marathon in July,' he says to Lindley.

'Not in the strict sense. I doubt that, like Philippides, we will be running for twenty-two miles.' His chuckle provokes a ripple of encouragement. 'Or, indeed that, like the heroes of today, we will compete for twenty-six.' He laughs alone. 'But I have persuaded our friend to join me on a peregrination through Macedonia. "Make way, you Roman writers; make way, you Greeks," as the poet put it.'

'Which poet was that?' Mrs Maths asks. Lindley ignores her.

'Do you know Greece, Miss Mulliner?' The Headmaster gives you a final chance.

'Oh yes,' you reply with a treacly smile, 'but I'm afraid I was disappointed.'

'With the monuments?'

'With the men. I'd been so excited by the vase-paintings; what I hadn't realised was that the men were wearing false phalluses. I expected every Greek to come similarly endowed.'

The Headmaster draws himself to his full height and the meal to a close. 'Yes, well, it's eleven o'clock and a school day tomorrow. Young, don't forget that you're seeing me in my study before chapel.'

'Of course, Headmaster.' I maintain the fiction. I lead you back to the guest room.

'Are you trying to destroy everything I've built up here?'

'Hole in one!'

'You're more likely to destroy our friendship.'

'Leo, I have to save you from these people.'

186

'They're decent, well-meaning people. Not the most scintillating company, I admit, but –'

'Do you want to grow into another Lindley, filling out shapeless clothes, laughing at your own feeble jokes. . . . "They have me, as Diogenes might have put it, over a barrel"? Oh tee-hee, tee-terribly-hee. How can you bear to sit at the same table, let alone walk across Greece, with that?'

'He's a highly erudite man.'

'What about sex?'

'Whose? His? Mine?'

'Yes, his/yours. Surely you can see through the guff about the purity of unbroken voices? You may channel all your passion into music, but one day the dam will burst. You'll be unable to stop yourself touching one of the boys. Maybe you'll pat him on the head or brush his leg accidentally. The next day it will happen again; only, this time, it won't be an accident. And, before you know, you'll be back at Covent Garden. Hello, Mr Meacham sir, welcome to St Bride's.'

'That's a foul thing to say.'

'Have I ever lied to you?'

'How do I know? I take people on trust.'

'Trust me,' you say, as you switch on the light of the sombre guest room with the old school photographs on the walls and the Headmaster's monograph on Palmerston by the bed. 'Trust me,' you repeat, as you kiss me on the nose and show me the door. Two hours later, I awake to find you standing over me in a man's short shirt, complaining that the constant patter of mice is destroying your sleep.

There may be no mice, but there is a trap, which you cunningly conceal, as you wheedle your way first into my armchair and then into my bed. 'You won't know I'm here,' you say, as you push me over the edge.

I elicit your promise to leave with the alarm which, unaccountably, fails to ring, so that, when Matron brings me my tea at seven, she finds us curled together like question marks. My attempt to establish my heterosexual credentials has misfired. It is not just that I have broken school rules but I have hurt Matron's pride; the tea being a sign of her special favour, which she accuses me of throwing back in her face. As you stifle a giggle, she throws

187

the cup in yours. In spite of her skill on sports day, she aims wide and hits the clock, setting off the alarm. My confusion grows, as she runs, sobbing, from the room and you insist that she is in love with me. I am unable to focus; there is a ringing in my head . . . but it is the alarm which has jammed. As I try to silence it, two drowsy boys appear at the door and ask if there is a fire. You stand and stretch; your shirt rides over your navel. Their eyes pop.

My meeting with the Headmaster is brought forward to before breakfast. The word of warning becomes a note of dismissal. I have disappointed him, insulted Matron, scandalised the boys and degraded my calling. When I return to my room, I find that you have already packed my bags.

'You'll thank me one day.'

'Will I?' Have I? I wonder how my life would have differed if I had dared to return to Gabbitas Thring. In the event, I join you in Brewer Street and tell my mother that I am taking private pupils. It is clear that I cannot advertise locally, so you spread the word among the girls in the clubs. I am amazed, first by the response and then by the voices. They may be untrained, but there is a passion, a power and, yes, a purity, utterly belied by the sallow complexions and tawdry clothes. I am fired with enthusiasm and feel that, given time and training, a couple might take it further. You warn me not to invest my dreams in theirs: I am just the latest diversion, a temporary release from the hazards of sore feet and tacky bar-stools. At first, I challenge your cynicism, but, after several weeks of late arrivals, missed lessons and drug-induced croaks and giggles, I am forced to agree.

My patience is petering out, when two girls from the Pink Lady suggest that if I use the piano in the club, they would be less likely to miss their lessons. I am sceptical of the idea and even more so of the setting. The word 'club' is hardly appropriate to the Meard Street clip-joint with its barred and wired, grimy windows, worn lino and rubbish-strewn stairs. The dark brown walls are too damp, the single naked light bulb too dark, the red plastic banquettes too hard, and the smoke-filled air too thick for singing, while the battered upright with its missing pedal and three broken keys looks to have been caught in the thick of a particularly violent fight.

'I can't play this. There are keys missing.'

'We can leave out those,' says Teresa.

'What if we swapped them with ones at the bottom?' says Janine.

'Come on, love,' says Teresa, 'it'll give us something to do while we're waiting.' And, as I have so little to do myself, I agree. The lessons – such as they are – take place in an atmosphere of ribaldry, jealousy and petty bickering, where even the sweetest love song is interrupted at the first whiff of a punter. But the girls seem happy. Even sour-faced Sonia approves of me and requests various Vera Lynn favourites, which she rasps with verve. 'I never had much of a voice,' she cackles. 'I did my bit for the troops in other ways.'

I am frightened of Sonia with her fat, jewel-heavy fingers, fronds of scarlet hair and eyebrows that have been plucked raw. She tells me, in a dubious compliment, that I add tone to the establishment. And yet, when her son, a real Walworth Road villain, pays a proprietorial visit, he is 'not pleased, not pleased at all' to see me and pins me to the piano lid. Louise runs for Sonia, who rescues me. 'He's just a poof,' she says, at which he slaps me lightly on the cheek and flashes a pungent grin. Sonia's own years on the game may convince the girls of her good faith, but I fear that they are deceived. As her son puts his hand up Teresa's skirt and visibly twiddles, she shoos him away. 'I won't let none of my boys go near this riff-raff,' she confides to me later. 'If they want some skirt, I send them to Shepherd Market. At least there's a bit of class.'

Sonia sometimes pays me to play in the afternoons when the girls are enticing their punters, who seem to be reassured by the presence of another man. I am torn between amazement at their naivety and pity for their plight, as they part with large sums of cash for imaginary rendez-vous outside local hotels.

Question: when is a prostitute not a prostitute?

Answer: when she has sex.

Very few of the men return and those who do have little redress. The most insistently irate are dispatched into the store room where Brenda, twenty-two stone and mentally

189

retarded, waits to engulf them. She has the strength of four men – as was shown when the police came to arrest her. An encounter with her is not one that anyone is likely to forget.

'That club provides the most moral service,' you say. 'Those men will go back to Birmingham' – for some reason, it is always Birmingham – 'and remain faithful for the rest of their lives.'

'It seems unfair. All they want is a little warmth.'

'Fairness is not an issue. Those men are scum . . . scum.' Your vehemence takes me by surprise, and I wonder if, like Patti and Velma, you might turn to one of the girls. But the experiments – at least those which you acknowledge – fail to fulfil you, and you remain dedicated to men.

The lure of low-life fades in the endless afternoons of waiting for punters who never appear . . . prostitutes, like prisoners, would make the ideal audience for Beckett. The only excitements are the irregular visits of the hoisters, who promise that they can shoplift from anywhere and yet always produce Marks and Spencer, and the five o'clock-work arrival of the drug dealers, with necessities, like heroin and barbiturates, and luxuries, like cannabis and cocaine. The cruel paradox of being on the game to pay for drugs and yet needing drugs to survive on the game sharpens when I discover that the dealers work for Sonia's brother. The world revolves in vicious circles . . . a revelation that leaves you unperturbed.

'That's life: dog eat dog.'

'More like dog eat bitch and puppy.'

'Some bitches bite back.' We are sitting in the Amalfi Café. 'Take a look at the women in here. Three work the strip clubs and four are Wardour Street researchers. I'll bet you anything you like you can't tell which is which.'

'I don't want to take your money.'

'Anything you like.'

I look around the room and the seven women are indistinguishable. There are no Louises or Teresas, with badly bleached hair and overemphatic lipstick, whose skimping on food and compensatory crisps and chocolate are written all over their spots. Nor are there any transsexuals, whom you insist can be most reliably identified by their feet.

'You know that I never bet.'

'Don't worry, I'm not trying to suggest that all women are prostitutes, any more than that all property is theft, just that it's not going to kill me. The girls at The Pink Lady will be dead by the time they're thirty; but not these ones. In their business browns and beiges, they might be any young executives. They're in control.'

The distance between The Pink Lady and The Pigalle may be the difference between the boardroom and the typing pool, but the product is the same. And, while the ideal of all the girls remains to take the money and avoid the sex, there are times when it is not that simple. I never know how many men you meet at the club or how many you meet up with later, although I fear the worst. You state that it is on my account that you never bring them back to the flat. I am surprised – and touched – until you add that it has less to do with sparing my finer feelings than with protecting them from the law; if there were ever any trouble, the police could arrest me as your pimp.

I shudder as I think of how Colwyn Bay would read it . . . and I try to blot out the memory of your picking up the Amalfi bill. Lewis has already given it the worst possible construction. His charge that I was living off you is doubly unjust when the bulk of the money from my lessons went on rent. And yet who can corroborate my story? If the Soho class of 76 held a reunion, who would be there? How many have survived the pimps and the pills, the injections and infections, and AIDS? Only Sonia . . . I imagine her living in bigoted respectability in Basildon, nostalgic for the days when villains had standards and old ladies slept in peace. I wonder if she ever associates the youth who played her piano with the man who opened her local superstore. I wonder if she ever spares a thought, or a tear, for any of those spiky, speedy girls.

Lewis claims that whoring destroyed your capacity to love. He writes that he has never known an ex-prostitute who was able to establish a lasting relationship . . . he damns himself with his own pen. I lack the benefit of his experience, but, if he is correct, then you are the exception that proves the rule. Your sexuality was confused long before Soho. . . . Robin told me how, at school, you went through the Upper Sixth as methodically as the Form

191

Master for his end-of-term reports. Whether that was in revenge on your father for being a mere bursar – and, indeed, The Pigalle was revenge on your natural father for being a meat-packer – I do not know. What I do know is that you hurt no one so much as yourself.

Nevertheless, your capacity for love far exceeded your capacity for passion. Your distrust of sexuality made you all the more appreciative of friendship, even when you courted cynicism.

'We have friends because we cannot bear to be alone.'

'No, we cannot bear to be alone because we have friends.'

Now I would add that we cannot bear to be alone because we have memories. And yet it is the very intimacy of my memories that isolates me. Sitting here, I feel a you-shaped emptiness, while the sound of my voice echoes through the void.

# 4

I am happy to do my bit for the Brighton hotel industry. The conference season may be over and the tourist season not yet begun, but the courts are as busy as ever. Pagan, Susan and I have taken up residence in the Grand, while Max and Rebecca have booked into the Metropole ... although her junior has, at least, gone home to Worthing. They are holding an expedited hearing to consider your parents' new evidence. Whatever else, it is open season on me.

The driver, who takes me to court, tells me how much he enjoyed last Tuesday's show, which put the most married couple and the most widowed woman in Britain together with a nonagenarian nun and the Registrar of Gretna Green. I am perplexed by his claim that 'at least you and I don't have to worry about any of that', until I see the *Nation* like a stain on the seat beside him.

'My friend always said you were one of us,' he adds. I force a smile and hanker for the bigoted cabbies of old. This new version comes with two furry dice bouncing lewdly from his mirror and a penchant for Broadway musicals. 'You don't mind . . .' he says, turning up the volume on the cassette. It is less a question than an assumption. I nod noncommittally and stare at the sheen of talcum on his neck.

'Is it cottaging?'

'I beg your pardon?'

'Your case. We have loads from London. My friend says it must be the sea air.'

'It most certainly is not!'

'He wasn't under-age?' His prurience is echoed by a barrage of hoots. He turns his attention back to the road.

'Once and for all, I am not on trial. I'm appearing as a character witness for a friend, who's embroiled in a custody case. I'll thank you to keep your observations to yourself.'

His eyes narrow and he drives on in silence, switching up the volume of the cassette and leaving the lyric, as so often, to speak for him.

> I set you free.
> There's not much longer to complain;
> I'll soon relieve you from your pain
> When I set you free.

We reach John Street. As I step out to pay the fare, I am horrified to find a phalanx of photographers bearing down on me. The in camera hearing is belied. I look away, while trying not to look shifty. The driver takes his revenge by counting the cash as slowly as possible. 'Seems like your friend must also be in the public eye.' I tell him to keep the change and thrust my way towards the building, only to find that the door is still locked and I am at the mercy of the photographers whose clicking cameras are reflected in the glass.

'You're pushing when you should be pulling.'

'That's the story of his life.'

As the one sympathetic voice breaks through the raucous laughter, I realise my mistake and pull the handle so hard that I knock over a sign instructing that 'No animals are to be brought inside this building'. The photographers remain outside.

I hurry up to the second floor, where Max meets me in the Solicitors' Assembly. He apologises for leaving me to cope with the cameras, of which he had no warning. Somehow – and he has no doubts as to the source – the press has found out about the hearing. Frustrated by the reporting restrictions, several journalists are snooping around for a story. I spot one lurking in the corridor and feel an overwhelming urge to pee. I enter the loo and scrupulously avoid glancing at the other occupant. It is only when he speaks that I identify Fred Docherty, the nation's favourite demolition man. 'What's a nice boy like you doing in a place like this?' he asks archly. My head pounds. My fly is open but I am numb. I look down in shock.

'Had a good eyeful, have you?' he asks, shaking himself vigorously. 'They say that the price of fame is never being able to piss in peace.' My sudden turn is almost an admission of guilt.

'Why are you doing this, Lewis? You can't still be bitter about Candida.'

'You'd never understand. You and I have very different morals.'

'In other words, I have some.'

'You should take care what you say: you're in a highly vulnerable position.' My penis feels exposed, but I dare not touch it.

'It may not be too late to withdraw your affidavit.'

'Are you trying to interfere with a witness?' He savours the innuendo. 'You wouldn't want to intimidate me, my old son? Not that that little thing would intimidate my grandmother.' He laughs. 'Better go; people may talk. See you in court, as the actor said to the agent.'

See you in Hell, as the chat show host replied.

In court, I feel like an actor at the start of a new series of a popular programme . . . The Judges: an everyday story of sentencing folk. All last season's favourites have returned: your parents, who are even wearing their trademark costumes; their legal advisers; my legal advisers; the Usher, a crusty character part complete with catchphrase 'Take the Bible in your right hand and read the words on the card. . . .' Waiting in the wings – or the witness rooms – are this week's guests: Vicky Ireland, Edward and Melissa, Jenny Knatchpole and, of course, Lewis, fresh from his own programme and a genuine star.

No sooner are we settled than the Judge enters with an apology. On account of an emergency application for an injunction, he will not be able to hear us until after lunch. We file out. Max warns that there is now no way that we will finish this afternoon. The delay will entail adjustments in everyone's schedule; as the Judge himself acknowledges when, on our return, he calls ceremoniously for his diary and consults his clerk. He informs Counsel that, by judicious switches, he will be able to continue the hearing on Monday. Although Rebecca thanks him for his consideration and says that all parties will be present, I worry about my witnesses; Vicky is due in studio, while, if Edward and Melissa stay here much longer, they will be confused with the couples filing for divorce.

At long last, your parents' Counsel stands to present his case. Now that I am more accustomed to my surroundings, I find time to observe him. Of average height and solidly plump, with bouffant silver hair, he exudes an Establishment urbanity that survives even his choice of tie. His dry tones border on detachment and, according to Rebecca, are informed by resentment at never having taken silk. To him, the law is an intellectual exercise, as formal as completing the *Criterion* crossword in Latin. In general, he finds family courts insufficiently gladiatorial; but, in this instance, there is compensation in her presence. He harbours an intense detestation of women barristers, which he masks with a show of old-world charm.

'He once offered me his chair at a Middle Temple dinner,' Rebecca recalls. ' "Don't worry," I said, "I'm not pregnant." "No matter," he replied slickly, "a gentleman should always give up his seat to a lady; he never knows if it's that time of the month." I stood there, as humiliated as if blood were trickling down my leg. He's of the breed of man who puts women at the front of the queue for lifeboats and at the back for life. As for women at the bar, I'm sure he feels that we're contaminated by our clients, particularly someone like me who specialises in assault and abuse. After all, are these papers you would wish your wife or your servants to read?'

He finds a kindred spirit in your mother, who, as a bursar's wife, was doubly domestic for thirty years and who, no doubt, subscribes to the traditional view that a woman's place is in the home, a man's is at work, and a homosexual's is in jail.

'I'm afraid I'm just a housewife,' she says, as he establishes her credentials.

196

'There's no need to apologise, Mrs Mulliner.' He beams reassurance. 'What better model for a young girl?'

He treats her with exaggerated courtesy, more suited to a rape victim who has to relive the ordeal in court. She plays her part by never once looking at me nor referring to me by name. And yet, however painful it may be for her to confront my sexuality, she makes it plain that her first duty is to Pagan. She describes her shock at hearing from both Lewis and Jenny after the *Sunday Sentinel* article and her sense of double betrayal that you should have entrusted your child to a homosexual rather than to your own parents ... in which case, perhaps she should ask herself why. She claims that she has no objection to homosexuality in principle – or even in practice – as long as it is in private, but that on no account do we ever have the right to involve children. I object to her choice of verb, which I am quite sure is deliberate. . . . I suppose I should just be grateful that Pagan is not a boy.

'And what about the health hazard? Does anyone know if Mr Young has been tested for AIDS?' At a stroke, she blasts all pretence of tolerance. Even her Counsel looks taken aback and rapidly sits, as if to contain the damage. I wait for Rebecca to press our advantage, but she seems strangely subdued. I realise that laying into a seventy-year-old woman risks losing sympathy. Nevertheless, there is a part of me that bays for blood.

'How many homosexuals do you know, Mrs Mulliner?'

'None,' comes the affronted reply.

'Are you sure?'

'Of course I'm sure.'

'Then how can you make such sweeping statements about their behaviour?'

'I have eyes.'

'To see for yourself or to read newspapers?'

'I'm not blind to what's happened in the last thirty years ... drugs and filth and pornography and not knowing where to look on the Brighton front.'

'And you'd lay all that at the door of homosexuals?' I begin to appreciate Rebecca's approach and wonder whether the Judge has the power to certify.

'And television; that's to blame too.' For the first time, she turns to me, as if to accuse me on both counts of the

197

moral decline of the nation. 'It makes everything seem normal. It puts strangers into your living room like friends. And they laugh at everything you hold dear. If that man is allowed to keep our granddaughter, she'll grow up with no respect for any of the things that decent people believe in . . . the Church, the Police Force, the National Trust. Look at the Royal Family'. . . . I do; although whether as an example of probity or laxity is unclear.

Your father follows your mother into the witness box. He presents himself as a man of the world, proud of his pragmatism, prepared to 'live and let live' . . . just as long as we do not live with children. To his mind, homosexuality is a handicap; at any rate by inference.

'Take my son, William. He's confined to a wheelchair; he'll never go mountaineering. It's no use pretending that he will. So he has to find alternatives, like fishing or table tennis. It's the same with Mr Young.' I see. And what is the ping-pong equivalent of a parent? A lollipop man? The ball is in his court. 'I've spent all my life in the company of men, first in the Army and then in a public school. I've known homosexuals, some of them first-rate soldiers and others first-rate school-masters – not that there's that much difference. But there are always doubts, dangers, you can never quite trust them. Take our senior arts master, excellent chap, even redesigned the school crest. He was with us for twenty years; everyone knew he was a bugger . . . excuse the vernacular. Then, one evening, he went out on a bender and paraded through Old House in the buff. Next day, he had to be dismissed.'

Poor man! Do you know what became of him?

'Your Honour, I object to this line of questioning. The issue for the Court is whether Pagan Mulliner should remain with my client, not the behaviour of individual homosexuals.'

'The two are linked, Ms Colestone,' the Judge sibilantly replies, 'whether you care for it or not.'

Your father brackets me with the sacked teacher. 'It's clear from Mrs Knatchpole's affidavit that Mr Young enjoys wearing women's clothing. I'm sure that there's no harm in it . . . I remember spending several hilarious evenings at the forces' revue, *Soldiers in Skirts*; but is it right for a young girl to be raised by a transveststite?' His difficulty with the word suggests his distaste for the practice. Who would have thought that your practical joke would have repercussions fifteen years on? 'If we don't take care, Pagan will grow up thinking such perversions normal. She's already far too mature for her years. I'm not saying that children should be wrapped in cotton wool, but I don't believe that a six-year-old should be familiar with fellatio.' What on earth . . . ? 'I wouldn't want my wife to use language like that, let alone my granddaughter.'

'I don't wish to add to your distress,' his Counsel prompts, 'but would you elucidate that last remark for His Honour?'

'Our son was taking a photograph of mother – that's Mrs Mulliner – Pagan and me. He said "Say Primula" . . . that's instead of "Cheese", an old family joke we learnt from Candida. And Pagan said that her favourite cheese – a cream-cheese, mind, a cream-cheese – was "fellatio". It was Mr Young's favourite too. He'd clearly discussed it in front of her. It was only when William laughed – out of embarrassment, of course – that I realised what she'd said. I had to explain to my wife what it meant.'

I scribble a note for Rebecca and wonder why it is that Pagan should find it so difficult to remember the capital cities of Europe and yet recall an off-the-cuff idiocy word for word.

Your father's tone is a perfect blend of pain and indignation, which his Counsel refuses to put to the test of further questions. Rebecca makes far less headway in his cross-examination than she did in your mother's. She taxes him with various inconsistencies . . . Pagan can hardly be happy to see them when she locks herself in my car, or feel at home in Hove when she repeatedly wets the bed. But these are details. And, as the Judge unctuously adds, 'children do not have the benefit of your rigorous logic, Ms Colestone'. She forces a smile and draws her interrogation to a close.

After a brief re-examination, your father steps down, and his Counsel takes up the affidavits from Jenny and Lewis. The Judge seeks to discover whether either contains anything controversial and, if not, whether the witnesses need to be called. On hearing from Rebecca that they do, he looks first at his watch and then at the heavens, before directing them to proceed.

Jenny enters the box, wearing a blue cashmere suit and that air of resignation which passes for authority in upper-middle-class women. She has lined; her strawberry blonde hair has faded and her creamy complexion soured. She fumbles for words, as if unused to any but canine contact, whereupon the Judge urges her to take her time.

Your parents' Counsel teases out the testimony of two parties: her engagement, where she was mortified by your revelations, and Eammon Lipton's birthday, where she was traumatised by my dress. 'Ever since, I've suffered terrible headaches when I watch television. I've written dozens of letters to the BBC to no effect. . . .' At last, I discover the source of all the anonymous letters naming me as a transsexual. Poor Jenny, even her vitriol falls wide of the mark.

It is clear from Rebecca's cross-examination that Jenny is consumed with jealousy. It torments her that you should have had a child and she should not. She appears to blame you for all the problems in her marriage; which is patently absurd. It can hardly have helped to have had Heathrow immigration officers laugh at her husband's penis at the start of her honeymoon; nevertheless, to my certain knowledge, you only ever met Guy by chance and in company after the show-down in Cadogan Square. 'Every time we went to bed, she came between us. . . .' As she breaks down, the Judge inclines towards her and offers her a glass of water, which she gratefully accepts. This, at least, requires the Usher to put down the paperback novel in which he has been engrossed and do some work.

'You are pressing the witness too hard, Ms Colestone. Not everyone is as inured to the rigours of the family court as you.'

With pointed delicacy, Rebecca asks about her experience of child-raising. The Judge looks impatient. Jenny looks frail. 'My husband and I have not been blessed with children. But that's of no consequence. I have my sheepdog sanctuary. I know how important it is that animals who have been neglected or ill-treated are looked after by someone who cares.' I wonder if she would have been equally vexatious if Pagan had been a pet.

I have to explain about the dress ... if only you had explained about the dress; it is the one and only time in my life that I have worn one. Unlike Robin, I have neither the inclination nor the build for drag. But you insist that it is the theme of the party and that I must humour my heterosexual friends. In the event, we arrive in Dorking to find the women in evening dress and the men in dress suits. Eammon and Lily are nonplussed. I explain that you must have misread the invitation; but one glance at your face reveals the truth. Lily alone finds our appearance droll. Disregarding my migraine, she thrusts me into the drawing room, where she introduces me as Leonora, my own twin sister. Conversation dies. You, of course, look chic in your double-breasted pin-stripes, borsalino and burnt-cork moustache. I look like an out-take from *La Cage aux Folles*.

The dinner-bell extends my ordeal, as Lily, who has become slightly hysterical, insists on amending her seating plan. I was originally placed between Jenny and Lydia, Eammon's partner's wife; but that would put three girls together. And yet she cannot simply swap us, as that would mean your sitting next to Jenny. The ark-like rigidity of her scheme seems to allow no resolution. Everyone waits, in mounting irritation, as she tries out different permutations. 'Isn't it fun?' you say, 'just like musical chairs ... with the emphasis on the musical.' Nobody laughs.

Finally, I am placed on Eammon's right. 'After all, Leonora is the guest of honour,' Lily exclaims. Eammon addresses only three words to me during the entire meal: 'Red or white?' They never invite either of us again.

You revel in having stuck a pin up the backside of the Home Counties. But the backside escapes with minor bruising; it is the pin that feels the strain. We do not speak for two weeks, following a row in which you deride me as bourgeois ... try telling that to Jenny Knatchpole, who has been storing up evidence of my deviance ever since. Your victories are proving to be pyrrhic. Whom would you rather credit, the Saint Clare of Little Kingshill or a transvestite exhibitionist? Don't answer; your opinion is hardly the norm.

'I used to believe that Candida Mulliner was evil; but, now, I think that the accused corrupted her.'

The Judge intervenes. 'The witness should remember that this is not a criminal court. Mr Young is not on trial.' Jenny looks disappointed.

'No further questions, Your Honour.' Your parents' Counsel concludes the re-examination.

'You may step down now, Mrs Knatchpole. Thank you for responding so graciously in such trying circumstances. I trust that we have not impeded your invaluable work.'

The Judge is unlikely to feel as benevolent towards Lewis, who saunters to the witness box with the cockiness of one more accustomed to the dock. He winks at the Usher and reels off the oath without reading the card. But, if his prolier-than-thou manner threatens to lose sympathy, his cheated-father act restores it. I have only myself to blame. I presumed that you must have told him about the abortion; but reading my affidavit was his first hint. Now I know how a murderer feels.

'I'm pregnant,' you say, flinging your overnight case on the kitchen table.

'Lewis?' You nod.

Maternity rears its mewling head, as you describe your dilemma. 'I don't believe in abortion. That is, I believe in a woman's right to choose, but not mine. Look at Imogen; she uses abortion as a means of contraception. I'm never sure if she considers it more convenient, chic or appropriately painful. But it's a human life. If abortion had been legal thirty years ago, there'd have been no Candida. I'd have been flushed down the pan at some soulless clinic. How can I do that to my child? And yet what chance does it have with parents like me and Lewis? "Bad blood!" my mother used to say, whenever I crossed her; "blood will out." And, for once, she was right. But this would be even worse.'

I am starting to see how your obsession with *Debrett's* owes less to snobbery than to genetics . . . bad blood to be purged by blue.

'Do you know if he even wants children?'

'He wants a son.'

'Would he be a good father?'

'He'd be the worst.' I picture his violence transferred

202

from you to a child: the black eyes from bunches of keys that you mysteriously fail to catch, the bruised arms from falls on the shallow, carpeted stairs. 'You'd make by far the best father of all the men I know, Leo.' It is the first time that you have mentioned it. I laugh away the tremor in my loins.

He refuses to accept your departure and arrives at the house, demanding entry. I bar the door, secure in the knowledge that you are out. He pushes past and darts up the stairs. He returns to the hall, doubly humiliated, flicks open a knife and holds it to my throat, threatening to kill me if I try to come between you. I laugh – I still do not know whether it is nerves or bravado – and he slits my arm. I shout; although there is no pain. There is a trickle of blood, but there is no pain. I must be in shock, which is why there is no pain. Then he scoops up the blood and forces it onto my tongue. It tastes disconcertingly bland. 'I'm an actor,' he says. 'Do you think I'd risk what I've got going for me by stamping out an insect like you?' He smiles and stabs himself with the retractable blade. 'Tell her, I'm expecting her back.'

You go back, having resolved nothing, determined to tell him the truth. In the event, he pre-empts you by returning from an audition where he was not even asked to read. 'You have to be queer to get anywhere these days. Bend over and you'll be a star.' He punches the wall; you giggle. He punches you; you run into the street and hail a taxi, which drives you straight to Holland Park. Safe behind the newly installed door-chain, you examine your bruised stomach and insist that he has damaged the child. The next day you make an appointment at the clinic and announce with dark-eyed desperation that 'babies are much over-rated; I fail to see the attraction. They eat; they shit; they spew. I'm surprised they don't all grow up to be men.'

'Is anything wrong?' Max notices my discomfort.

'Just a fluttering in my head.' I must pin down my butterfly mind.

So Lewis knew nothing of the baby . . . not even in recrimination. However hard Rebecca tries, she cannot dispel the impression he creates when your parents' Counsel asks about my fitness as a father. 'What do you think I think? He forced the woman I loved to have an abortion. He took away my chance of having a child. And now he throws it in my face as if it were history.' He breaks down in tears; are they as stagy as the blood? 'He was terrified of ending up alone. He cast some sort of spell on her . . . I know; I've played Svengali. He took my child away from me. He has no right to hers!'

After a brief re-examination, Counsel declares that he has no further questions and the Judge adjourns proceedings for the day. Rebecca will present my case on Monday. 'Let's just hope that the English cricket team puts His Honour in a good humour over the weekend.' She has no time to confer, as she is rushing back to town to prepare for her grandson's circumcision.

'Chin up,' she says, 'there's light at the end of the tunnel.'

'Then it's the glare of an oncoming train.'

Pagan and I spend Saturday morning on the pier. She has her fortune told by 'the amazing computer palm scanner', which, among much else, reveals how she will fare as a child, as a wife and as a husband, and that her lucky number is two. 'Famous Twos are Bart Lancaster, Sophy Loren and May Quant.' We have our photograph taken in a mock-up of Prince Charles and Princess Diana, which I trust will not prove to be an omen. We enter a stall selling personalised Brighton rock, but, among all the Kevins, Kirstys, Laurens and Melanies, there is a predictable lack of Pagans. So I settle for one marked 'daughter', and she picks me one marked 'Dad'.

'Grown-ups don't eat rock,' I say.

'Dads do.' She rests her case. We walk down the promenade, where three young women ask if I would mind taking a photograph. I pause wearily, pulling up my tie and smoothing my hair. Then I realise that what they want is for me to take a picture of them. They have either failed to recognise me or else they are uninterested, and, as they fall into a candy-floss huddle, I laugh for the first time in days. 'Look at the birdie and say. . . .'

After lunch, I leave Pagan and Susan to visit the Sea Life Centre and drive to London to record the show. Vicky is waiting for me at the camera rehearsal. She is remarkably cheerful about yesterday's wasted journey and promises that she is doing all that she can to rearrange her schedule for next week. Her chief concern is that I look strained. I assure her that it is nothing that a tub of Max Factor and a tube of Eye Light cannot fix. And yet, as we sit while the crew set the unusually complex video cues and indulge the pop group $E=mc^2$'s U2 fantasies, the strain starts to tell. I escape before I snap.

The buzz as I walk on stage should be bottled. It is a relief to be back on the right side of the questions. The familiar line-up of guests offsets any lack of preparation . . . although it turns out to be far too familiar for one loudmouth in the audience, who yells 'Not him again!' on Ian Botham's entry. As Vicky hisses in my ear and Botham carries on regardless, I reassess the benefits of broadcasting live.

Question: what sort of man allows his guests to be insulted?

Answer: the sort who allows his child to be taken away.

My after-show hospitality is limited to a single round of drinks as, with Arundel Castle on the morning's programme, I am anxious for an early night. I race back to Brighton and jump bathless and bookless into bed. Sleep eludes me; my thoughts prove to be harder to dim than the lights. I try music, masturbation and Mogadon in turn and in vain. The pillow chafes my cheek. I sweat as though it were a siesta. In despair, I reach for a glass of water, which spills all over the sheets.

I awake in a tangle of sodden bedding. I wash, dress and join Pagan and Susan for breakfast in a half-empty dining room. Pagan orders a basket of fresh fruit.

'What are these?'

'Lychees.'

'They don't look like cheese.'

As Susan pours me some coffee, an elderly man, with relief map veins and a zip that has lost the battle with his stomach, approaches the table. 'If I had my way, you'd be shot,' he declares. 'There were men like you in the jungle; we regarded them as lower than the Japanese.' He walks back to his wife who butters him a croissant. I am bewildered. I suppose that he may have taken exception to the remarks I made to Botham on the state of English cricket or to several of $E=mc^2$'s lyrics; but, surely, neither constitutes a shooting offence? The mystery deepens, when we are intercepted at the door by the assistant manager who advises us to avoid the lobby and, instead, to use the service stairs.

'Has there been another bomb?' I ask, as he leads us through the kitchens. 'Why has no one been evacuated?'

'Not so much a bomb as a bombshell, sir.' He laughs limply. 'I thought that you might wish to see this.' He holds up the front page of the *Nation*. I read my own obituary. My *Double Life* has become my *Rent Boy Shame*.

Pagan complains that the stairs are making her tired. I take her in my arms; the warmth outweighs the weight. The assistant manager warns us to be on our guard. 'There are several journalists in the lobby. One has already tried to bribe a chambermaid, who quite properly reported it to me. But I'm afraid that some of the staff are only casual. And had it been anywhere else but the Grand. . . .'

'I'm very grateful for all your trouble. I'm sorry to have brought scandal into your hotel.'

'Think nothing of it, sir; we have politicians here.'

Susan leads a protesting Pagan to her room. 'You promised we'd go to a castle.'

'I need to have a quick look at the paper. It's work.'

'You promised!'

I lock the door and turn the pages. My head swims at the thought of four million copies rolling off the presses. The facts of the story are sordid rather than sensational; I am at the nuts and bolts end of vice, not the whips and chains. The one perversity of which they can accuse me is a taste for foul language. And that was because it was the boys' language; it seemed to make them more themselves. It is reported, in bold type, that I kept my socks on during sex as though it were the height of decadence . . . but the room was so filthy that I would have kept on all my clothes if I could. In terms more suited to an assault, I am charged with having 'performed fellatio on the boy'.

'What's fellatio . . . ?' I eavesdrop on breakfast tables throughout the land.

'It's a cream-cheese to which chat show hosts are extremely partial.'

'I had to explain to my wife what it meant.'

Will he have to explain rent-boys too when they make their inevitable appearance in court tomorrow? I can recall a time when they had to be explained to me ... when I supposed that the boys lingering on Soho corners were playing the waiting game of adolescents, not the mating game of adults. Then, one night, a soft-spoken, middle-aged man, with bone-white flesh, accosts me as I stroll home.

'Are you rent?' I thrill to the blatancy of the question. The term is unfamiliar but I presume that it must be a synonym for queer.

'Yes,' I say equally boldly, although he is far too old to attract me during the day.

'Shall we go to your place?' I take him to Brewer Street. 'I like you,' he says, 'you're a cut above the rest. There's no quibbling, no haggling.' And I fail to understand, even when he makes demands which are unacceptable on a first date and noises which I am afraid will rouse you. The next morning I awake to find him gone, having left three ten-pound notes on my pillow. My immediate thought is that he must have stolen something and then had a pang of conscience; but a quick check reveals that the only thing lost is my self-respect. Do I look like a tart to you?

I look around the Amalfi. Which are the researchers and which the strippers? I find it impossible to say.

I never tell you about the man, nor, a few years later, about the boys. The first comes on my thirtieth birthday; a present from me to me. With David moved out and you abroad on an assignment, I feel miserably alone. But I have an advert in my wallet and I realise that I am rich enough to buy 'relief'. What a euphemism! What a lie! ... along with so many others, like 'discretion guaranteed'. I fling the paper to the floor and curse their bad faith. But then, if they put a price on their bodies, what price anything else? It is not that I am naive enough to believe that such visits dispel my loneliness, but they at least give it an identifiable form ... and an identikit face. The payment is for my own protection. The boys manipulate but never touch me; though naked, I am clothed in cash.

When my television face becomes too familiar for such ad hoc arrangements, I use agencies, on the assumption that exposure threatens them more than me. In the meantime, I destroy any chance of love. I sell my ideals more cheaply than the boys sell their bodies; I am so certain of disappointment that I pre-empt hope. The young Andy Warhol bleached his hair so that he would never have to watch it grow grey; I drain my life of passion so that I will never have to watch it go wrong. Now, I even dream in monochrome.

It was not always thus. I was once a confirmed romantic . . . for which I still bear the scars of your scorn. I climbed up Juliet's balcony; I sailed to Tristan's island; I languished in Abelard's cell. Now, I see only the death of love: the poisoning, the stabbing, the castration. We live in a culture that subordinates every other myth to the myth of romantic love and hence to the inevitability of loss. We idealise self-sacrifice as reverently as a priest raising the communion cup. And, when I allowed Lady Standish to seduce me into giving up Robin, I drained the cup to the dregs.

Robin accused me of moral cowardice; David accused me of self-oppression; I accuse myself of romantic illusion. I visualise this room as a courtroom . . . even an anonymous hotel bedroom has a dignity that the Brighton Court lacks. I press the trouser-press into service as a dock. I want to subpoena Lady Standish as a witness for the defence; but she stands firm in the Maid's Causeway kitchen. Will you allow her to give her testimony from there?

She examines Exhibit A: the 'life's a bitch and so's my mother' poster that has already caused such offence. She tells me of her love for Robin, of her fears for Lydia and of her troubles with her husband. She asserts an alliance. 'I felt that we understood each other from the moment we met. We are linked by our feelings for Robin' . . . she links arms as if in illustration. 'He's a very special person but weak – wouldn't you agree? – he can be so weak. He doesn't know his own mind, not least when it comes to Jennifer. You and I who are strong have a duty to guide him. He looks on you as a brother; you must give him the benefit of your advice.'

I have always longed for a brother, someone who would be close but not claustrophobic. I am coaxed into submission. And, even if I ignore her remarks about the influence of school and the inadequacy of his father, I feel sure that he will be happier with Crierley and Jenny than with Earls Court and me. I have as strong a sense of the sanctity of his family as you, albeit one linked less to its history and more to an ideal of married life. Lady Standish never confronts the reality of our relationship but rather presents her restraint as a sign of intimacy. By the time that Robin returns from having shown Jenny around Cambridge – she takes the Amnesty protest on King's Parade to be a quaint medieval custom – his mother has wrung a promise from me to speak to him of his obligations, social and sexual. Do you still wonder that I cry at every showing of *Camille*?

Now my tears burn my cheeks like acid. I have disappointed everyone: you, Pagan, my mother. I twice pick up the phone to call Gleneagles; but my courage fails. I remember your contempt for the punters at The Pigalle. What would you have thought if you had known that your best friend was among them? Whatever else, I doubt that you would have named me as Pagan's guardian. It is a far cry from consorting with heroes on the slopes of Mount Olympus to cavorting with rent-boys on a floor in Notting Hill.

I remain in my room, safe from journalistic intrusion, although every creaking floorboard chills me like a haunted house. I ask Susan to take Pagan to the toy museum in the hope that the change of venue will make up for the change of guide. But the visit is cut short. They are joined by a woman whose wheedling questions rouse Susan's suspicions and whose language, when she refuses to answer, confirms her fears. Her accusations fall flat, as Susan replies that she has never known a more devoted parent than me . . . an assertion which she repeats at the hotel. But, while I find her pledge of loyalty touching, I worry that it may be overruled. What will happen when her parents agitate and Geoffrey surfaces? She is twenty-three years old; her life has moved from nursery to school to nursery. I am the stranger lying in wait at the gate.

After lunch, I swear a fresh affidavit before a local solicitor, which will allow Rebecca to question me on the *Nation*'s story in court. She and Max insist that, in spite of the risk of hostile cross-examination, it is wiser to address the allegations than to shy away. The most galling fact is that, if we had not lost the whole of Friday morning, the

209

case would have been resolved within the allotted day. I even wonder if the injunction application might have been engineered by Brian Derwent. He was determined not to be beaten by the reporting restrictions. Prevented from printing one story, he has simply produced another. Moral: no one can muzzle a rabid press.

The next morning I order a wide range of papers, to my immediate regret. Rather than risk a return to the law of the jungle, we breakfast in Pagan's room, where I sit beneath an inauspicious print of 'The Arraignment of Princess Caroline'. At nine thirty, Max arrives to fetch me and to lend Susan his mobile phone.

'How are you feeling this morning?'

'The condemned man ate a hearty breakfast.'

'That's not true! You ate kippers and toast.'

I press Pagan to my chest. As we kiss goodbye, her whole life seems to flash before me; I gulp for air. We go down to the lobby, which, to my relief, shows no sign of reporters. They have decamped to the court steps, which Max propels me up so fast that I feel both giddy and guilty. I am surprised that he does not throw a blanket over my head. . . . Young, write out a thousand times: 'I am not on trial; I am not on trial; I am not on trial.' After three lines, I run out of ink.

The Court is tense with anticipation, even the Usher seems to think that developments are of sufficient interest for him to leave off his book. I walk up to Rebecca's junior, whose face betrays the distaste of a man who exhausts all his excess energy playing squash. Rebecca herself burns with indignation. I smile gratefully at the long, handsome head, with the nut-brown eyes and perfectly poised bun that inspire such confidence. She considers that the *Nation*'s story may well constitute contempt; but, in a statement at the start of the session, the Judge makes it clear that he sees it as less grave.

'The article in question has been brought to my attention by my clerk' . . . who sits, inscrutably, typing out Orders on his lap-top computer. 'I wish to make it quite clear that I shall be trying the case on the evidence before me and not on scurrilous gossip. You may rest assured that I shall not allow it to colour my judgment in any way.'

Nevertheless, the morning's hearing becomes less of an

examination of my relationship with Pagan than a tribunal on my sexuality. Rebecca starts by asking leave to present new evidence and files my third affidavit. I enter the witness box and take the oath. 'I swear by Almighty God that the evidence I give shall be the truth, the whole truth and nothing but the truth.' As I add 'So help me God!', I realise that it comes from Hollywood, not the card, and cough. Rebecca leads me first through my own statements and then through the prosecution's . . . the applicants' accusations. I explain that, whether for better or worse for myself, I have kept my sexuality separate . . . but it has certainly been better for Pagan. As she has no awareness of sexuality, it is an irrelevance; what counts is my love.

I add that you knew everything about my sexuality (So help me God!) and that, even though several of our married friends offered Pagan a home, you entrusted her to me. I state my case to my own satisfaction but not, it would seem, to the Judge's, who gruffly asks Rebecca to move on to other matters. For the first time, she challenges him.

'Should Your Honour decide against my client, he might feel that his case has not been pursued'. . . . Gloves off – and wigs on – with the threat of an appeal.

'Your client may not be as conversant with the ways of this court as you are, Ms Colestone. You may proceed.'

Her acknowledgement of his antipathy is manifest in the speed with which she takes me through my remaining evidence. As she refers me to specific paragraphs, I fumble with the papers and lose my place. Eventually, the Judge hands his copy to the Usher and asks him to show me the relevant passage. He dismisses my thanks with a grunt.

I fear that I am creating a bad impression . . . which is one that your parents' Counsel is determined to underline. Dispensing with preliminaries, he asks about the discrepancy between my first and second affidavits. . . . I am a twelve-year-old boy at the door of the Headmaster's study. 'I see. So, this was a deliberate invention on your part. You lied in the affidavit and thereby lied to the Court. What was your purpose in lying?' I want to reply that it was to protect myself from the prejudices of men like him, but, instead, I say that I was afraid that the Court might be reluctant to let Pagan remain with a homosexual.

'I'm sure that that is a well-grounded fear.'

'Your Honour, I object. My learned friend should reserve his comments for his speech.'

'I think that's right, Mr Digby-Lewis.'

I am disconcerted by his cross-examination technique. Whenever I say something that threatens him, he snaps 'I hear what you say' as if to dismiss it; and, whenever he wants to make sure that the Judge registers my reply, he repeats it with a roll of his eyes and a pained 'oh well'. How I hate those 'oh well's, as insidious as a cab-driver's 'know what I mean?'s. His manner towards me is far more hostile than Rebecca's was to your parents. I begin to fear that she may have been right and my case has not been pursued. One of the reasons which Max gave for instructing her was to identify my cause with a woman. But what use is that when the whole thrust – the cut and thrust – of the Court favours the bully-boy tactics of men?

'What will you do if – I should say, when – Pagan asks about your homosexuality?'

'I shall explain that it's a different kind of love.'

'And would you say that it's equally valid?'

'Yes.' I answer him and, for the first time, I answer myself. 'Yes, I believe that it is.'

'I doubt that there are many in this Court who would agree with you,' he comments, and I wonder why Rebecca does not intervene.

'As you and I both know, majorities aren't always right.'

'I hear what you say. What will you do if she is ostracised or bullied by other children on account of your sexuality? Children can be very cruel.'

'Only when they learn it from adults.'

'Some adults may disapprove of their children associating with her . . . or with you.'

'I would doubt that. So far, everyone has been most supportive.'

'Hampstead intellectuals?'

'We live in Holland Park.'

'I put it to you that, whatever your intention, you are abusing her ignorance.'

'And I put it to you that you're wrong. I distrust current notions of childhood sexuality; I believe that children should be protected from sexuality, both their own and other people's. I'm determined that she should remain

212

innocent, but that doesn't mean keeping her in ignorance. The only innocence that lasts is based on knowledge –'

'I hear what you say.'

'Which, to prevent misunderstanding, I should stress is not the same as experience. Knowledge is experience without pain.'

'I hear what you say! So you would have no objections if she became a lesbian?'

'She's six years old!'

'You haven't answered my question.'

'There's not a shred of evidence to suggest that children of gay people or, indeed, those adopted by gay people are more likely to grow up gay than any others.'

'You still haven't answered my question.'

'I shall be proud of her whatever her sexuality, whether she choose to marry or to stay single, have children or be celibate, a prostitute or a nun.'

'A prostitute?'

'That's a figure of speech.'

'A very telling one.'

'What I mean is I'll love her whatever.'

'Oh well. And, after all, you have considerable experience of loving prostitutes.'

'Your Honour, once again, my learned friend is making personal observations,' Rebecca objects.

'Yes. Mr Digby-Lewis, would you restrict yourself to asking questions of the witness.'

He takes that as a mandate to grill me on the rent-boy allegations.

'I can only say that I bitterly regret the incidents, not because of the adverse publicity, but because they diminish me as a person.'

'That's all very well. But you show remarkably little concern for your victims.'

'Your Honour,' Rebecca rises; 'I consider that to be a most inappropriate remark.'

'I agree. There is no reason to suppose that Mr Young was the first – or indeed the last – man to avail himself of these unfortunate boys' services.'

'Your Honour, may I ask you not to be misled by terminology?' I can no longer keep silent. ' "Rent-boy" is a popular phrase, which bears no relation either to the men's

213

age or experience. I resent the suggestion that they were immature, inadequate youths and my activities somehow akin to child abuse. Indeed, a friend of mine, Duncan Mossop, is currently engaged in research for a television documentary on prostitutes –'

'Not another one?'

'I fear so, Your Honour. And the oldest he interviewed was seventy-three.'

'Seventy-three?' His incredulity emboldens me.

'Yes, Your Honour. In fact, he lives here in Brighton. He took it up eight years ago when he retired.' A smile flickers through the Court and remains fixed on the clerk's face. 'He claimed that his busiest periods are during party conferences.' The clerk's grin fades in the Judge's grimace. I fear that I have gone too far.

'Your witness, Mr Digby-Lewis.'

'No further questions, Your Honour.'

Rebecca's re-examination is brief. I step down. She then explains that neither Edward nor Melissa has been able to leave London. 'There is life outside the law courts, Ms Colestone,' the Judge replies, although his supercilious smile denies it. 'Their statements appear to be uncontroversial and I have noted what they say.' My only character witness is Vicky Ireland, who pays tribute to my personal integrity and my devotion to Pagan. Even the Judge seems impressed by my missing the Paul Newman lunch in order to catch her in *Toad of Toad Hall* and refusing the *Wisdom of the East* series to avoid six months filming abroad. Your parents' Counsel is surprised – and I am cheered – by her ringing endorsement of my future with the BBC; although I suspect that she speaks from the heart and not from the Board.

As soon as her evidence is over, Vicky has to rush back to London to revise tomorrow's programme. Although she insists that the revelations will be a nine days' wonder, it is unfortunate, to say the least, that we have scheduled one of our more hard-hitting Tuesday discussions: with survivors of sex scandals, including an actor, a politician and a priest. To proceed would be provocative. So we are obliged to fall back on two subjects that I have hitherto vetoed . . . Zsa Zsa Gabor and talented pets.

The sole professional witness is the Welfare Officer who

declares roundly for me and, moreover, does so, courtesy of Pagan. She reports that she remains a happy, lively little girl and that her only signs of disturbance are caused by her visits to your parents. 'It's clear that any bond between them has yet to emerge and that Pagan feels hurt and bewildered by the continuing contact. She insists that she wants to stay with Mr Young.'

'I hear what you say,' your parent's Counsel interjects. 'May I ask how long you have been in your present post, Miss Dixon?'

'Eighteen months.'

'Just over a year. Oh well. And do you have any children of your own?'

'I'm not married.'

'You're not married. Oh well. Nevertheless, and in spite of such limited experience, you will admit that Mr Young's sexuality puts Pagan's at risk?'

'I most certainly will not.'

'Miss Dixon, I grant that I may be out of touch with current social work thinking, but do you no longer believe that children need role models?'

'Of course they do.'

'Then wouldn't you agree that the best model for a well-balanced child is a healthy, heterosexual couple?'

'The best perhaps.' She looks uncomfortable. 'But there are alternatives.'

'Alternatives? Oh well. Alternatives. I think we've all had occasion to see where those have led.' He leaves the place ominously unspecified. 'No further questions, Your Honour.'

With all the witnesses heard, the Judge declares that it is an appropriate time to break for lunch. He inquires as to Pagan's whereabouts and, on being told that she is in Brighton, requests that she be brought to court in preparation for his judgment. I am delighted. It appears that, against expectations, she will be given the chance to express her views. Max is less sanguine and warns that it may simply be an attempt to forestall any problems. His words plunge me into despair. I long to be alone. I am too full of foreboding to eat, and Rebecca's insistence seems insensitive. Nevertheless, I allow myself to be lured to a local pub, which is packed with *Nation* readers. I stare at

215

the window and feel the hostility beating on my back. After an hour of condemned-cell conversation, we return to court and a brief reunion with Pagan, who has confused the corridors with Television Centre and expects to be entertained. The best that we can offer is a box of crayons.

'I'm going to draw you a picture of the sea.'

'Be sure to make it calm.'

Nausea overwhelms me as we are summoned into court. The walls dissolve and reform as a crematorium. In our serried ranks, we are no longer litigants but mourners, rising for the Judge as though for a coffin. I grip the pew . . . I seize the seat and propel myself into the present. The Judge puts on his spectacles like a black cap and injects a note of gravity into his voice.

'I have reached my decision, which has by no means been an easy one'. . . . I urge him to reconsider; I demand the deliberations of a jury. . . . 'In my view, the most disturbing element in this entire case is the mystery surrounding Pagan's father. He may be unaware of her existence; he may be prevented from playing his natural role in her life. I would go so far as to say that, were he here today, my task would be a great deal simpler. But he is not, and I consider Candida Mulliner's silence in this matter to be grossly irresponsible' . . . your mother nods. . . . 'Miss Mulliner did not enjoy a close relationship with her own father, or, indeed, her mother . . .' whose head is suddenly still. . . . 'It may be that, in my previous judgment, I was unduly influenced by their estrangement; it is, after all, the way of the world for children to consider parents ungenerous and parents children ungrateful. I have found it hard to assess Pagan's relationship with the applicants' . . . which is scarcely surprising since it does not exist . . . 'but their concern for her well-being and devotion to her interests have been exemplary, not to mention their acceptance of the changes that a young child will bring to their lives. Furthermore, I believe that their home background is more stable and conducive to normal development than that of the respondent' . . . so much for psychological parenting; so much for his own Welfare Officer's report . . . 'who, it must be said, has cared for Pagan conscientiously – to the best of his ability – over a long and difficult period, and to whom she has formed a close attachment. Nevertheless, I

216

am obliged to look to the future, not to the past. I therefore order that Pagan reside with the applicants, while the respondent be granted regular visiting and staying contact.'

I feel flayed. I watch your parents embracing like footballers. Visiting and staying contact: is that all that we have left? He will make strangers of us. He will replace intimacy by outings. I will join the legion of Sunday fathers leading protests against the closure of the zoo.

Justice is not blind but blinkered. He does not see me but a newspaper headline. Your father is seventy-four; your mother seventy-one; and yet they are still considered fit to bring up a six-year-old. 'Age is, of course, a factor, but not, I am convinced, a decisive one'. . . . No, and there are no prizes for guessing what is; let's hear it for our old friends, John Thomas and Lady Jane. Your parents' childlessness was a tragedy; mine is a judgment. Why? It takes two people to produce a child – although Lucy Paynton managed well enough with a syringe – but does it take two to raise one? Isn't there an Indian tribe where gay men are put in charge of the children? Or is homosexuality solely a disease of the decadent West?

I force myself to focus on the aftermath of the judgment. I long for a Hollywood ending: a quick cut to Death Row or a close-up of a grieving mother. Instead, Digby-Lewis makes an obsequious speech thanking the Judge for his discernment and asking that his clients be awarded costs. To my surprise, the Judge refuses, declaring that, since both sides were acting in Pagan's best interests, it would be unfair to penalise either. . . . I speculate on your parents' savings. Might they be forced to sell their house? Will Pagan be returned to me by default? I shall be laughed out of court. . . . Meanwhile, Rebecca implements our contingency plan.

'As it is my client's intention to appeal against the Court's decision, I would ask Your Honour to stay the Order pending that hearing.'

'The request is refused. I might add that I consider any further action to be both foolish and futile.'

'Your Honour will appreciate that I am acting under instructions. May I at least ask Your Honour to indicate that it is an appropriate case for an early hearing?'

'You may ask, Ms Colestone, but, as I have already stated that I consider any appeal to be groundless, I shall be making no such recommendation.'

Max whispers to me that, in view of Pagan's youth, the Registrar of Civil Appeals is bound to agree to an expedited hearing. I am no longer reassured by words.

There is a flurry of movement as the Court rises. The Judge bows and everyone else bows back. I stand stock still, although more from paralysis than protest. The clerk fades into insignificance, as he gathers his papers and leaves. Is it my imagination, or will no one look me in the eye? Your parents huddle with their advisers, wallowing in congratulations as they wait to collect their prize. Rebecca takes my arm and leads me towards the door. She asks if I have considered what to say to Pagan. I shake my head. I am as tongue-tied as on the day of your death. Moreover, I fear that my approach will be barred by a tipstaff. Rebecca reassures me with a squeeze of the hand. Her warmth in the wake of such legalised cruelty threatens to unnerve me. I have barely had time to compose myself when Pagan appears.

'It's boring. Susan won't let me dance. Can we go home?' She holds up her drawing: a sea of blue swims before my eyes. I take her in my arms.

'I have to talk to you, my darling.'

'Don't you like my painting?'

'It's lovely.'

'It's for you.'

'Do we have to stay here?' I plead with Rebecca. 'Can't we have just half an hour to ourselves?'

'I'll try to find an empty room.'

'Why are you sad?' Pagan asks.

'You have to be brave, my darling' . . . I am taking her to the dentist. 'You have to be strong' . . . I am leaving her on her first day at school. 'You have to show everyone how grown-up you are' . . . I am driving her to the crematorium. 'We will always have each other' . . . I am a liar. 'The Judge wants you to live with Granny and Grandpa for a little.'

'No!' I press her to my chest, half to comfort, half to silence her. Rebecca returns to show us to a room. From the corner of my eye, I see your parents standing by the stairs and their Counsel, now all affability, sharing a joke with Max; I feel betrayed. Pagan throws herself onto my legs, doubly threatening my balance. We enter the consulting room. The air is as stale as before, with an added stench of deodorised vomit. I gag; Pagan wails.

'It won't be for long, my darling. We're going straight to another court.'

'I want to stay with you.'

'I wish it were up to me, but it's not.'

'I hate them. I'll die. I'll do suicide' . . . which she pronounces like a Chinese meal.

'Somebody help me.' Rebecca is looking away and Susan is wiping her tears. 'You mustn't say those things. You're six years old; you have so many people who love you. Susan loves you. Rebecca loves you.' I draw them into the circle of deceit.

'You don't love me.'

'Of course I do, my darling. I love you most of all.'

'You promised I won't go there. You promised.'

'I have no choice.'

'You're a liar.' She hits me. 'A nasty, nasty liar. And I hate you.'

'Don't say that. You know you don't mean it.'

'Yes, I do.'

'Soon you won't. And it's not as though we won't see each other. I'll come and collect you every fortnight.'

'When's a fortnight?'

'Every two weekends. I'll bring you home and you'll sleep in your own room, where everything will be the same as always. And we'll go out and have such fun that every time we meet will be a party.'

'I don't like parties; there's always lots of people.'

'This time, there'll only be us.'

'She slides onto the floor in a heap of sobs. Your parents enter the room. 'Have you said your goodbyes?' your mother asks. 'If we don't go now, we'll be too late for tea.'

'I won't go. I'm not going.'

'Now don't be a show-off.'

'What about her clothes? She hasn't even got a bag here. Everything's at the hotel.'

'We'll manage tonight, thank you. She can wear one of my nighties. Would you like that? It'll be an adventure. . . . The solicitors will be in touch about the rest.

. . . Now, come along dear, don't be tiresome. Say goodbye to Nanny and –' she looks at me – 'Uncle.'

Pagan starts to scream and clings to my ankles. Your mother loses patience and tries to pull her off. 'This is not the sort of behaviour I expect from a big girl of six.' The big girl of six looks so small at my feet, wriggling out of your mother's clutches. 'Will you kindly let go of her?' she shouts at me.

'I can't shake her off.' I raise my arms in proof. 'If you'll just give us five more minutes.'

'You've had far too long already. Father!' She summons your father, who responds with reluctance. Rebecca tries to intervene, but your mother thrusts her aside. Your parents divide Pagan's legs as though they were pulling a wishbone. As they tug, I topple, and she lands on my chest. My hurt and humiliation are complete.

'That's better,' your mother says. But her victory is punctured by a sharp bite. 'You wicked girl!' She slaps her. 'Look!' She displays her hand for all to see. 'You've drawn blood!' If Rebecca were not restraining me, there would be more.

I screw up my eyes, as your parents haul Pagan out between them. She kicks and squirms and squawks as they drag her down the stairs. I seem to hear the scuffle extend into the street, but it may just be the screaming in my head. There is a rush of silence. I feel as cold as an empty mirror. I look at Rebecca and Susan, but their faces are blank. I catch sight of the Families Need Fathers poster and, with no thought for any other family, rip it off the wall.

# 5

I return to an empty house but a crowded pavement. As I park the car, I am beset by a pack of middle-aged women. At first glance, I take them for reporters, but they are readers, with the sneer of yesterday's headlines reflected in their eyes. It is women like these who have been my most faithful fans; who bake me cakes and knit me scarves for my birthday . . . the Gloucester Road Oxfam shop will lose its most profitable line. Now they stand in shapeless coats and sensible shoes baying abuse. One of them whacks me with an umbrella, although there is no sign of rain; another plucks the braid off Susan's sleeve. We escape up the path. They make no attempt to follow, even as I fumble with the key. They respect my property, if not me.

We stumble inside, where Susan's cracked voice belies her calm words. I rage at the *Nation* for printing my address. It adds nothing to their story; unless they are hoping to provoke a sequel . . . *Disgraced Star Lynched By Disgusted Readers*. I wonder at the hatred that has lured these women from their comfortable homes – for they are comfortable, that much is clear – in order to wait in the street on a freezing February evening for a momentary shot at me. How did they know when – or even that – I would return? Will they come back tomorrow? Are they a group? A secret cell from the Women's Institute . . . flying bigots? Or did they make their way here independently, like the thousands who cheer outside Buckingham Palace . . . 'We want the Queen'.

I peer through a gap in the sitting-room curtains, as though I have something to hide. They are still there. I half-expect them to launch into a chorus of *Jerusalem*. What are they waiting for? A party of under-age rent-boys to arrive for a post-trial orgy?

'I don't understand what drives them,' Susan says.

'Anger . . . with me, with themselves. Resentment. Revulsion. They've invited me into their living rooms twice a week, only to find that I've crapped on the carpet.'

And yet the explanation is too glib. The expression on their faces is more than indignation. I have not just affronted their sense of decency but aroused their deepest anxieties. My sexuality threatens them, of course; but is that because it is 'unnatural' or, rather, unknowable? Do they fear for their husbands and sons, or do they suspect them? Are they blaming me, by association, for the disaffection of their marriage beds? I long to convince them that sexuality is no guarantee of intimacy . . . quite the reverse. Sex is no respecter of personalities or persons. Friendship is about 'you' and 'me'; sex is about itself. As you told me years ago, women mistrust men because they know that, at the moment of truth, they are an irrelevance. My lover . . . my fiancé . . . my wife . . . are all swept aside in the rush of an orgasm; only the female remains.

I trace the remark back to Cambridge. We are sitting in your room at King's discussing our childhoods, when, as so often, conversation strays to sex.

'As a girl, I thought that pubic hair was public.'

'And you've lived the rest of your life on that principle?'

'Don't be such a prude. The only thing wrong with sex is when it's confused with love.'

'I can't work out if that's the most profound paradox or utterly perverse.'

'Sex is so powerful that we have to protect ourselves from it; or else it'll tear us apart. So we invent love, or rather the troubadours did. At least it means that our partner will be there in the morning. Sex keeps love alive; love keeps sex controlled.'

'What about friendship?' I proclaim my own article of faith. I watch all my women-friends – not only you but Imogen, Laura and Virginia – jumping on the merry-go-round of sex, only to see it turn into the helter-skelter or the dodgems. I pick them up, battered and bruised, or comfort them when they are dumped at the end of the ride . . . I may not share the thrills and spills, but I always come up with the candyfloss. I am closer to you than your boyfriends. Our relationship does not run on the roller-coaster of the orgasm; it is built on sympathy and humour and respect. So I want to go outside and tell those women that they have vilified the wrong man. I am their ally. If they want intimacy, they must look to friendship not sex. But, as I peep through the curtains, I see that they have left.

I telephone Hove. Your father answers. He is reluctant to summon Pagan and claims that she is having a bath. I insist that I can wait. I am resolved to remain calm, even when it becomes clear that the delay is deliberate . . . I start to wonder if it is a slur on my standards of hygiene. She finally comes on the line, and I greet her with the forced gaiety of a shop-soiled Father Christmas. She replies in a plaintive whisper which seems to sift through the gap in her teeth. I struggle to unravel her speech, which is more full of sobs than sense. I urge her to take a deep breath . . . but my advice is waylaid by your mother, who grabs the receiver and accuses me of purposely seeking to unsettle her.

'It's clear we will have to set a time, once a week, for you to call, or else all our good work will be undone.'

'She's not a prisoner. I have the right to speak to her at any reasonable hour. And vice versa. Though, don't worry, it'll cost you nothing. I shall tell her to reverse the charges.'

'It's not a question of money but of principle. If you have something to say to her, send a letter. All this telephoning isn't good for children. No wonder the standards of literacy have declined. In my day, writing was an art.'

'There's also an art to conversation.'

'I'd expect you to say that; it's your job. In my view, it's just so much idle chatter.' She hangs up. I blame myself for not teaching Pagan to use the phone. When we showed her how to answer it for you, we should have added how to dial. In any case, I am afraid that she will forget my number. Susan suggests that we have it inscribed on a necklace or a bracelet. Yes, I reply, then all we need is a disc marked Reward . . . we can take it off the cat.

Trouble slinks off with a show of supreme indifference to the fate of his mistress. Susan and I go up to her bedroom to decide what we should pack for Hove. I propose that she should have enough to feel at home but not so much as to forget that it is only temporary. I find that it helps to think of her as an evacuee and to speak of 'for the duration'. We move to the nursery, now a mockery of childhood with its Wendy house (soon to be repossessed), rocking horse (destined for the knackery), and piles of cuddly toys, testament to our naive belief that her life would be equally cuddly. We should have offered her spikes and blades; we should have left off the safety gates and the fireguard. Do you remember Melissa's horror when Edward put Dougall and Sweeney on the garage roof so that they would leave him undisturbed to watch the Test Match? For months, she lambasted him for being an unnatural father. But she was wrong; he was preparing them for the fall.

'Where do we begin?' I ask Susan who, ever practical, makes successive rounds of elimination on the grounds of size, acceptability and mess. She suggests the *Easy Stitch* (suitably feminine), the *Etch-a-Sketch* (creative but clean) and any number of dolls (role models) . . . although I draw the line at Barbie. From the games' chest, she picks *Hedgehog's Revenge*, *Junior Cluedo*, and *Treasures and Trapdoors*; but, given their need for 'two to six players', I suspect that she will have more use for *Solitaire*. My contribution consists of books, paints and her flute, to which, in a spirit of rancour, I add a mouth-organ, bugle and drum.

The choices are made; and Pagan's life is tied up in string. As we return downstairs, Susan asks me how long I want her to stay. I am shocked that she should consider leaving and insist that the dark days will not last – in my wartime scenario, I now place your parents in Hamburg not Hove – and that she will be needed on Pagan's return. I confide Max's view that, if we serve notice of the appeal right away, it is likely to be held in April. I would regard her departure as an admission of defeat; although, after the *Nation*'s revelations, it would be quite understandable. She pours scorn on the report and protests that she will be delighted to stay. Besides, she quit her previous post when the husband tried to seduce her on the night that his wife gave birth; there is no danger of that here. I suggest that she, at least, consult her parents and Geoffrey. She smiles shyly . . . slyly, and adds that there are some advantages to having a fiancé two hundred feet under the sea.

Consuela returns from canasta in Shepherd's Bush. She is surprised to see us and distressed not to see Pagan. I explain the gist of the judgment. She nods and says nothing; but her face conveys all the pity – and pain – of one who knows what it is to give up children. For the first time, I feel that I understand her. I sense a bond between us where there has hitherto been only a contract. I have always supposed that her anguish at leaving Alicia and Roberto was balanced by relief at escaping from the tyrant-in-law who excoriated her first for stealing her son and then for allowing him to die. Now I know that nothing balances the barrenness.

I drag myself to bed. I go through the motions of going to sleep. My eyes acknowledge their exhaustion, but my mind mocks it. I feel as though Pagan is dead to me and there are no words to express my grief. As my head pounds and my chest cramps, I lack even the analgesic of analogy. I console myself with the closest thing that I can find to her . . . the fleecy Bo Peep blanket from her cot. Although it has lost several sheep, it retains all its slops and spills and smells. How could it do otherwise when, despite every inducement, she refused to relinquish it to the wash? Now I am grateful for her obduracy. Each stain is a map of her childhood. Her comforter has become mine.

I awake to a vile game of postman's knock. Consuela brings me the mail, which includes a parcel. I open it to discover two coils of brown in a box. They emit such a putrid stench that, at first, I take them for decomposing rats. Then the truth hits me. I gulp . . . I gag; but I refuse to crack. I put on gloves and examine the specimens like a pathologist (although the disease is in the mind). There are no clues, not even a note, as if the connection speaks for itself . . . even a rat would have been less insulting. I flush away the contents, but I fail to expel the smell, which defies disinfectant to linger beneath my nails; I clip them to the quick. I try to picture the mental processes of the sender, but even the physical processes are beyond me. Was he – or she (I must make no assumptions) – at such a loss for words? Your mother was right; the art of letter-writing is dead.

I open the rest of the mail with foreboding; I have never been so grateful for an estate agent's speculative designs on the house. In fact, I find nothing but messages of support. The sole unwelcome note is sounded by Duncan Treflis who, from the respectability of the Garrick, sends me a membership card for the Stallion, a club which, on the evidence of its logo, caters to a rather different clientele. The scrawl, like the man, demands a disproportionate effort. I decipher 'A stable door that can be closed even after the horse has bolted' and determine not to reply.

Susan is screening my calls but lets through my mother. Her voice sounds as if it has been filtered through muslin: not soft but dead. I clasp at straws. There was a distribution problem; the *Nation* never reached North Wales. The straws give way in my hand.

'How are you keeping, Mother?'

'Poorly. My asthma has come back. The doctor says it's stress.'

'I thought that from New Year to Easter was your quiet time.'

'Oh, there's no one staying; that's one blessing. Mrs Coombes says we'll be lucky if we ever get any bookings again.'

'She's always a comfort.'

'She's been a good friend to me. She came in an hour early on Sunday morning to show me that paper.'

'Mrs Coombes reads the *Nation*?'

'Her Donald had rung with the news; he thought I should be warned.'

'I bet he did.'

'He was your best friend; he always asks after you.'

'He's two hundred pounds of prime malice. The only news he wants is bad news. He can't forgive me for having got out and made something of my life, while he's stuck there in a dead-end job and a dead-beat marriage.'

'What do you mean? He has four children. They've called the youngest after Enid.'

'Poor girl!'

'So what have I got? What have you? And don't go giving me Pagan.'

226

'I won't . . . I can't.'

'She had to read it out loud to me because I couldn't find my glasses. I came over so bad that I couldn't go to chapel. It's the first Sunday I've missed since your father's attack.'

'I'm sorry, truly.'

'Why didn't you warn me?'

'I knew nothing about it. It was hardly one of those A Day In The Life Of My Favourite Things In A Room Of My Own features. I was as shocked as you.'

'You are going to take them to court? They've no right to print such lies.'

'I think I've spent enough time in court lately. No one wins but the lawyers.'

'What about Elton Donovan; he won, didn't he?'

'It's not always that clear-cut. I may have met one of those men at a party.'

'At the BBC?'

'Who knows?'

'Then why did they pick on you? Why not Terry Wogan?'

'Because I'm gay, Mother. And don't pretend you don't know or that it's a bad line. It's hard for you and I'm sorry; but it's what I've been for twenty years, so nothing's changed.'

'What about Candida?'

'What about her?'

'You lived together all that time.'

'So?'

'It was a mockery.'

'No. Marriages may be mockeries, but not friendships. Marriages have to stick to the rules; friendships make up their own.'

'I don't know what to say.'

'Shall I ring you back when you've had a chance to think?'

'I always brought you up to know what was right; I always brought you up to know what was clean.'

'Oh yes, I remember' . . . I remember sitting in the kitchen reading library books in a pair of rubber gloves, because she was convinced that public pages spelt disease. She even sprinkled them with flea-powder, until she found that it brought on her asthma. 'I was as clean as a boy in an oxygen bubble.'

'So what happened?'

I bite my tongue as the bubble bursts. 'I grew up. I discovered life.'

'You discovered a lot of fancy ideas. What made you any different from Donald Coombes or any other boy? Your voice, that's what. I wept when the Bishop of Bangor called you an angel.'

'I grew up. I fell from grace.'

'This is what comes of all those books.'

'I've done nothing I feel ashamed of.' I struggle to convince myself as much as her. 'I've slept with a few men whom I wouldn't ask to dinner, but is that a sin?'

'Yes. I've never lied to you, Lenny, and I don't mean to start. It may not be a crime any more, but it's still a sin. That's the difference between God's law and ours; and all the fancy talk in Parliament can't change it. There's one truth, same as there has been for two thousand years. But, these days, everyone thinks they can pick and choose for themselves. They treat right and wrong like the sweet counter at Woolworth's. They want to serve themselves with life/God/the Bible –' she elides them in word as in spirit – 'just like they do with the coffee creams and the hazelnut clusters. "We'll take a few adulterers but no murderers, a few blasphemers but no thieves." But you can't pic'n'mix the Ten Commandments. You can't leave out the soft-centres. They all weigh the same to God.'

'No, they may have done to Moses, but Christ made distinctions.'

'What would you know about it? You don't even go to church.'

'Not now, but I did. Fifteen years of sermons leave their mark. A friend once gave me a pamphlet, *Christ's Words on Homosexuality*. I opened it like a tax demand. But I needn't have worried; every page was a blank.'

'We know you're very clever. You can twist anything; you can make black seem white. But, in your heart, you know what's right.'

'Exactly, it's my heart, not my conscience or my memory, but my heart.'

'What about mine? It's breaking, doesn't that count for

anything? I'm sixty-three. I don't ask much of life. Who knows how much time I have left? For twenty years I've had to care for your father and watch him grow as simple as a child. At least there's one consolation; he's been spared this.'

'Don't you think he might have understood?'

'Oh, very likely; when it was two of them – two of you – who did it to him.'

'Don't blame me. I didn't hit him. I wasn't even in the country.' I am guilty none the less, and of the utmost depravity, as I allow his attackers first to enact my desires and then to embody them.

'I know. Who was it who had to deal with everything?'

'You could have sent me a telegram.'

'I wanted you to have the chance to sing; I wanted you to enjoy Venice. How I wish I'd never heard of the place! I always knew that girl was out for no good. And so it's proved. Come home, son; come home, and we'll see this through together.'

'I can't, Mother. You haven't even asked about Pagan. In case you're interested, the judgment went against us.'

'I didn't need to ask. After that story –'

'I'm more than that story. I'm more than any story. I'm in despair.'

'You must never despair, Lenny. Do you think I've given in to despair in all these years with your father? He's alive. You must count your blessings. It's God's will.'

'That's codswallop!'

'I'm sending you a book. I got it from the new minister. He means well, even if he does want to make changes.'

'Let's hope it's nothing like the book the old minister gave me: Sex for Boys . . . no, sorry, Boys and Sex, complete with anatomical drawings by Picasso. For years, I expected women to have three breasts.'

'That's right; turn everything into a joke. You're not on television now.'

'Believe me, it was no joke.'

'Promise me, you'll read the book. It's full of true-life stories of men who've repented their sin and turned to Christ.'

'I promise that I'll read it; I can't promise that I'll turn.'

229

'I'm praying for you, Lenny; and so is Mrs Coombes. Whatever happens, you're still my son.'

There is no answer to that, so I put down the telephone and run my face under the tap. I curse myself for my craven capitulation to her tablets of stone/heart of stone morality. I should take a leaf out of your book, or, at least, a page from my Cambridge diary. The ferocity of your attacks not just on Christianity but on the whole concept of ethical values was deeply disturbing to a boy from North Wales who had grown up on a diet of chapel with everything. And yet, while I rejected your position, I admired your passion, which I try to recapture twenty years on.

'Christian morality is moribund. It should be thrown out like absolute monarchy and courtly love.' We are walking along the Backs after a lecture on T. S. Eliot.

'Throw out the history, throw out the mysticism, throw out Heaven and Hell if you like, but spare the Good Samaritan and the Prodigal Son.'

'I'm afraid it comes as a package, all-inclusive.'

'Then it's time to split it up. God's dead . . . Einstein exploded him; but right and wrong weren't destroyed in the blast. We're rational, sentient beings; we can create our own ethical code.'

'Based on what? One man's assassination is another man's murder, one man's property another's theft; promiscuity is one more than me . . . Did you say ethics or semantics?' You rip the leaves off a branch and scratch your hand.

'It doesn't have to be subjective. I believe that we're each born with an innate morality. It exists within us like the capacity for speech; it predates kisses and smacks and carrots and sticks. We may lose sight of it, but it's always there.'

'Where?'

'In that part of us that isn't separate, the part that connects to the earth, the part that says "we" not "I" and "love" not "give".'

'And exactly what part is that, Leo? The soles of our feet? Connected to the earth? Please! Why not admit it? All morality is just glorified self-interest; and Christian morality is the worst. "Thou shalt love thy neighbour as thyself." That says it all. Self ... self ... self. You don't steal my ox because you don't want me to steal yours.'

'No, I don't steal from you because I respect what's yours ... the feelings you have towards it.'

'Towards my ox, Leo? Whatever can you mean?'

'Be serious, can't you?'

'The only reason that you don't steal from me is that you're afraid of being punished, either here or in the hereafter. Morality is just the excuse made by people who are too weak to assert themselves in any other way.'

'No, there's another morality, one based not on paternal pressure but on fellow feeling, which has its roots in not wanting others to feel pain or to lose dignity. We respond to them; we put ourselves in their place.'

'In other words, selfishness.'

'No, sympathy. Imagination, not conscience, is our saving grace. That's why art – and, above all, literature – is more moral than any religion and we must tell children bedtime stories rather than teaching them bedtime prayers.'

'I take my hat off to you, Leo. You'll part the Red Sea next. You've remade morality in your own image and called it art.'

'I thought that you believed in art.'

'I believe in artifice; there's a subtle difference.'

'What's subtle about it?'

Your answer is lost as you drift away, down the tow-path and out of my memory. I am once again conscious of the room. I want you to see ... I want my mother to see how I have practised what I preach – no, what I propose – with Pagan. She learns how to behave through analogy not instruction; 'Thou shalt not ...' has been replaced by 'Imagine if ...' But the past has preoccupied me for too long, and, when I look up, it is time for lunch.

At three o'clock, Consuela summons me to the front door, where there is a boy asking for me and for money. All she can report is that he is 'a boy from school; very thin'. I presume that it must be the paper-boy; I fear that, in all the furore, I may have forgotten his Christmas box ... no wonder that the deliveries have been late. I go down, to discover an acned adolescent of about fourteen, in a purple shell-suit and a back-to-front cap.

'Sorry to bother you, mate. I'm just knocking on a few doors; I wonder if you can help us out with a few quid.'

'Are you my paper-boy?'

'What do you mean?' He seems nervous and looks out into the road.

'Are you in charge of my papers?'

'Fat chance. I ain't got nowhere to stay. Homeless me.'

'How old are you?'

'Old enough.' He grins cockily.

'I've no doubt. But you should be living with your parents. Or else in a hostel. Have you heard of the St Mungo Trust? I can give you the number.' An instinct of self-preservation prevents me from asking him in.

'Yeh, yeh,' he says impatiently. 'Been there, done that. All I'm asking is a few quid. A fiver for some food.'

'I'm not giving you any money.'

'Why not? You're on TV. You must be loaded.'

'Who are you?'

'Look, I'm sure we can come to some arrangement. Like you did with those other kids; know what I mean?' His crude wink accentuates his wall eye.

'Go away,' I shout. 'I'm not giving you a penny.'

'Fair enough,' he says and points to a car; 'they gave me a tenner for asking.' Following his fingers, I see two figures in the front seats: a man with a phone and a woman with a camera. He invites me to 'Have a nice one!' and runs into the road. I rush after him, only to trip over the bottom step. I taste the gravel. The photographer darts to the gate, but, far from coming to my aid, she snaps me supine in the path . . . no doubt, by the time it is printed, it will have become a gutter. She jumps into the car which speeds away. I drag myself indoors and, shrinking from Consuela's concern, grab a phone. I dial Print House and demand to speak to Brian Derwent. I am tossed from euphemism to excuse, until I finally reach the man himself. His tone of sugared menace feels as if an icing-horn has been plunged in my ear.

He claims ignorance of the photographer. I have to admit that she may have been from the *Sentinel* . . . but only because he did not think of it first. 'Can you tell me why you're persecuting me?'

'You're becoming paranoid, my friend. News is news:

232

you mustn't take it personally. If the *Nation* hadn't broken the story of those boys, the *Sun* or the *Sentinel* would. Wouldn't you rather keep it in the family?' He laughs without a trace of irony.

'On that basis,' I suggest, 'treachery would be preferable to an enemy attack.' But he will acknowledge no analogies except his own.

'If you take my advice, Leo, you'll keep your head down and this will all blow over. Don't go making too many phone calls. Today's headline is tomorrow's history; no one knows that better than me.'

'Thank you, Brian, but I intend to keep my head up, only from behind a different parapet. I'm writing to Ian Hastie to resign my *Criterion* column.'

'I wouldn't do anything rash.'

'Oh, but it's not rash. I've been plucking up the courage for years.'

I put down the phone with a flourish, but my elation fades as I become aware of the ache in my ankle. I call Consuela who proves to be a dab hand with a bandage. Immobility forces its own rhythm, and I spend the evening listening to a new recording of the *Missa Solemnis*. Consuela interrupts the Sanctus with the news of another young man at the door. I begin to fear that I will be plagued by an endless round of photogenic beggars and insist that, on no account, must she let any stranger into the house. 'No, this time,' she says, 'it is good . . . is your friend . . . is David.' I am taken aback for, although she volunteers no surname, there is no chance of confusion. I know a dozen Davids but only one who can be remotely described as young.

He walks into the room and fills it with so many lost possibilities. I make to stand but my leg is too painful. I prop it on the gout-stool like a plea for sympathy. The music swells to the heights of the Hosanna; I flick off the sound and am scared by the silence. I wait for him to speak.

'I don't usually barge in on people; but I wasn't sure that you'd want to talk to me. It's easier to slam down a phone than a door in a face.'

'I'd never slam anything in your face; it's one that I'm far too fond of.'

'I'm being serious.'

'So am I. Won't you sit down.' I indicate an armchair; but he keeps his distance, settling onto the sofa and casually crossing his legs. I am transfixed by the patch of pink between his turn-up and his sock.

'You're looking good.' His tactics are obvious.

'I'm growing old. As Candida says –'

'Says?'

'Used to say, you know you're growing old when your age exceeds your waistline.'

'You must have a very trim waist.'

'Thank you.' I refuse to be disarmed. 'Why have you come?'

'I had to after Sunday's paper. I'm afraid it's my fault. I set the ball rolling.'

'Maybe. But I think it's rolled about as far as it can. I suppose they might try to make out that I'm Lord Lucan or Shergar. . . .'

'Same old Leo.' Does he mean it as a compliment? 'You should publish your memoirs; you could call them *Smiling Through*.'

'As long as I'm free to plug them on a chat show. . . . Why did you do it, David? It's so unlike you.'

'No, it's so unlike how you think of me; that's different.'

'Did you really resent what I wrote about Candida?'

'Yes, but it wasn't because of that; and that bitch of a journalist knew it. What decided me was your Sigourney Weaver interview last summer. You asked how she dealt with accusations of being a lesbian . . . accusations! It's not a crime to be a lesbian, any more than it is to have red hair.' I smooth my parting.

'It was just shorthand.'

'The limitation of liberalism is always its language. Scratch a liberal and you'll find a dictionary of oppression underneath.'

'My mother used to tell me I'd swallowed the dictionary. Perhaps that was it.'

'I wanted to highlight media hypocrisy. Instead, they made it seem so trivial, like a jilted lover's revenge.'

'David . . . this is the most powerful print group in the country. Did you really think they'd agree to your agenda?'

'She seemed so sympathetic. She told me she knew Derek Jarman.'

'I can't believe that you'd be so naive. Far from endorsing your cause, they've used you to promote their own foul values. Do you suppose it was an accident that they held the story back for six months, only to run it a few weeks before I was due in court?'

'I know nothing about any court.'

'No, but they did . . . I've been locked in a custody battle for Candida's daughter. Their timing was perfect; at a stroke, they proved me to be unfit for both family viewing and family life. And would you care to hear the result?'

'Not really.'

'Surprise, surprise, I lost. Still, at least media hypocrisy was exposed.'

He moves towards me. I am overwhelmed by the smell of him: the fresh, doughy, hot-buttered-toast smell that is truly good enough to eat. I start to shake. He grips my shoulders; I shrug him off. He kneels on the floor and manoeuvres himself around my foot. He berates the *Nation*, the Court and his own folly. I suggest that he pour us some drinks, which he does, but, instead of bringing me mine, he returns to the sofa and balances both glasses on the arm. We exchange glances; his challenging, mine confused. I respond to the challenge, hauling myself up, hobbling across the room and sinking onto the seat beside him. 'That's better,' he says and lets his hand rest lightly on my thigh. My skin sizzles as though on fire.

I am disturbed that so casual a gesture should create such an impact. I strive not to misconstrue it and to remember his theory of 'non-intrusive touch'. I ask for a full account of his life, not his work – the Bush House bush telegraph has been buzzing – but his family, his friends, his lovers . . . the lightness of my tone is deceptive, for I am starting to entertain the most incongruous second-time-lucky hopes.

'Where should I begin?'

'Why not the lovers?' I smile to hide the blush.

'There's not that much to say. After we split up, I was determined to stay unattached . . . to hedge my bets – play the field. Then I met Cass on a meditation week in Devon. He was very spiritual. For a time, I got involved with a lot of New Age groups . . . you know the sort, "let's all sit in a circle on the floor and share our brains"; until, after a while, I began to feel that I had no brains left. Sleeping in a squat under a sign proclaiming "One man's meat is another man's toxin" didn't quite chime with life at the World Service. So I left and bought a flat in Brockley. Then, last year, I met Griffin, who's an opera critic.'

'Griffin Lennox?'

'The same.'

'I read his column; he writes well.' The hand on my thigh starts to feel like a cold compress.

'An opera queen was just about the last man I saw myself going out with. I've always held that Covent Garden is to the arts what the House of Lords is to democracy. But it's his passion and, I suppose, he's mine. He's helped me to grow in so many ways. He's very active in Queer politics.'

'Hence the tee-shirt.'

'It's about much more than tee-shirts!' He withdraws his hand. 'He's heavily into s and m. I can tell you disapprove; but that's because you hate sex. You consider it dark and disgusting and degrading. Why else do you waste yourself on rent-boys? It's weird; you assert the power of the imagination in every other aspect of life, but not sex. There, you insist that we must all stick to the strictest rules ... as though it's the only way you can deny your deviance. I've never understood why so many gay men try to adopt their own version of the missionary position, when most missionaries want to prevent them adopting any position whatsoever.'

'In my case, it's hypothetical.'

'Well it shouldn't be. For all your hang-ups, you're a very attractive man. I saw an ad in *Boyz* last year, from a young guy who was "looking for a Leo Young type". I cut it out to send you.'

'There was no need.' Two less considerate friends have already rectified the omission ... and supplied the context: 'Young man seeking uncle to pamper me. Must be solvent. Leo Young type preferred.' 'It'd be like the *New Statesman* competition for a Graham Greene parody in which Greene himself only managed to come third.'

'You'd come first, Leo; believe me.'

He leaves me with an expansive hug and a profound sense of emptiness which is unrelieved by our arrangement to meet for lunch next week. He has aroused feelings that I have suppressed for years. How long is it since I have had any sense of myself as a man, rather than as a collection of mannerisms – the cocked forefinger, the tutting teeth, the staccato laugh – that render me screen-sized, fit for the bi-weekly bite? The bow tie and the horn-rimmed spectacles of the opening titles may be instantly identifiable, but I am struck by the fact that there is no face in-between.

I throw myself into my work with such zeal that Kaye and Vicky each report the other's fear that I am overdoing it. They insist that I have nothing to prove. My position with the programme is secure; ratings are sustained and even Disgusted of Tunbridge Wells has stayed silent. I am grateful for their concern, which is, nevertheless, mis-placed. My aim is not to prove myself but to protect myself . . . who knows what demons lurk in the blank pages of a diary? I determine to keep them at bay and embark on a hectic round of lunches, launches, first nights and private views. Pain is absorbed in champagne, as I enter a world where time is replaced by fashion. I swap small talk and finger food with people whom I have avoided for years.

Once a fortnight, I become a father. I regain my sense of purpose on the road to Brighton; only to watch it fade on the journey back. Pagan has grown so distant. Her visits feel as formal as school trips; with treats turning into chores which she listlessly endures. She seems indifferent to the prospect of returning home, greeting my questions with evasions and talking more to her teddy bears than to me. Even bedtime brings few confidences. I ask about her new friends ('boring'), teachers ('boring'), neighbours ('bor-ing') and grandparents ('I'm tired'). To my dismay, I realise that she no longer trusts me; instead of her all-loving Leo, I am another adult liar. I cannot blame her; like everyone else, I have betrayed her. The only way that I can prove my good faith is in court.

The appeal is heard on Maundy Thursday in the Thomas More building in the Royal Courts of Justice – all of which I find ironic. Protocol is surprisingly informal. The one excitement is that, at last, the revue artist has the chance to dress up. I fear that he fails to do it justice . . . the ill-fitting wig on top of the mop of curly hair has a distinct air of robing-room improvisation; although it may be in

237

protest at his continued lack of lines. I am equally frustrated by my role in the proceedings. There is no new evidence; neither I nor any witnesses are called. Rebecca simply argues that Judge Flower misused his discretion, attaching too much weight to my sexuality and not enough to the stability of the relationship. Your parents' Counsel counters that my sexuality is itself a threat to stability. The Judges retire to confer. I have a firm belief that there will be safety in numbers . . . but I am forgetting the stranglehold of the old-school tie. It scars them for life and cuts off their supply of compassion; they are wracked with guilt for what they did as boys. Their disgust distorts their judgement . . . and their judgment is unanimous. The appeal is dismissed with costs.

Those costs, in Max's rough estimate, will be around £10,000 . . . £6000 for me and £4000 for your parents. 'Adding invoice to injury,' I parry the blow with a quip, but he fails to respond. Or insult to injustice. I keep that one to myself. I feel like the man who received a bill for the gas that escaped in the explosion that blew up his house. It was only when he appeared on my show that they withdrew the final demand.

'It may take a while to raise the cash,' I warn him. 'In the past month, I've had two personal appearances cancelled. Rent-boys and superstores just don't mix. I guess I'll have to wait until they build a Soho Sainsburys.' This time I raise a smile.

'What I admire most about you, Leo, is that you never give in. Whatever else you may lose, you keep your sense of humour.'

It is easier to hide what I feel than to express it. I am bereft even of words. Friends make the appropriate noises and pull compassionate faces; they rally round – or, at least, they expect me to rally – but they cannot begin to comprehend my loss. They require simple shorthand like 'widow' and 'orphan' to engage their sympathies and ease their minds. They regard my 'once a fortnight's as a reasonable allowance. Laura declares that I will have more free time in a holiday weekend than in any two working weeks . . . as though time can be counted in hours. Edward tells me horror stories of a friend whose ex-wife has remarried and exiled their children to New York . . . as though distance can be measured on maps. Melissa blithely equates banishment with boarding school . . . as though my sanity can be saved by the bells of Mallory Towers.

I have not felt so empty since the morning of your miscarriage. I try to black out the image, but it multiplies as on the screens in a studio control room. As I close my eyes, I see you stumble into my bedroom, your hand to your belly, your vagina an open wound . . . as I open my eyes, I awake to another nightmare; the blood seeping through your night-dress, the clots sticking to your legs. You lie prostrate on the floor. I try to lift you, but my hands slide in the sweat and the slime. Disconnected thoughts rush through me: doctor . . . no, funeral . . . no, ambulance. By the time it arrives, you are delirious, imploring me to forgive you and wailing that this is your punishment for aborting our child.

With blood on my hands, I fear misunderstanding. I want to make it clear to the men that the abortion was Lewis's, the convalescence mine. I no longer court ambiguity; I could never cause a woman such pain. But they are too busy negotiating the stairs to pay heed to your rambling. When they ask, I admit to being the father to prevent them dismissing me as a friend. . . . Friends do not shiver by your stretcher in a pyjama jacket and corduroy trousers; they are left at home, biting their nails by the phone. Friends are not raced to hospital with sirens blaring like a film chase; they amble in during visiting hours bearing flowers. And yet, as I watch you convulsed by contractions, I wish that I had claimed to be a lodger . . . a burglar . . . anything to be anywhere but here.

At the hospital, we are admitted straight to obstetrics. I can barely keep pace with the trolley and break into a trot. I follow you into the ward, where I stand helpless, while the doctor and midwife jab and scan and attach you to a drip. As you rasp and rave, I plead with the doctor for something to ease your pain; he tells me to take your hand while you push. I feel the force swelling inside you, digging through your nails to my skin. Then, suddenly, it is over; I am aware of a bubble of sound and of moisture. I stare at the wall. I do not want to see what has spilt out of you. I just want to know that you are safe. The midwife jabs you

again and asks if you wish to hold your baby; you screech
'no' in a voice as raw as your flesh.

You jerk your head as I stroke your hair. The midwife
insists that I leave you to rest and directs me to the quiet
room, where I sit flicking aimlessly through a book of
remembrance. Five minutes later, she appears with a
cloth-covered basket. I presume that she has brought me
some fruit and allow myself to feel hungry. 'Your wife
doesn't want to see him,' she says, 'but I was sure that you
would. It's so important to give yourself time to grieve.'
Then, she takes out this perfectly formed . . . form – I don't
want to think of it as a baby – and slips it into my hand. It is
no bigger than my palm; and yet everything is in place
except the eyes . . . the starkly staring swellings of its fused
eyes. And, as she spouts her empty homilies, I glimpse an
image of my destiny: to stand, the phantom father of a
miscarried child.

# Three

# The Origins
# of the Specious

*In the first of two articles, the writer and broadcaster* **Leo Young** *reflects on his trial by tabloid and the deep-rooted homophobia of our society.*

The English vice is not flagellation or pederasty but hypocrisy. Earlier this year, when researchers from my chat show were looking for survivors of sex scandals willing to discuss their ordeals, they found a positive embarrassment of heterosexuals – adulterous ministers, kerb-crawling colonels and promiscuous priests – eager to receive the ultimate rehabilitation: absolution on air. The homosexuals – I'm sorry, bisexuals – were less forthcoming. None of the MPs caught in cinemas, actors in lavatories or bishops in seminaries would contemplate a public confession; they knew that theirs was the one sin which even a clap-happy studio audience would be unable to forgive.

I myself have felt the jagged edge of this hypocrisy. It must be common knowledge, even to readers of this august journal, that, in recent months, various tabloids have vied to reveal details of my sexuality. I have been propelled from the listings to the front pages, with my private life a matter of public prurience (how the Editors square their graphic and gratuitous reporting with their commitment to a family readership is not for me to say).

It may seem disingenuous to be shocked by such attention, but, as the presenter of a chat show, it is easy to forget that you too come under scrutiny. The primary role of the host is to ask questions; he is the audience's conduit to celebrity ... indeed, he is constantly exhorted to efface

243

his own personality and censured should he interject too much. And yet, at the same time, he is expected to be a 'personality'. It is his programme; he may well be better known than many of those he interviews. And he is subject to that peculiarly contemporary form of iconoclasm: the urge to prove that every public figure has not just feet but genitals of clay.

One result of my exposure has been requests to appear on several rival chat shows; all of which I have declined, but for reasons of policy rather than funk . . . no one knows better than I the uncanny ability of a studio audience to turn conversation into performance art. Instead, I have taken the opportunity to quiz myself . . . with far more rigour than I would dare to apply to any of my guests. And, while it may seem odd for someone who is more familiar as a face than as a by-line to present his personal credo in the pages of a newspaper, the choice does have a certain symmetry.

Conventional wisdom declares that it is in a crisis that you come to know your friends . . . personal experience confirms this; and I have been heartened to find that,

amongst mine, I can count over five hundred viewers who have been moved to send letters of support. The obverse is that you come to know your enemies; and I have also received razor blades, a noose and excrement. Any old television hand is hardened to hate mail – my secretary has a policy never to show me anything addressed in green ink – but it is rarely specific (I still cherish one envelope with the instruction 'If undelivered, please direct to Terry Wogan'). This particular batch, however, harps on a single theme (which could not be directed to Terry Wogan): my sexuality. I am no longer a person, nor even a personality, but simply a penis.

It may be possible to know my enemies, but it is far harder to identify them, since the one – the only – word that almost all such correspondents fight shy of writing is their name. Nevertheless, it is essential to understand them. After eight years of prize-winning broadcasts, I am told that I pollute the airwaves. Is it asking too much to ask why? Am I behaving differently towards my guests? Are actors no longer safe when they sit next to me on the sofa? Is there propaganda in my posture? Or do they fear that I am giving off subliminal messages the way that their predecessors found subversion in pop songs played at slow speeds? (As an experiment, try videoing a programme and freeze-framing it to read 'gay is good' on my lips.)

The analogy may be absurd, but it is no more so than their arguments. They bring to mind those of a Texan evangelist whom I interviewed, years ago, for a documentary on Dallas. He deplored the influx of Mexicans with their Catholic faith and Spanish language. 'If English was good enough for Jesus Christ,' he said, 'it's good enough for us.' The eccentricity was almost endearing; until one remembered the murder rate among recent immigrants.

Homophobia is equally ridiculous and equally lethal. The homophobe, like the fundamentalist, finds it impossible to accept that any other history, any other culture, any other viewpoint than his own exists (expedience justifies the pronoun; for the purpose of this article, I focus on men). Of the hundreds of phobias, from arachno- to zeno-, there is a key ingredient which makes homophobia the most insidious. Whereas its fellows are fears of the 'other', it is fear of the 'same' . . . of the 'self'. Sufferers hate no one so much as themselves. They are disgusted by their own desires; but, rather than acknowledge or explore them, they yearn to be rid of them. So they seek to be purified by women . . . a search that is doomed to failure, not least because of the contradictions in their attitude to women (who are seen as both superior for not having men's desires and inferior for desiring men). It is often said that you can only truly love someone else if you love yourself; I would go further and, at the risk of misinterpretation, say that a man can only truly love a woman if he can love a man.

The phobia that homophobia most resembles is agoraphobia. The homophobe wants to stay safe – supposedly safe – within the familiar concepts of his closed

245

mind rather than opening himself to new thoughts and larger realities. His symptoms are varied; from the man who bashes you in person to the man who does it by proxy . . . from the man who sends you shit in the post to the man who does it from a great height and metaphorically. The latter often wears a horsehair wig; like the high court Judge who, in August 1992, gave a child molester a suspended sentence for the rape of a nine-year-old girl, describing it as 'a breath of fresh air' since he had previously abused two young boys and was afraid that he might be gay.

This belief in the homophobe's self-hatred is what separates me from those who see every queerbasher as a queer at heart (the theory being that he kicks your face in to stop himself kissing it). I maintain that every queerbasher is a queerbasher at heart, who, far from expressing hidden desire for another man, is revealing his deep revulsion from himself, and that gay men who read anything more into it are displaying, at best, naivety and, at worst, dangerous fantasy (the desire to be roughed up by rough trade). Self-hatred also prompts the homophobe's aversion to the least sign of gay affection, since even he

cannot seriously believe that a tentative kiss between two soap-stars will turn little Johnny gay. After all, many thousands of screen kisses from Scarlett's and Rhett's to Charles's and Diana's have done nothing to reclaim me.

One thing about gay men that homophobes do find secretly attractive is our imagination. From puberty onwards, we stand at one remove from the world. We have to transform heterosexual myths (whether Scarlett and Rhett or Charles and Diana) in order to create images to sustain ourselves. At street level, this produces 'camp', with its unique, double-edged double vision, at once frivolous and hard-hitting . . . the limp wrist in the iron glove; on a more elevated plane, it creates art (as elevated as the ceiling of the Sistine Chapel) and accounts for the disproportionate number of gay men who feature in every list of the world's cultural giants.

Another attraction that gay men hold for homophobes is our freedom. In castigating our 'irresponsibility', the homophobe attacks that which he most desires. Society trains men from birth to take certain roles. Pinstripes, overalls or uniforms are all variations on the same strait-jacket. The captives resent the Houdinis who are able to escape. You need only see a father cradling his baby son to be aware of his capacity for love and then see them again ten years later to be aware of how much has been lost. The former babe in arms is kept firmly at arm's length.

And yet even the attractions of imagination and freedom pall besides the homophobe's perception that the gay man is having more sex than him . . . to the homophobe, the gay man's sole identity is sexual, since it is that which sets him apart. The homophobe at once wants sex and denies it. He fears his body as much as he does the darkness of his desires. In this, he is tutored by two thousand years of Christian tradition, which takes as its first commandment not 'Thou shalt love the Lord thy God' but *'Noli me tangere'*; a primacy further discredited by recent discoveries that the phrase itself may well be a mistranslation and what we read as 'Don't touch me' should in fact be 'Don't cling to me'. . . . The Church's one foundation is condemned.

In the Christian tradition, sexuality is set at the service of procreation; the charge against homosexuals is that we use it for recreation. Time and again, fundamentalists and their fellow-morallers liken gay men to beasts. But surely the reverse is true? It is gay men who have moved furthest from sex as a biological imperative and hence from the animals. And, if fundamentalists refuse to consider the beams in their own eyes, they should at least look to the motes in their myths. There are as many different sexualities as there are people and there have been since the Garden of Eden. . . . I recall a friend's reply to a bannered bigot proclaiming that 'God created Adam and Eve not Adam and Steve'. 'Oh Eve,' he taunted, 'wasn't she the world's first snake act?'

The *'Noli me tangere'* tendency constantly yokes sex and violence as the Scylla and Charybdis of contemporary society, when, in fact, the two are polar opposites. Sex is about giving pleasure – however inadequate – not pain. There may be bad sex, but there is no such thing as good violence . . . and, in the case of sexual violence, the emphasis rests squarely on the noun. Gay men are frequent victims of sexual violence and yet they continue to be regarded as its instigators, both directly and indirectly ('they bring it on themselves'), along with women who wear short skirts or travel by tube at night.

Homophobia, whether latent or blatant, is a sickness which poisons the perpetrator even as it assaults the victim. It remains the one prejudice that dares to shout its name. Thus it is that, far from homosexuality being a social ill, it is the acceptance of homosexuality that marks a society's health. When I first read Christopher Isherwood's assertion that he judged every political party and government by its treatment of gay people, I deplored his limited vision. After experiencing the horrors of homophobia, both individual and institutional, I am convinced that he was right.

*Next week: the eternal romance between gay men and straight women and the homosexual as family man.*

*The Observer*, 6 June 1993

# Exploding
# the Nuclear Family

*In the second of two articles, the writer and broadcaster **Leo Young** declares war on hetero- sexual exclusivity and neo-Victorian values.*

S ome of my best friends are heterosexual . . . so I regret that my article last week should have been taken as a blanket attack on straight men [*See Letters Page 22*]; it was intended as nothing of the kind. My own experiences of the past few months have, however, con- vinced me that homophobia is latent even in the most liberal men. And, although I remain grateful for the sup- port of friends and col- leagues, I am aware that they have granted me as a favour what they themselves assume by right.

The one aspect of gay life that all heterosexual men view with suspicion is our relationship with heterosex- ual women. Wary of any inti- macy that is not based on bed, they suppose that the bond between gay men and straight women must be equally sexual, founded not on intercourse but on lust. By claiming that our mutual interest in men is what binds us, their pride – although not their curiosity – is satisfied. Such an attitude is, itself, a prime example of why women turn to gay men. They may sleep with straight men, but they can talk to us. Besides, if shared desire is all, how do these men explain their own antipathy to les- bians? Far from making com- mon cause, they regard them as material for pornographic fantasies and sexist jokes.

It was when I started mak- ing friends at university – rather than making the best of those who had been thrown in my path – that I learnt to value my relationships with women. One, in particular, with the photographer Can- dida Mulliner, became the

249

fulcrum of my life. We first met in Venice, in a chance encounter which, if I had faith, I would call fate. We shared our lives for nearly twenty years; and, although she died eighteen months ago, she remains my prime confidante. I report to her on everything and (I am aware that the admission courts derision) gain strength from her replies.

While Candida and I were always honest with each other, we were less so in our dealings with the world at large ... a deceit which I perpetuated by what I wrote after her death. I should stress that I never lied, but then there was no need. After centuries of ambiguity, the English language offers scope enough for evasion. My assumption that my sexuality was a private concern was not shared by the thugs of the tabloid press, who smeared it all over their front pages. I see now that no one's sexuality can be private when, by his silence, that of others weaker than himself is threatened. The truth is that Candida and I enjoyed an all-embracing and yet non-sexual love. Hollywood may have eroticised the relationships of Christopher Isherwood and Sally Bowles or Cole and Linda Porter; the rest of us should acknowledge them for what they were.

It is ironic that the very people who condemn gay men for founding their lives on their sexual preferences should feel threatened by a relationship that is asexual. When an American comedian claimed that women, by kissing their gay friends, were importing AIDS into the heterosexual community (Is this the Mary Magdalene kiss to rival the Judas one?), he was resorting to the age-old practice of using a joke to attack what he was unable to understand. Words can be weapons and just as they have long been directed at gay men, so they are now used against their women friends; whether it be the English 'fag hag', with its hard-toned hints of Morgan Le Fay, or, even worse, the American 'fruit-fly', which makes the woman sound parasitical and the man putrid.

My relationship with Candida may not have been protected by law or respected by language, but it was no less real or potent or committed. It was not an escape from sexual relationships, still less a parody of one. It was resented both by her men friends and (I have to admit) by my boyfriend; and yet its supreme strength was the quality of its love. It was not a love without issue; for, despite all the gleeful-gloomy

250

predictions of my lonely old age – the sterile senility which is seen as the just reward for a misspent youth – we had a daughter. I say we, although I am not the child's natural father. For years, I jibed at Candida's refusal to say who was, but I have finally understood her reasons. She was intensely superstitious (remaining on palm-crossing terms with several fortune-tellers); it is as if she had a premonition of her death and wanted to pre-empt disputes. She was determined that her child should be mine.

I know that there are many who consider this to be the height of irresponsibility, and I have no doubt that their objections would have been stronger still in the case of a boy. If gay men did not exist, society would have to invent us . . . by stigmatising strangers, it conceals the far greater dangers that lurk within the home. Far from threatening the family, we are its prime defence . . . a smokescreen to obscure the prevalence of paternal abuse. Even Freud, who first unearthed the evidence, chose to treat it as infantile fantasy for fear of offending his wealthy patrons. He knew not to go a taboo too far. We would do well to learn from other cultures, such as the Mohave Indians in America, where homosexuals are traditionally placed in charge of children: a role for which they are felt to have special aptitude.

Candida's hope of avoiding disputes was thwarted and her daughter has been removed from my charge. This is not the place to inveigh against what I regard as a gross injustice; but I should like to examine the forces that underlie it. I have recently received a pamphlet from a group calling itself Focus On The Family, which claims that 'In the increased tolerance of homosexuality lies the greatest danger to the survival of civilisation'. This begs the question not only of the vast number of homosexuals whose work stands at the heart of civilisation (avoiding the familiar roll-call of artists and philosophers, I would single out the mathematician Alan Turing, without whose code-breaking skills 'civilisation as we know it' might have fallen to Hitler) but of why the boundaries against barbarism must always be drawn in the bedroom. Surely the ever-worsening problems of homelessness, nationalism or Third

World debt – to take three glaring examples – represent a greater threat to civilisation than society's tolerance of two men making love?

I too would like to focus on families and on the place of gay people within them. Families are bigger than conventional definitions. As adoptive parents know, they are not limited to those who share your blood; as stepparents know, they are not limited to those who share your name; as homosexuals know, they are not just about procreation . . . a view that is as outdated as that of the nineteenth-century politicians who wished to restrict adult suffrage to those who had a stake in the land. The struggle for the right to a family is as pertinent at the end of the century as the struggle for the right to vote was at the start.

We are frequently exhorted by politicians and pundits to reassert family values. What are family values about if not love? Is that solely the province of two parents with two cars and two point four children . . . or of their counterparts with two point four servants a hundred years ago? Survey upon survey has shown that the rise in single-parent families has no bearing on the

rise in crime and yet rightwing politicians continue to link them. Another recent survey has exposed the myth that teenage girls become pregnant in order to jump council housing-lists and yet it is still put forward by people who have never been near a council house except during an election campaign (which explains why they persist in regarding a fifteenth-floor flat in a tower block as a coveted prize).

To give their sophistry authority, these politicians claim historical precedent and call their values Victorian. That may satisfy their yearning for a golden age of imperial power and social hierarchy, but, as historians have shown, the idea of the ideal Victorian family is an illusion. In 1861, for instance, at the height of Victoria's reign, sixty per cent of first children were born out of wedlock; and, as for Victorian child care, it was not until 1885 – a mere two years before the Queen's Golden Jubilee – that the age of consent was raised from twelve to sixteen. The proposal provoked outrage in the House of Lords, where peers declared that they had long enjoyed access to this 'unripe fruit' and demanded the same rights for their sons.

There is currently much talk of the problems posed by the break-up of extended families. I maintain that gay men and women are those extended families ... we are brothers and sisters, uncles and aunts, and, not infrequently, fathers and mothers. But, instead of opening its heart and mind to acknowledge our contribution, society prefers to exclude us. Mrs Thatcher famously – fatuously – spoke of 'pretended families'; but the true pretence is the perfect nuclear family. Now that all other nuclear protections have been exploded, is it not time to explode this one too?

In fact, the rush of reactionary politicians to shore up the 'traditional' family is a sure sign of its obsolescence; a decline that is inevitable since the very forces that led to its creation – the rise of capitalism and the need for a stable work-force – are themselves threatened by the flexibility of modern capitalism and an economy that no longer requires so many jobs. And yet, afraid to confront new ideas and structures, conservatives (both large and small) are fighting a rearguard action to defend the status quo, retreating behind rusty ideologies which buckle under the strain.

To return to the language of my post-bag: homosexuals are not freaks or perverts; our increased visibility over the past thirty years might best be described as a process of normalising the natural. There is still a great deal to be done; the ghetto is no answer to the closet. A Buddhist monk once told me that the purpose of existence is not to strive to become perfect but to strive to become human ... the whole life is the holy life. In which case, just as the integration of all the aspects of one's own personality is the key to a healthy life, so the integration of all its members is the key to a healthy society. Exclusion risks unleashing the twin forces of repression and revolution. This is why, although gay people may be a minority, securing our rights is not a minority concern. Homophobes must confront their prejudice and liberals their privilege to ensure that we are not merely tolerated on the fringes of society but are enabled to take our places at the heart of family life.

*The Observer*, 13 June 1993

# 1

I rap your father's head against the door . . . a personalised knocker seems such a strange – and telling – retirement present.

'Who is it?' your mother calls superfluously.

'Leo Young.'

'It's not five o'clock yet.' She slams the window shut. I shuffle on the mat with its inappropriate wording. This is absurd. Do they intend to keep to the letter of our agreement and the chime of the clock? I gain momentary satisfaction from switching the tail of their fretwork cow from 'No milk today' to 'Six pints please', until the futility of the gesture overwhelms me. Your mother opens the door. 'I'm prepared to make an exception this time, but it really is most tiresome. An arrangement is an arrangement.' I look at my watch. It is four fifty-four.

'Is Pagan ready?'

'Patience!'

'I beg your pardon?' Even after three months of forced fortnights, I am not expecting this degree of rudeness.

'Patience. We have no Pagan here.' For one flesh-creeping moment, I take her at her word, but reassurance appears at the top of the stairs.

'I told you to stay in your room until I called you, miss.'

'I want to see Leo.' The miss in question darts down the stairs and throws herself into my hug.

'Must you make such an exhibition of yourself? Whatever will Uncle think?'

255

'What did you mean "we have no Pagan here"?' I ask, although I fear that I am beginning to understand.

'We don't, do we, Patience? We have a new name, or rather a name . . . since Pagan's not so much a name as an act of defiance.'

'You have no right!' I rage.

'We have every right. Patience has started a new school . . . begun a new chapter.'

'It's monstrous. A name isn't just a tag on a uniform. It's how she thinks of herself.'

'And more importantly, how others think of her. What's Pagan? Drugs and drums and child sacrifice. Whereas Patience is a virtue . . . an opera.'

'And a card game for old women so lonely that they have no one to cheat but themselves.'

'I hate it,' Pagan says.

'Nonsense! You're far too young to hate anything.'

'This is the height of cruelty.'

'*Pas devant.*'

'What?'

'*Pas devant l'enfant,*' she insists in her worst wogs-begin-at-Calais tone. 'Patience dear, will you see that you have everything ready for the weekend?'

'I've already seen it.'

'Would you like to come into the living room?' she asks me. She turns to Pagan. 'Remember what happened to Miss Answer-back!'

I walk into the room where every cushion is plumped, every fringe primped and every surface polished, and recall your story of the royal visit for which your father told his groundsmen to whitewash the coal. He now sits, with his face concealed behind a newspaper like a cornered husband in a farce.

'Father,' your mother calls, 'Mr Young is here.'

He greets me gutturally, stands and holds out his hand. On a glance from your mother, he reconsiders and scratches his head. She picks up the paper, shakes it, folds it and places it in a rack marked Magazines.

'I've been explaining to Mr Young about Patience.'

'I heard,' your father confesses. 'We thought it for the best, old man. Not much of a change, really. Just a few letters but they make all the difference. You'll soon get the hang of it. Fairly trips off the tongue.' I think of how, despite every entreaty, my mother never came to terms with Leo. Now I am glad of the occasional Lenny; it is a passport to a vanished world. Will I be the only Pagan-speaker? Will I rule myself out of her present and become a relic of her past, by turns obsolete and quaint? 'We had little choice. It was hard enough getting her into St Andrew's in the middle of the year. If it weren't for Mother sitting on the preservation committee with the Headmistress. . . .'

'She thought that the name might be disruptive.'

'Of what?'

'There was a lot of disquiet among parents when she let in a boy called Saddam.'

'He doesn't eat food; he sits on a bench in the corridor,' Pagan interjects. 'I wish I could.'

'Don't you like the food?' I ask.

'It tastes like poison.'

'What a thing to say! Think of all the little black girls who are starving.'

'Apart from the food, are you enjoying it more?'

'I hate it. I want to go back to Miss Lister's.'

'She's just had a few teething problems.'

'Miss Hewson pulled my tooth out with a piece of cotton.' She flashes a lop-sided grin. 'Then I put it under the pillow, but the fairies only gave me a pee.'

'Ten pee.'

'The hotel fairies gave me a pound. I thought seaside fairies were kinder.'

'Ten pee is quite enough for one tooth, young lady,' your father says. 'What do the fairies want with your mouldy old molar?'

'They can sell it.'

'Who to? Would you like something from someone else's mouth?' He leers at her.

'I would if I was old.' She turns to me. 'He has no teeth. He takes them out like a trick and snaps them and . . . ' she falls silent.

'Really, Edgar! What on earth possessed you to do that?' I am cheered by this sign of dissension.

'I was just trying to buck her up; she looked glum.'

I repel the image of your father stripped to the gums and return to the matter in hand. 'What teething problems?'

'Settling down, making friends, obeying her teachers: that sort of thing. It's a traditional school which believes in the three "r"s.' To listen to your father, you would think that she learnt nothing at Cottesmore Gardens but potato-prints and plasticine.

'Patience has to realise that she's not as special as she thinks she is,' your mother adds.

'What nonsense! What do you mean?'

'Of course she's special to us. I mean in regard to other children. Her teachers say that she fails to concentrate. She answers back; she's a disruptive influence.'

'I'm amazed. There've never been any problems before. Her general reports were excellent. And her drawing was considered exceptional.'

'Ah, drawing,' your mother says.

'Drawing,' your father echoes.

'There's been too much drawing.'

'She's six years old!'

'I won a prize for my painting last week,' a small voice speaks out.

'That's wonderful. Do you have it here?'

'They wouldn't buy it.' Her eyes water. 'It was for the dolphins. Everyone else had someone to buy theirs and they didn't win.'

'So that's what all this is about?' your mother says. 'All this fuss over a little picture.'

'It wasn't little. It was of me and Leo.'

'So it shouldn't have been eligible for a prize. You were supposed to paint your family. The others chose mummies and daddies and dogs. How do you think that Grandpa and I felt to see a picture of a little girl – if it was a little girl, I really couldn't tell – staring at a head in a box?'

'It was a television!'

'It made me shiver.'

'I'd like to buy it, if I may.'

'You can't,' she says sadly, 'they've pulled it off the wall.'

We return to London, pursued by your mother's strict injunction against my attempting to unsettle Pagan. She insists that she has no wish to question the Court's decision, and yet she cannot help feeling that it has been far too liberal in allotting my weekends; no sooner have they accustomed her to her new routine than I reintroduce her to the past. . . . She need not worry. Pagan appears to view the prospect with indifference, as she sits listlessly in the car, rubbing breathy drawings on the glass. She disdains all her favourite songs, leaving me to accompany the teddy bears on their picnic and Cliff Richard on his summer holiday alone.

Her arrival is marked by none of the extensive toy- and doll-kissing of previous visits. She even shrinks from Consuela, squirming out of her embrace on the grounds that the smell of onions on her apron is making her cry. She opts out of her prandial guessing-game and, on hearing that we are having tortilla, shows neither pleasure nor surprise; until the sight of Consuela's pained face prompts her to relent and confide that she too is learning to cook.

'For school?'

'No, in the kitchen. *She –*' the word 'Granny' is still taboo – 'taught me how to make jam tarts. But she wouldn't let me taste them except the broken ones. She said they were for her ambulance. I said people who weren't well won't be hungry. She said they were to sell. . . . I hope no one buys them and they go green.'

Consuela's offer to bake a cake which she can eat elicits no reaction. I take her into the living room, where she shuns her customary place on my knee in favour of a space under the seat of my armchair. I suspect that she is angling for a game of hide-and-seek, although there would be precious little mystery about where to find her; but she rejects the suggestion and insists that I stay where I am. She crouches with her face to the floor and clings to my ankles, as though they were the bars of a cage. She chatters to herself, rebuffing my response with the charge that it is naughty to listen. When I ask whether she feels cramped, she replies that she feels 'safe'.

She returns to her refuge after dinner and settles down to watch television. It seems that your parents limit her viewing in the early evening and ban it completely after 7 p.m. 'They won't even let me switch on you, cos they say I see too much of you already.' At the risk of extending the gulf between the 'no' of Hove and the 'yes' of Holland Park, I allow her to watch her fill . . . which she does through the

259

frame of my calves. Her one distraction is the arrival of Trouble, although even he fails to arouse the expected enthusiasm.

'Would it hurt if we cut off Trouble's tail?'

'What do you think? It's not like clipping his fur . . . more like chopping off a leg.'

'Are there some cats who don't have tails?'

'Yes. Ones from the Isle of Man.'

'When Trouble dies, will you buy one of those?'

'Trouble's not going to die. He's only five years old . . . younger than you. No one's going to die . . . is that what's worrying you? Besides, a cat has nine lives.'

'I don't like tails! I don't like tails!'

I try to make sense of her vehemence. The next morning, the evidence is at once clearer and more confusing. After disturbing me twice in the night – and not merely by waking me – she rouses me with a series of scrapes and slams and thuds. I rush to her room, which looks as if it has been visited by the drug squad. Dolls are eviscerated and fluffy animals vivisected; books are spineless and favourite toys smashed. A clockwork goose, accidentally animated, waddles across the floor. I am unsure which shocks me more: the devastation, or the sight of its perpetrator, cowering in a corner, waiting to be smacked. I do what I can to reassure her. I hold out my arms, but she shies away. As I try to fathom why she should have destroyed her most cherished possessions, my only clue is the memory of you shearing your entire wardrobe after the abortion. I dismiss it as an irrelevance and question her. She says nothing except 'she's a bad girl; she's a bad girl'; as though her identity were slipping from her grasp.

I call Consuela to clear the mess. She crosses herself and speaks at speed in Spanish. I take Pagan into the bathroom. She is uncharacteristically coy and I suspect your mother's influence. She will no longer let me help her wash or see her without her clothes. 'It's rude,' she insists, and I think better of arguing. She is too young for such modesty; the distinctions of male and female should be subsumed in those of adult and child. Your mother, with her antiseptic notions of purity, is going the fastest way towards destroying it. By trying to guard against the threat of sex, she is putting the thought in her mind. Pagan will grow up like a convent girl bathing in her shift and her shame. . . . And yet what if it is not repression but reaction? What if someone has made her hate her own body by imposing his? As I bring her back to her bedroom to dress, I voice my fears.

'Darling, no one is in any way . . . hurting you, are they?'

'What sort of hurt?'

'Any sort. Is anyone at school or at home, a friend or a grown-up, hitting you or hurting you or touching you in any way that they shouldn't?' I am lost in the Moscow metro, unable to read the map.

'She's a bad girl. So bad.'

'That's not true. We all lose our tempers and break things . . . grown-ups too. Married people throw plates at each other. You must have seen them on TV.'

'Married, like *them*?'

'Like lots of people. So it's not important; we'll buy some new toys. What is important is that no one's doing anything to you that they shouldn't, anything that's . . . rude. You told me before that you were a big girl and could bath yourself. Is that what you do in Hove, or do Granny and Grandpa help you?'

'I'm a big girl.'

'Yes, of course. Though it's alright with Granny. She's another girl . . . woman.'

'No, it's still rude.'

'So, she never goes into the bathroom with you . . . and Grandpa neither?'

'Cruel Leo, making all these questions. My head hurts. I'm hungry. When can we have breakfast?'

I surreptitiously search her legs for bruises, while she shifts and squirms and tries to turn putting on her vest into a game of peekaboo. I am unable to respond; my suspicions raise a barrier between us. Am I allowing my hatred of your parents to distort my judgement? I need advice – I must try to snatch a word alone with Susan after lunch – above all, I need you . . . and not just as a confidante. Can't you give me a sign? I know: if she chooses her white jumper, my fears are justified; if she chooses her blue, I can forget them. . . . Against all precedent, she chooses her pink.

'I thought you didn't like pink. Wouldn't you rather wear the blue? It goes better with your culottes.'

261

'I'm not a boy!'

At breakfast, where she wreaks havoc with the honey, I spring my Saturday surprise: Susan is coming up to town from Hampshire.

'You must say a big thank-you to her, because she's leaving Geoffrey, even though he's only home for a week.'

'Can't he come too?'

'No. . . .' No. He has never approved of me and was evidently relieved when the Appeal decision made it impractical for Susan to remain. Her departure has, at least, brought forward their wedding plans. 'They're going to be married when Geoffrey leaves the Navy next June.'

'Then I'll be a bridesmaid!'

'Don't get too excited; it's not for a year. And careful with that spoon on your sleeve.'

'She said when she was married, I would.'

'She may not have any bridesmaids. She told me that she wanted a very quiet wedding.' She added that Geoffrey's family was appallingly stuffy ('horse-hair rather than goose-down'), which I suspect was to prepare me for exclusion. The front page of the *Nation* and the back pages of the *Tatler* do not mix.

Susan is her old self, which is just what we need at this time of enforced new identities . . . although not her old face, after an ill-advised attempt to revamp her make-up, which has left her a hybrid of Rive Gauche and village green. Pagan clamours for confirmation, first of the wedding and then of her own role in the ceremony, and insists that we spend the morning looking at dresses. Susan is happy to oblige, although not to the extent of endorsing her choice: a diaphanous cloak over a skin-tight satin sheath. 'It'd almost be worth it to see my future mother-in-law's face.' I feel an infidel in this temple of femininity, and, on hearing Pagan proudly proclaim to the assistant that 'when I'm eighteen, I'm going to marry Leo', I break out and take them for lunch.

After lunch, we attempt to repair the morning's damage in the Regent Street Disney Shop. Pagan revels in her purchases but objects to being kissed by Mickey Mouse.

'It's naughty.'

'It was just a peck on the cheek.'

'Men aren't allowed.'

'Mickey Mouse isn't a man.'

'He is underneath.'

As the till rings up a Christmas Eve total, I decide against burdening Susan with the reasons for our unseasonal spree . . . I refuse to plant briars in her bridal bouquet. I will find out the truth alone.

Pagan's bedtime mood almost allays my suspicions. Unlike last night's gloom, she appears quite relaxed as she gives me an open-armed cuddle. I pre-empt Sunday's surprise and tell her that I have invited Stephanie and her parents for lunch. Before switching out the light, I broach the subject of names. She has been Pagan all day, which I feel sure has comforted her; but I have no wish to foster a split personality. If she is happy to be Patience, so am I. The choice could be worse – it could be Prudence – and, as you know, I have never been a proponent of Pagan per se. I am sure that I will find it easier to accept from people other than your parents. I tell her that it is entirely her decision; but, if she chooses Patience, we must warn people in advance.

'No!' she shouts. 'I want to be me. I don't want to be them.'

'You're you whatever. You'd still be you if you were called Catherine or Jennifer or Stephanie.'

'But not Patience. I don't like Patience. I hate her.'

'Very well, then we'll stick to Pagan. You'll be Pagan for me . . . for all your old friends.'

'I'll be me when I come here. And the rest of the time'll be like I was sleeping. Like a hedgehog.'

'A hedgehog?' My mind prickles.

'That goes to sleep all winter.'

'Oh, I see. But that would be a bit sad. You'd be asleep for most of the time.'

'But only till I'm eighteen. Then, I'll come home to live with you. I'm six now; I'll soon be seven. So it's not that many years. I'm going to get a big piece of paper and draw on lots of lines; one for every day till I'm eighteen. Then I'm going to cross them off, one at a time.'

'Pagan, darling, you know that there's no one in the world that I love as much as you and there's nothing that I want more than for you to live here; but it isn't possible. Sometimes grown-ups can't do all that children think.

263

There are other people telling us what to do. We have to learn patience.' The word is too quick for me.

'No, I hate Patience. She's naughty. She does naughty, naughty things.' I picture your mother's reprimands and pray that they will not leave her as bitter as they did you.

Lunch is a great success. Consuela cooks roast beef and Yorkshire pudding to the manner – and the nation – born. Mr Stephanie – Stephen – gives us an insider's view of the progress of the Channel Tunnel, while Mrs Stephanie – Delia? Dahlia? – reveals an unexpected gift for mimicry. The girls play quietly together until four o'clock, when Stephanie runs screaming downstairs in a stream of tears. Her mother calms her sobs but fails to secure an explanation. Pagan proves to be equally reticent. Stephen and I make paternal noises about tiredness and tiffs, while we stand around at a loss. With our children at odds, our common ground is eroded, and I am relieved when they seize the first polite opportunity to depart.

'I never want to see Stephanie ever, ever, ever,' Pagan insists in the middle of the A23.

'Don't you like her any more?'

'Patience doesn't like her.' I am jolted by the name but presume that, with London receding, her Hove side is moving to the fore.

Your mother answers my knock, barring the door in such a way as to preclude the possibility of my entry. 'Did you have a good weekend? What did you do? Are you tired after your journey? Don't you have a kiss for Granny?' She pre-empts any answer but the last by pressing her cheek into lip-range. Pagan makes no move. 'A kiss, Patience, please. People are watching.' I swivel around, but the only sign of life is the cherub peeing in next-door's garden, his incontinence writ in stone. I recall your mockery of her maternal mantra. . . . ' "People are watching you; people are watching" . . . to hear her talk, you'd think the world was full of voyeurs. Though I suppose that was no surprise when God himself was apparently fixated on my genitals, his celestial telescope steaming up every time a foreign body strayed anywhere near. As kids, we were constantly on display. "Don't slouch" . . . "Don't scratch" . . . "Smile" . . . "People are watching." Until one day, I said the unsayable. "Of course, people are watching. William's in a wheelchair; they're trying to see inside." And she screamed that I was a wicked girl; she should never have taken me in; I hadn't given them a single moment's pleasure.'

Pagan slides back into focus. 'I hate Patience. She's naughty. She does naughty, naughty things'. . . . I thought that history repeated itself, until I started to live in the past.

Having elicited a kiss for herself, your mother prescribes one for me. 'Kiss Uncle goodbye then and thank him for having you.'

'She doesn't have to do that; she knows she's always welcome.'

'She has to learn manners; she's a big girl.'

As I drive back to London, I try to erase the expression on Pagan's face while retaining the sensation of her kiss. On my return, I find a message from Mr Steph – Stephen Tickell – whose audible distress lends weight to his demand to ring him as soon as possible. He sounds even more agitated in person; and, when he claims to have news about Pagan which he would rather not divulge on the phone, I offer to go straight round. He invites me into the den and, after much circumlocution, tells me that Stephanie has revealed the reason for her outburst. It seems that Pagan made her lie on her bed and pull down her knickers; then she inserted a lizard in her vagina.

'A lizard?' I ask incredulously.

'A model lizard. Stephanie said she had a green lizard.'

'She has a crocodile . . . a green rubber crocodile.'

'I didn't go into details. All I know is that, when we arrived home, Stephanie started crying again. She said that she had a pain "down there". My wife looked, found her skin was chafed and persuaded her to explain. Look here, old chum, are you alright?' I feel sick. A large whisky does little to ease my mind; although it helps to settle my stomach. 'We weren't sure whether to tell you. We don't want to overreact; it may just be innocent fun. Birds and bees . . . lizards and crocodiles. But Stephanie said she was quite vicious. Has she done anything like it before?'

'No, never, nothing . . . nothing vicious. You know the position: for the past three months, she's been living with

265

her grandparents. I only see her once a fortnight. How can I know what's going on?'

'Look, I never said anything was going on –'

'No, but I did.'

I tell him what occurred on Friday night; I have hesitated to admit it even to you . . . especially to you, who can only look on in horror, but I woke up to find Pagan rocking on my bed. My first thought was that her bad dream had become mine. 'I can't sleep. Can I come in with you?'

'You know the rules. You can come for a cuddle on Sunday morning, but only married people sleep together.' I am scrupulous; I am over-scrupulous. My bed has become a courtroom with Judge Flower presiding at the head.

'*They* don't. They have two rooms.'

'It's different when people are old. They find it hard to sleep.'

'You said old people don't need to sleep as much.'

'They still need some. And middle-aged people like me need even more. So let's take you back to bed.' I throw off the duvet.

'Please let me come in with you. Please. Just for one minute . . . half a minute . . . a bit of a minute.'

'Are you trying to be naughty?' I ask; at which she pulls down her pyjama trousers, rolls her hips and pokes her fingertip in her vagina.

'I can come in now, can't I?' My brain spins with her finger. I do not know where to look. I take her hand, pull up her pyjamas and guide her gently back to her room. My desire for an explanation fights with my determination to shield her from guilt. I crouch by her side, stroke her cheek and ask whether anyone – any man – has done anything to hurt her. It is three in the morning; I cannot find the words for myself, let alone for her. 'No,' she replies with a certitude that I grab on to. I remind myself that all children masturbate, especially if they are unhappy (my own blank memory merely confirms my repression); it is an involuntary impulse, on a par with sucking her thumb or clinging to her cot-blanket. It would be a mistake to make too much of it. So I switch off the light and promise to sit with her until she falls asleep.

'I wish we didn't have to have dark, Leo. There are monsters with faces which frighten me.'

266

'Don't worry. They're not in the dark; they're in your head.'

'That's worse.'

'Not at all; it means you can make yourself see other things.'

'Can I?' . . . Oh yes, you just have to model yourself on your Uncle Leo. He is doing it now.

Stephen Tickell is out of his depth. He picks up a string of amber worry-beads, which he twists tensely through his fingers. He wonders whether we can attribute Pagan's behaviour to the move or if we must look for a more sinister explanation. I reply that I am as mystified as he is. I presume that your parents watch her carefully, but who knows who may have eluded them? Workmen, teachers, friends, the entire Sussex St John Ambulance brigade . . . my voice cracks. I try to compose myself as Stephanie and her mother enter; their marked resemblance now extends to red eyes. I feel more isolated than ever. Stephanie stares at me in mute reproach, while her mother flashes a strained support-group smile.

'We wanted you to be quite sure that Stephanie was telling the truth,' she explains.

'Don't worry.'

'So dear, tell Mr Young exactly what you told Daddy and me.'

'There's no need, really.' A maternal hand signals silence.

'We were in her room, playing. She said we were going to play Night. She made me lie on the bed. She pulled down my knickers. . . .' She looks to her parents for reassurance. 'Then she picked up my legs and hit me in my wee-wee with a lizard.'

'It was a crocodile.'

'Not now, Stephen!'

'She went in and out, in and out, although I said I didn't like it; in and out, calling "Come, come, come".'

'What did she say?'

'You never mentioned that before.'

' "Come, come, come".'

I hear Stephanie's words . . . Pagan's words, in a host of male accents, echoing like an elocution lesson on my journey home. Pagan is in danger; and yet, if my suspicions

267

are correct, there is no way that I can alert your parents . . .
I picture your mother's 'What! In our house?' and the glint
on your father's blade. I decide to ring Max. He will hit
them with the full weight of the law. . . . But he is not at
home. Sylvia informs me that he is at some cinephiles'
convention; she promises to have him call me the moment
(however late) that he returns. In the event, he waits until
he is at work the next day.

I am unprepared for his reaction. It is clear that he does
not want to believe my story, which is understandable;
and equally clear that he thinks I do, which is insulting. He
declares that her behaviour is just a sign of disturbance.

'Tearing up her toys may be a sign of disturbance . . .
breaking up her room may be a sign of disturbance; but
masturbating by my bed and forcing a crocodile up her best
friend's vagina is a sign of assault!'

'Whoa, there! That's a very serious allegation.' I remind
myself that he is a lawyer. 'Have you any evidence to back
it up?'

'I've just given you the evidence.'

'That wouldn't stand up in a police cell, let alone a
court. . . . It seems to me that we're all too quick, nowadays, to cry "Child abuse". How many people do you know
who were abused as children? How many do I? And yet, if
statistics are to be believed, they're everywhere.' He
laughs and seems to sip some coffee. 'Have you any idea
who might be involved?'

'How do I know who she sees in Brighton? I'm a four-
day-a-month man. In any case, I'm not interested in
retribution. I just want to make sure she's removed to a
safe environment.'

'Such as Holland Park?'

'I'd like to think so, eventually. But the crucial thing is
not to delay.'

'Can't you see how it'll look to outsiders, say social
workers or the police? Having failed to keep Pagan by any
other means, you resort to these wild allegations . . . the
stench of sour grapes will be stifling. What's more, you
may end up with your own contact cut.'

'Mine?'

'Suppose the grandparents counter-allege . . . claim
they've seen similar behaviour and blame it on you?'

'That's preposterous!'

'Absolutely. Without a doubt. But you're in a very vulnerable position.'

'She's a six-year-old girl; I'm a gay man. Isn't there a slight conflict of perversions? Or am I so depraved that I'd even stuff the holes in a Gruyère cheese?'

'I'm your legal adviser, Leo; it's my duty to alert you to the consequences. Trust me, don't mention it to anyone. You haven't, have you?'

'Only the parents of the other girl.'

'And they said nothing to suggest they suspected you?'

'No!' I ransack my mind for a memory. 'Not a word. Their first concern was for their daughter and, then, to make sure that it didn't happen to anyone else. And suppose it does; won't it look worse for me if I say nothing now?'

'Leave it to me. I'll have a quiet word with the Mulliners' solicitors. We'll see if we can't get to the truth of it. Make sure that her grandparents are extra-vigilant, without making it seem they're at fault.'

'But what if they are . . . no, I can't say it . . . but I must; however loud you cry paranoia. What if it's one of them . . . that's to say, him?'

'Don't say it. Don't even think it. You'll drive yourself mad. He's seventy-four years old; he has a dicky hip; you saw him in court. For God's sake, the man's a Dunkirk veteran! Start accusing him and you know how it will look.'

'I'm not accusing him; I'm not accusing anyone. I just want Pagan secure.'

'And she will be. Trust me.'

I trust him, as the days turn into weeks. I occupy myself with two articles of faith for the *Observer* and the final batch of programmes before the summer break. I welcome the break more than the summer. My chronology has contracted; I measure time like a prisoner living for fortnightly visits. Then, as in the aftermath of a riot, all privileges are withdrawn; I am refused access to Pagan. Your mother rings to tell me that she has a heavy cold.

'In June?'

'Summer colds are so much more treacherous. The doctor says she must stay in bed.'

I am not allowed to speak to her ('the doctor says she must stay in bed') and, when I send her a parcel of books, it is returned with a ring round the name Pagan and the message 'Not known at this address' printed at the top. I am no match for such pettiness and send a second parcel addressed to Miss P. Mulliner, with the letter inside headed 'darling'. The compromise is evidently acceptable; for, when I phone again, your mother confirms that she has received it. 'I'll make sure she writes to say thank-you.'

'That really isn't necessary.'

'Manners maketh man . . . and lady.'

She informs me that the summer cold has settled on her chest and a second weekend has to be cancelled. I am incensed and suspicious. I feel sure that they are hiding something. . . . Is she covered in scars? Do they want to keep me away until they heal? I determine to alert the Welfare Officer, but I defer to Max. 'Children fall ill. I should know; I had to cancel holidays, parties, even a bar mitzvah. You must watch out; this is becoming an obsession. It used to be that heterosexual men thought all gay men were child molesters; now gay men appear to think all fathers are child abusers.'

I convince myself that he is right. I affirm my faith in fathers, but it is as routine as a recital of the Lord's Prayer. I cannot clear my head of doubts, even on an early morning run. The park is full of Pagan. I jog past the pond where she refused to throw stale bread to the ducks, claiming that it was cruel to give them food that was too hard for us. I circle the playground where she had her first brush with machismo when an eight-year-old bruiser pushed her off the slide. At which moment . . . with which memory, she appears in front of me. I marvel at the power of thought while despairing of its mockery. Then I see that it really is her. She must have run away – hitched a lift or taken a train – and given her address as Holland Park. Incongruity is banished in joy. I race towards her and clasp her to my chest. She screams and squirms, in spite of all my avowals, whereupon a man bounds up and wrests her from my arms, yelling that she is his daughter. As Pagan melts into Linda, I see that my tears have blinded me. I explain to the man that I have mistaken his child for my own . . . my niece. He fixes me with a stare first of hostility and then of recognition. Whatever else, I retain the authority of the screen.

He defers to the image and tells the girl that there has been no harm done; she has no need to make such a fuss. Then he reminds her that she saw me on *Jackanory* and asks me to autograph a paper bag.

'Of course; should I sign it to Linda?'

'No . . . Ron.'

The following Friday, I ignore your mother's protests that Pagan is still not fit to travel and insist on my right to collect her, adding that I will apply to the court if I am refused. She gives way, grumbling that she will be the one who has to nurse her when she falls ill. I drive down in a deluge, am delayed by an hour and meet with an icy welcome.

'We'd given you up. I was about to put Patience to bed.'

'I'm sorry, but you see the weather. . . .'

'She was wretched. You should never do that to a child.'

'If I'd known, I'd have rung. May I come in now?'

'You expect me to welcome you to my home after what you've done?'

'I'm an hour late. Is that a crime?'

'You know what I mean . . . spreading wicked lies about my husband.'

'I spread no lies; I simply told my solicitor that I suspect Pagan is being abused.'

'Be quiet! Don't repeat it! Think where you are.' She pulls me into the house. I try to wipe my shoes on the mat but she prevents me. Pagan runs down the stairs.

'Leo! Leo!'

'One at a time, if you don't mind. It's not the Grand National.'

'How are you, my darling?' As I take her in my arms, I see no sign of illness. It is clear that I have been punished for my allegations.

'She said you weren't coming. She said you had something better to do. But I knew you would.'

'How could I ever have anything better?' I turn to your mother. 'How could you say that?'

'Poppycock! She doesn't understand; she's six years old. That's what you forget.'

271

'How are you, my darling? You look well.' I turn relief into accusation: 'You look very well.'

'I was raped.'

'What?' My heart rams against my ribcage.

'In the swimming pool, yesterday.'

'You mean you were robbed. Grandpa left your bags in the café and they were stolen.'

'I know. I had my towel in it. It was wet.'

'You were robbed? Your bags were taken? Nothing else?'

'Yes, yesterday. They were thiefs. He said they ought to be hung up.'

'Patience dear, would you go into the kitchen for a minute? I need to say something to Uncle.'

'No, please. If it's about me, I should listen.'

'Just for a moment, darling. I promise we won't be long.' I follow your mother into the living room.

'You see?' she tells me. 'Words. She's six years old. She doesn't know the meaning of words.'

Your father stands stiffly by the fireplace. Manners clash with morals as I formulate a greeting. I opt for a noncommittal nod; he does not respond.

'Why can't you accept the Court's decision?' he asks. 'Magnanimous in victory; dignified in defeat . . . that's the British way. No gentleman would resort to such lies.'

'Look!' your mother screeches, 'you've brought filth into my house.' I am about to challenge her metaphor when I realise that she is referring to my shoes.

'Shall I go outside and wipe them?'

'It's too late; the damage is done.'

'How can you bring yourself to say such things?' your father asks. 'A six-year-old girl exposing herself by your bedside . . . what kind of man are you?'

'What kind of perverted imagination do you have?'

'It wasn't imagination. I woke up and saw.'

'It was the middle of the night. You don't know waking from sleeping.'

'You don't know truth from lies . . . an innocent child.'

'What's innocence?' I ask . . . and answer: 'Innocence is being free from fear. Innocence is being free from guilt. Innocence isn't not knowing the meaning of words; it's having no call to use them.'

272

'Don't throw Cambridge at us,' your father says, 'we had all that with Candida. We won't stand for it again.'

'Besides, it wasn't just the masturbation –'

'Please!'

'I'll ask you not to use language in front of my wife.'

'It was the crocodile. Didn't your solicitor mention that?'

'Oh yes. Along with what she said or, rather, is said to have said.'

' "Come, come, come!" ' he enunciates with disgust.

'My husband has never used words like that in his life . . . I should know.'

'But I never accused Mr Mulliner; I never accused anyone. I just want to protect Pagan.'

'You're sick,' your father says. 'If I had both my hips, I'd thrash you.'

'What about you?' your mother asks. 'If she was doing . . . those things you say she was doing . . . why was she doing them in London rather than here? She's even stopped wetting the bed except when she returns from you. Last time, her pants were so soiled that I had to rub her nose in them.'

'What?'

'To cure her . . . like a dog.'

'She's not an animal!'

'Don't tell me how to bring up children!'

'If she is soiling herself, it's because she's frightened of coming back here.'

'I told you he'd brazen it out.'

'The thing is, old man,' your father changes tack and tone abruptly, 'I'm of the old school. I believe in discipline. A good smack on the b-t-m is worth a thousand talking-tos . . . not too often, mind, or it loses its value, but as a last resort. Patience may not like that; she's always been used to having her own way.'

'And look where it's led,' your mother interjects.

'That's right. . . . She sees you as a soft touch. She's a cunning little thing; manipulative. All children are. People talk about feminine wiles, but they're nothing compared to children's.' I find his man-to-man mode shaming. 'We had cases at school: boys accusing other boys and even masters. I'm not saying there was never any truth in it; but, nine times out of ten, there was a motive. I remember one boy – that friend of Candida's – went so far as to accuse the chaplain.'

'Robin Standish?'

'That's him. Turned out that it was in retaliation for being caught presiding at some sort of black mass.'

I am strangely cheered by this mention of Robin, although I fail to see the connection with Pagan. Your father explains it by adding that 'it just goes to show you can't believe a single word any of them say. All children are born liars.' With that, he pats me on the back and escorts me to the door. I try to keep to the trail of footprints to avoid further soiling of the carpet (might she rub my face in it?). There is no need to call Pagan who is poised at the door. To prevent further chiding, I grab her coat, her case, and leave.

Our reunion is soured by recriminations. She doubts my explanation for our two lost weekends and dismisses her heavy cold as a runny snuffle. She is tired and tetchy all through dinner and spills a jug of apple juice to provoke me ... now that she is paid in a currency of slaps, she is anxious to know the exchange rate; if 'a good smack on the b-t-m is worth a thousand talking-tos' in Hove, what is the value in Holland Park? One hundred, two hundred, five? She remains suspicious of my tolerance and tests it again at bedtime by insisting on changing from her room to Susan's to yours. Before settling down, she demands that we both kneel to pray. She recites a number of simple petitions, although, when she reaches 'God bless Granny and Grandpa', she confides that she always inserts 'don't' under her breath so that it won't count. She adds that she wants to say 'God bless Leo' but they won't let her, so she says it herself later ... 'Will it still work?'

'Don't worry.'

'She says you're already part of "God bless all the world" and anyway there's no point cos you don't go to church. I go to Sunday school.'

'I know.'

'I don't think we should have school on Sundays; God said it's a day to rest. Why don't I have a daddy?'

'What?'

'Everyone has a daddy except me. A girl in my class said I came out of a tube.'

'You came out of a tube in Mummy's tummy.'

'No, a tube like in science where they make smells.'

'That's nonsense. You had a daddy like everyone else. I know that Mummy would have told you about him when you grew up.'

'If I had a daddy, I'd have another granny and grandpa, wouldn't I? I wouldn't have to stay with *them*.'

'It might still depend on the Courts.'

'Will Jesus love me if I don't have a daddy?'

'Jesus loves all children. Haven't they at least told you that?'

'He wouldn't love me if my name was Pagan.'

'Your name is Pagan. And I'm quite sure that Jesus doesn't care about names.'

'Pagan means someone who doesn't believe in God.'

'Pagan means someone who doesn't believe in Granny and Grandpa's God. That's rather different.'

'Why didn't you marry Mummy? Then you could be my daddy.'

'That's enough. It's late . . . time to sleep.'

'Is it cos you want to stick your bottom in little girls?'

'What? Pagan, who said . . . who did . . . has someone done that to you?' She turns not only mute but rigid. 'Darling, it's very important that you tell me the truth.' She presses both hands across her mouth. 'Believe me, I won't be cross. Not at all. If someone's hurting you, I can stop it. You want me to stop it, don't you?' She relaxes a little and nods. 'Has someone put his bottom in you?'

'Patience is naughty; Patience is bad. Patience does naughty, naughty things.'

'No, it's not Patience . . . it's not you. It's the nasty, nasty man who did it to you. Tell me, was it Grandpa?' She shakes her head. 'You're sure?' She nods. I am amazed at the extent of my relief. 'Was it someone who came to your house?'

'He said that, if I told, I'd be put in a prison like the Princes in the Tower. I wouldn't ever see you; it'd be like you were dead, like Mummy.'

'Who said? Who?'

'Patience is naughty; Patience is bad; Patience is sore.'

'Who said it? Who did it?'

'Him.'

'Grandpa?' She nods.

'He stuck his bottom in Patience's bottom.'

I dig my nails into my palm. I force myself to demand details. 'In your front bottom or your back bottom?'

'Yes. He hurt me. Sore. He said "Come, come, come". And it was all white, like school pudding, on my tummy. You won't put me in a prison?'

'No, my darling. No one's going to put you in prison; I'm going to set you free. But I am going to put Grandpa in prison and then I'm going to throw away the key. He'll never hurt you . . . no one will ever hurt you again.'

She nestles in my arms. We are united by touch and tears. Later, I let her sleep in my bed; I know that I have nothing to fear.

At eleven the next morning, we drive to Wimpole Street for an appointment with Patrick Dudley, a paediatrician friend of Stephen Tickell. I first spoke to him a month ago, after the incident with the crocodile. He was reluctant to see her, insisting that he always required a referral from social services; but, when I explained the dangers of publicity and assured him that I remained her legal guardian, he agreed to examine her informally. To secure Pagan's cooperation, I have made no mention of his being a doctor. She distrusts the entire profession after their treatment of you.

We inhale the airy confidence of the consulting room. Dudley's candied condescension recalls the radio 'aunties' of my youth. With glazed indifference, he asks her about her school, her friends, her hobbies.

'Who's your best friend?'

'Leo.'

'Not counting Leo.'

He plants her in a corner with a pile of superannuated toys, while he questions me. I describe the disruption at school and the flirtation at home. I mention the wet beds, the soiled knickers and the signs of vaginal discharge. I spell the word protectively and am taken aback when she puts the letters together, albeit endowing vaginal with a hard 'g'.

Having registered her presence, he proceeds with the

examination, performing a perfunctory sight test before leading her behind a screen. She asks me to accompany them; but he explains that it is not allowed, adding that he normally has a nurse 'but she looks after her own little girl on Saturdays; though that won't matter, since you and I are already such good friends'. His demeanour, designed to put her at her ease, has the reverse effect on me. I catch a glimpse of her thinly screened modesty and the drift of his pill-sugaring speech. 'Can you climb up on this? Do you enjoy PE . . . ? Lie down and pretend to sleep. Do you think you'd make a good drum . . . ? Take big breaths. Open wide. Pant like a dog. This is just going to tickle. . . . Let your legs go floppy. Lift up your knees. Good. This is just going to tickle. . . . Now turn over and we'll take a little look at your bot. Good. Another tickle.' Why should it tickle? What is he doing to her? Did your father use the same phrase? She yelps. I have to clench my fists to stop myself toppling the screen.

'That didn't hurt now, did it?' Dudley claims in the face of the evidence. Pagan does not reply; I picture the eloquent accusation in her eyes. 'All over. You've been a very brave girl. Put your kit back on and we'll see what we can find for you in my drawer.' What he finds is a lollipop, with which he bribes her into the waiting room. He then returns to his desk and takes out a silver art-deco cigarette case, which he presents to me. 'Do you partake of the weed? No? It may shock you, coming from a doctor, but I can't help regretting the fact that so few people do nowadays. It was such a serviceable convention: an instant ice-breaker. Courtesy . . . comradeship.'

'Cancer?'

'Yes, well, to the matter in hand. . . . I'm afraid that there's nothing conclusive. Her vagina is a little red, which is consistent with mild incontinence. And there's slight scarring to the hymen.'

'What's that consistent with?'

'Children play with themselves; little girls as much as little boys. Inserting a finger –'

'Or a penis?'

'As I said, there are slight scars on the hymen and mild anal dilation.'

'Is she fingering that too?'

277

'An open bot is generally trying to tell us something, but I wouldn't be prepared to make a diagnosis based on anal dilation. We don't want another Cleveland.'

'This is one girl, not the whole of Hove!'

'Now anal fissures would be a good sign . . . that is, from a clinical point of view. In a baby, they might be due to a bowel problem; but not in a six-year-old.'

'So what action should we take?'

'The trouble with anal dilation is that it tends to clear up fairly fast. We'd need a photograph; and, to be frank, I'm not too keen on taking pictures of six-year-old bots, especially when the consultation has been somewhat irregular.'

'So we leave her exposed to further abuse?'

'You mentioned that you suspected your father?'

'He's not my father; he's Pagan's grandfather.'

'Make it clear that you have your eye on him. Abusers are cowards. More than likely, he'll run scared.'

'They're far more than suspicions. She described what he did to her in gross detail.'

'Let me give you a word of advice. In thirty-five years in this field, I've seen case after case collapse in court. Any half-competent barrister would wipe the floor with her story. The Judge has to direct the jury that it's dangerous to convict without corroboration. Do you want to put her though all that to no purpose?'

'All I want is to protect her.'

'There's something else. You said yourself that the grandfather was a disciplinarian. She may have thought to herself: I don't like this man; I'm going to make trouble for him.'

'Her grandmother is equally strict and yet she hasn't accused her.'

'Children are devious.'

'His very words. I'm beginning to smell a conspiracy.'

'Come now, Mr Young; that's unworthy of you.'

'You heard what she said about bottoms.'

'There may well be confusion; she may mean smacks. . . . So he believes in a good slap on the bot; that doesn't make him an ogre. He's in keeping with one out of every two normal families'. . . . I, of course, am not a normal family; I am a pervert who believes that children

278

learn at their parents' knees, not by being spread across them.

'And the "Come, come, come" and the spilt school pudding?'

'Playground talk.'

'In a primary school?'

'I'm afraid so. Either she or one of her friends will have watched a pornographic video. Word gets around.'

'So I'm to do nothing?'

'My advice is to stay vigilant but silent. You'd be stirring up a hornet's nest and the little girl would be the first to be stung.' He walks me to the door. 'I feel that we're altogether too precious about children these days; it's like all the fashionable, faddy diets . . . we mustn't eat this; we mustn't eat that. We need a little grit in our food to protect us; just like we need a little grit in life.' He exhales smoke in my face. 'And, even if there has been a degree of what we might term "sexual inappropriateness", it doesn't automatically mean that she should never visit her grandparents. Pros and cons, my friend; ride the seesaw. Pros and cons.'

We discover Pagan turning a clockwork TV with a permanent showing of nursery rhymes. I remind her of our date with the dinosaurs at the Natural History Museum. She says a guarded goodbye to Dudley, who asks if she enjoyed her lollipop.

'Grandpa gave Patience a lollipop when he tickled her too.' Dudley looks startled. I hear the thump of a slumped seesaw.

'Pros and cons, my friend? Pros and cons?'

# 2

I sit in the lounge of Brown's hotel, like a lonely hearts
lover mocked by the freshness of his rose. I am waiting for
your mother. Making contact proved to be easier than I had
feared. A direct approach to the bank in Stamford established that her husband had been promoted and transferred
to Peterborough; an indirect one, via the BT archives, left
me with photocopies of the last eight years' entries of
Sextons. I embarked on a process of elimination.

'Hello . . . Mr Sexton? You may not remember me; but I
think that we worked together at Barclays in Huntingdon,
thirty years ago.'

'You've got the wrong man, I'm afraid. I don't think I've
even been to Huntingdon; I'm an optician. Besides, I bank
at Lloyds.'

'Hello . . . Miss Sexton? I'm sorry to bother you. But I
think that I may have worked with your father at Barclays
in Huntingdon nearly thirty years ago.'

'Not mine. Not unless you're psychic. Pop died in
Plymouth in 1960. Look, what is this? Are you from Cilla
Black?'

'Hello . . . Mrs Sexton? I don't expect you'll know me,
but I used to work with your husband nearly thirty years
ago in the bank in Huntingdon.'

'Well I never. Thirty years. He's out at his committee
now, but he'll be ever so disappointed. Mr . . . ? I didn't
quite catch your name.'

'I'm sorry. I'm afraid I've got the wrong number.'

280

A trip to Peterborough and a tour through the avenues and cul-de-sacs of suburbia confirm that I have the right number, both of the phone and the house. These are the streets that witnessed wife-swapping in the seventies, Trivial Pursuit in the eighties, and negative equity in the nineties. 'Lilac Time', with its loft-conversion, satellite-dish and white wrought-iron gates, looks the perfect setting for a bank manager. Rejecting the impulse to knock on the door, I return home, where I write her a letter, recounting our friendship and requesting a meeting to fill in some of the gaps left by your death. I guarantee my complete discretion . . . until I recollect the men who did as much for me.

Three days later, she telephones me. She introduces herself without mentioning you; and, for a moment, I fail to put a history to the name. She explains that this is the first time that she has been alone in the house and free to talk . . . I feel like a conspirator. It seems that she had no idea that you were dead and has been unable to stop crying since receiving my letter; fortunately, her husband attributes it to the change of life. 'I thought that all my tears were dried,' she says . . . or is it 'cried'? I am distracted by the accent. 'When I was younger, they'd come on without warning. Floods of tears: I couldn't control them. They don't tell you about that when they make you give up your baby. I only saw her for a few hours and yet I wept for her for years. "It's just Mum in one of her states," my family would say. I have two girls.'

I overcome her resistance to a meeting. Even so, she rejects my offer to drive to Peterborough, in favour of tea in London, which she can combine with a morning's shopping.

'How will we recognise each other?'

'Oh, I'll recognise you. I never miss a programme. My favourite this year was Zsa Zsa Gabor.'

I wait in the plushness of Brown's, my privacy preserved by the host of American tourists, when I am greeted by something overwhelmingly floral. 'You look redder than you do on the BBC,' she says, smoothing her skirt and sitting down; 'your hair, that is. Though it may be our set; it doesn't do you justice.'

'How was your journey?'

'Very A to B . . . that's what my daughter says. And the toilets weren't fit for a football fan. I couldn't live in the capital.' She points the word as though it were the concept that scared her.

'You don't seem to have had much success shopping.'

'Oh, I never meant to buy anything. Just to shop.'

I order our teas. She toys with the sandwiches and reserves her serious attention for the cakes. 'I shall pay for this tomorrow,' she says with a mouth full of meringue. 'A minute on the lips, a lifetime on the hips. Still, everything in moderation.' She reaches for a millefeuille.

I examine her features for signs of yours; but I see no resemblance. Your face is all animation; hers is set in its folds, its expression framed in excess flesh. She squeezes the pastry into her mouth and a dollop of cream squirts out. She meets my gaze with a guilty blush; and I sense the intimacy of her relationship with food. I avert my eyes as she dabs her dewlap. Between bites, she introduces me to her family. Both daughters are married. One lives in Leeds with a cricketer . . . I politely pretend to have heard of him; the other has stayed in Stamford and works part-time in her husband's office. 'Two of the kids are under five, so I help out three days a week. My husband thinks it's too much for me. But she's my daughter.' She gulps.

'Yes.'

'Besides, I gave up my job when we moved back to Peterborough; so what else do I have to do?'

'Candida told me that you were a cashier in Boots.'

'I was a supervisor!'

'Of course. I'm sorry. My memory.'

'She came out of the blue. There was no letter . . . you sent a letter. I didn't have time to collect my thoughts.'

'She was always impetuous. It was her nature.'

'I don't know where she got it from.' She is silent.

'It was her middle name.'

'It's not right, you know: that law letting kids track down their parents. Opening a can of worms on their eighteenth birthday, when it should be a bottle of champagne.'

'People need to know where they come from.'

'What about the parents? You can have no idea what it's like to give up a child.' I decide not to disabuse her. 'I was seventeen years old. I couldn't tell the difference between her growing in my body and my own body growing. It didn't feel anything special . . . just another change; until she came out: that perfect, squashed bit of me. . . . Look at me. You've made me cry again.' I apologise and hold out the cake-plate. 'Why not?' she smiles, 'what have I got to lose?' . . . I refrain from remarking 'weight'. 'It's strange but I remember her birth so much better than my daughters' . . . my other daughters. Then there were cards and flowers and my husband and his mother. But, with her, I was completely alone.'

'Didn't your own mother visit?'

'No. . . . It was a hard labour. Sometimes I feel it's been forty years' hard labour, which is no less than I deserved. I used to think she was giving me something to remember her by, if only rips and stitches. They let me hold her, but they wouldn't let me feed her, even though I had all this milk . . . for months, I had milk that I had to get rid of. I remember there was some famine; I think . . . I expect it was Africa. People were starving, and there was I wasting all this milk. I used to dream of mouths. . . . The woman from the society came to collect her the next day and I howled. I howled and howled until the nurse gave me an injection; I was disturbing the other mothers on the ward . . . the real mothers. I was kept there for five days, watching the comings and goings: the husbands and the children and the chocolates. I could see all the visitors looking at me and asking the story of the girl without so much as a bottle of Lucozade on her locker.'

'What happened when you were discharged?'

'I went home. To Mum and Dad and six years of silence. Oh, I had some good times . . . laughs with the girls, fun with the lads. But inside there was pain; in my heart . . . in my head . . . in my breasts, there was pain. There was love and guilt spilling into each other. There was pain. I couldn't tell anyone. Everyone knew; but they were doing me a favour by saying nothing. I had to be grateful, even though it was eating me up. And the worst day of all was her birthday. For weeks before – long before I remembered – I'd get this ache in my stomach and this rash on my skin: bright blood-red lumps. . . . Mother's Day was almost as bad. Every year, in the shop, we had more and more gifts:

bath salts; so many sorts of bath salts . . . what does anyone want with bath salts? And my daughters would write me cards. And my husband would say "it's Mum's day today, so she's not going to lift a finger" . . . though I always did. And all I could think of was those few hours in the hospital with that little baby on the pillow.' She breaks down in dry tears. 'There's a Grandparents' Day now, you know,' she recovers herself. 'My grandson – he's eight – sent us a card for the first time last year. He put "To the best Gran and Grandad in the whole world". And that didn't hurt at all. . . . Look at me, chattering away nineteen to the dozen. I can see you're a professional; you know how to make people talk.'

'Were you never curious to find her yourself?'

'No, I gave her – I tried to give her – to a good home. I insisted on church-goers, though I wasn't one myself . . . perhaps that was why. And, six years later, I married. If Andrew could see me now . . . I don't mean talking about this, but talking to you. He's a great fan. He wrote a letter to the paper after they published . . . well, you know. They didn't print it. He said they had no call to do that to someone who brought pleasure to millions. He's very broad-minded.'

'And yet you haven't felt able to tell him about Candida?'

'That's the past. It's dead and buried. Oh, I'm sorry. I didn't mean. . . .'

'Don't worry.'

'Ever since I heard the news, I keep thinking: was it psychopathic?'

'What?'

'Like cancer. She seemed so unhappy. I don't know what she expected from me. We were strangers . . . strangers who happened to share the same blood.'

'She had an almost mystical belief in the power of parenthood. All the emotions that others attach to their lovers or art or God, she attached to you. There was no way that you could live up to her expectations . . . her fantasies. The biggest shock was to learn about her father.'

'She told you?'

'Of course. But there was far more to it than snobbery. She seemed to be living out a fairy tale, with herself as a

284

princess in disguise. Then she found that the king was a genuine peasant. . . . I don't suppose you know if he's still alive.'

'Who?'

'Her father.'

'I go to visit him once a week.'

'Really? I'm sure she told me he'd run off. I must be confused. She was so disillusioned by the story. She threw herself into . . . a life that wasn't good for her. I've always believed that one of the reasons she never named Pagan's father was to spare her a similar pain.'

'You don't know who he is?'

'No. And, at the risk of sounding like Candida, I'd give anything to find out. I'm desperate for an ally. He's the only one people will listen to. Even the Judge admitted that, if he'd known his identity, he'd have come to a different decision. I'm no relation so I'm nothing . . . I wouldn't even be allowed in the ward if she had an accident. But a father has rights. He could apply to the Courts; he could have Pagan removed from her grandfather.'

'Her grandfather?'

'I don't want to distress you, but I suspect . . . in fact, I'm convinced that she's being abused.' The word sounds shrill amid the understated elegance of the lounge.

'Pagan?'

'I have proof.' The blood drains from her face.

'It can't happen again. It can't.'

'Is everything satisfactory, sir, madam?' The waiter's intervention is insufferable. I ask him curtly to leave.

'I must go. I knew that I shouldn't have come. Why did you insist?' She takes out a mirror, more to occupy her hands than to look at her face.

'The last thing I want is to hurt you. I thought you'd understand.'

'Of course I understand. Who better? She told you about her father.'

'The meat-packing?'

'What? I mean that her father was my father; her father was her grandfather. I was her mother and her sister.' She looks aghast. 'You said that you knew.'

'No, I knew something different . . . thought I knew.' I

285

try to assimilate this new pattern. Is this blood enough for you? I am drowning in blood.

'I'd never told anyone except my mum. It killed her. Oh not with shock, nothing sudden. But, from then on, she went through life like she was always laying the table and never eating. She stopped talking; the house felt as cold as a convent . . . God forgive him for what he did. He'd been after me for years. He was always switching off lights; she used to tell him he must have Scotch blood and he'd laugh to make her feel safe. But it was so as he could come at me in the dark . . . with his breath and his hands. To be honest, I never thought much about it, not until the hands got rougher. . . . The last thing I meant was to tell Candida – such a pretty name, don't you think? I could never have picked such a pretty name – but she was so pushy. She reminded me of him. I don't like to say it but she did. She wouldn't let go of me. When I asked her to leave, she began to accuse me . . . it was my fault that I hadn't kept her, my fault that her dad had run off.'

I suddenly see a resemblance, not in your features but in your self-disgust. You are sitting opposite me on so many mornings-after, insisting that you are nothing but a slut and blaming it on your bad blood.

'That was when she told me that the same thing had happened to her.'

'What?'

'She said that her father – her adopted father – had interfered with her.'

'I don't believe it'. . . . I won't believe it. . . . It is all too believable. Is that why you never named Pagan's father? Is he yours? Are the sins of the fathers alive in the wombs of the daughters? The idea is absurd; it defies both credence and chronology . . . when Pagan was born, you had not seen him for ten years. Or had you . . . ? My thoughts turn on surprise visits and forced entries. The future contracts and the past fills with fearful possibilities.

'She said she'd never told anyone, as though I'd feel honoured. But we'd just met. I couldn't take it in. It was my day-off.'

I spin in a spiral of betrayal; the ties of a twenty-year friendship have slipped loose. In despair of romance, I romanticised our relationship; but what was it worth

286

when you denied me the most fundamental fact of your being? Were you too ashamed? Did you picture yourself as a Lilith or Lolita luring him to destruction? Did you take on yourself all the stigma of woman and the depravity of men? For the first time, the wrist-slitting side of your character makes sense. Is that what you feared: not that I would fail to understand but that I would understand too well . . . that I would lay you on a threadbare couch and analyse away your mystery? Now that child abuse has filled the place of original sin, were the associations too banal?

'I wish she'd never told me . . . is that cruel? I'm sorry. I wish you'd never told me; I have a home to go back to tonight. What did she want from me? I know the answer. But how could I be a second mother to her? I couldn't even be a first. I had two daughters, Sheila and Louise. They were fourteen and twelve, on the brink of everything. I had to protect them. And me . . . what sort of life do you think I had stuck in the shop all day? Varicose veins and corns, in a word. I couldn't even put my feet up at night; there was always something to cook or clean. And then there was Andrew. He knew nothing . . . he still knows nothing. I always meant to tell him, but it was never the right time. Until, after a time, it became impossible; it would have made our whole marriage seem like a lie. Do you think I did wrong?'

'It isn't a case of right and wrong.' I resent her plea for sympathy.

'But, if I'd kept her with me, none of it would have happened.'

'What about your father? Parents can abuse their children, whatever the circumstance. You're the proof.'

'But hers used it against her. She mentioned a time when she was a kid, just six or seven years old. She was trying to push him away, so she told him that he shouldn't touch her. It wasn't right; he was her daddy. And he said it didn't count because she was adopted. They weren't related; they didn't share the same blood.'

I excuse myself and head for the lavatory, clinging to the wall as though aboard ship. Once inside, I turn the taps on full blast and shriek. I forget about the concealed cubicles and am startled by a flush. I loudly clear my throat to appease the emerging occupant, trilling a couple of scales as he washes his hands. Unconvinced, he peers in the mirror as if to determine whether I am musical or mad. I flash a smile, and he cowers as though it were a penis. He hurries out, leaving me the freedom of the basin. I splash my face, but I fail to clear my head, which is bursting with memories of you.

I see you lying, sprawled on scarcely ruffled sheets, your naked breasts gilded by the hazy Venetian sun. 'Sex is nothing to write home about,' you declare; and I picture my mother reading the postcard. 'Who wouldn't swap the squelch and sweat of sex for the warmth of friendship?' . . . I realise now that this is no guff to console me for my impotence but a cry from the heart.

'Sex is power,' you say later, months later . . . years later, as both a caution and a creed. 'Your mistake is to confuse it with love, or even with passion.'

'What about with pleasure?'

'You're squandering your most valuable asset. You should take pleasure in what you can do with sex, not in the sex itself.' I wince as the wit curls with desperation. I flinch from your bitter smile as you scrawl 'premature ejaculation' in response to a *Cosmopolitan* questionnaire on what a woman most looks for in a lover. Is this what your father has done to you? At last, I understand the men who take the law into their own hands and shoot their children's attackers, although, in this case, he should turn the gun on himself. I start to think in tabloid headlines. I want Old Testament morality with New Testament modifications . . . not just an eye for an eye but a head on a plate.

I return to your mother, who is gazing like a gypsy into her tea-cup, although, on inspection, the cup is empty and her eyes are blank. She sniffs a smile at me.

'I had to make myself hard. I had to act as though Mother was the last name anyone would call me. I was scared. I told her the truth to get rid of her but she seemed to feel closer . . . like we'd been through something together that we'd been through apart . . . like she wanted me not as a mother but as a sister.'

'She was able to adjust that quickly?'

'No, I don't mean blood, but like women talk about in

lectures, in London. She poured out her heart and I wanted to listen, but I was expecting the girls home from school; all I could hear was the clock. As it turned out, Sheila walked in just as she was leaving. "Who was that?" she asked; and my brain went like a sponge. So I said she was selling cosmetics. "Looks like she could do with some herself," she replied . . . well, of course, her eyes were red and black from crying. And I slapped her, hard across the leg. She looked at me in amazement . . . believe me, I never raised a finger to my girls. I slapped her, and, the way she looked at me, I was sure she knew. For weeks – or was it months? it felt longer – I lived in fear of every knock at the door. But she said she'd say nothing to anyone and she was as good as her word. That was the only time I ever saw her. I came across some of her pictures in a magazine; I cut one out and stuck it on the fridge. But Andrew took it down. He doesn't like anything gloomy. He says he gets enough of that at work.'

'So how do we stop it happening again to Pagan?'

'There are people: doctors, policemen, social workers . . . they didn't have so many people when it was me.'

'No one believes me. They think I'm out to make trouble. But if you told them what she'd said to you.'

'No, I couldn't. You promised . . . one meeting.'

'Your husband need never know.'

'What about letters and papers and . . . no, you've no right. It was forty years ago – next year'll be forty years – I met her for two hours in forty years.'

'Pagan is six years old; Pagan is today and tomorrow.'

'What can I tell them? Joan . . . Candida is dead. I have no proof . . . no authority.'

'You have a mother's authority.'

'I'm not her mother! I'm just the woman who gave her birth.' She looks down. 'I've never been to court in my life.'

The waiter brings a pot of fresh tea, which he pours with extended ceremony. He leaves; neither of us lifts a cup.

'I'd best be going. I have to catch the six ten. I'll be back in time to fetch Andrew his supper.'

'Does he know you've come . . . shopping?'

'He thinks I'm staying late with my father. He's in a home in Huntingdon.'

'You still see him?'

'I've told you. I go every week.'

'I don't understand how you can.'

'He's eighty-five; I'm all that he has. He never touched me after ... after. ... He never even kissed me on my wedding day. There's a picture of him and my mum outside the church and all you can see is their clothes. Andrew likes him. They used to play chess and argue about the news. He said he should move in with us when my mum died, but I was having none of it. Not with –'

'Sheila and Louise?'

'When things got too much for him to manage on his own, he went into the home. And I go by every Thursday, so that they don't start taking him for granted. No matter what they've done, no one should be taken for granted.'

'But you'll miss this week.'

'I popped in yesterday after I'd finished in Stamford. He was in disgrace; he'd misbehaved in a game of charades.'

'Cheated?'

'Worse. He'd taken off all his clothes to demonstrate *Naked Video*. I didn't know where to look.'

'You were there?'

'When the matron was telling me. It was during the WI afternoon on Sunday. The ladies were very shocked. He's eighty-five.'

'So you said.'

'Such a silly title, when there are so many others to choose from. It has to be TV for the old folk. So why not *Through the Keyhole* or *Surprise Surprise*?'

'I suppose they thought they were safe with the over-eighties.'

Her face darkens. 'No one's ever safe.'

'And yet you still visit him?'

'He's my father; I'm his daughter. That's all that's left.'

'I don't understand anything any more.'

'Best not to try. All I know is that time's so short ... Andrew retires in three years; my next-door neighbour's already made her Christmas pudding. I have four grand-children; I want to be able to enjoy them growing up.' She stands. 'I'd better go now. You've no idea what a thrill it's been for me to meet you. I just wish it could have been ... well, you know. If I told my friends, they'd think I must have won a competition. Not that I can tell them. It's another secret. I've lived with so many secrets. I used to think they'd tear me to pieces; now I feel they're holding me in place.'

A moment later, there is nothing to show for her presence but some crumbs by her plate, a smear of lipstick on her napkin and a confusion in my mind. I picture your family tree turning in on itself like a weeping willow. Images coalesce of you and Pagan and your father . . . your two fathers: the one stripping off in the residents' lounge and the other clutching Pagan in the swimming pool. . . . 'Open your legs. Kick like a dog. Close your mouth. The water's to swim in, not drink.' He strides in further; she screams. 'It doesn't count,' he insists, 'we're not related.' I watch helplessly from the edge as he drags her into the deep end. 'Don't be a baby. Open your legs. . . .'

# 3

December 1993 ... March 1994 ... June 1994 ... even March 1995: your pills have outlived you but not their potency. I empty a bottle in my hand and weigh the prospects of deliverance. I have an irresistible urge to taste one: to enjoy a foretaste of oblivion: to suck on the teat of death and swallow the sweetness. I wish that I had faith and could believe that, by taking them, I would be somewhere else tomorrow; I wish that I could believe that tomorrow was already somewhere else today; I wish that I could translate my sense of the continuity of life into the eternity of God. But the hopes of my childhood now sound as hollow as the hymns.

I toy with the concept of rebirth. I would be happy to trust to karma and come back as a lama in Tibet or even a llama in Peru. Then I remember Imogen in her Buddhist incarnation chiding you for swatting a fly.

'It might be your mother.'

'Don't tempt me,' you say and redouble the attack.

Memories cloud my mind ... and my purpose. I promised that when your life became irreversibly horizontal, when it shrank to a round of bed-baths and pans and sores, I would feed you the pills. Death would be the final bond of a lifelong friendship, murder the consummate act of love. But, when the time came, you were unable to signal your wishes. I refused to risk all on the ambiguity of an eyelid; defying your desires, I demanded that the doctors found ways to keep you alive. With no hope of cure, I pinned my hopes on remission. It was not so much your death that I could not face as my life without you. Is this the chance to atone for my betrayal?

I turn to Pagan. How many pills would it take to release her, while leaving enough for me? To miscalculate would be too dreadful to contemplate. I feel sure that this is what you would want . . . and yet the last time that I heard your voice – your own voice and not the synthesised sibilance of the computer – was when you saw her stretching for some capsules which I had left on the chest. She was counting them out like jujubes. I rushed upstairs just in time to prevent her putting them in her mouth. Your head was writhing on the pillow, your lips were blue and covered in spume. It was as if so much strength went into that final warning that you never uttered another sound.

I need to hear your voice again; I need a sign. Will you make the leap from my memory to my imagination? Will you prove that there is an after-life, if only in my mind? Help me. Give me a flash of inspiration so extraordinary that I know that it can only come from you.

Nothing . . . I sit and wait but there is nothing; my imagination is as empty as my life. I have not felt so helpless since Donald Coombes used to lie in wait for me at the school gates and my mother told me that I was big enough to fight my own battles. But what can I do about Pagan's? No one will let me take up arms on her behalf. I have failed her . . . I have failed you. You should have entrusted her to Tristan and Deborah or Fergus and Penny or any of the other couples who offered. With them, she would have been protected by the law; with me, she is denied basic justice. I have no right of appeal. My morals are despised, my motives compromised. How can someone so limp-wristed point a finger at anyone else? Since meeting your mother, I understand better than ever why you left Pagan with me; but the very thing that made me safe in your eyes makes me suspect to the rest of the world.

My fears take flesh as I watch Pagan toss in her sleep, clenching her fists into powerless punches. I wipe beads of sweat off her forehead and blow wisps of hair from her eyes. 'Forward . . . fast forward,' she shouts; once again, the late-night video is whirling. Is it fanciful to speculate on the films that she is seeing? Are they suitable for all or do

293

they demand parental guidance? Who shot them? Who is showing them? Who has censored them? What home horror movies are playing on her mind? As she bangs her teddy bear on the pillow and flings it out of bed, I visualise the daddy bear disturbing her dreams.

I take her in my arms and try to clear her head without waking her. She shies away as though she senses my maleness before she identifies me . . . as though your father has filled her with an indiscriminate fear of men. I cannot let her go through life with your confusions, fixed in her sexual distastes by the age of six.

'Men are animals, Leo. They fuck women and fight each other. The processes are the same; they just involve different parts of the body. I realised when I went to the bare-knuckle boxing with Brian.'

I identify seven stages of sexual awareness: curiosity; naughtiness; game; passion; obsession; depravity; incapacity. The ideal is to settle in the middle. But what of those who start too young or peak too soon?

I fear that your parents are taking steps to stop me seeing Pagan. Their latest complaint concerns our visit to the paediatrician, which she let slip, in spite of all my warnings, when your mother took her to the doctor to find out why she was not eating and she said that she had already been to one the week before with me. . . . This evening, when I go to fetch her, I am attacked.

'You have no right to take her to see anyone without our permission.'

'I was concerned about her; I wanted a professional opinion.'

'So you creep off to a doctor?' Your father sneers as though at a schoolboy sneak.

'And would you like to know what he found? She had a bruised and dilated anus and scars on her hymen.' Your mother covers Pagan's ears; she squirms as though they were pincers. 'It's not Pagan's ears that are hurt.'

'Patience! Patience!'

'There's a word for men like you,' your father says, 'who foul up your own lives and see foulness everywhere, who sully our decency with your perversions. It's a word that begins with a "c".' I think of the obvious. 'Cad!' He takes me by surprise.

'What's dilated?' your mother asks. Pagan slips free and runs to me.

'Dilated like a gaping wound; dilated like something's been forced inside.'

'Suppositories,' your mother exclaims in triumph. 'Patience has been constipated and I gave her suppositories.' I have never seen a suppository and try to picture the size. 'I used to give them to her mother and uncle. Ask William, he'll tell you.'

'Gladly. Will you give me his number?'

'And as for scars . . . she fights when I try to insert them. I have to force her. I may have caught her with my nails. You see,' she turns to Pagan. 'I told you not to wriggle. Now look at all the trouble you've caused.'

'So who applied them? You or your husband?'

'Me, of course. Father has never so much as changed a nappy. He can't bear anything to do with the t-o-i-l-e-t.'

'Pagan will say otherwise, won't you, darling? Just tell your grandmother what you told me.' She stands quaking. 'No one's going to punish you. You can say whatever you like.'

'They most certainly will punish her if she tells lies.' Your father cracks his knuckles like a whip. 'She has to be taught to tell the truth.' She starts to cry.

'Now look what you've done,' I accuse him.

'Now look what you've done,' your mother accuses me. 'Patience, come to Granny.'

'Pagan, stay where you are.'

She shrinks from us both and runs from the room.

'See, she can't face the truth,' your father says. 'She's trying it on. She says the worst thing she can think of because she knows you'll believe it. It's what you want to hear.'

'How does she know what to say? She's six years old!'

'I wouldn't be surprised if he put her up to it,' your mother says, 'putting lies in her mouth to try and scare us and then repeating them to the lawyers. Well it won't work.'

'Can't you see how unhappy she is? Doesn't that worry you, if nothing else?'

'It's only when she sees you; the rest of the time, she's fine. You overturn everything. You take her back to her old

295

life. You call her by her old name. Is it any wonder she won't settle? I tell you, I've had as much as I can take. I'm going to talk to our solicitor; I'm going to prepare a file –'

'Easy, Mother.'

'How can you say that? You're the one he's accusing . . . such vile accusations.'

'We have to think of the girl.'

'Precisely. We must free Patience from his evil clutches. Which is why I intend to have his Contact Order revoked. . . . So, I suggest that you make the most of this weekend. If I have my way, it will be the last.'

I discount her threats and drive Pagan home. In the car, she reproaches me bitterly for betraying her to her grandparents. I apologise and suggest that she smacks me hard as soon as we stop at a traffic-lights; but every one that we come to is green. I am horrified to find that my intervention has made things worse. Far from being deterred by detection, your father seems to have grown more confident. The message is clear; he is at liberty to renew the attack, while I am threatened with exclusion. Moreover, according to Max, by demanding that Dudley conduct an internal examination without the consent of her guardians, I may well be charged with aiding and abetting an assault.

From assault to murder . . . I look at Pagan and again at the pills. Why not leap to the logical conclusion and kill the pain once and for all? But I fear the obloquy that would grow on my name like mould. I would become the all-purpose pervert, star attraction in the Chamber of Horrors. My mother would be forced to do public penance for my birth, while your parents wallowed in tabloid grief. And yet it is they who are the monsters so beloved of banner headlines. I accuse them both since, at the very least, she must suspect his guilt and be trying to protect him. How else does she explain why she would treat a child for constipation, while at the same time rubbing her nose in her soiled pants?

I am incensed by the inconsistency and put down the pills. There is no way that I will play into their hands by doing away with myself, let alone with Pagan. Come what may, I will find the means to expose them. Meanwhile, I flush temptation down the lavatory, saving two Mogadon as a pledge of sleep.

Thank you . . . thank you. I slept far better than I dared hope. I saw a sign and one so simple and yet so bold that it bears your hallmark. My dream developed into a vision. I realised that, instead of struggling against insuperable odds, we should run away; I glimpsed both the disguise and the destination. As I apply the regulation fifty brush-strokes to her hair, I put the proposal to Pagan.

'How would you like to be a little boy? Just pretend. So that we can hide somewhere that no one will find us.'

'Oh yes,' she claps her hands. 'No one could hurt me if I was a boy, could they?'

'No one at all. You'll be totally safe.'

'No one could do naughty, nasty things'. . . . I push my thoughts back under the stones where they belong. 'Will I have to be someone else again; or will I still be Pagan?'

'We could call you Paul. That's almost Pagan but not quite. Just like a boy's almost a girl but not quite.'

'Paul. I'm Paul . . . Paul.' She bounces up and down on the bed.

'Sh-sh. You mustn't let Consuela hear; it's a secret.'

I have forgotten the burden of secrecy on a child and the frustration that comes of not being able to reveal and relieve it. She drops heavy hints over the coco pops ('if I were a boy, I'd have two helpings'), and her chuckles echo the crackles of the cereal as she adds the milk. Fortunately, Consuela is content just to see her looking so cheerful and picks up nothing more substantial than the dirty plates.

After breakfast, we drive to the bank where I withdraw the £4762 that I have on deposit and then to the Halifax, where I take out my entire entitlement of £500 in cash. We then go shopping, or rather stocking. Our first stop is Marks and Spencer, where Paul is kitted out as extensively as for the first day at school. We buy vests, socks and underpants – authenticity being the keynote – together with shorts and jeans, tee-shirts, sweatshirts ('Will I sweat cos I'm a boy?'), pullovers and tops. There is no call to invent a twin brother – like the burly transvestites with weight-lifter wives – since ages are prominently marked. 'I'm nearly seven,' Pagan protests as I place her in the five-to six-year-old range. 'But you're not tall,' I say deter-minedly. 'Besides, boys are bigger than girls,' I add as a sop to her pride.

Our visit to Russell and Bromley turns out to be trickier. 'That's a boy's shoe, sir,' the assistant insists. 'Oh, I didn't realise . . .' he blushes and hurries to find me its pair . . . I feel like the Princess of Wales being let off for speeding.

'She's a tomboy. What can I do?'

We head back up the street to Snow and Rock, where we buy a tent, mattresses, stove and fuel-canisters, flashlight and batteries, kettle, pans and sleeping-bags.

'How can we sleep in a bag?' Pagan asks.

'It's not a real bag; it's just a word.'

'Like when *she's* a bag of nerves?'

'But much nicer.'

The spending-spree elates me. I intend to use my credit to the limit. Who knows when I will be back to pay the bill? We move on to Dixons, where I buy a small transistor radio, more batteries and a Sony Watchman as a surprise for Pagan.

'Now you'll be able to see yourself wherever you are,' the assistant says blithely.

'My show's live.' I resent the imputation. 'Besides, the screen isn't a mirror.'

After returning home for lunch, where we make up for our lateness by our appetites (for the first time in months Pagan not only finishes her food but asks for seconds), we set out for the rest of our supplies. To avert suspicion, I alternate between several stores. The watchword is tins. I think back to the programme which I made with a group of survivalists in the States; they had provisions to last ten years. Our requirements may be more modest, but I am in no mood for restraint. So I buy salmon, sardines, mussels, tongue, turkey and tuna; vegetables, soups and bisques; spaghetti hoops and golden syrup (by special request); truffles, *marrons* and *foie gras* (for special treats); orange juice and orange squash, coffee and Coffeemate, ginger beer and gin.

I feel as if I am entering the world of Bunter and Robin and making up for all the midnight feasts that I missed along with boarding school. I break my own 'tins only' rule by taking two fruit cakes, with sell-by dates by which we should have long left the country, and a selection of comfort-chocolates. For a few weeks, I intend to forget both my waistline and Pagan's teeth. The imperative is to survive.

Toothbrushes and toothpaste, soap and soap-powder, deodorant, hair-dye and fly-spray, a mirror . . . I congratulate myself on covering all contingencies. Aspirin, junior Disprin, antiseptic, disinfectant, bandages, throat sweets and vitamins . . . your mother's ambulance can hardly come so well stocked. Pagan views every item as further confirmation of her freedom. Our only argument arises over cat-food. In three separate shops, at three separate stands, she attempts to slip tins into my trolley. I explain that we have to leave Trouble with Consuela. Her lower lip trembles. Much to my disgust, I hear myself saying that boys don't cry.

'I'm not a boy yet.'

'It takes a lifetime's practice.'

It is Consuela's cards evening, and I put Pagan straight to bed, insisting on an immediate lights-out in view of the busy day ahead. I scan the shelves for the perfect books to occupy my leisure . . . as well as long-deferred classics and my *Desert Island* Proust, I take Anaïs Nin's *Diary* in honour of you. I pack three suitcases of clothes and load the car, while trying to avoid the attention of the unofficial neighbourhood watch. I write to Max, my mother and your parents, with explanations for our departure, and to Consuela, with instructions on seeing to Trouble and the house. I ask Max to pay her wages and any bills and leave him a letter of authority to draw on my accounts.

The next morning, as soon as Consuela goes to church, I cut off Pagan's hair. My model is Dennis the Menace; but she squirms so much that it almost becomes Van Gogh. 'I am a boy!' she exclaims with delight. And, with the addition of a Yankees baseball shirt and shorts, the illusion is complete. I cannot hope for such a drastic transformation; the memory of Ernest Lipton's party precludes drag. But, by dyeing my hair, I hide my most distinctive feature, while my freckles will disappear beneath my beard. Then, giving thanks for my magpie mentality, I dust down my old St Bride's corduroy jacket and trousers, which smell

299

somewhat musty from the attic but still fit perfectly after eighteen years . . . eighteen years, I hope you take note (I am inclined to buy another dozen bars of Lindt to celebrate). I am thrilled to find myself anonymous again.

We are let down only by our headgear. As we leave the house, I sport an old Cambridge boater and Pagan a school hat, to hide our hair from any intrusive gaze.

'I can't wear this; it's for a girl,' she insists with all the scorn of Just William.

'We'll throw it away as soon as we're out of London.'

'Shan't we give it to the poor children?'

'Maybe one of them will pick it up.'

We are halfway down the avenue when I think 'passport' and make an abrupt turn.

'Are we going to another country?'

'Not straightaway but soon.'

'When?'

I start to explain that, when my beard has grown and our safety is assured, we will hire a boat to take us to the Continent.

'That's why I drew out so much money. We won't be free to go through airports. For a start, I no longer have your passport. And, anyway, we might be recognised. But do you remember Aunt Imogen?'

'The lady with the funny hair?'

'Sometimes. When she came back from living in America, she wasn't allowed to bring her dogs.'

'Why?'

'It's a rule. So she took them to France.'

'Don't they have rules in France?'

'Not the same ones. Then she paid some fishermen to sail them across the sea.'

'Did they put them in boxes?'

'That I don't know.'

'Will they put us in boxes?'

'Of course not. We shall stand on deck and wave England bye-bye.'

I wish I were as certain about where we would be waving hello. Spain is the obvious choice, although I have no desire to spend my life among the beer-bellied brutality of the Costa del Crime. . . . In the past, Sweden has provided a haven for terrorists and deserters, and yet, whatever

David and his friends might say, I am hardly a political refugee.

'Will we live in abroad?'

'Yes.'

'For ever?'

'For as long as we want.'

'Will I be a girl again?'

'You can be whatever you like.'

I post the letters before we hit the Westway, where I fling Pagan's hat out of the window. She laughs. I proceed to discard a far more precious package: her hair. I intended to keep it, next to her baby curls, as a souvenir of a second rite of passage; but the dangers of discovery are too great. So I release the strands, which drift like thistledown as we roar up the road to Herefordshire.

'Where are we going?'

'Do you remember when Mummy died and we drove to have lunch with an old lady and we said a wish and scattered fairy-dust by a lake?'

'Are we going to live in a van?'

'No. There was a little house by the gates, which no one has lived in for years. It won't be very comfortable or clean; there won't be any heat or light. But it's June, so we won't be cold. And we'll get up when it's day and go to bed when it's dark. At least I will; you'll be asleep far earlier.'

'That's cruel.'

'But we'll be together, which is all that matters, isn't it?'

'Will we have a TV?'

'Wait and see. If you're an especially good girl . . . sorry, boy'; I respond to her exasperated elbow. 'You may have a surprise.'

We stop for petrol near Malvern. I work the pumps and worry about recognition. The further we go from London, the more self-conscious I feel about the boater. I long for something less jaunty, better suited to the cords. I find myself in rare agreement with my father, who complained that 'No one wears a hat any more, no one shows respect' (although, in his scheme, the main purpose of putting one on was to take it off to your betters). I push mine over my eyes and approach the till with trepidation. My fears turn out to be groundless. The attendant is so engrossed in conversation that it is as much as he can do to count my change.

We picnic in a field, which is a great success and pee behind a bush, which is not. Pagan finds squatting in the undergrowth undignified and fails to function.

'It's like a tramp.'

'What do you know about tramps?'

'*She* told me.' Her forehead furrows. 'She doesn't like them.'

'All the more reason to behave like one,' I suggest with vengeful logic. Her bladder instantly agrees.

A little before four, we reach Crierley. Pagan recognises the pineapples. I examine the gatehouse, which is even more ramshackle than I remembered.

'Are we going to make it tidy?'

'No, I've explained. No one must know that we're here.'

'Will we go to prison?'

'If they find us. At least, I will. You'll go back to your grandparents.'

'That's worse, that's like going through Traitors' Gate!'

I park the car behind the cottage, hidden by a wall from the road and a hedge from the house. I ineffectually kick over the tracks. Pagan ignores my instructions and runs up the path.

'Wait for me; it may be dangerous.' I suddenly feel a tug of despair. I have never before acted on impulse, and, walking around the walls, I see why.

'Don't you have the key?' Pagan asks, as I rattle the front door, which I had somehow assumed would be open. 'How are we going to get in?'

'I'll find a way,' I say, with vain confidence. 'This is an adventure. In adventures, you don't use doors; you climb through windows. Don't you know that?' Her silence suggests doubt. We continue our circuit of the cottage. I lift her over fallen slates, broken glass and crumbled plaster, but I cannot save her from the gorse bushes. 'Never mind,' I say. 'Little boys' legs are always a mass of scratches; it'll look much more authentic.'

'What's authentic?'

'Real.'

I choose the window which appears to offer the easiest access. The sill is covered with viscous slime; and, as I press my fingers on the frame, they sink in, releasing a kaleidoscopic colony of ants. Pagan screams, while I berate myself for omitting to bring gloves. Two of the panes are smashed; so I grab a stick and shatter the shards. Wrapping my hand in a rag, I wrench the wood; but it fails to give way. I pick up a large stone, taking care to avoid the crawling vermin, and, pushing Pagan well back, hurl it through the frame. From the subsequent cracks and crunches, I am convinced that I have destroyed the entire wall and wait for the rush of rubble. When none occurs, I move forward and try to dislodge the remnants.

'It's like a shark. Look, the window's the mouth and the bits of glass are its teeth.'

'Then take care not to come too close, or it may bite.'

I contemplate how best to brave the jaws. If I put a leg over, I am in danger of castration; head first, it's decapitation; feet first, and I may be split in two. I begin to regret my well-spent youth. Why was I singing in choirs when I could have been breaking into houses? Surely every child should know how to negotiate splinters of glass without risking serious injury? And, to my amazement, ours does.

'Why have you stopped?'

'I don't want to chop my head off. Strange as it may seem, I'm rather fond of it.'

'Why don't you push it with your hand?'

Facing me is a handle which, with a Test-Your-Strength whack, I nudge down. The frame flies open, spraying glass like melting snow.

I congratulate Pagan and ease myself over the edge. I feel myself sitting on something yellow. 'Me too,' she calls; and I lift her over, trying to avoid the sludge on the sill. Her shoes scrape on the debris. 'It smells like pooh,' she says, pulling a face midway between a grimace and a pout.

'It's just damp,' I snap, stung by her honesty.

'It's pooh,' she reiterates . . . and she is right. As we move into the hall, the stench grows stronger, and, as I open the kitchen door, I realise that we are not the first to have sought refuge here. Like a prison cell in a dirty protest, your dream cottage has become a giant midden. And, in the corner of the room, padding and panting, lurks something alive.

I slam the door and haul Pagan back the way that we came. I thrust her through the window and quickly follow.

'Aren't we going to stay there?'

'No.'

'Then where?'

'I don't know.' I picture a salesman asleep in his car.

'Can't we go to a hotel?'

'You know that no one must see us.'

'But now that I'm in my clothes and my legs are scratched. . . .'

'We have to wait till my beard grows.' She puts her hand to my cheek.

'That's scratchy too.'

I squat against the wall; Pagan makes to mirror me and tumbles into my lap. I wonder whether it might be feasible to rush back to London and intercept the mail. I could ask Consuela not to cook for six months while we used up the tins; I could tell your mother that I had to cut off Pagan's hair on discovering lice. But that still leaves your father. . . . .

'What are we going to do?' Pagan asks me.

'I don't know. We must both put our thinking-caps on.'

'What's the problem?' I start and look up to see Robin; moonlight marbling his skin. 'Why must you always look on the black side? No one comes near it for months on end. We'll be perfectly safe.'

'It seems sacrilegious.'

'It isn't St Paul's! It's a fake, a folly. It's dedicated to Aphrodite . . . it was made for us.'

'Lead on then,' I say with a smile. . . . 'Don't worry,' I turn quickly to Pagan; 'I've thought of the perfect place . . . the Temple of Love.'

Robin darts down the path, while Pagan and I remain at the cottage, along with *My Naughty Little Sister*. At half-past six, she pronounces herself starving, and I prepare a meal. Unwilling to set up the stove, I open tins of cold ham, coleslaw and pineapple chunks . . . I promise you that, once we reach Spain, we will live on nothing but fresh fruit and vegetables. . . . After eating, we return to the car, where she complains about the seats, her stomach and boredom, before falling fast asleep. At eleven o'clock, I decide to risk the drive. I wish that I knew Lady Standish's habits. Does she lie awake, nursing her grievances and measuring the nights with cheap thrillers? Or is she lulled to sleep by Lydia's snores? What will I do if she hears us? . . . So far, there is no need to answer. I give thanks for the lack of gravel and park at the front of the house.

'Is it still an adventure?' Pagan asks, as she stumbles into the night.

'The adventure's barely begun.'

Taking the torch and tent in one hand and Pagan in the other, I make my way to the back of the house. Across the courtyard, I see the caravan and the cold flickers of a black and white TV. Creeping across the cobbles, I am conscious of a world of wild noises: burrs and buzzes and hums and twitters and whoops. We make our way past the walled garden and into the copse. I find the path instinctively; I have trodden it so often in my mind that my feet follow suit. All at once, we see the temple. I am strangely reluctant to walk up the steps.

'It's teeny,' Pagan says.

'Do you remember it from last time?'

'I thought a temple was big like a church.'

'This is a temple just for us.'

I touch the balustrade. I half-expect to find evidence of my former visit . . . perhaps our conjoined initials scratched into the stone, like the graffiti on the Acropolis. But I have evidence enough welling in my eyes.

'Why are you crying?'

'This is a very special place for me.'

'Are they happy tears?'

'Oh yes.'

'I don't want to be a grown-up; you cry when you're happy as well as when you're sad. . . . Where are we going to sleep?'

'Here, under the stars.'

'I can't see any stars.'

'It's what it's called.'

'That's silly.'

'Look!' As if on cue from a celestial stage-manager, a star shoots across the sky. 'Who's silly now?' She snuggles against my arm.

'Why can't we go inside?'

'It's locked.'

'How do you know?'

'It always is. Still, we'll be warm enough in the tent.' I begin to unfold it. Pagan moves to the door. She turns the handle, which opens. Amazement defers to triumph. 'Who's silly now?' she asks.

The interior is clean and fresh and empty. I am seized by the spirit of Dionysus . . . or, more prosaically, the urge to dance. As though reading my thoughts, Pagan enacts them, pirouetting across the floor. In the semi-darkness, I catch the gleam of marble and shine the torch on Aphrodite, Zeus and several other immortals gazing down in Olympian disdain.

'Is it Jesus?' Pagan inquires of a beard.

'These are pagan gods.'

'You mustn't say that,' she says intently, as though I were implicating her.

'I suggest we pitch camp here. We'll soon have you tucked up.'

'Aah!' She screams with a cry so feral that I do not fear disclosure.

'What's wrong?'

'Something touched my leg. Look.' She kneels beside the carcass of a bird. 'Is it deaded?'

'Don't touch it.' The temple turns into a tomb, as I picture its frantic last flight, flapping itself to death in a doomed bid for freedom.

'What sort is it?' she asks. I look and shudder.

'A blackbird,' I say, gently cupping its blood-red breast.

She refuses to remain alone in the temple, so I take her to fetch supplies. But bleary eyes and dragging feet only make my task harder, and, after two trips, I insist that she stay in the car. She agrees, on condition that I lock the doors. I return to work. It is a long haul, but the moon lights – and memories lighten – it. All goes well, until I spot a figure leaving the caravan and crossing the courtyard. I freeze and a butane-canister rolls out of its box. Fear amplifies the clatter and I anticipate discovery. But, after a momentary hesitation, she proceeds on her way. From this distance, it is impossible to know whether to credit Lydia's myopia or her mother's age.

With everything transferred, I think about hiding the car. It is too metallic to trust to the trees and there are no handy piles of autumn leaves. I am struck by a sudden whim to drive it into the lake. . . . Then I see that I am standing beside the stables. I heave open a rotting door. The stalls offer the perfect hiding-place, and I steer it slowly round. In a corner, I spot a heap of tattered horse-blankets (which put me in mind of Robin's Aunt Waverley). I fling them over the chassis. 'That's it then,' I say to Pagan, 'time for bed.'

'Lift! Lift!' She holds her arms outstretched.

'Lift what?'

'Lift me.' Too tired to press for a 'please', I pick her up and carry her down the path.

'You didn't buy me any boy's pyjamas!'

'Never mind. You can be a boy during the day and a girl at night, when it doesn't matter.'

'No, that's wrong. Night's when it matters most of all.' She slumps, and I tuck her into her sleeping-bag. I lay out the mattresses, which are self-inflating. I only wish that the tent worked on a similar principle . . . after grappling with it for an hour, I gain new respect for the truth of situation comedy. I decide to leave it until morning and bag down. Sleep keeps a watchful distance, and I lie awake, dreaming of dawn.

In the morning, I realise that I have also forgotten to buy loo paper. We are left to improvise with ferns and dock leaves. While wiping Pagan, I come across the sores on her anus. I ask if they hurt; she pretends not to hear. 'Would you like to rub on some ointment?' She pulls up her pants. Then I remember the form. 'Does Patience's bottom hurt? Would she like some ointment?' She looks at me sharply. 'You said I'm called Paul.'

My third omission – and a deliberate one – is a camera. Given my beard and Pagan's hair, I felt that a mirror would be ample record. But, as we settle in the temple in our drum-tight tent (to my MA [Cantab], I shall now add my DIY [Crierley]), explore territory, cook meals, read, relax, and generally enjoy each other's company, I realise that I want to preserve every moment, and not merely for myself in memory but for posterity on film. I need an independent witness . . . but it is stuck in a drawer in my study, so I develop a series of snapshots in my mind.

The first shows us by the lake . . . don't worry, as long as we keep behind the reeds, we are well concealed. That is me bathing and beckoning Pagan to enter. Although the chill knocks me back like whisky, I pronounce it warm. Nevertheless, nothing will induce her to set foot on the mud. So, there I am, picking her up and pretending to throw her in. And there she is back on dry land . . . which is not out of sequence; I have to put her down fast when she forgets herself and starts to scream. The next is one of my favourites; I am lifting her in the air and dunking her. That way, she can enjoy the splash without the squelch. Incidentally, this one is not out of focus; it is lost in a cloud of spray as I fall in.

It is as hard to persuade her to drink from the lake as to swim in it, especially once we have used it to wash.

'You wouldn't drink the bath.'

'This is different. There are organisms . . .' (or in my mother's telling phrase 'orgasms') 'plants and little fish that clean the water.'

'I don't want to drink little fish.'

'Besides, where do you think the water at home comes from?'

'Taps.'

'Which lead back here. Do you know that the water that flows from every London tap has passed through seven and a half people?'

'That they spit out?'

'No, that they pee.' That picture of her with her tongue out perfectly captures her reaction.

'I'm never going to have another drink in my whole life.' The next one with the orange squash is to remind her not to make such rash claims.

'Anyway, how can it pass through half a people?'

We have now been here three days, and I continue to record our daily routine in order to rebut any future suggestion that we must have been bored. There I am with *Clarissa* . . . well she is boring, I have to admit; but, as you see, I soon find a far more congenial companion in Anaïs Nin. This one shows Pagan declaring that I have read quite enough grown-up books and must now turn to hers. With the title hidden, I cannot tell if it is *The Wind in the Willows* or *The Worst Witch All at Sea* . . . although I plump for the former, since there we are, an hour later, scouring the lakeside for role-models. Look at Pagan, in every sense a portrait of delight, as I point out a potential Toad.

If the colouring in the next batch of shots looks different, it is not due to the light or to inferior film, but rather because, after a week of blue skies, gentle breezes, bare skin and purging sun, we are turning a golden brown. My beard is growing fast and, even without dye, appears several shades darker than my hair. Every morning Pagan examines it, as though she were cultivating water-cress for school.

'It'll soon be ready,' she says. 'You don't look like you at all.'

I agree, as I gaze with a stranger's eyes at the stranger's reflection. In many ways, I will be reluctant to leave. I have gained a deep sense of peace here: with Pagan; with myself; and, if it is not too fanciful, with Nature. No longer Mr Metropolis, I feel like the American businessmen who strip off their suits, enter the forest and find their souls. I am learning to appreciate solitude, for its own sake and not just as a break between engagements. I can finally understand Robin's identification with the landscape . . . and yet that only makes his absence harder to explain. I presume that it holds too many memories, which would also account for his mother's and sister's avoidance of the lake . . . although not for their neglect of the rest of the grounds. I have not caught a glimpse of either of them since the first night.

Even in the wild, we cannot escape the television. Pagan reserves her broadest smile not for the discovery of a bird's nest or a badger but for my present of the Sony Watchman. To my *Desert Island* books are added her lakeside programmes. Then, one evening, she runs to me, not with her usual glum face at the close of children's broadcasting, but the picture of excitement as she catches our appearance on the six o'clock news. I borrow the set. The story leads on every channel: I have abducted my former ward; we are believed to be still in the country; we may be travelling in a silver-grey BMW, registration number J 473 ELF; and, while the police have no reason to fear for our safety, they are very anxious to speak to me or, indeed, to anyone with information regarding our whereabouts.

The next day, all the bulletins carry a tearful interview with your parents. 'If you're watching this, Patience,' your mother says, 'we just want to tell you that we miss you and want you home.' I note that, even in the glare of the cameras, there is no mention of love. As she sees them, Pagan starts to shake, first her fists and then the set.

'Look out, or you'll break it!'

'I don't care! I won't ever go back. Never, never, never. I want to stay here for ever, like Mole.'

'You won't have to go back. One evening very soon, I'll walk down to the village, find a telephone box and call Aunt Imogen'. . . . I have decided to enlist Imogen's help, less for her experience with the dogs than for her love of conspiracy. It will appeal to her for all the wrong reasons as well as the right.

So that is my Crierley album . . . or, at least, the captions; the pictures have to be taken on trust. . . . No, I refuse to look at any more. I ought to tear those up. They are so grey and grim, which is the fault of the weather. After two days of driving rain, the romance of the landscape is shattered. The foliage wilts under the weight of moisture; the purples of the foxgloves darken into decay. The fairy ring becomes a clump of toadstools and the magic glade a tangled scrub. Deprived of our morning swim and evening stroll, we are confined to the Temple, with as little to occupy our minds as to keep us warm. Boredom is now Pagan's constant complaint. 'You said we're on an adventure. Things are supposed to happen on adventures.'

'They will. Shall I teach you a new game of cards called rummy?'

'I hate cards. Why won't your stupid beard come quicker? I'm going to pull it so hard that it grows this big.' At a stroke, she wills me into Bernard Shaw.

'You'll just pull it out. Then we'll have to wait for it to grow all over again.'

'I'm bored. I want to go home.'

I hold depression at bay as if it were an assailant; I talk it down like a suicide off a ledge. It is time to make plans for our departure. The radio confirms that, although we are no longer headline news, we have not been forgotten . . . one report suggests that we may be in Germany (my remarks at the bank are paying dividends). And yet I refuse to become complacent. We need to stay here for at least another week. It is essential that Pagan should not lose heart. And I think that I have found the answer. . . . Do you remember when Robin took us to the top of the house for a tour of the nursery, with the rocking-horse and the doll's-house and the dressing-up box which licensed his illicit fantasies? In the museum that his mother has made of her life, they are bound to be prime exhibits. I propose to Pagan that we should take some of them out on loan.

'Will there be a video?'

'There were no videos when Robin and Lydia were little.'

'But you said they were rich.'

Having broached the subject at breakfast, I am forced to spend the rest of the day curbing her enthusiasm. Although I am confident of negotiating the house, I am wary of the caravan, and I refuse to make a move before nine o'clock. At which point, she insists on accompanying me, 'so as you know what to bring'.

'Don't you trust me any more?' I ask. She pretends not to hear.

As we approach the house, I am filled with a dull dread like the dawn of a Colwyn Bay Sunday. I stroke my beard and determine that, no matter what, I will ring Imogen tomorrow. She must know dozens of Cornish fishermen . . . the association makes me laugh; Pagan presses an admonitory finger to her lips. We creep around the walls. When I urge her to keep to the shadows, she responds by walking on tip-toe and toppling onto me.

I move to a side door, which is, as I expected, unlocked . . . no doubt Lady Standish believes that even burglars have abandoned them. Walking down a short corridor, we find ourselves in the trophy room. The furniture is covered with sheets, as if all that the house requires is a coat of paint. I shine my torch onto walls packed with family portraits and animal pelts. Pagan screams as the beam picks up a polar bear's grin.

'Don't worry; it's stuffed.'

'It's a zoo.'

We proceed to the hall and the staircase, where she grips my hand at the sight of a suit of armour.

311

'It's scary.'

'Think of the Tin Man in *The Wizard of Oz*.'

My light is reflected in the richness of the panelling, where centuries of polish hold out against years of neglect. I aim the torch up to the ceiling; crumbling plaster and missing timbers attest to the gallery's collapse. I wonder whether it is safe to proceed.

'Why have we stopped?' Pagan asks. 'Where are the toys?'

We climb the stairs. The first-floor landing is blocked by a row of chairs, on which stands a crudely written notice 'Unsafe! Keep out!' I do not allow my beam to linger. We continue to climb. Pagan takes exception to Robin's great- (or is it great-great-?) grandfather's kelims, which brush her head as she follows the wall. 'Carpets should stay on floors,' she says severely, adding with equal stricture, 'these stairs are too steep for children.'

'Hold on to the rail,' I suggest, ignoring the implicit plea to be carried. Instead, she grabs the fringe of a kelim. 'Take care,' I warn, 'it may not be very secure.' My fears are justified as the rug rips off the wall. I hear a scream and a thud, followed by a gut-wrenching groan, as the dead weight crashes down on her. I swing the torch through varying degrees of darkness. I try three steps and then six, by when it is clear that she has rolled to the bottom of the flight. I run down to her; I tug at the cloth, raising a miasma of dust. 'Don't worry, darling; I'm here.' I scramble to reach the source of the moan.

She lies very still at the centre of the rug, like a princess smuggled from a harem. 'It's alright, you haven't hurt yourself,' I assert, as though she had fallen out of bed. 'Come on, we must go up to the nursery. I'll carry you. Would you like a piggyback or a fireman's lift?' She mewls. 'You can't have hurt yourself. You were wrapped in the carpet; it broke the fall. You can't have broken anything.' She whimpers. 'Oh my darling, tell me where it hurts.'

'I hurt.'

'Yes, but where? Can you walk? Shall I try to help you up?' I put my hands under her body and lift; she screams. I lower her gently. 'Is it your back that hurts?' She does not answer. 'I'll carry you downstairs.' It is immediately clear that my slightest touch induces agony. My brain pounds. I am racked by a vision of her lying in bed as immobile as you, the victim not of creeping but permanent paralysis. I see the same console and collar and the stair-lift no longer a game and . . . and I can hardly breath. 'Pagan, darling, I'm going to fetch a doctor . . . an ambulance.'

'Don't leave me.'

'I have to. I'll come straight back. I'll call the lady in the caravan.'

'Don't leave me without the light.'

After wedging the torch in the crook of her arm, I run down the stairs and feel my way through the house. I bang on the caravan door. Lydia opens it, all pink and teeth and glasses. Her hands flutter between her bosom and her face.

'Lydia, where's your mother?'

'Go away!'

'Lady Standish, it's Leo Young!' I peer into the caravan; but Lydia blocks the view.

'Go away! Go away! She has a dog.' She snaps and growls.

'It's Leo, Lydia; you remember me. I'm a friend of Robin's. Where's your mother . . . mama?' As a foetid smell wafts towards me, I fear that the reason for their not appearing is that Lady Standish is dead and Lydia living with her corpse. 'Where's your mother, Lydia? Oh God, why does it have to be you?' I push past her and into the empty caravan.

'She's seen you on the programmes.'

'That's right; but we've stopped for the summer.'

'You stole a little girl. Mama! Mama!' She runs outside. 'She won't let you steal her.' I follow her into the courtyard. She bangs on the door of the outhouse. Lady Standish emerges with a flush. 'What is it? What's the matter?' Her words are slurred as though from a stroke. Lydia stutters and sobs. I intervene.

'Lady Standish, please don't be alarmed, it's Leo Young. I need your help.'

'You are a criminal. You are on the run,' she barks through biteless gums.

'My little girl is hurt. She's fallen downstairs in your house. You must help me.'

' "Must"? I am not a woman to be moved by "must"s. Oh do stop snivelling, Lydia. And fetch my teeth.' Lydia

313

stands bewildered. 'My teeth, Lydia!' She hurries into the caravan. I start to explain what has happened. Lydia brings her the dentures, which she inserts as smoothly as a party trick.

'I need a telephone.'

'We have no telephone here.' A note of imperious mockery returns with her teeth. 'The nearest is in the village. Lydia will take you while I attend to the girl.' Lydia swallows her objections.

'No, we can drive.'

'You have a car?'

'It's parked in the stables. And – of course, what am I thinking of? – I have a phone!' I dash to the stables and throw off the blankets. I grab the mobile and run back through the courtyard, just as Lady Standish comes out of the caravan in a coat.

'Would you ring?' I ask her, 'would you say that a little boy –'

'Boy?'

'You could tell them that he was your grandson. Please. You know what it is to have children. They're trying to take her away from me. It's our only chance.'

'Enough, Mr Young. It's degrading to watch a man beg.' She makes the call. 'Lydia, an ambulance is coming to fetch a boy who's hurt in the house. You must wait in the drive to show the men in. Say nothing, do you understand?' Lydia nods her lumpish head like a puppet. 'Except that your mother is on the stairs with the boy.'

'But she's wearing her pyjamas.'

'They're doctors. It's what they expect.'

I take Lady Standish to Pagan, who is lying where I left her, clutching the torch like a teddy bear, its beam shining on her feet.

'Darling, it's me. Are you alright?'

'You said no time. No time always takes the longest time of all.'

'How are you feeling?'

'Sleepy. It doesn't hurt any more. Can we go for the toys?' I ease the torch out of her hand and direct the light onto her face. Lady Standish gasps.

'What is it?'

'No, it's nothing. It must just be seeing a boy in the house again.'

'Will you go with her in the ambulance? Will you do this for me?'

'I have been trying to remember whether I ended up liking you or despising you. Perhaps tonight will settle it once and for all.'

'Thank you.'

'I shall take Pagan –'

'Paul.'

'Paul – such an obvious name – to the hospital. You will wait with Lydia in the caravan. When I return, we'll talk further.'

'There may be a price to be paid for helping us.'

'Do you suppose that someone who has gone from this to a caravan fears anything that the world can throw at her now?'

I hear steps on the stairs and dart up to the second floor.

'Aren't there any lights, lady?' I catch the wheeze of resentment in the ambulanceman's voice.

'My lady, if you wouldn't mind.'

'We asked the . . . other lady, but she just laughed.'

'My daughter is an innocent. Why do you need lights? We want you to take the child to hospital not to operate on him here.' She trains the torch on their faces to pre-empt any show of protest and then onto Pagan, who makes no sound, as they strap her in the stretcher. 'You remain in your room, Lydia, like a good girl. Should you require anything, ring the bell. You men, follow me.' For a moment, my fears are lost in admiration as she is once again chatelaine of Crierley, striding steadfastly down the stairs, as though to live in darkness were a minor eccentricity and she had never heard of the phrase 'unpaid bill'.

I wait for the blue light to disappear down the drive, before emerging to join Lydia in the caravan.

'She wanted to go to hospital. Lydia likes hospitals. People are nice to her there. They show her pictures and ask her to do drawings. They always say "Very good.".'

'Would you like a drink?' I ask, 'a cup of tea or coffee?'

'You'll burn yourself on the water.'

'I'll take the risk.'

She cowers and covers her ears, as the water boils and

kettle bounces. 'It sounds cross, like the fire is biting a hole in its bottom. One day, it's going to burst out.' I prepare the coffee and let her words roll over me. 'You came to see her with her brother.'

'Yes. Do you remember?'

'Her brother's a bird. He's flown away, but he'll come back. Birds always come back in the summer.'

I black out the Christmas card robins. 'Yes, I'm sure he will.'

'Why did you steal the little girl?'

'I didn't. The television made a mistake.'

'Do you want to marry her?'

'She's a child.'

'Do you want to marry Lydia?'

'What?'

'Mama's going to die soon. And no one's going to marry her; so what will she do?'

'She . . . you mustn't worry.' I tangle myself in her pronouns. 'Your mother is strong.'

'Why won't you marry her? Is it because she's ugly?'

'That's not true. You're very pretty.'

'She's not pretty; she's ugly. They measured her face in a machine. They put a hat on her head that held it hard and counted why she was ugly. All down here and along here.' She traces a slow path over her bulbous forehead, across the lost line of her eyebrows, down her squashed nose to her harelip. I feel an overwhelming rush of pity for her maimed self-awareness, mingled with hatred for the father who passed on his disease in place of the family profile. The 'fatherhood is in the blood' line looks even less tenable when that blood is ninety per cent proof.

'She's ugly, ugly, ugly,' she squalls, as she tears at her cheeks with a vehemence that might do damage, were her nails not bitten to the quick. Pulling her hands from her face, I try to project warmth without encouragement. She starts to spout gibberish – 'She wants to be a swan, she wants to be a swan' – and I fear that my coming may have unhinged her. But snores replace sobs, as she sinks slowly into sleep, lolling her misshapen head on my shoulder.

I drift in a sleep-waking void as I wait for Lady Standish to return. Guilt weighs as heavily on me as Lydia. As dawn seeps warily through the window, I realise that my only course is to admit defeat. My rescue attempt has exposed Pagan to worse dangers than your father. Even if she escapes tonight without serious injury, both of our identities are sure to be revealed.

I snap into alertness as a car crosses the courtyard. I free myself from Lydia, who slips onto her side. Numbness grips my shoulder and I revolve like a giddy sheep. Straining to make out the voices above the snores, I seize on the peremptory 'That will be all, we can manage the rest ourselves.' So they are back . . . I give thanks to the gods of temple, church and forest; what is more, she can walk. . . . As she confirms a moment later by stepping into the doorway, her left arm in a sling.

'Pagan has fractured her wrist.' Lady Standish forestalls my question. Guilt turns to relief and then back to guilt at feeling relief.

'I was sure that she must have broken her back.'

'She has some very nasty bruises, but she'll live.'

'Darling, let me help you.' I lead her by the undamaged elbow. She feels as fragile as a bird that has been winged.

'You may use my bed.'

'Does it hurt?'

'They gave me a drink of blackcurrant and two needles, but they said not to look. And they took pictures of me, but I didn't let them take my pants down –' She drops her voice to a whisper – 'so they can't tell the police. Was I good?'

'You were very good.'

'They said I was a soldier. That's even better than a boy!'

'No more talking now,' Lady Standish insists, 'it's time to rest.' She covers her with all the warmth of one who is given too little licence to be gentle. As she kisses her shyly, I see a long line of longed-for grandchildren. 'Remember what you promised me.'

'What was it that she promised you?' I ask a few minutes later as, leaving Pagan and Lydia to sleep, we cross the lawn in the brittle morning light.

'That if she did what I asked, I would tell no one about you.'

'And have you kept your word?'

'Are you trying to insult me?'

'I'm sorry, I'm still in a state of shock. I'm amazed that you were able to fool the staff.'

'We weren't. Of course, they saw nothing on the X-rays; but they had to check for internal injuries. I gave her name as Pauline . . . known to her friends as Paul. Luck was with us. The doctor wanted to keep her in hospital. She said it was the rule for children injured at night to see a social worker in the morning. I directed her attention to the portrait in the hall. "My husband's grandfather founded this hospital," I said; "his father endowed it; for twenty years, I was President of the League of Friends". . . . She gave way, on condition that we came back to the fracture clinic. Remind me to let you have the card.'

'You've been brilliant.' She shivers. 'But you're exhausted. How thoughtless of me! You've been up all night; you need to sleep.'

'I never sleep; I just dream differently.' She walks on. 'You haven't yet told me why you came here.'

'I tried to explain: her grandfather –'

'No, not why you left London; why you chose Crierley.'

'It sounds fanciful, but it was almost as though something drew me here. I pictured the grounds . . . the isolation.'

'And what about the rain? Did you seek shelter in the house?'

'There's a temple in the woods . . . I spent a night there once before.' Her face clouds with a long-suppressed memory.

'I should never have come between you and Robin. You were the one person whom he loved.'

'We were very young, finding our way through our feelings.'

'He assured me.'

'We were finding our way through our words.'

'I put blood before nature. It was the greatest mistake of my life.'

'But . . .' I temper my question with discretion; 'you didn't appear to object to his friendship with Duncan Treflis.'

'Duncan was a family friend. We hoped to flesh out that friendship when Robin married his niece.'

'Only he wouldn't have it.'

'I put it to him that it was his duty, but he refused to see. He talked of his duty to himself. I told him that there was

318

no such thing. Duties, by definition, are to other people. He claimed that I needed him to sacrifice himself in order to justify my own wasted life. Men are so melodramatic. How could my life ever be wasted when I had him? He accused me of thinking only of Crierley and not of him. I tried to explain that they were one and the same. Duncan is a very wealthy man. With the money that he was prepared to settle on Robin and Jenny, the house would have come alive again. Instead, it has been left to decay.'

'And it almost claimed Pagan as its victim.'

'Which would have been doubly ironic, considering that her mother was the cause of the rot.'

'I don't understand.'

'I don't expect you to. I didn't myself until it was too late. . . . Instead of sending him to a Catholic school, where he would have grown up with boys from his own faith . . . his own background, his father insisted on sending him to one where he came under the influence of a girl . . . a girl who'd sneaked in by the back way . . . a girl who, because she hated her own family, taught him to hate his. She left him to care for nothing and no one but himself.'

'Please don't forget that she was my dearest friend.'

'She was no friend of yours.'

'What?' She does not elaborate; I dismiss her hyperbole. And yet it pains me that Robin's mother should think as ill of you as mine.

'And now you are on the run with her daughter?'

'Hardly on the run.'

'Another few steps and she might have broken her neck, then where would you be?' I say nothing; she does not seem to expect it. 'You've had a very narrow escape.'

'I know. I came to a decision while you were at the hospital. As soon as it's civilised – I'd like to rephrase that – I'll call my solicitor. I'll ask his advice, frame my doubts in the form of questions. Of course, I shan't say where I am.'

'Say whatever you choose. Who will pay any attention to us: a crabbed old woman and her crazy daughter? In the village, they call us witches. I often wish that we were.' She shivers. 'We should go back; I'm starting to feel the chill. Besides, I have to wake Lydia. She'd sleep her life away if I let her . . . perhaps I should.'

319

'I don't know how I can ever thank you.'

'By not trying. In my position, gratitude is too great an encumbrance.'

She makes her way back to the house like a miner's widow lost in the shadow of a pit. Touched by her frailty, I want to take her arm, but I am afraid of causing offence. I wait while she catches her breath.

'May I ask if you've remembered?' Her eyes fill with a confusion of memories. 'Whether you ended up liking or despising me?'

'Oh that!' She dismisses my foolishness. 'Yes.'

# 4

As The Judges returns for its third and, we trust, final series, the producers have instituted changes. The plot-lines are tougher; the mood on the set is more sombre. Some of our old favourites are missing. The Usher has been written out – or perhaps died – and replaced by a far more photogenic young woman. Rebecca, too, is absent (engaged in a long-running saga in the Strand), so I am being represented by her junior, who seems confident in the face of his first leading role. Digby-Lewis is back, his sour smile suggesting a dearth of alternative offers, along with all the other principals: your parents, their solicitor, and Max. But, as we wait for the entrance of Judge Flower, I pray that someone – anyone – will take over from me.

My only surprise is that I am not in the dock. But, far from being arrested the moment that I deliver Pagan to Max, I find that I am charged with no offence . . . not even abduction. Liberty is as unsettling as it is unexpected, and I return to Holland Park like a man who, having been cured of cancer, has lost his reason to live. Meanwhile Max takes Pagan to your parents who, from the evidence of the tabloids, see her fractured wrist as a perfect photo-opportunity. Captions range from *Patience shows her hand* and *In Plaster and Tears* to a shot of her reunion with your mother dubbed *The Patience of a Saint*.

The *Nation* may have canonised your mother, but her catalogue of virtues fails to include forgiveness (to my mind, a far more appropriate caption would be *The Plaster*

*Saint*). Two days after my return, I receive your parents' application for an Order to revoke my contact, together with an affidavit in which they couple a long list of my failings, ranging from negligence to insubordination, with the claim that I have shown that I cannot be trusted and will undoubtedly take the first opportunity to 'kidnap' her again. They state that she has come back both physically and mentally scarred, citing a horrific incident, only a few hours after her arrival, when she rushed into the kitchen and grabbed a scalding pan from the stove. . . . Am I the only one who can read between the lines?

My own affidavit is made mealy-mouthed by Max. Insisting that, if I continue to produce such 'wild allegations', I will turn the Court against me and lose any hope of retaining contact, he tries to excise all reference to my suspicions of your father, even though they constitute my entire defence. We eventually hit on a compromise, whereby I agree to preface each charge with 'of course I now realise that there is not a shred of evidence' or 'at the time I believed that something was amiss', which I cannot believe has fooled anyone. I sign my name as though to a blank cheque.

I wish – how I wish – that I had followed my instincts, especially when I receive your parents' second affidavit, which is as outspoken as mine is restrained. They claim that I have made my imputations against your father in order to provide a smokescreen for my own activities and then proceed to blow – no, blast – it away. They base their case on the changes in Pagan's behaviour after her weekends with me. They produce evidence: physical . . . the rawness around her vagina; psychological . . . her violent mood swings; verbal . . . the 'fellatio' (which they fear may now have gone beyond words). They save their gravest concern for our ten days in hiding; the potential for abuse was immense. Pagan has volunteered nothing and they respect her silence (being loath to remind her of an ordeal which she longs to forget), and yet the question remains: for what reason other than perversion would a man cut off a girl's hair and dress her as a boy?

I feel as though I have fallen into a septic tank . . . I may climb out, but the smell will always cling to me. How can your parents suggest that I would ever do such a thing to

Pagan? I love her; I have never abused her. I truly believe that I have never abused anyone in my life ... except perhaps myself. I glance to where they are sitting, so much more composed than on previous occasions ... your father even sports a cravat. I ache with exhaustion; I shrink from the prospect of another hearing. I would offer to give her up, if only I could rely on a judge with the wisdom of Solomon rather than the prejudice of Judge Flower.

Sages are, sadly, in short supply on the present-day Bench. Their replacements are stooges, as Judge Flower proves with his opening remark that he is sure that the proceedings need not detain us long and his instructions to Counsel to be brief ... which provokes a pun from mine that he would have been well advised to resist. In the event, with neither side calling witnesses, the pace is fast (although I fear that the plot contains too few twists to sustain the ratings). The only frisson occurs during my cross-examination, when Digby-Lewis deliberately provokes me into repeating my fears about your father with his wheedling 'Not a shred of evidence, is there? ... You say you realise now that it was all a mistake?' Max looks wretched, while Rebecca's junior seems to suggest that, if this is drama, he would rather remain in revue.

As Max warned, the Judge takes against me ... although, if he turns, it is by the full 360 degrees. After rebuking me for my offensive and unsubstantiated conjecture, he makes an order that a new welfare report be prepared on Pagan and adds that, in the interim, she is to be kept from me.

We leave the Court and face the cameras. I fail to see why the newspapers go to such expense, when they might just as well use library pictures; it is only when I see my reflection in the windscreen that I remember my beard. Even my return home is deemed worthy of record, although the solitary photographer is a welcome indication that my star has waned.

His lens is the closest that I come to human contact. The house is as mournful as a morgue. Consuela has gone back to Spain. She left only garbled word with Max, but it seems that the events of the past few months – faecal parcels, abusive phone calls, abrupt disappearances – have reconciled her to the matriarchal bosom. Even Trouble has deserted me, although I suspect that, in her confusion, Consuela forgot to make arrangements for his food. I like to think that he may have been adopted – or rather, picked up – by more responsible owners, and yet, given the financial incentive, they would surely have returned him. So I fear that he must have been run down. Still, his departure removes one source of grievance from my mother, who is making her first trip to London for years.

'I had to come,' she says, as I collect her at Euston, 'when I saw a picture of you in a beard. You looked the very image of your father's cousin Norman: the one who went to the bad.'

'He went to Australia.'

'Well he never wrote.'

'Anyway, you know you're always welcome.'

'You don't have to put on a brave face for me, son; I washed you and dressed you for ten years.'

'What? You'd have had me changing my own nappy if you could.'

'You'll have to speak up; I'm getting hard of hearing.' Her elaborate mime underlines her obvious lie. 'Mrs Coombes is looking after your father. She always says that, if I ever decide to trade him in, I must be sure to give her first refusal. She's joking, of course,' she is quick to reassure me. 'Who could feel anything for your father? He's like a child.'

Trouble may have gone, but, the moment that we reach home, she is seized by a fit of coughing. 'Didn't I tell you? I had tests at the hospital. They found it isn't cats I'm allergic to, after all, but dust.' I call in the contract cleaners. Their efforts fail to allay her fears. She snipes at everything ('I'm a plain woman; I speak as I find'), while reserving her heaviest fire for the kitchen. It is as if she projects all her resentment of my deviance from heterosexuality onto my cooking with electricity rather than gas. 'I'll never get used to it; I like to see what I'm dealing with. I need a flame.'

In a desperate search for alternative targets – boys with long hair; girls with short dresses; anyone wearing purple – I propose an excursion.

'Would you like to visit Buckingham Palace? They've

opened it to the public for the first time. They say you can't move for the queues, but I'm sure I can pull some strings.'

'No, not now.' She is horrified. 'You must do nothing that draws attention to yourself. Ask favours of no one. You never know when you'll need them for something important.'

'Mother, I've done nothing wrong; I'm not going to place myself under house arrest.'

'If you've done nothing wrong, why has the phone stopped ringing? Whenever I call, it's always engaged.'

The silence is suddenly tarnished. 'It's July,' I flounder. 'Everyone's in Italy.'

'Keep yourself to yourself. People will respect you for it. Remember Mr Profumo – you're too young – but his life was in ruins. He took himself off to the East End . . . ten years later, he was hobnobbing with the Queen.'

'Then there's hope for me yet. I must find myself a good cause. I rather fancy the Boy Scouts.'

'It's not a joke, Lenny. I've had to take your photographs down from the hall. There's been muttering. It's a family hotel.'

'And I'm a family man. I was trying to protect my family.'

'When have you ever spared a thought for your father or me?'

'I mean Pagan. She's my family now . . . at least she was.'

'That poor little mite: she's brought you nothing but trouble.'

'Do you like me, Mother?'

'What sort of a question is that?'

'A very simple one: do you like me?'

'One thing I don't like is playing games.'

'I remember, when I was a kid in primary school, asking Miss Shelley to explain the difference between "love" and "like".'

'You were always one for words. We could never keep up with you.'

'Please listen to me. She replied that we had to love everyone, because that was what Jesus taught us, but that we only needed to like the people we chose, which struck me as strange, since loving seemed far more special and

325

intimate than liking. Now, of course, I know that she was right. So do you like me?'

'All this talk! You can always say anything with talk. I'm here, aren't I? "By their fruits ye shall know them." Matthew chapter seven verse twenty.'

After five days, I feel as though I have lived on a diet of crab apples and sour grapes. The relief of her departure is tempered by tedium. Time hangs as heavily on me as a hand-me-down suit. I have nowhere to go but Television Centre, where I am greeted by the consolatory smiles which irked you so much in your illness. Colleagues racing down corridors are suddenly free to stop and chat, which might be cheering if it were not so sinister. In a bid to discover where I stand, I confront Kaye Blake, who has just flown back from three weeks in Goa ('No meal cost us more than a pound . . . the poverty's horrendous'). I confide my worries, competing for sympathy with her fading tan.

She welcomes me to a 'bullshit-free zone' and scratches her peeling shoulder. She explains that some of our masters – the irony is unconvincing – have serious reservations about starting the new series while I remain under a cloud. When I object, she looks pained and moans that she does not find this at all easy. I am stunned . . . I stand there with a knife in my back and she expects me to feel for her bleeding heart. She asks what I want her to do. I make it very plain; she must back me . . . back me, as she would put it, a hundred and fifty per cent. I am fighting for my life. If they axe me now, people are bound to think that they – that is I – have something to hide. She retreats into a frenzy of scratching, detaching a large piece of skin. Her phone buzzes. She answers and turns to me.

'I'm sorry, Leo. First day back. I'm late for a meeting.'

I thought that she was having a meeting with me.

My appearance on *Jackanory* has been cancelled. I was due to read five stories from Peter Makeson's *Dougie the Dormouse* books; but Ianthe Snowdon rings to say that they have run into a problem with the rights. I offer my wider services and boast of a zoomorphic range that extends from prickly hedgehogs to cuddly bears. She replies that they have decided to programme a week of repeats. 'Fave raves. Golden oldies for the under-fives.' She giggles, as though she had a feather under her nose. 'Kids love the familiar. I'm sure you understand?' . . . Oh yes, I understand very well. I know what it means to be faceless. I shall resist their attempts to blank me off the screen.

'Is this the kind of man we want corrupting the nation's youth?'

'No, he's not nearly adept enough. Find someone better.'

My only diversion is to answer my mail. My postbag is heavier than ever, but its contents have changed. Nit-picking is replaced by vitriol. I am amazed that such sophisticated tortures can be devised by such unsophisticated minds. Castration would appear to be the least of my worries. One particularly inventive correspondent proposes that I be used in laboratory experiments instead of rats . . . and yet he does not sound like an animal-lover; he simply hates me. Most write anonymously and, to judge from both style and paper, in conditions of extreme constipation. I make a point of replying to all who enclose their addresses, hoping by a show of reason to put their lack of it to shame.

The one person to whom I yearn to write, I cannot. Tomorrow is July 26th, and I hardly need to remind you of the significance. But, when I ask Max about sending her a card, he advises against it. He can see no harm himself but feels that we will do best to stick to the letter as well as the spirit of the Order. . . . I am struck by a remark that your mother – your real mother – made about the pain that she felt on your birthdays and wonder if mine is the same. For the first time, Pagan and I will be apart. I try not to think how she will spend it. Surely they must give her a party . . . in letter if not in spirit? I picture your mother issuing strict instructions against dropping crumbs on the carpet, while your father plays hunt-the-thimble with a houseful of seven-year-old girls.

My first thought, when Susan rings in the morning, is that, remembering the day and suspecting my mood, she is on a mission to cheer me up. In the event, the call does quite the opposite. She describes how she has received a visit from two Brighton police officers investigating allegations of child abuse against me. I correct her; she must mean my allegations against your father. No, she insists, against me. Her indignation is intense. She reports how she told them that the charge was an outrage: she had

327

never known so devoted a father. I thank her, but my words are detached, for I am already making a call to Max in my mind. When, a few minutes later, I do so in earnest, he promises to inquire informally. Damn informality, I say, this is not a discreet examination of my eligibility for a club! He advises me to remain calm and promises to ring back as soon as he has news.

I sit by the phone, waiting for hospital results, exam results and word from a lover, all rolled into one. At four thirty, it arrives. 'Susan was right. It appears that the Mulliners have confided their suspicions to the police.'

'Surely that man must realise that, in the course of any investigation, his own guilt is bound to come out?'

'He may be running scared. If what you say is true –'

'If . . . if!'

'I'm your friend, Leo . . . ! I repeat; if what you say is true, he may be afraid of what Pagan will tell the Welfare Officer and want to get his own story in first. Attack is the best form of defence . . . don't forget he was a soldier.'

'But his wife wasn't. And I'm sure she suspects him. She wouldn't be so rash.'

'Maybe she's afraid of the welfare report too, though for different reasons. If it exonerates you, then we're back at square one. She'll do anything to prevent your gaining access to Pagan.'

'Well this time they've gone too far. I shall sue for libel!'

'You'll accomplish nothing by overreacting. Whatever their motives, you know that you're innocent. You have nothing to fear.'

My confidence sags as soon as I put down the phone. The one person who can boost it is your mother. I wait for banking hours and make my appeal. I explain that it is no longer just Pagan who is in danger. I describe your father's tactics, my position and her options . . . if she will only tell her story – your story – I will be cleared and the true perpetrator exposed. Her voice drops so low that all I can hear is her fear. I ask her to speak up; she begs me to leave her in peace. She reminds me of my promise and adds that it is not as though she has any written evidence . . . only memories; and she has grown increasingly forgetful. So she cannot be sure of what she told me. It is quite possible that she has muddled the two stories. . . . And I realise that I am on my own.

My isolation becomes self-perpetuating. Such invitations as I do receive I refuse, and those which I cannot avoid I regret . . . none more so than that to Lily de Trivelle's memorial service, where, after a dreary piece of Haydn and a misjudged address, I gaze across the nave to find Duncan Treflis striving to catch my eye. His repertoire of nods, winks and nudges would be more suited to an auction room . . . although its flagrance might prove to be costly. I decide that a wan smile is the safest compromise between his determination and my distaste. To my annoyance, he takes it as a licence to waylay me on the way out. After chiding me for failing to reply to his letter, he asks me to lunch. I explain that I am otherwise engaged.

'Come now, you forget that I am a master of the diplomatic excuse: white lies and half-truths a speciality. Yours I attribute to a well-meant but misguided desire not to impose on me.' Neither his vanity nor his loquacity permit of correction. 'I should warn you that, if you refuse, I shall collapse comatose at your feet – since we last met, I have had a nodding acquaintance with diabetes – leaving you duty-bound to rush to my aid, which will be far less amusing for both of us. So, where's it to be? My club?'

'The Stallion?'

'Ha!' His laughter rings around the portals of St Paul's, Knightsbridge. 'This time, I think the Garrick.' I shrug and loosen my tie.

I shrink from his peppery proximity in the taxi. He rests his hat on my knee as though it were his own. We arrive at the club after a jittery journey. . . . 'I'm not altogether sure that they allow beards in the building. Do you, Hedley?' The porter's smile gives nothing away.

'If there's a problem, I'm happy to go elsewhere.'

'I jest. I'm an old man; why can't you humour me?' He mixes petulance with pomposity. 'Besides, it suits you. It supplies an air of mystery. It reminds me of the one I myself grew during the war.'

We move up to the dining room, where he makes the most of the waiter's hand on his chair.

'Poor Lily. . . .' I have no chance with the menu. 'Not the most impressive of turn-outs. If you remove all her

329

husbands, there was practically no one there. You, I take it, knew her professionally.' He makes it sound as though I shone her shoes.

'She appeared on my show several times. The viewers loved her.'

'They didn't know her. You'd have heard a very different story from her friends. I was amazed to see Davinia Rutland . . . her sister. She was disowned by the entire clan in the forties, when she abandoned everything for an Irish jockey . . . though I'm told he was hung like a horse.'

'Perhaps you'd warn me when I should start taking you seriously?'

'Always.' He bares his yellowing teeth. 'You may not take me accurately, but that's not the same.' He breaks off to flatter the waiter, who fails to respond. 'I understand that you've recently returned from Crierley.'

'Did Lady Standish tell you?'

'I haven't spoken to Evelyn Standish for years.'

'May I ask why?' I contain my surprise.

'Her pride. That ridiculous caravan. It's as though she's trying to park it on all our consciences. Well, believe me, there's no room on mine.'

'Oh, I do.'

'I offered to help her, provided that she moved away from that deadly house; as did her sister. But she's stubborn. It's a family characteristic.'

'It's a characteristic of anyone who's used to having his own way.'

'Was that last remark aimed at me?'

'If the barb hits. . . .'

'It barely scratches.' We eat. 'It may be that I deceive myself, but I've never understood why you took so violently against me. I've always thought most highly of you.'

'Thank you.'

'I suppose it's because we're so similar. I look at you and see so much of myself when I was young.'

'Do you mean the beard?'

'Way beneath the beard. . . .' Only his solipsism saves me from panic. 'I suspect that you must also see yourself in me – shall we say forty years on? – sinking slowly in the quicksands of time.'

330

'I'd say that you'd kept your footing with uncanny ease. Anyone would think you'd made a pact with the devil.'

'Why thank you.' He picks up the blunt edge of the compliment. 'It's true that I may no longer be under guarantee, but I'm still in full working order. Of course, I'm dogged by that disagreeable new acquaintance I introduced in church. And my gait is not all that it was –'

'Do you mean that you suffer from stiff joints?'

He smiles and leaves me to speculate on the extent to which his verbal convolutions reflect his moral turpitude. This is the man who once described Robin's insensitive father as having 'a multi-layered epidermis' and then added insultingly that it was an allusion to his thick skin.

I turn my attention from his speech to his person. As I contemplate the pampered, too-well-preserved face and the hands that bear witness to a lifetime of manicures, I am satisfied that there is not the slightest resemblance between us. I have been saved from a life of such sterile futility by Pagan. . . . At which point, the truth hits me like a swing-door and I remember that she has been taken from me. Posterity is now a thing of the past. I have fallen for the most insidious of all illusions: hope.

I look up to see him staring at me like a mirror; the frame may be cracked and the glass silvered, but the image is clear. 'Whatever else, we share a taste for what Oscar described so piquantly as feasting with panthers; and poor Leslie Meacham amended to fighting with alley-cats.'

'Why poor?' I kick myself.

'Haven't you heard? He was caught making a nuisance of himself in a public convenience and went to live with his sister in Torquay. . . . Still, whatever feline metaphor you choose, you must agree that there is no more exciting sight than that of an inarticulate boy grubbing for his pleasure.'

'Was that what attracted you to Robin?'

'Who, as you may recall, was exceptionally articulate.'

'Even at fourteen?'

'Robin was special. He was thrust in my path. I tried to resist; and yet: Temptation like a plump, pubescent boy. . . .' A Shakespearian actor at the adjoining table looks startled. My courtesy has been strained to the limit.

'I really must go. I have an appointment.'

331

'About your troubles, I expect? Well, don't despair. As an old friend – sadly no longer with us – used to say, "Rules are made to be kept and laws to be broken." It's a precept to which I've adhered all my life. So, break on, dear boy, with my blessing. And next time you need a bolt-hole, come to Buckstone. It has all the charms of Crierley, plus what I believe are commonly known as "mod cons".'

I make my escape and hurry home to shave. As I am halfway through one cheek, the phone rings with news that I feel sure is an augur: a woman informs me that her son has found Trouble. I rush through the rest of my beard and drive to Acton. I do not identify myself, and she is nonplussed when I press the doorbell (which offers further assurance that Happy Days Are Here Again). She fails to connect our calls and scans the street for a camera. Only when Trouble bounds into my arms does she give up hope of her fifteen minutes of fame. She asks me in for a cup of tea. I sit in the striped living room, stroking Trouble who purrs with self-satisfaction. I am so relieved that I quite overlook the promise on the collar, until, as I prepare to leave, the boy asks shyly, 'Is your cat's name Large Reward?'

Any hope that Trouble's return marks a revival in my fortunes is dashed at seven thirty the next morning, when I am woken by a knock at the door. Assuming that it is the postman with a package of dubious import, I ignore it . . . but to no avail. Cursing, I stumble downstairs to be greeted by two police officers.

'Leonard Young. . . .' I am not sure whether it is a question or a statement. 'I'm DI Hopkins from the Special Inquiry Unit at John Street police station in Brighton; this is DC Bridges. We're investigating the case of Pagan Mulliner. I'm arresting you on suspicion of indecent assault. I must caution you and tell you that you do not have to say anything unless you wish to do so, but what you say may be given in evidence. I'd ask you to come with us to John Street station to continue the inquiry.'

I try to unpeel the layers of my reaction: shock . . . disbelief, certainly . . . but also relief, that I no longer have to struggle to prove the truth of my story; although I shall have to struggle even harder to prove the truth of my side. I am entering into a dangerous arena. This is not the children's bullfight of the family courts, where death is still in training; but a full-blown corrida. Fear gores my mind. I try to focus on the officers. I am unsure of the protocol; do I ask them in or wait for them to push past? In the event, I issue an invitation, which they politely accept and then immediately abuse by calling for reinforcements to search the house.

I am trapped in an episode of *The Bill* . . . which reminds me of my right to a solicitor. The Inspector gives me permission to ring Max, who promises to follow us to Brighton, at which point the spectre of Kafka recedes. I ask if I may shower and shave (the beard is too recent a memory). The Inspector has no objections, provided that the Constable accompanies me. I steal a glance at the thickset young man with the thinning blond hair, but his cold blue eyes give nothing away. He stands by the bathroom door, his gaze stripping me of modesty, and I forgo the shower. I resent his morbid interest in my razor.

'I'm not guilty, you know.'

'No, sir?'

'So I'm not going to slit my throat . . . or try to electrocute myself with the hair-dryer.'

'No, sir.' He 'sirs' me with all the contempt of Cambridge porters.

It is not until I put the blade to my cheek that I realise the extent of my terror. I am trembling so hard that I dare not risk a cut. I retreat to my bedroom to dress. I ask Bridges what to wear; he pretends to ponder. 'Something casual, I'd say, sir. This isn't one of your black-tie affairs.'

'I don't mean fashion. I've never been to a police station before. Are they hot or cold? What will I need?'

'I think we can take it that you'll find it hot. '

We go down to the kitchen, where the Inspector has made coffee. However intent she may be on keeping our relations amicable, I find the forced informality unnerving, like a child meeting a teacher out of school. Through the door, I glimpse her men rifling my study.

'Couldn't I help? Those are private papers; I don't want them disturbed.'

'Don't worry, sir; leave it to us.'

'They won't find anything; there's nothing to find.'

'Leave it to us.'

The coffee is wasted, since the Inspector insists on setting out before it has time to cool. As we quit the house, my attendant photographer snaps into action. The officers suspect a tip-off; I explain that he has been keeping watch for weeks. I suddenly feel benign towards him. 'Well done,' I shout. 'Patience pays off.' Which sounds like another caption.

I search for a police car, only to be told that we are travelling incognito in a Toyota.

'Nifty little motor, though I say so myself,' says Bridges. 'Of course, it eats petrol. . . .' I feel sure that he cheats on the mileage. In the middle of Brixton, I let out a shout. Bridges swerves. 'What the fuck! Sorry, guv. Don't do that!'

'I've forgotten the cat.'

At the station, I am ushered into a cheerless charge room and placed in the hands of the Custody Officer. After taking details of the arrest, logging my cash and removing my belt and tie (I wore the wrong clothes after all), he leads me down a labyrinth of corridors. Reaching a door, he pulls back the wicket and lets me into my cell. It is larger than I expected with heavily glazed white tiles, like a municipal Gents. The only light is a single bulb behind thick, dust-stained glass and the only furniture a broad wooden bench built into the wall. At one end is a mattress with a naked pillow . . . I think of all the heads that must have greased it and start to itch; at the other is a hole which serves as a lavatory. He seems to take particular pleasure in showing me the button by which I can call them to clear it . . . the button that is my only point of contact with the outside world. 'Ah,' I say caustically, 'it must be the latest thing in sanitation: an inside toilet with an outside flush.'

He departs in the jangle of bangs and bolts and crashes that accompanies him like a signature tune. I am left alone; and yet I am not afraid. I am apprehensive, which is different. I know that, as long as I keep a clear head, I will clear my name. But it is difficult to think above the oaths, yells and caterwauls that emerge from the neighbouring cells. My only escape is to speculate on the previous occupants. Who were they? Drunks? Murderers? The Grand Hotel bombers? There is no way of knowing . . . which is where my metaphor breaks down; in a lavatory, there would at least be names scratched on the walls, along with messages to give even the loneliest men hope.

It is midday when the Custody Officer collects me for interview. He takes me into a small room, sparsely furnished with a table, four chairs, a tape-recorder, and microphones on the wall. After repeated requests, I am finally allowed ten minutes in private with Max, who has been waiting for over an hour. Indeed, once he has satisfied himself that I am not suicidal, his chief concern appears to be his own maltreatment . . . stuck in the lobby 'with Joe Public'; kept in the dark; not even offered a cup of coffee. 'For God's sake, this is a provincial force!' I point to the microphones, but he snorts. 'We're talking PC Plod not MI5.' He then dismisses my arrest as 'a local difficulty. They'll never get a charge to stick.'

'I'm innocent, Max.'

'Even so, conviction in child cases is a lottery. Last year, the police were so hamstrung by a client of mine whom they suspected of buggering his children that they charged him with buggering his wife, about which they couldn't have given two hoots.'

'I don't have a wife.'

The officers return. Now that she has taken off her coat, I am aware that the Inspector is pregnant. I speculate on how her hormones might affect her questions. She switches on the tape-recorder, which emits an ear-splitting hum.

'This interview is being tape-recorded. We are in the interview room at John Street police station. I am DI BH176 Hopkins of the Special Inquiry Unit. The other officer present is . . .'

'DC AB472 Bridges of the Special Inquiry Unit.'

'It is 12.30 p.m. on Thursday August 11th 1993. I am interviewing . . . please say your name.'

'Leo . . . Leonard Young.'

'Also present is your legal representative.'

'Maxwell Isaac Barrowman.'

She explains the recording procedure and repeats the caution.

'Have you understood everything so far?'

'Just about.'

'What didn't you understand?' I make a note to eschew

335

irony. 'As you know, you've been arrested for indecent assault on a child. Did you take it in when I told you at the house or was it a bit of a bolt from the blue?'

'I was aware that you were conducting an investigation.'

'If I may intervene for one moment?' Max does so. 'I have discussed the charge with my client and advised him not to answer any questions.'

'I'm sure you appreciate that that doesn't prevent me from asking them.'

Inspector and Constable conduct the examination with the timing of an expert double act. My refusal to participate allows me the chance to admire their skill, although I admit to some disappointment that the roles of 'good' and 'bad' policeman should be allotted so predictably by sex.

They ask about my relationship with Pagan, concentrating on moments of intimacy. When the Inspector asks if I was strict about enforcing bedtimes, the Constable wants to know if I was strict at other times ('Did you smack her? Where did you smack her? Did you smack her through the knickers or on the flesh?'). When she asks whether she wore a nightdress or pyjamas, he asks whether she slept in my bed ('How often did you touch her? Would you say you were a touchy sort of person? Did you cuddle close?'). When she asks about bathing her, he asks about drying her ('Did you sometimes give her an extra-special rub? Did your hand ever slip?').

I am finding it hard not to comment. I start to ration my 'no comments'. I fail to see why Max is so insistent on my right to silence, although I continue to note his instructions from the corner of my eye.

'Why did you abduct Pagan Mulliner?' the Inspector asks. 'Why did you dress her up as a boy? Did you know that a paediatric examination has revealed tears to her anus?'

'What did I say?' I turn to Max. 'Now will you believe me?'

'Later, Leo.'

'No comment.'

'What would you like to do to someone who tears a little girl's anus?' Bridges leans over me. I feel his breath on my cheek. 'What do you think we should do to someone who

336

tears a little girl's anus?' His stance renders any comment redundant.

'What's a tongue sandwich?' The Inspector takes me by surprise.

'How do you know about that?'

'That's better. If we can turn this into a dialogue, we might get somewhere.'

'I've already informed you that my client neither wishes nor intends to answer your questions. So would you produce whatever evidence you have against him or else allow us to leave?'

'You'll leave when we're good and ready,' the Constable snaps. 'The sooner he starts to cooperate, the sooner that will be.'

The Inspector adopts a more wheedling tone. 'No one's suggesting you're a monster. It's easy to see what must have happened. You were left on your own with a little girl. Her mummy was dead; you were all she had left. She came to you seeking comfort; you tried your best to give it. Sometimes she came in the middle of the night. . . . You never planned it. It's just that one thing led to another. Come on, admit it. Aren't I right?'

'No! . . . no comment.'

'Tell us about your sex life.' Bridges edges close enough to become part of it. 'Do you have a boyfriend?' No comment. 'It must be hard to meet people with a face like yours . . . I'm speaking professionally, of course. Always looking behind you as it were – in case someone's shopping you to the tabloids. Whereas, with a six-year-old kid, you knew you'd be on safe ground.'

'You disgust me!'

'I disgust *you*?'

The Inspector insinuates more slyly. 'I think that you love Pagan, Leo. Truly, I do. And I know that she loves you. Which is why she was willing to do whatever she could to please you. The trouble is that you wanted too much. When did it all start to get out of hand?'

'May I have a glass of water?' My throat smarts from the silence.

'No.'

'I must protest. My client is not accustomed to this sort of treatment.'

337

'Nor was the little girl.' The Inspector is heavy with her unborn child. 'Tears to her anus: will you think of that for a minute?'

'I've thought of little else for months! Why do you suppose that I took her away, if not to rescue her from the man who was abusing her?'

'Leo. . . .' Max interjects.

'We know why you took her away: so there'd be nothing to stop you having your way with her.'

'You were scared, weren't you, Leo?' The Inspector's sympathy is as insulting to my intelligence as the Constable's bluster is to my character. 'Her grandparents had started to suspect; they were threatening to blow the whistle.'

'No, that's not true!'

'So, you decided to strike first and at the most vulnerable target . . . a frail old man. Oh yes, he made no bones about your allegations. "I've had my life," he said; "I don't care what I'm put through, so long as I can protect my granddaughter".'

'And you believed him?'

'Can you give us one good reason why not?' Bridges asks. 'A man of seventy-four, well liked, respected. A man who worked in a school for thirty years without one breath of scandal. And, what's more, has been happily married for fifty. Why would he want to bugger her?'

'You tell me; you're the detective.' I am appalled; this is the first time that anyone has mentioned buggery.

'What interest would a man like that have in an anus?'

No comment.

They decide to conclude the interview. The Inspector removes the tapes from the machine, asking me to choose one, which she then places in an envelope. I sign on the seal. I assume that I will be allowed to go, but she informs me that I am to return to the cells. Max protests that she has no right to detain me further, to which she replies that, not only does she have every right to hold me for the full thirty-six hours but, if necessary, she will apply to a magistrate for an extension. She and the Constable exit, leaving Max in mid-threat.

The Custody Officer collects me and repeats the ceremony of the keys. The cell has been occupied in my absence and exudes the foetid smell of cornered fox. I gag and rush to the hole, which is rank. I ram the button. An officer appears and peers through the wicket. I shout that the lavatory is a disgrace; he derides my complaint. 'We've got a psycho going ape-shit down the corridor, and you're kicking up a stink about a blocked khazi!' He slams the wicket shut. I stand in the corner of the cell at the furthest distance from the bench. My despondency takes on a regal note, and I wonder if I am being deliberately baited, like Edward II imprisoned in the bowels of Berkeley Castle. Five minutes later, I am startled by the flush.

The afternoon drags on, marked only by the clatter of the wicket, as uniform faces stare at me like keepers in a zoo. In which case, I must belong to a very rare and exotic species (I am resolved to think positively). Perhaps they are hoping that I will breed in captivity. The image cheers me, while the faces continue to intrude. I have no idea whether they want to intimidate or to humiliate me; but, whatever the intention, the effect is the same.

At five o'clock, I am collected by the Custody Officer and taken to the interview room for a second examination, which repeats the procedures of the first. As they launch the attack, they load their questions with fresh ammunition seized in the search. This includes a selection of your photographs, notably the child whores in Manilla and Mexico (what are to me bitter indictments of sexual tourism are to them clear indication of sexual tastes); the much-chewed dildo that you bought as a bone for Texas (I am only grateful that they never found his collar or they would have had me on all fours); and various remnants of your wardrobe. I blush once, when Bridges pulls out a small pack of American magazines with covers that leave little to the imagination. These I acknowledge (to you, though not to them); they provide me with tame stimulation, tapping into a collective fantasy when I am too exhausted to create my own.

I shall spare you the monotony of my 'no comments'; not that they spared me the monotony of their commentary. I only hope that Max's judgement that my silence will secure my release is correct. For the moment, they are determined to maintain the pressure. Bridges pulls out a television and explains that they are going to play me part of Pagan's video evidence; which, for the purpose of the tape-recording, he describes as Exhibit BPB I, in reference to the fact that he produced it (which he relates as proudly as if it were *Citizen Kane*). The Inspector adds that it was shot last week in a special room in a local children's home. She was one of the interviewers and Marcia Dixon, the Welfare Officer, the other. Your parents were present in an adjoining room.

'Then it's no wonder she never accused him. How could she when he was there?'

'He was in another room. They had no contact.'

'But she would still have sensed his presence. She's terrified of him, and with good reason. Time and again, I've said "Just tell the truth and you'll be free"; and, every time, she's been sent back.'

'Both Marcia Dixon and I are highly trained in interview techniques and well able to assess the child.'

The video lasts for about an hour, during which they repeatedly fast-forward, promising that I will be able to re-run anything later, but I have seen more than enough. It is a shock to discover Pagan, her face haggard, her short hair forced into ribbons, and her hands . . . one in plaster from the fractured wrist, the other in bandages from the burns. At first, she relaxes with Marcia and the Inspector, who ask if she wants to watch herself in a film and point out the image on the monitor. 'Like Leo,' she says, 'yes, yes.' Marcia then plays truth games with pens and asks if she knows what 'safe' is. 'Yes,' she says; 'it's like when Leo pushes me on the swing and I won't fall off.' Instead of welcoming the assurance, she immediately asks if I pushed her hard. 'Oh yes,' she says laughing; 'he pushed me so hard, I could kick the sky.'

'That part,' the Inspector informs us, 'was basic rapport-building.' But, as soon as they try to build further, the flimsiness of the foundations is exposed. Using words like cuddly toys, they ask whether anyone has ever hurt or done 'naughty things' to her; she refuses to be drawn. So they adopt a more pictorial approach. The Inspector presses a box of felt shapes into her hands, while Marcia picks out circles and squares and figures and demonstrates how to stick them on a board. She ignores them in favour

340

of the monitor. Faced with such intransigence, their words become blades.

'Has Leo ever touched your bottom?' Marcia asks.

'Leading question,' Max mutters under his breath, but loud enough for the Inspector to scowl.

'Course.'

'Was that your front bottom or your back bottom?'

'Yes.'

'Did Leo touch your front bottom or your back bottom?'

'Yes.'

'Has Leo ever touched in your bottom? Has Leo ever put anything in your bottom?'

'Yes.' I start. What? When? Only a thermometer when she was a baby, and there is no way that she could have registered that.

'When was that?' She shakes her head.

'Don't you remember?' She shakes her head.

'Were you at home?'

'No.'

'Were you on holiday?'

'No.'

'Were you in somebody else's house?'

She nods. 'He said we were friends and then he hurt me. He made me lie on a bed and it was sore.' I sense Max tensing.

'Don't worry. You mustn't be scared. If you want to say naughty things . . . if you want to say nasty things . . . no one will be cross.'

'It was the consultant,' I shout out. The Inspector stops the video. 'The paediatrician I took her to see.'

'If you have any comments, write them down and we'll go over them at the end.'

'But it's important.'

'That's why I gave you the paper.'

'What's the point? You won't listen. You hear only what you want to hear.'

I push the pad away. The Inspector restarts the film, while her screen image resumes the questions. What I find most disturbing is the level of Pagan's replies. It may be that the subject makes her shy or the setting nervous, but she seems to have regressed by two or three years.

'Have you ever slept in Leo's bed?' Marcia asks.

'Lots.' She gives another one-word, four-year-old answer.

'In the morning or the evening?'

'Yes.'

They ask her to demonstrate, in felt, how my bed fits into the room and how she and I fitted into it. She slaps the pieces on the board with considerable accuracy . . . apart from making me black. They then press her to show them how we slept when we ran away. She ponders for a while before saying that she can't because she can't make a church. The ecclesiastical reference surprises them (I feel sure that they suspect satanism); but she refuses to elaborate. Sticking with Crierley, they want to know why she was dressed as a boy. I will her to reveal our escape-plan, but she keeps faith and stays silent. When they ask if she liked what I did to her as a boy, her only reply is 'I fell downstairs'.

They then give her dolls, whose pronounced genitalia come as a double shock after the rigid sexlessness of Barbie and Ken. 'It's naughty,' she says, 'it's like Leo's bottom.'

Was she to grow up in a house of locked doors? Was she to grow up in a world of lowered glances?

'Is it like anyone else's bottom?' She shakes her head. 'Is it like Grandpa's bottom?' Her eyes gape. She shakes her head violently and throws the doll onto the floor. The Inspector picks it up and yet does not – or will not – pick up on the clue. 'So it's not like Grandpa's bottom?'

'No.' She shakes her head.

'If this doll were Leo and this doll were Pagan, what would they do together?'

She takes the male doll, purged of its grandpaternal threat, and the female doll, freed of its fear, and holds them together in a full-faced kiss.

'Are you saying they'd kiss one another?' She nods and then gives the Leo doll a big kiss in person. Do you find that sinister or touching . . . ? They, of course, found the opposite.

'When will I go home and see Leo and Trouble?'

'Don't worry, there won't be any trouble. Leo will never put you in any trouble again.'

I sink my head in my hands. Their obduracy fills me with despair. I am a single man . . . a gay man, ergo I must be an abuser, whereas that kindly old cove, her grand-father, with his marital and military records, is above suspicion. Very well then, let them take me to court. Let them try me. Let them build their case on the name of a cat!

The Inspector freezes the frame and waits for me to look up. She asks if I am ready to continue. I signal my indifference. She moves on to a point where she is questioning Pagan with, at least, a display of detachment.

'Has anyone else ever hurt you? Has anyone ever made your bottom sore?'

'Whose bottom? Leo's?' She picks up the doll.

'No, has anyone else ever made Pagan's bottom sore?' She shakes her head. 'Not Grandpa? Has Grandpa ever made Pagan's bottom sore?'

'No! He has never hurt Pagan's bottom! He has never hurt Pagan's bottom!' Her vehemence disturbs me even more than it does them. Why is she lying? On the screen, Marcia is comforting her.

'No, of course not. Grandpa is a good man, who loves you.' She has changed her stance considerably since her appearance in the witness box. 'That's the end of the nasty questions. You're a very clever girl; we're all very pleased with you. Shall we play with some of the toys? Afterwards, the police lady has promised to take you to see the station; would you like that?'

'I'd like to see the trains.'

The interview is over, the television switched off. Looking at the officers, it is clear that we have been watching different films. Whereas I am convinced that every frame exonerates me (the mystery is why she should have protected your father), they view it differently: my bed, my bottom, my hand on her bottom, my cutting her hair. . . . What I see as pain at the memory of her grand-father hurting her, they see as horror at the very idea. The Inspector asks whether, considering the evidence, I still have no comment. 'I have only one,' I reply. Max looks nervous. 'Take care if you ever ask your parents to babysit for you.'

'You think you're very clever,' she says, with such scorn that I fear the effect on the child in her womb. 'People like you, you think you live in a different world from the rest of

343

us; you think you're above the law. Well, I'm here to show you you're not. I believe that you repeatedly assaulted that little girl, and, believe me, I'm going to throw the book at you.' She calls the Custody Officer. 'Sergeant, you can take him back to the cells.'

At half-past eight, I return to the charge room, where the Custody Officer, Inspector and Constable are all waiting, along with Max, who looks grave. Losing no time, the Custody Officer declares himself satisfied that there is sufficient evidence to charge me on a count that I did 'between 1st November 1991 and 31st July 1993, at a place within the jurisdiction of the Central Criminal Court, commit buggery on Pagan Mulliner'.

I interrupt while he is cautioning me. 'Why buggery? It was indecent assault this morning. What's prompted the change? Is it that you feel more confident of gaining a conviction? Do my sexual tastes mean I'm halfway there already? Or is it that, to your mind, the anus is more inviolable than the vagina?' He ignores me and repeats the caution, after which I am led into an adjoining room, where another officer photographs and fingerprints me, before taking down a physical description.

'Hair red. Eyes green. Freckles. . . .'

'I flatter myself that I am quite well known.' If they pull rank, then I shall pull reputation. 'Five million people watch me twice a week.'

'Watched,' he says and continues with the form, after which he accompanies me to the cloakroom, where I am unable to wash the ink off my hands. Max joins us and tells me that he has spoken to the Inspector who has no objections to bail, which makes the shock all the greater when, five minutes later, the Custody Officer refuses it. He claims that, in view of the gravity of the offence and my recent absconding with Pagan, he has good reason to suspect that I will jump bail. So I am to be kept at the station overnight and appear before the magistrates in the morning. I take a dazed leave of Max and am returned to the cells.

The Duty Officer asks if I want an evening meal; and, for the first time, I feel hungry. He hands me a tray of pie and chips and cold banana custard, along with a sardonic apology that he is sure that it is not what I am used to. 'Not

344

so far,' I say, 'but who knows?' One look at the thick-crusted pie and the mound of chips makes it clear why Bridges is running to fat. I tentatively pick at the food, but the plastic fork fails to establish a grip. The chips slide in their own grease and the crust collapses on its gristle. When I press on the knife, it snaps. Despair gives way to fury. I grab the pie in my hands and stuff it into my mouth. At which moment, a face appears at the wicket and laughs.

Sleep is an impossibility. The light in the cell burns my eyes; the bench is hard and I dare not trust to the pillow. The clatter in the corridor grows louder; to the slamming of doors and the clanking of keys is now added the murder – no, betrayal – of *Land of Our Fathers* by two Welsh drunks. And yet even that is preferable to the constant visits of the Duty Officer, who rattles my wicket as though it were the bars of a cage. His attitude has changed with the charge, which, by removing any ambiguity from my status, has removed all checks on his resentment. I am numbed by the transition from deference to derision and disgust.

At four in the morning, my resistance flags. The drunks are stuporous, and the only sound is the murmur of muffled violence from a distant cell. I ache with cold, but there is no warmth in the blanket. I cheer myself with the prospect of every guest from the last eight years of shows (I cannot begin to guess at the number) petitioning the Queen for my release . . . my fantasy makes a mockery of my hopes. I start to blame you. You should have warned me about your father; not just for Pagan's sake but for mine. I should have been given the chance to protect myself. I would have put a padlock on the bathroom door, consulted a female doctor, and renamed Trouble Joy.

What I find most baffling is her refusal to tell the truth. When Marcia called the red pen green, she saw that she was lying. I suppose that she might be colour-blind . . . now I am being perverse. And yet why should she name him, when it has only made things worse for her so far? . . . Or might there be another reason? One that I cannot – that I have to – consider. Is it possible that I did do it . . . no, not me: some separate, dark part of me, connected to me not by mind, but merely by muscle and tissue? The idea is unthinkable; and yet others have thought of it; they have endorsed it. Might they be right? Have I committed the crime and suppressed the evidence? Have I buried the memory as deep as the taboo?

Whenever I despaired of my sexuality in the past, my comfort was that at least I was not a pederast. Whenever I heard of some unfrocked clergyman caught with an unbuttoned choirboy, my response would be 'There, but for the grace of God, go I'. . . . But now that I no longer believe in either grace or God, the consolation is as empty as the phrase.

At seven o'clock, the Custody Officer slides back the wicket. A minute later, he is bashing open the bolts on the door.

'What the fuck have you done to your face?' I am startled. He examines me. 'It's ink, for Christ's sake!' He laughs. 'Out there, it looked like blood.'

He leads me to the basins at the end of the corridors. The soap is more lather than substance and the bowl encrusted with hairs. The ink appears to be indelible; I have dark grey lines on my cheeks to match the bags under my eyes . . . I look like a French film. After breakfast – that is, after the offer – I am handcuffed, in a parody of intimacy, to a constable and driven to court . . . I am grateful for the warmth of his leg. There are six prisoners in the van, five men and one woman. Two of the men recognise me and start to hurl insults. They are slapped to silence. As we leave the van, one of them lurches away from his shadow and lunges at me, hitting me hard in the side.

'Are you hurt?'

'It's too early to say.'

I am bundled into court and down to the basement where I am locked in another cell. Shortly after ten o'clock, I am taken in front of the magistrates. The clerk reads out the charge and the prosecuting solicitor requests that I be remanded in custody. Max replies that I am a highly responsible citizen who, far from planning to abscond, is eager for the opportunity to clear his name. The magistrates agree to grant bail. My relief on hearing the chairman's 'I feel that nothing will be gained by locking up Mr Young' dissolves with the qualifying 'at this point'. Liberty comes within limits: I have to surrender my passport, remain at home, and report to the local police station twice a week. I must also undertake not to contact Pagan, your parents, or anyone connected with the case.

Max drives me back to London, generously attributing his silence to indigestion and his open windows to the heat. I arrive home, longing for a bath and then a day, if not a lifetime, in bed. . . . But, first, I have to tidy a mess far worse than any burglary. And, as I delve through the debris, I discover that the police have treated me even more callously than in the cells. As if they cannot trust me with so much as an image, they have removed all my photographs. There is not one picture of Pagan left in the house.

# 5

Fear shakes hands with envy and shakes its fist at difference as I make my way to the Court. I find the faces of my studio audience transposed to an outside broadcast and hear their voices raised above the City din. 'Bastard . . . pig . . . pervert': the insults are interchangeable but the intentions are clear. A man in a clerical collar brandishes a spidery sign claiming that 'The Maastricht Treaty Demands Legalised Sodomy On British Children', and I feel like a cross between Jacques Delors and Gilles de Rais. My sole support comes from three young men in the red wigs and overemphatic freckles of the Leo Young fan club who hold up placards inscribed with the letters LEO, in a dangerous gesture of defiance.

I have my reply ready for the BBC reporter who asks how I feel. 'Fighting fit,' I insist. 'The six months since I was charged have been bleak. As you know, I've had my show – my livelihood – taken away from me. I've been subjected to a campaign of harassment, while remaining under suspicion of a horrendous crime. And, worst of all, I've been kept away from the little girl in question: the girl whom I've loved as a daughter for the past seven years. Today, at last, I shall be able to clear my name.'

I push my way to the door and turn in response to a photographer. I flash him my most determined smile. As I do, I spot my three supporters involved in an altercation. One of them has his wig knocked off and another has his pushed over his eyes. Nevertheless, when they see me, they lift their letters aloft. My name, which has been scrambled in the scuffle, now reads EOL.

Max escorts me through the vestibule. As I step through the metal detector, I recall David's story of a friend whose pierced nipples set off the alarm at Amsterdam airport. I laugh out loud, to the fury of the functionary, who frisks me roughly. We take the lift to the first floor and into the Grand Hall. The wealth of colour, marble, columns and carvings comes as a relief after the brutal monochrome of Brighton. This is a cathedral of the law not a nonconformist chapel, and Max identifies the statues of its secular saints: Thomas Gresham, Charles I and II, Elizabeth Fry. I stare up at the lunettes, filled with allegorical figures of national life and justice. I admire King Alfred, Emperor Constantine and Magna Carta, and scowl at Moses with his tablets of stone.

We proceed to number three court, where we are greeted by Rebecca and Anthony, her junior. I am heartened by their assurance, which seems so much greater than before. Rebecca has no qualms, in spite of its being only her third case to involve video evidence; for, having had the chance to study Pagan's interview, re-running every statement and freezing every frame, she is convinced that we are way ahead of the prosecution. I have answered all ambiguities; my vindication will be complete.

I enter the courtroom, as confident and controlled as if it were the stage of the Greenwood Theatre. Glancing at the gallery, dotted with latterday *Mesdames Desfarges*, I feel that the police should have searched for knitting-needles rather than guns. Scattered among them are my supporters. I recognise almost as many faces as on my *This Is Your Life*, or rather *Lives*, for it is the mark of my fragmented existence that they all remain separate . . . I swear that, as soon as the trial is over, I shall endeavour to make myself whole. My mother sits at the front, wearing her funeral coat and funereal expression, next to her sister Violet. She allows herself a pained nod on catching my eye; Aunt Violet waves. In the row behind are David and his boyfriend Griffin, sporting tee-shirts which, I am sure, must constitute contempt of court. More soberly dressed are Edward, who intends to discuss the case in his column, Melissa, who will no doubt disguise it in her next-but-one novel, and Sweeney, who is working it into his Sociology GCSE. Vicky Ireland, Beth Lowden and Ginny Lawson have come from the Beeb, together with Imogen, Laura, Tristan, old Uncle Duncan Mossop and all.

On scanning the back row, I come face to face with myself. For a moment, I presume that they have planted a decoy in case the verdict should go against me and the crowd should bay for blood. Then I realise that he is one of the two professional Leo Young look-alikes who advertise their – my – services in the back pages of *The Stage*. He wrote upbraiding me shortly after the news of the charges. I found that I was not the only one whose career was in ruins; he depended on me even more than I did myself. I could at least resume my research on Chaliapin; I might have travelled to Russia, had it not been for the conditions of bail. But who would employ him to stand in at small-town fêtes and preside at village hall chat shows when I was awaiting trial for abuse?

I did not answer his question, let alone his letter. I could find more deserving objects of sympathy closer to home. Imitation may be the sincerest form of flattery, but impersonation is nothing but parasitism. And yet, now that I see him, I feel a degree of loyalty towards him. Does the natural affection which you ascribed to the people who share your blood extend to those who share your features? Can we respond to our mother's nose and our father's mouth on a stranger's face? Where does the mystery of resemblance lie? Is it simply a lucky dip in a universal gene-pool? I feel an inexplicable kinship with this man who mirrors me in public and in private . . . my identical, yet non-fraternal, twin.

Max leads me to the dock and chats with me as I step inside. Observing that the leather seat is more cracked than any in the body of the Court, I determine to sit stony-still. I sense the gallery's glare on the back of my neck and pray that my mother is not finding fault with my morning wash. Max moves to his place behind Rebecca, and we rise for the Judge. It is Mrs Justice Campbell . . . although her wig destroys all distinctions of sex. The Court Associate announces the case of Regina versus Leonard Young, which makes me feel as if I had broken into Balmoral. He puts the charge to me and asks how I plead. My shout of

350

'not guilty' comes out like a squeak. I find myself clawing the chair.

The jury are brought in; their racial and sexual mix seems to reflect a mythically integrated society. I am intrigued to find that all the men wear grey or black and all the women blue, as though respectability were set within strict, colour-coded limits. I harbour fears of two of them: a skeletal man in a pince-nez and a fierce woman who looks as if she has hidden her 'all men are rapists' badge beneath her lapel. Once they have been sworn in, the Judge informs them that they must put out of their minds anything that they may have read in the newspapers or seen on television and try the case solely on the evidence that they hear in court. She reminds the press that they must print nothing that identifies the victim. At the reference to Pagan, I realise that much of my elation derives from the prospect of seeing her again, albeit at a distance, for the first time in seven months.

The prosecution's first witness is Detective Sergeant Bridges, who, from the strain on his shirt, appears to have celebrated his promotion in every pub and restaurant in Sussex. He walks so smugly into the witness box that it is a particular pleasure to hear him stumble over the oath. With the aid of a notebook, which he removes reverently from a sealed plastic bag (as though it had been vacuum-packed to preserve its freshness), he answers a litany of questions on my arrest and interrogation, Pagan's injuries and interview, and the objects discovered in the search of the house.

The Judge commends the clarity of his evidence: a view which Rebecca manifestly does not share. Any forbear-ance that she may have shown in the family court disappears, as she cross-examines him harshly, probing his attitude to sexuality and his knowledge of homosexuality. He claims that, for a policeman in Brighton, ignorance is an impossibility.

'The other week we were investigating a rent-boy racket and my colleague, DI Watson, arrested a man of seventy-four.' I swivel round and catch Duncan's eye.

'Is it his age or his occupation that offends you?'

'It just goes to show; they'll go with anything.'

'Does that include six-year-old girls?'

351

'If you'd dealt with as many abused kids as I have. . . .'

'Oh but I have, Sergeant. I was appearing in such cases, if not before you were born, then very soon after. And I know the distinction between evidence and prejudice.'

'I hope that you also know that between question and comment, Miss Colestone,' the Judge interjects.

'I appreciate Your Ladyship's reminder. May I turn to the matter of the photographs seized from my client's house . . . Exhibit P3, My Lady. May I ask the jury to examine these photographs once again and to take particular care, as they are original prints by Candida Mulliner and therefore highly prized . . . and priced.' The Usher passes the pictures to the jury. 'Are you aware, Sergeant, that, although now exhibited in court, these pictures and many others on a similar theme are far more frequently exhibited in galleries world-wide?'

'No, I can't honestly say that I am.'

'Are you then unaware of Candida Mulliner's reputation as a photographer?'

'Didn't she take some pictures of Madonna on a tank?'

'Yes. And many thousands of portraits and landscapes from around the world. Were you aware that Miss Mulliner specialised in studies of prostitutes?'

'No.'

'Although, unlike the many celebrated male artists who have dealt with the subject, her images can in no sense be described as seductive.' I search for a flicker of feminist sympathy from the Judge. 'Some of the prostitutes whom she depicts are as young as seven. It is these pictures – a small selection from a vast archive – that you have chosen to remove. Why? Do you consider them to be erotic?'

'Anything can be erotic to a pervert.'

'How true, Sergeant.' He looks confused. 'Did you know that my client is Miss Mulliner's artistic executor?'

'No,' he replies, 'I didn't.'

'Since this makes him responsible for dealing with all inquiries about her work (including both its exhibition and reproduction), wouldn't it be surprising if he did not possess examples of her photographs?'

'Yes, but you tell me; why weren't they on the walls like so many others or, at least, filed in cabinets downstairs? Why were they stuffed in a box at the back of a wardrobe?'

'Mightn't it be the case that Mr Young kept them there precisely because he didn't want them to be part of his everyday life . . . these disturbing, degrading, incriminating images, but incriminating of a whole society, a whole culture, not one individual?'

'It might be, yes.'

'Yes, Sergeant, it might well be; and, indeed, it is. For Mr Young is not one of those men – those heterosexual men – who travel regularly from this and other Western countries to the Philippines or Brazil or Thailand, where girls as young as these are freely on offer. As one look at his passport – let alone at the stories in several scandalous newspapers – will show.'

'I'm sorry? Was that a question?' Bridges asks cockily.

'Miss Colestone, I do not consider this a relevant matter for the witness.'

'I apologise, My Lady. Now I should like to turn to the matter of the black rubber dildo with teeth marks. This is not exhibited in court. May I ask why?'

'It seems to have got lost somehow,' Bridges shrugs.

'Lost?'

'Mislaid.'

'A black rubber dildo has been lost – I beg your pardon, mislaid – in a police station?' Rebecca's tone delights the gallery. 'Is this a common occurrence? Wouldn't you have been wise to keep it under lock and key?'

'It was under lock and key.' He is growing sullen.

'Then may I ask who was in charge of the key?'

'No, you may not, Miss Colestone.' The Judge is losing patience. 'I think that we have established that the article in question has disappeared. Would you either demonstrate the point of this line of enquiry, or take up another.'

'Of course, My Lady.' She turns back to her witness. 'You say that the dildo in question was bitten?'

'Yes. Large tooth marks. As if a mad dog had chewed it.'

'A mad dog, really? Fortunately, My Lady, I have a replica of the item here.' She flourishes a dildo to a further burst of laughter. 'Of course, sizes vary, as I am sure you are well aware, but would you say that this is approximately the equivalent of the one which you confiscated from my client's house?'

'As far as I can tell, yes.'

'My Lady, would it be convenient for this to be marked as Exhibit D1?' She summons the Usher. 'Would you show this to the witness.' She does. 'Thank you. Now, Sergeant, would you say that this was about the same consistency, thickness, malleability, as the one which has been so mysteriously mislaid?' Bridges holds the object as though its very touch was compromising.

'I should think so. I'm not an expert in these matters.'

'Would you bite it, Sergeant.'

'I'm sorry?'

'Bite . . . with your teeth.'

The Prosecuting Counsel stands. 'My Lady, I really cannot see what this has to do with the case in hand. My learned friend is attempting to embarrass the witness.'

'Not at all, My Lady. As I intend to show, it is of crucial significance.'

'I hope so, Miss Colestone.' The Judge smiles sweetly at Bridges. 'If you'd be so kind, Sergeant. Would you oblige me by biting it.'

'Of course, M'lord . . . I mean M'lady.' He bites it and holds it up.

'Any toothmarks, Sergeant?'

'I didn't want to damage it. I wasn't sure what you might want to use it for.' His attempt to play to the gallery falls flat.

'Don't worry, Sergeant. This is precisely what I want to use it for. So bite away.' He does and examines it. Evidently unhappy with the result, he attacks it as though he had not eaten for a week. He takes it out of his mouth, sticky with saliva. 'Would you pass me the exhibit.' The Usher hands it back to Rebecca with distaste. She studies it carefully. 'Would you say that your teeth were strong, Sergeant?'

'I've tackled some T-bones in my time.'

'I can well imagine. And you see, there's barely an impression on this.' She addresses the Usher. 'Might that be passed to the jury.'

'I think that I'd better look at it first,' the Judge interjects. The Usher hands it, via the Court Associate, to the Judge, who examines it warily. She then returns it to the Usher who takes it to the jury. From the intensity of her inspection, I suspect that I may have misread the 'all men are rapists' juror.

'It seems clear, does it not, Sergeant, that the marks you've described could not have been made by a human?'

'If the rubber were as hard as this, yes.'

'Which you've testified that it was. In fact, you told the court that it looked as though a mad dog had chewed it . . . are you aware that before they were given a cat – a cat to whom I shall be returning shortly – my client and Miss Mulliner owned a retriever?'

'No, I was not.'

'Then may I take it you are also unaware that, for a joke, instead of a rubber bone, Miss Mulliner bought Texas a dildo; which has remained forgotten in a cupboard for years?'

'A joke? What sort of a joke was that? It seems to me in pretty poor taste.'

'Oh surely not as poor as hiring Tarzan-grams to strip off and embarrass WPCs or sending them letters in envelopes headed "Confidential: AIDS Test results"?'

Bridges blushes beetroot. 'How the hell did you hear about that?'

'The truth is, Sergeant, that you see what you want to see.' She ignores his question. 'A little girl has been horribly abused, so you pick the obvious candidate. You were determined that Mr Young was guilty, partly because of his celebrity – and there's an element in us all that longs to see the rich and famous take a tumble – but mainly because he is gay. It is not my client who is standing in the dock; it is his sexuality . . . and your prejudice.'

Rebecca so effectively demolishes Bridges's credibility that nothing the Prosecuting Counsel says in his re-examination can restore it. She goes on to deal a similar blow to the police paediatrician, accepting his diagnosis at almost every stage but dissenting from his conclusions. In her view, there is as much significance in the scarring of Pagan's hymen as in the tears to her anus. 'Is it not true,' she asks, 'that in girls of Pagan's age, the anus displays considerably more elasticity than the vagina, and that buggery, far from being indicative of sexual tastes, is, in fact, the only practical means of penetration?' The paediatrician is forced to agree.

With the medical evidence in ruins, the Court rises for lunch . . . although the Judge instructs me to remain in the room for a further ten minutes, in order to reduce the risk of confrontation. As I sit beside a tattooed and taciturn prison officer, I feel more than ever like Ronnie Kray. My request for his estimate of the morning's progress is met with a grunt. I receive a more considered response when I am released to join my defence team in the corridor. Max and Anthony are jubilant, although Rebecca remains as circumspect as a producer in the middle of a shoot. Since our delayed start gives no guarantee of immunity from the prosecution, we choose to avoid the cafeteria. Anthony is dispatched to assess the position in the street. When he reports that the crowd has dwindled into single figures, we decide to head for a nearby pub.

As we walk through the hall, I experience a Mozartian tingle when my name appears to emerge from the statue of Charles II. A moment later, a wheelchair rolls round a pillar, which I at once identify as William's. Glancing at his face, I am struck by a resemblance to you, which is patently absurd . . . unless it has been shaped by shared memories, the experiences of childhood which leave their mark as physically as accidents of birth. He asks if we might have a few words in private, so I tell the others to go on ahead. At first, I suspect that he simply wants to justify his conduct during your illness. He sniffs and fumbles for excuses like tissues.

'It was my mum and dad. When Candida refused to have anything to do with them, they made me promise not to see her. They said it would be disloyal. My father's very hot on loyalty.'

'I suppose it's inevitable when you've spent twenty years in the Army and thirty in a public school.'

'I wouldn't know about that. He wouldn't send me to his school. It was alright for Candida; but not for me.'

'I could never understand that. I'd have thought that as a boy. . . .'

'But I wasn't a boy, don't you see? I was a chair. What sits four foot off the ground, has a head, four legs and runs on wheels? Come on, Leo; if you don't know, have a guess.' I am unable to deal with his pain. 'He was ashamed of me, of my – that's to say, his – disability. He claimed it was

356

impractical. Old buildings . . . narrow corridors . . . stone flags . . . steep steps. "You're the bursar," Candida said, "make them build a few ramps." I said nothing. Instead, I was sent to a school for children with euphemisms.'

'Euphemisms?'

'Learning difficulties. Physical handicaps. Half of us in our chairs, the other half off their trolleys.'

'Candida never forgave him.'

'Candida didn't have to forgive him. This isn't Candida's story; it's mine!' He looks down. 'I should have come to the funeral. I wanted to come to the funeral. But I could imagine you introducing me to everyone. "This is Candida's brother." "I never knew she had a brother; she kept that very quiet." Yes, this is Candida's quiet brother, only sometimes he wants to scream so loud.'

'Then why don't you?'

'Oh, it's harder when you're sitting down all day; it's not just your muscles that atrophy, but your vocal cords. Life shits in your face and you're supposed to be grateful to anyone who wipes it off. I need my parents, see. They're getting old and one day they won't be here; but, while they are here, I need them. I'm not Mr Disabled Person of the Year; I'm not running marathons in the Wheelchair Olympics. I live by myself, sure, and I drive my own car, but that's it. My mother cooks for me. She brings me food marked Monday, Tuesday, Wednesday, and so on. And I always eat it in the correct order . . . as if they were medicines not meals. Why's that, would you say?'

'I'm afraid I don't know.'

'You should do; you're clever. You were always so much cleverer than me, you and Candida. I need an answer . . . I'm sorry, I'm embarrassing you. They'll be wondering where I am.'

'Are both your parents in court? I only saw your father.'

'My mother's a witness. I'm sure it's quite unethical, but my father's giving her a blow-by-blow account of the morning's events over cod and chips.'

'How did you escape?'

'I need the lavatory. I asked a waitress in the canteen for the way. "Do you want the disabled toilet?" she said. "That's right," I said; "I only want one that won't flush."

Why aren't you laughing? She didn't either. In the past, everyone's always roared.'

'Perhaps another time. The setting's not conducive to laughter.'

'You didn't do it, Leo; I know you didn't do it; you'll be OK.'

'How do you know? What do you know? You haven't seen me in years.' I am perplexed by his change of tone.

'I must go. I really do need the lavatory. "How do you do a wee-wee?" a kid asked me the other day. "Girls wee sitting down; boys standing up." '

'Was it Pagan?' He does not answer but makes for the door. 'Why won't you tell me? Why did you want to see me? Is that all you wanted to say?' He suddenly seems frightened and eager to escape. 'At least let me help you.'

'No need, there are lifts and ramps. Even this venerable old building has put in ramps. Wonderful things, ramps.' I watch him disappear and then make my way to the pub.

I return to find the Court transformed for Pagan's video evidence. Screens are set up for Judge, Counsel and jury, and one for me in the dock. Cameras are fixed for the cross-examination. The Prosecuting Counsel introduces the film. Having pored over the transcript, I am able to anticipate most of the dialogue as if it really were *Citizen Kane*. Familiarity does not make the material any less painful, and my one consolation is that, whatever else, I will never have to sit through it again. I watch for the jury's reaction, which is impossible to gauge in the pin-drop silence ... although, when Pagan speaks of my touching her bottom, the 'all men are rapists' juror ominously fingers her lapel.

At the end of the tape, the Judge explains the procedures for cross-examination; Pagan is waiting in an adjoining room and will be questioned via a closed-circuit video-link. She herself is in control of what appears on the screen, which will be seen only by those directly involved. She is particularly anxious that there should be no noise in the gallery and that every effort be made to minimise Pagan's ordeal. With that in mind, she asks Counsel to remove their wigs and reminds them to sit still in their seats. She then ascertains that Pagan is ready and introduces herself and the two barristers.

'Are you the Judge?'

'That's right.'

'But you're a lady.'

As the film constitutes Pagan's examination-in-chief, the first to question her is Rebecca. She leads her gently through her evidence, quickly establishing that it lends itself to more than one interpretation.

'When you said that Leo had touched your bottom, was this after you'd done a wee or a pooh?'

'You shouldn't say that. *She* says it's naughty.'

'Who's *she*, Patience? Is it Granny?'

'Yes.'

'I understand. We don't like to talk about pooh; it's not a very nice thing to talk about. But sometimes we have to. Sometimes, when we're not very happy, we do pooh by mistake. Is this what happened to you?'

Pagan nods. She looks so grave and grown-up. The Judge intervenes.

'Patience, it would help me a great deal if you spoke out loud rather than nodding . . . if you said "yes" or "no"; so I could hear what you said. Is that alright?'

'Yes.' She speaks and nods at the same time.

'So you'd done a pooh and Leo was cleaning you?'

Pagan nods and then remembers. 'Yes.'

'And did you feel better when he'd cleaned you?'

'Yes.'

'You didn't feel hurt?'

'No.' The Judge intervenes again.

'Patience, if you ever don't understand a question, you will tell us, won't you, so we can explain it to you?'

'Yes.'

'Good girl.' I am grateful for her composure but sad that she should answer so freely to her new name.

'Patience, on another occasion that Leo touched your bottom, do you remember – and I know that it's not easy when you're a little girl to remember all these things – but do you remember telling him that you felt sore?'

'Yes.'

'Do you remember when it was?'

'When I came home.'

'By home, do you mean London?'

'London's my home . . . my house . . . my room.'

'Yes of course. And do you remember where you were coming from?'

She squirms in her seat. The Judge addresses her.

'You can tell us whatever you like, Patience. No one is going to be cross with you, and no one's going to hurt you. I promise.'

'Hove.'

'Home?' the Judge asks.

'Hove, My Lady. Patience's grandparents live in Hove.'

'Of course. Thank you, Patience.'

'So you were coming from Granny and Grandpa when you said that your bottom was sore?'

'Yes.'

'Was this your front bottom or your back bottom?'

'Both.'

'Did Leo do anything to help?'

'He gave me some cream on it.'

'Did that make it feel better?' She nods. 'Now, I want you to think very carefully, Patience. Did Leo ever put anything inside your bottom?'

'No.'

'He never touched it or put in a finger?'

'No, no, no!'

'It's very important that you understand me, Patience, and that we all understand you. Did Leo ever touch your bottom at any time except to clean it or rub in some cream?'

'No. I said so already.'

I turn away from the screen and gaze up at the gallery. I want to catch everyone's eye.

'But Patience, on the film that we've just been watching: the film with you in it –'

'They promised to show me the trains.'

'I beg your pardon, I don't quite follow.'

'The trains at the station. But they never did.'

'I'm sure that, another time, they will.' Rebecca looks lost. 'Now, in the film, you say that Leo put something in your bottom in another man's house.'

'No!'

'Can you remember Leo taking you to see a doctor in London after you'd told him that your bottom was sore?' She reflects for a moment. She has matured so fast; she is

360

starting to think, rather than just to express the thoughts that appear in her head.

'Yes.'

'Do you remember why that was?'

'He said that, if the man saw that my bottom was hurt, I wouldn't have to go back to Hove.'

'And he was the one who put something in your bottom?'

'Yes.'

'Not Leo?'

'No. I keep saying.'

'Do you know what it was?'

'It was cold.'

'And did he touch you anywhere else?'

'He touched everywhere.'

'Thank you very much, Patience. You're doing very well. My Lady, the man in question was a paediatrician whom my client consulted when he began to suspect that Pagan was being abused. He will confirm this himself later.'

'Thank you, Miss Colestone. Patience, are you tired?'

'No.'

'Do you mind if we ask one or two more questions?'

'It's alright.'

'Patience,' Rebecca continues, 'when you ask on the film, when you will be able to go home and see Leo and Trouble, what do you mean?'

'I want to see them.'

'Yes, I know. But, if I say to you "you'll be in trouble", you know what I mean, don't you?'

'Like *she* says when she tells me I'm naughty.'

'And *she* is still Granny?'

'Yes.'

'But you didn't mean that when you were speaking about Leo, did you?'

'Course not. Trouble's my cat.'

'Her pet cat, My Lady, nothing more sinister. So, Patience, it wasn't that you felt scared that you'd be in trouble with Leo for talking on the film?'

'I love Leo; I love him best in the whole world . . . in the whole universe. But he doesn't love me.' Is it her eyes that mist or mine?

'Why do you say that?'

'He won't come to see me any more.'

'Perhaps he will soon.'

'I want to go home.'

'Where's that?'

'I've only got one home . . . one real home. I hate the seaside; I'm not on holidays.'

'Patience, please don't upset yourself,' the Judge says. 'This will soon be over. We're all trying to find what's right for you.'

'It's right to go home.'

'Carry on, Miss Colestone.'

'When Leo took you to live by the lake last summer, did you want to go?'

'Oh yes.'

'Do you know why he cut off your hair?'

'Course. So I'd look like a boy.'

'Why was that?'

'So that *they* wouldn't find us. And they wouldn't have. But I fell downstairs. And I had to go to hospital in an ambulance. And I had to come home. And I can't ever see Leo again.'

'You may very soon.'

'When?'

'Let's answer the rest of these questions first. Did you like being a boy?'

'I was Paul. People don't hurt boys.'

'Did Leo ever hurt you when you were a boy?'

'Leo never hurt me when I was a girl; Leo never hurt Pagan.'

'No, of course not. Tell me, when you were in the woods, did you have beds to sleep in?'

'No.' She looks impatient.

'So where did you sleep?'

'In bags.'

'Would they be bags with zips in?'

'Course.'

'And you each had your own bag? You didn't sleep in Leo's?'

'No, we put them together; but he said they were too small.'

'Leo said that the bags were too small for you to sleep together?'

'Yes.'

'But you wanted to?'

'Yes. I want to at home; but he won't let me . . . only as a special treat. He says I'm too big.'

'I can understand; you're growing up. Tell me, why do you want to sleep in Leo's bed?'

'He's warm.'

'And when you're in his bed, what are you wearing?'

'Pyjamas.'

'And what's Leo wearing?'

'Pyjamas.'

'Always pyjamas?'

'Course; you're not allowed to wear any other clothes in bed.'

'No, of course not.' Thank you . . . it will be a sad day, when a man who has looked after a little girl for the whole of her life cannot give her an early morning cuddle as a special treat. 'Thank you, Patience, we've nearly finished. I want to ask just a few more questions. When they gave you the dolls in the film, do you remember saying that one had a bottom like Leo's?' Pagan giggles. 'Did Leo ever show you his bottom?'

'No, it's rude.'

'So you've never seen Leo's bottom?'

'Oh yes.' I suddenly feel sick.

'When was that?'

'When I was small and there was Mummy. We made him a pie bed. Well she did and I helped with the edges. Then we hid in the cupboard, with a little crack for air. And he came in and took off all his clothes. And Mummy thought it was funny so she laughed and he was cross.'

I am trapped in a maze of memory; how could I have forgotten that?

'So you were with your mummy?'

'I said.'

'What about when you were by yourself?'

'No, it's naughty.'

'That's right, it's naughty. And is Leo ever naughty?'

'No, Leo's never naughty.'

'Is anyone else ever naughty?' She says nothing. 'Does

363

anyone else ever hurt inside your bottom?' She says nothing.

'My Lady,' the Prosecuting Counsel interrupts, 'I consider that Patience has been questioned for quite long enough on this matter. In the film, she clearly denies that anyone else has interfered with her.'

'My Lady, I maintain that my learned friend is mistaken. That is precisely what she does not deny, as I shall endeavour to prove.'

'Please do so, Miss Colestone, and as quickly as possible, so that we can avoid any further distress to the child.'

'Patience, when you saw the doll, you said that it wasn't like Grandpa's bottom? Do you remember?' She nods. 'Have you ever seen Grandpa's bottom?' She looks away from the camera. 'I know this is hard, but everything will be alright, as long as you tell the truth. So, have you ever seen Grandpa's bottom?' She nods.

'Was that a "yes" nod or a "no" nod, Patience?' the Judge asks.

'Yes.'

'But Grandpa's bottom didn't look like that, did it? What did Grandpa's bottom look like?' I stare at the screen. Pagan holds her arm rigid in front of her.

'Your arm? Are you saying that Grandpa's bottom looked like your arm?'

'It pointed.'

'Thank you, Patience, I see. I'm sure that we all see. Now, in the film, you say that Grandpa never made Pagan's bottom sore; do you remember?' She nods. 'You're not a liar, are you, Patience?' She shakes her head. 'Of course you're not. So Grandpa never made Pagan's bottom sore. But did Grandpa ever make Patience's bottom sore?' She does not reply.

'I'll go to prison,' she says, after a pause in which I break every record for holding breath. 'If I ever tell anyone, I'll be sent to prison.'

'That's not true, Patience. Believe me, there's no such thing as a prison for little girls.'

'There is too. And I'll go there if I tell anyone. Especially Granny. I must never tell her.'

'Who said that, Patience?'

'Grandpa.' I turn to where he is sitting next to William's wheelchair, staring at the floor.

'What did he tell you not to tell her, Patience?'

' "Come come come." ' She starts to sway. 'He said that. He put his bottom in my front bottom and then in my back bottom. It pointed; it hurt. "Come, come, come," he shouted.' She shouts, ' "Come, come, come." '

'No,' your father shrieks. 'It's lies, all lies. She's lying.'

'Silence in court, silence in court!' On the screen, I see Pagan cower and an unidentified arm reach out to support her.

'Thank you, Patience, you've been a very brave girl.'

'Pagan.' She pushes the arm away. 'My proper name's Pagan.'

'Of course it is. Thank you, Pagan. I have no more questions, My Lady.'

'Thank you, Miss Colestone. Your witness, Mr Strachan.'

'My Lady, I feel that, under the circumstances, there is nothing to be gained from subjecting the witness to a further examination.'

'Thank you, Mr Strachan, I entirely agree. Patience . . . Pagan, you've been most helpful; I wish to thank you on behalf of us all. In a few minutes, I'll come and talk to you myself.' Pagan looks uneasy. 'First, I'm going to turn off the pictures. Is that alright?' She nods.

The Judge switches off the monitor; the screen goes blank. She turns to the Prosecuting Counsel.

'Well, Mr Strachan, how does the prosecution case now stand?'

'My Lady, I'd be grateful for the opportunity to take instructions.'

'Will ten minutes give you enough time?'

'I would hope so.'

'The Court will rise for ten minutes.'

As the Judge leaves the room, there is a marked release of tension. The Prosecuting Counsel turns to a man sitting in the row behind him and leads him out. Lawyers arrange their papers; journalists consult their notes. The Usher chats to the jury, while Rebecca confers with Anthony and Max. I am at a loss. I have an almost irresistible urge to confront your father, who stares at the floor as intently as if he were trying to start a fire. Then Sweeney shouts from the gallery, 'Well wicked, Leo!' I swivel round in time to see Melissa and an officer scold him. There is a smatter of applause and my vision blurs. David waves; Imogen blows me a kiss; my mother has her hands clasped in prayer.

Rebecca comes to congratulate me, which seems to be the wrong way round. 'I hope you have plenty of champagne on ice.'

'I was afraid of tempting fate.'

'Don't worry,' she says. 'At long last, fate has taken up your case.'

She is proved right a few moments later, when first the Prosecuting Counsel and CPS clerk and then the Judge return to the Court. When asked if he has reached a decision, Strachan replies that, in the light of Pagan's statements, it would appear that the prosecution is no longer sustainable and therefore the Crown proposes to present no further evidence.

His words provoke a swell of applause in the gallery, which the Judge makes no attempt to quell. When it dies down, I expect her to turn to me; but, instead, she addresses the jury. It seems that, even though the case has collapsed, they are still required to deliver a verdict. I remain terrified of a maverick juror, but the Judge's directions are acquittal-clear.

'Members of the jury, you have heard the evidence of the last witness. It is plain that the defendant has no case to answer. I therefore direct you to deliver a verdict of "not guilty". Would you appoint one of your number to act as foreman in this matter.'

I watch them form a huddle. Pince-nez stands up; he would certainly not have been my choice. The Judge speaks to him.

'Members of the jury, have you reached a verdict on which you are all agreed?'

'We have.'

'Is your verdict on the charge of buggery guilty or not guilty?'

'Not guilty.'

'And is that a verdict on which you are all agreed?'

'It is.'

'Thank you very much, members of the jury.' She turns

to me. 'Mr Young, I have no doubt that you are totally innocent of the charge. There is not a scrap of evidence to suggest that you have been anything other than a loving and responsible guardian. You leave the Court with your reputation unblemished.'

I listen to her words. I pick my way through the sentences. It is only when I hear another roar of applause from the gallery that I realise their full import. I am free. The sword of Damocles has been rendered as harmless as Lewis's retractable dagger. The Judge continues.

'While it is clear that there is no substance to the charges against the defendant, it is equally clear from both the medical evidence and the child's own testimony that she has been abused and by someone who may well be a member of her family. I trust that the officers conducting the inquiry will continue their investigations and take whatever steps are necessary to apprehend the perpetrator.'

The Judge rises. I sit dazed in the dock. Everything that I touch tingles. I have regained my faith in human decency . . . and not on account of twelve good men and true but of one seven-year-old girl. If you were to challenge me now – if only you could challenge me now – to justify my belief in an innate and uncompromised ethical code, I would look no further than Pagan. She had no system of words nor any means of comparison, but she knew that what your father did to her was wrong. It violated her natural morality. Why else did she hide behind Patience? A name which had at first threatened her sense of self became its safeguard. As soon as I understood the truth behind her claim that 'he has never hurt Pagan's bottom', I knew that we would win the case. What is more, I am confident that her scars will heal. Patience's pain has failed to penetrate Pagan. She has been protected by something stronger than flesh.

I become aware of people. I switch my thoughts to thanks. I am warmed by the wisdom in Rebecca's eyes.

'You made it all seem so easy.'

'It was.'

Max is shuffling impatiently beside us, like a little child shouting 'me, me, me', as his parents embrace. I clasp his hand; he slaps my back. Several of the jurors come to congratulate me. The badge-lady throws her arms around my neck. I turn to the gallery, where the spectators are dispersing. Only my mother remains seated, clutching her handkerchief to her face. I am startled; I cannot remember when – if ever – I have seen her cry. She has always regarded tears as an indulgence on a par with the Catholic liturgy. Now that she has given into them, I am strangely moved.

Max directs my attention across the Court, to where your father is arguing with Bridges. I catch the words 'outrage, conspiracy, abuse'; although I cannot tell whether the allusion is sexual or judicial. I move towards them, followed by the rest of the group.

'I will not go,' he shouts, 'I demand to see a lawyer; I demand to see my wife. The child is lying. She hates me. I never go near her; it's my wife who puts her to bed.'

'I should remind you, sir, that you're under caution.'

'William, tell them who I am. Tell them I'm Edgar Mulliner. This can't be happening to me.' Bridges snaps handcuffs on his wrist. 'Take care; I'm arthritic! William, fetch your mother.' William sits stock-still; his hands lie limp on the wheels. 'Your mother, you useless lump!' William rolls slowly away from him and towards us.

'Where's his wife?' I ask Max.

'Presumably in one of the witness rooms downstairs. He was allowed in court, as they weren't going to call him.'

'Too risky,' Rebecca adds, 'I intended to play on that.'

I make my way to Bridges. 'Look!' your father snarls at me. He holds out his manacled wrist. 'Are there no depths to which you won't sink?'

'I was acquitted. What more do you need?'

'I've been in charge of men,' he shouts, 'fighting men.'

'I think you can close your case now, Sergeant.'

'Yes, sir, I'm inclined to agree. I'd like to apologise for any misunderstanding ... though I'm sure you can see what it looked like to us.'

'Give a dog a bad name, eh?'

His eyes stray to the dildo on the Court Associate's desk. 'Or else a bone,' he grins and leads your father out. I turn to William, whose entire chair is shaking.

'I'm so sorry. I can understand how you feel.'

'You understand nothing.'

368

'Hadn't you better explain to your mother? She's still waiting to give her evidence.'

'My opposite number should have alerted her to the verdict,' Rebecca says, 'although not to the aftermath.'

'I'm saying nothing,' William asserts. 'I owe her nothing. She'll hear nothing from me.' I find his fervour perplexing; but my reflections are curtailed by the Usher's request that we clear the Court.

As we walk back into the Grand Hall, I become aware of a figure stumbling towards us. 'What's happening?' your mother asks. 'They told me you'd been acquitted. Why?'

'Because I'm innocent.'

'Where's Mr Mulliner? Where's my husband? William!' She pounces on your brother, who has swerved his chair to the back of the group. 'William, where's your father? Answer me!' He says nothing but wrenches her hands off his arm and turns his chair to the wall. She tries to pull it back; but, even in her frenzy, she fails to lift the brake. She gives up and veers round towards us. Three lawyers from another court stop to watch.

'Will someone tell me where to find my husband?'

I step forward. 'He's been arrested, Mrs Mulliner, for abusing Pagan. She identified him in court.'

'You're a liar, a poisonous liar! Tell me the truth. Where is he?'

'He's in the hands of the detective who dealt with me. I expect they're setting off for Brighton. If you're quick, you may be able to hitch a lift.'

'No! He's a good man, a decent man. William, tell them.' He keeps his face averted and an eloquent silence. 'They hate him; they've hatched a plot between them. Never have children. You must never have children. They'll picnic on your grave.' She sags; her strength ebbs before my eyes. Rebecca goes to her aid.

'You should sit down, Mrs Mulliner.'

'Who are you? No!' She shakes her off. 'We've been married for fifty years; I was a war-bride. And this is how you repay him.' She hurries from the hall, sliding dangerously on the marble floor. William wheels himself to the lift, while the Usher leads the rest of us to Pagan.

She is sitting in a small ante-room playing with Marcia,

whose arm I failed to identify. She has her back to the door and does not turn as we walk in.

'Hello, darling.' Her spine tenses. She slowly swivels, drops a domino and bursts into tears. 'What sort of hello do you call this?' I squat and open my arms. She runs into them so hard that I lose my balance, and then buries her face in my jacket. Somehow I feel the wetness through the cloth. Then she looks up, throws her arms around my neck and half-punches, half-smacks my shoulder.

'Where did you go?'

'They wouldn't let me visit you.'

'I wanted to see you.'

'I wanted to see you too.'

'They said you'd been gone to prison.'

'Here I am.'

'Marcie says I won't ever have to see Grandpa again.'

'You won't.'

'You said that before.'

'This time it's not just me.'

'Can we go home? To Holland Park.' She turns to Marcia. 'I'm sorry, but I won't be able to finish the game. I'll say you won.'

'We'll declare a draw,' Marcia concedes. 'But I'm not sure that you can go home quite yet.'

'Why not?' She clings to me. 'You said!'

'What's wrong?' I am equally perturbed. 'Surely you can't send her back to her grandparents now?'

'No, of course not. . . . Maybe we can discuss this somewhere private. Then we can come back to Patience.'

'Pagan!' I say. 'And I refuse to decide anything more behind her back.' I appeal to Max and Rebecca. 'How can they stop me taking her now?'

'I see the problem,' Max declares with maddening moderation. 'It's the Court Order, isn't it?'

'That's right,' Marcia replies. 'Whether we like it or not, you've been denied contact. And until we can get it revoked. . . .'

'You'll what? Return her to her grandparents?'

'No, I'll do suicide!'

'Don't worry, darling, they won't take you.' I press her to my chest. 'What if they let Mulliner out on bail?'

'We'll apply for an Emergency Protection Order. I can

ring up a magistrate who'll give me one within the hour. We'll transfer her to a local children's home.'

'She has a home with me.'

'I'm sure that it'll only be temporary, but it's the best we can do.'

'It sounds exactly like the prison that her grandfather held over her head.'

'I don't want to go to prison.'

'Don't worry, you won't.'

'The law is the law. There's nothing we can do until we go back to court.'

'Not again! I seem to have spent the best part of the past two years in court. I wonder why I don't take up permanent residence. Yes, there's a thought. Instead of cutting legal aid, they could raise money by hiring out rooms.'

'It's no use upsetting yourself,' Max says. 'She won't be sent back to her grandparents, and it's only for a few days. But we have to go through the correct channels. You wouldn't want them to hold it against us later.'

'Can't we make a special application? Is there no legal equivalent of a late-night chemist?'

'This is the last lap, I promise,' Rebecca says. 'Not much longer to wait.'

'Pagan's keeping calm, aren't you?' Max says. 'You'll show Leo that he's being a silly old fuss-pot.'

'Why?'

'So you'll come back with me,' Marcia tells her. 'We'll go and play with all the other girls and boys. And we'll see Leo again very soon.'

'When?'

'Tomorrow, if you like.'

'Really?' Pagan and I ask in one voice.

'No problem.'

'Will you come tomorrow?'

'I promise. So you'll be a brave girl, won't you?'

'I don't want to be brave. I hate being brave. When people say brave, it means horrid.'

Marcia takes Pagan out. I walk with Max and Rebecca down the main staircase and into the reception area. A policeman warns us that a large crowd has gathered outside, along with journalists, photographers and camera-crews; but, this time, I am not alarmed . . . quite the reverse. I step into the street to a burst of audience applause, which is, for once, not orchestrated by a studio-manager. I tell the reporters what I feel in new-minted clichés: I dismiss all the doubts of the last six months; I thank my family and friends and everyone who has stood by me; I stress how much I look forward to resuming work on the show and, most of all, to being reunited with Pagan.

I am surrounded by loyal supporters.

'You did it; you showed the bastards,' Edward says.

'We're so proud of you,' Melissa adds.

'I did nothing. Apart from entering my plea, I never uttered a word. It was all down to Rebecca.' Smiles and sentimentality abound.

'Of course, it's goodbye to my project. I'll never make a diary out of a single day.'

'Sweeney!' his mother sounds affronted, as though selfishness were confined to the young.

'Joke, Mum. I'm really glad you were let off, Leo.'

'I'm sure we'll be able to find you something else.' I feel responsible for his abortive research. 'Maybe Rebecca knows of another trial you can watch.'

'Great. Do you? I'd like something sexy. Especially with a pop star or an MP.'

'I'll see what I can rustle up,' Rebecca laughs.

Another wave of well-wishers reaches us. My mother pushes her way to the front. Her eyes are raw. 'Thank God!' she says, 'thank God!' But, for once, the words appear to be an expression of relief rather than an injunc-tion. 'I love you, Lenny,' she says, pressing her lips to my cheek. Aunt Violet, no longer intimidated by either my height or my notoriety, envelops me in the same ample hug that she did when she was still Auntie Vi. Further friends are distinguished solely by their sex: male hand-shakes and female kisses. Then David crosses the divide and gives me a long kiss full on the mouth. My mother looks uneasy. I remember my courtroom pledge and introduce them.

'This is David Sunning. He used to be my researcher.'

'Is that all I was, Leo?'

'And my lodger.'

'Is that all?' He looks at me and I know that this is my one chance to piece together the fragments.

'And my lover. He used to be my lover.'

'Thank you.'

'Pleased to meet you,' my mother gulps, clutching her handbag to her breast. For the moment, I feel that this is as much as I can expect and leave her to Aunt Violet and a celebratory visit to St Paul's.

I edge my way across the pavement and through the throng. There is no sign of the Maastricht man or any of this morning's bigots. No doubt there will be more trials for them to picket tomorrow, but I refuse to think of that now. A woman thrusts a large bunch of lilies in my hand and disappears before I can thank her. Across the road, I see the three young men from my fan club, lifting their LEO placards high above their heads. I have never before been aware of my name's anagrammatic potential. I walk over to them, shake their hands and shift their letters, so that they reflect my overwhelming emotion: OLE!

# Four

**ROYAL BOROUGH OF
KENSINGTON AND CHELSEA**

---

# Schedule Two Report

Under Rule Twenty-Two (Two) Adoption Rules 1984

In the matter of the proposed adoption of Pagan Mulliner by
Leonard Peter Young.

## 1. The Child

a. Pagan Mulliner was born on the 26th July 1986, at the Portland
Hospital, London W1. Her current address is 64 Addison Avenue,
London W8.

b. She is illegitimate.

c. She is of British nationality.

d. She is 4'1" tall, of medium build, with long chestnut hair and fair
skin.

e. She is a sensitive, intelligent child, with a warm disposition,
who is loving and loyal to her friends but wary of strangers.
Though naturally docile, she is prone to sudden mood-swings
and to temper-tantrums when crossed. Her general development is appropriate for her age.

f. She has no religious background, apart from attendance at
Sunday School when staying with her grandparents.

g. She is the subject of a Residence Order in favour of Leonard
Peter Young, the prospective adopter, made on the 12th May
1994 in the Brighton County Court.

h. Not applicable.

i. She visited her maternal grandparents between July 1992 and
February 1993 and lived with them between February 1993 and
March 1994, at which time her grandfather was charged with
abusing her. Since then, she has had no contact with either
grandparent.

j. She was taken into the care of East Sussex County Council and placed in a Brighton residential unit between March and May 1994. While this served to remove her from an abusive environment, it was clearly unsuited to her long-term needs. The rapid turn-over of children and staff only increased her insecurity. The Manager of the Unit recommended that she be returned to the care of the prospective adopter.

k. Apart from the fourteen months between February 1993 and May 1994, she has lived with the prospective adopter all her life.

l. She attended Thomas's Kindergarten, 19 Ranelagh Grove, London SW1, between September 1989 and July 1991.

She attended Thomas's London Day School, 17 Cottesmore Gardens, London W8, between September 1991 and February 1993.

She attended St Andrew's School, Monmouth Street, Hove, between March 1993 and May 1994.

She returned to Thomas's London Day School in May 1994.

m. Following a recommendation from the Court, she sees Dr Ruth Lister, a consultant child psychiatrist at the Tavistock Clinic, London NW3, twice a week.

n. She is the prime beneficiary under her mother's will and heir to her artistic estate. The property is held in trust for her until she reaches the age of twenty-one. The prospective adopter is the sole trustee.

o. It is her express wish to live with and be adopted by Mr Young, whom she regards as the one stable factor in her life and as her father in all but name. She has no strong religious feelings, apart from a general distaste for Christianity which she associates with her grandparents. (It is unclear what she means by her various references to a 'Temple of Love'.)

## 2. The Natural Parents

### The Mother

a. Candida Millicent Mulliner was born on the 12th October 1954 in Peterborough District Hospital. She died on the 15th November 1991.

b. She was unmarried.

c. She first met the natural father at school and remained close to him for the next twenty years; although, after university, their paths diverged. Pagan was conceived during an isolated sexual incident.

d. She was 5'10" tall, of medium build, with long raven hair, fair skin and dove-grey eyes. Her strong features were striking

378

rather than beautiful and she enjoyed experimenting with her appearance. Indeed, she is often unidentifiable in photographs.

e. From information furnished by the prospective adopter, it would appear that she had a magnetic personality and was always at the hub of any gathering. She had an incisive mind and a witty tongue, with a tendency to favour the latter. She was a strange blend of the anarchist and the conformist, who longed for acceptance and yet revelled in outrage. She would keep even her closest friends at a distance, while at the same time craving their intimacy. She doted on her daughter and cared for her constantly until incapacitated by illness. She faced death from Motor Neurone Disease with inspirational strength of character.

f. She was brought up in the Church of England but, in later life, became a committed atheist.

g. She obtained a Bachelor of Arts degree (Aegrotat) from Cambridge University.

h. On leaving university, she took various unskilled jobs while trying to establish herself as an actress. Her performing career failed after a season as a dancer in a London nightclub. She found her vocation in photography, for which she received international acclaim. A major retrospective of her work is planned for the spring of 1996 at the Museum of Modern Art in New York; it will then visit the Pompidou Centre in Paris and the Institute of Contemporary Arts in London. This revival of interest in her mother may well affect Pagan.

i. She was adopted as an infant by Edgar and Muriel Mulliner. She was the illegitimate daughter of Linda Davies, a seventeen-year-old sales assistant, and an unidentified father. Linda subsequently married and raised two daughters, both of whom now have children of their own. She has never told her husband of Candida's birth and is adamant that she wants no contact with Pagan. There is no known hereditary disease in the family.

j. Candida Mulliner's view of adoption was resolutely black, coloured by her own unhappy experience. Nevertheless, she placed her total trust in the prospective adopter, whom she asked to be her co-parent while she lived and made the child's testamentary guardian on her death.

k. It should be noted that, owing to the mother's death, all the above information has been provided by the prospective adopter.

l. Not applicable.

## The Putative Father

a. Robin Perceval St John Standish was born on the 13th August

1954 in Crierley, near Fownhope, Herefordshire. He died on the 25th April 1987.

b. He was unmarried.

c. See under mother.

d. He was 6'0" tall, slim, with golden hair, full lips and cornflower-blue eyes. He had rare physical grace and, throughout his life, retained a boyish charm.

e. From information furnished by the prospective adopter, it would appear that he was genial and generous with a relaxed intelligence, which he played down in order to trade more easily on his physical allure. His surface confidence was belied by inner doubt, which drove him to excessive and self-destructive behaviour and, ultimately, to suicide.

f. He was a practising Roman Catholic.

g. He obtained a Bachelor of Arts degree from Cambridge University.

h. On graduation, he worked as a film critic for *Scoop* magazine. He spent some time managing the family estates in Herefordshire but refused to follow a conventional career path, believing that 'one should work to live, not live to work'. He travelled extensively and took part in various counter-culture activities on the Continent.

i. His parents are both dead. His father, an alcoholic, died in the mid-1980s. His mother died of heart disease in October last year (there is no suggestion that this was congenital). He has a surviving sister, Lydia, who was born suffering from Foetal Alcohol Syndrome, which has left her physically scarred, emotionally withdrawn and mentally retarded. No one in Robin's family is aware of his relationship to Pagan.

j. He never expressed any desire to see his daughter or any opinion on her future.

k. It should be noted that, owing to the father's death, all the above information has been provided by the prospective adopter.

l. Neither parent ever revealed to anyone, including the prospective adopter, the truth of Pagan's paternity. The facts have only recently and unexpectedly come to light. It is thought likely that the Standish family would resist any claim against it made by, or on behalf of, the child.

### 3. The Prospective Adopter

a. Leonard Peter Young was born on the 1st May 1955 at Nant-y-Glyn Maternity Hospital, Colwyn Bay, North Wales. His current address is 64 Addison Avenue, London W8.

b. He is the child's testamentary guardian.

c. He is homosexual and, while currently unattached, does not rule out the possibility of a relationship in the future. He nevertheless insists that Pagan's needs will remain paramount. In the past year, he has discussed his sexuality with her and found her to be wholly sympathetic. He has many close women friends, who will provide her with appropriate role models.

d. He has never married.

e. Not applicable.

f. Not applicable.

g. Not applicable.

h. He is 6' 2" tall, broad-shouldered and lean. He has copper-coloured hair, pale, heavily freckled skin and sea-green eyes.

i. He has an exuberant, outgoing personality which is well suited to his media role. He leads a busy social life with diverse friends. At the same time, he is a deeply private man, sensitive, reflective and warmly empathetic, particularly with children. He has a sharp wit and a shrewd sense of humour.

j. He has no religion but was brought up a Methodist. He declares himself neutral on the subject of God, while deeply hostile to the myths and teachings of the Christian church, claiming that 'the Garden of Eden is no place for a child; I would rather that she grew up with Ken and Barbie than with Adam and Eve'.

k. He obtained a first-class Bachelor of Arts degree from Cambridge University.

l. On leaving university, he taught for fifteen months in a preparatory school and then joined the BBC where, for several years, he worked in radio. In 1983, he moved to television and, for the past ten years, has hosted a chat show. He has presented numerous documentaries and arts programmes. He is also an experienced journalist, who, since last autumn, has written a weekly column in the *Observer*. He has wide cultural interests, particularly in music, which he once thought to make his career.

m. He owns a large detached house with a substantial garden in a quiet, residential neighbourhood. The house is beautifully furnished and maintained, without being over-formal. Pagan has her own bedroom and playroom and shares a bathroom with her nanny. The garden is well tended and equipped with a slide, swing and sandpit. Holland Park, with its children's playgrounds, is a ten-minute walk away.

n. He has a high disposable income. In April 1994, he signed a new contract with the BBC, worth £350,000 a year over the next

381

five years. In addition, he commands considerable fees for after-dinner speeches, personal appearances and newspaper articles.

o. There are two other members of the household: Juliet Croome-Clark, Pagan's nanny, and Una Wilmott, the housekeeper.

p. He is an only child. Both his parents are living. His father is a permanent invalid following an assault. His mother is asthmatic but otherwise in good health.

q. After initial opposition, his mother has given her full backing to the proposed adoption. Mr Young believes that, once the relationship is legally endorsed, she will finally accept Pagan as her grandchild. His father is unable to express a view.

r. He has lived with the child all her life, playing a major role in her upbringing. He assumed sole responsibility for her on her mother's death.

s. He has a good understanding of the nature of the proposed adoption. Given the Residence Order currently in force, it will have little effect on their day-to-day lives. On the other hand, it will profoundly alter the way that both he and Pagan perceive their relationship and provide them with much-needed security. He remains bitter about the way in which he has been treated during the past three years, considering that he has been victimised on account of his sexuality. The adoption will mark official accept-ance of his love for the child.

t. His principal goal is to ensure that Pagan enjoys a peaceful and happy childhood in which she can put the anguish of abuse behind her. He aims to be protective but not possessive, encouraging her to form friendships and to develop talents that will sustain her throughout life. He places a high – though not exclusive – value on academic progress and is particularly keen that she should pursue her interest in art.

u. He is well informed on the sexual issues that affect a young girl, especially one who has suffered such trauma. He has a strong support network and appears highly qualified to care for the child both now and through adolescence.

## 4. Actions of the Local Authority Supplying the Report under Rule Twenty-Two (Two)

a. The Local Authority was notified of the proposed adoption by Mr Young on the 12th May 1995.

382

b. The Local Authority was required by the Court to submit a Schedule Two report on the 26th May 1995. Mrs Charlotte Walsh of the Family Placement Unit Adoption Team was appointed as the Social Worker in the case. She proceeded to interview the prospective adopter and the child and to prepare the report. The Adoption Committee agreed on the 3rd August 1995 that it was in Pagan's best interests to be adopted and that Mr Young was suitable to adopt. Pagan Mulliner was placed for adoption on the 15th August 1995.

c. Not applicable.


## 5. Generally

a. Not applicable.

b. Not applicable.


## 6. Conclusions

a. See attached medical reports (Schedule Three) for detailed assessments of the health of both the prospective adopter and the child. Pagan continues to show signs of disturbance associated with the abuse but has established a good relationship with Dr Lister and is responding well to therapy.

b. Adoption is clearly in the long-term interests of the child, who is devoted to the prospective adopter and determined to have their relationship legalised – and, in her eyes, legitimised – as that of father and daughter. It should also allay her remaining fears of being removed from home.

c. Not applicable.

d. Adoption is clearly in the long-term interests of Mr Young. It will enable him to be the father *de jure* which he has long been *de facto*. It represents a recognition of all that he has done for Pagan in the past and a declaration of faith in their future.

e. Renewal of the Residence Order would be an inferior option. It would confirm Mr Young's sense of himself as a second-class parent and might well divert his attention from caring for the child towards nurturing his grievances against the authorities.

f. I conclude that the Adoption Order should be made. If the Court, however, takes a different view, then the Residence Order of the 12th May 1994 should be renewed.

*Charlotte Walsh*

Charlotte Walsh,
Social Worker, Family Placement Unit,
Royal Borough of Kensington and Chelsea.

# 1

I walk up the gravelly path past a forlorn patch of primroses. I pull the doorbell like an organ-stop. Another pane in the fanlight has been boarded up since my last visit. I speculate on the cause . . . deliberate vandalism, a fit of rage, an escape attempt, or just the natural process of decay?

I am relieved when the Manager opens the door. On Thursday, the only adult on the premises was an agency worker who had not been informed of my visit. She left me kicking my heels on the step and Pagan pressing her face against the window, while she phoned for authorisation. When she finally let me in, she made no apology, seeming to feel that I was at fault for disturbing her shift. After all, none of the other children's parents had come.

The Manager asks if we might have a word while Pagan finishes her lunch. He shows me into his office and then immediately departs in search of some coffee. I peer at the portrait of the home's benefactor, Sir Johnson Gurnett, Victorian industrialist turned death-bed philanthropist who, after a lifetime spent exploiting their parents, left his Kemp Town home, suitably endowed, for the care of indigent orphans. His expression puts me in mind of Judge Flower.

The house is an impenetrable labyrinth of faded formal rooms, connected by cavernous corridors in which the least sound becomes an echo. And yet, although the council has run it down, in every sense, it cannot afford to

385

close it completely. So, several passages are roped off, while an entire wing is abandoned, unfurnished and unheated. Ten children, aged between three and twelve, occupy a space originally intended for thirty; which only adds to their sense of loss.

The Manager comes back with the coffee, apologising, firstly, for having spilt it; secondly, that the milk is powdered; and, thirdly, that it is in a Thomas the Tank Engine mug. Once settled, he returns to the subject of the late lunch, which he blames on an incident in the dining room involving two boys and a billiard cue. He mops his mug with a dirty handkerchief and, the next moment, uses it to blow his nose. Stirring his coffee with his biro (he regrets the lack of spoons), he makes further excuses for Thursday's confusion over my arrival.

'It's good to see that you haven't given up on us.'

'I've no wish to sound rude, but I don't come for the pleasure of the company. I'd be back even if your assistant had set a pack of Alsatians on me. I'm here for Pagan.'

'Yes, of course. Point taken. I only hope she realises how lucky she is.'

'Lucky?'

'Relatively speaking,' he qualifies quickly. 'I really don't know what some of these kids have done to deserve this . . . that is, I know that they've done nothing. They're dumped here through no fault of their own and then we dump on them twice over. I tell you, you should make a programme.'

'Perhaps I will.'

'Naming no names, of course?'

'Of course.' He looks relieved.

'It means so much to Pagan that you come down three times a week. We have some parents who can't even be bothered to cross the road.'

'I want her to know that I'm always here for her.'

'Believe me, she does. The other day, she was in one of her "shouty-shouty" moods, as she calls them. She was having a bit of a ding-dong with another girl . . . oh nothing to worry about. She told her that, if she didn't leave her alone, she'd cut her up and serve her to her daddy for dinner.'

'Is that good?' I am alarmed by this vision of myself as a modern Moloch.

'Oh sure. It shows that she feels protected by you but not dependent.'

The telephone cuts short his explanation. He reaches to answer it and knocks his coffee over a pink file marked Confidential. As he flounders, I offer him my clean handkerchief and take the opportunity to escape. 'As soon as the meal's over, they'll head for the rec. room,' he says. 'Make yourself comfortable there.'

I walk out into an atmosphere of sanitation and Savlon, damp clothes and wet beds. I move down corridors hung with posters of dolphins and defaced by graffiti. I enter the recreation room which, with its mixture of expensive curtains and furnishings, chipped plaster, torn lino and ancient mashed potato calcifying on the ceiling, embodies all the home's incongruities. I swear loudly as I trip over a model car and am startled to discover a woman sitting in a sagging armchair, hidden by its high back. We have met before. She is the mother of a gangling, snub-nosed boy, who propositioned me on a previous visit. 'Don't let it worry you,' said the Manager, whose response to my report showed that he has never faced a charge of child abuse. 'He was sodomised by his father and uncle; it's the only way that he can relate to men.'

I turn to the woman and hope that she was not as offended by my 'Fuck' as I was by her son's offer. She flashes me a fuzzy smile and I pick up on the Manager's description of her as high on valium and low on self-esteem; to which he added that she is in and out of clinics so often that even her dog has a social security number. In a voice eerily drained of emphasis, she tells me that she has come to see her son Ronald, whom they named after the President. I ask politely if his father is American; she stares at me as though the suggestion were insane. She informs me that, for the moment, all four of her children are in care, but she wants to have another three because seven is her lucky number. I despair to think that parenthood can be entered so lightly . . . at least she had to buy a licence for her dog.

A mob invades the room and demands my attention. I am surrounded by older children who know my show and younger ones who have seen me on *Jackanory* (I smile at the thought of the olive branch recently held out by Ianthe Snowdon). Pagan detaches herself from Shona, the mournful, disfigured girl who has become her new best friend, and runs into my arms, planting a creamy kiss on my cheek. 'I'm going out, I'm going out,' she shouts. I fear that she may incite envy – or worse – in the others. 'My daddy's taking me to a castle. I'm going to live there soon. We're going to pull up the bridge and drown everyone outside in the moat.'

I am disturbed by the increasing violence of her speech and its connection to her environment. Even now, Ronald, who has yet to acknowledge his mother, is engaged in a frenzied row with Eugene, the one black child in the home, a deeply disturbed boy with cigarette burns and razor slashes covering his arms like tribal markings, who sought me out last week to explain that he had not been born black but that he had been bad to his parents and God had put a curse on him. I asked who had filled his head with such wicked nonsense.

'My parents.'

'How could they? If it were true, it would mean that God had put a similar curse on them.'

'He did,' he said. 'It made them blind; which was why they adopted me.'

The pattern of prejudice recurs, as Ronald takes off his trainers and hurls them at Eugene, yelling, 'Own up, you black bastard; I'm not going to be stuck indoors all day because of you.' His mother reproaches him, her words at odds with her permanent grin. Ronald quickly turns the full force of his fury onto her . . . 'Don't tell me what to do! You're a fucking schizo.' He mimes lunacy; she obediently backs off. Aware that the children are looking to me to take a lead, I gently suggest to Ronald that that is no way to talk to his mother, at which he rounds on me . . . 'What do you know about it, you great poof!'

The word hits me like an electric shock, the charge intensified by Pagan's presence. She grabs my hand; 'I want to go out; you said we were going out; I want to go to the castle.' I promise her that we will, just as soon as Ronald and Eugene stop rolling around on the floor. And yet, although all my instincts are to intervene, I fear that, in this world of loud whispers and long shadows, I may lay myself open to censure and decide that the wiser course is to inform the Manager, whom I find in the kitchen, washing up. He listens wearily to my account and explains that it stems from one of the children setting off the fire alarm in the night. As no one has admitted to it, this afternoon's cinema trip has been cancelled . . . 'I tell you, you should make a programme. You really should.'

I follow him back to the recreation room where the fight continues, watched by two excited four-year-olds as though it were *Tom and Jerry*, while the other children, Pagan included, ignore it completely and play among themselves. I am not sure which depresses me more: the brutality or the indifference. I resolve that, as soon as I return home, I shall ask Max to make another attempt to advance the residence hearing. I dread to think how a month in this world of rage and anguish has affected Pagan. She has been rescued from one kind of violence, only to be subjected to another. Nothing can be more calculated to sustain her sense of guilt.

I can, at least, offer her a temporary respite; and we walk upstairs to fetch her coat. I am relieved that Jess, the fearsome deputy manager, is not on duty, or I would never be allowed in the bedroom unsupervised. In her view, I am a man and therefore innately guilty, whatever the verdict of the trial.

'You must know what Oprah Winfrey says about child abuse. Or don't you watch your women rivals?'

'I can't bear to. I get too depressed by the thought of her salary.' Her sour face seems to take me at my word.

'That if you're asked whether you were abused as a child, there are only two possible answers: either "yes" or "I don't remember".'

'Come on. I'm the last person to underestimate the problem; but nothing is served by such wild exaggeration.'

'It's in your interest to say that; you're a man.'

My mistake was to think that she might feel some sympathy towards me by virtue of our linked sexuality when, in fact, she regards all men as equally poisonous. She told me quite openly that she became a vegetarian, not out of concern for animals, but because the meat that she ate might be male.

A general gloom appears to have pervaded the house. As we enter the bedroom, we find Shona lying on her bed, her body heaving, her face buried in the counterpane. Pagan runs up to her and lovingly rubs her forehead on her shoulder; I am moved by this gesture of compassion, which contrasts sharply with her apathy downstairs. I sit down next to them but jump up fast when I sense the dual disapproval of Oprah and Jess. Like a radio actor, I am forced to convey all my emotion in my voice. I ask what the problem is; Shona does not reply. Pagan speaks for her. 'It's her face.'

I am startled by the baldness of the statement, which appears to confuse the general with the specific. Shona's face is, self-evidently, a problem: a patchwork of burnt skin and plastic reconstruction, as angular as a cubist painting with its distinct and highly coloured planes. The moral of her story is so stark that, if I had heard it anywhere but here, I would suspect poetic licence. She is the sole survivor of a family of five who had their electricity cut off after failing to pay the bill. They were forced to use candles. One fell and started a fire which consumed her mother, father and two younger brothers. Her face bears the scars.

'Why? Does it hurt?' I ask. I have assumed that the dead flesh lacks sensation. Now I fear that it creeps with the crackling of flames.

'It did in the night,' she says, 'with the bell.' The association harrows me. 'Then, at lunch, Julie-Anne called me bacon-face.' She cries again. I dare not take her in my arms. 'Everyone hates me because I'm ugly.'

'I love you,' Pagan says, with a hug. 'Next to Leo, I love you best in the world.'

'But you'll go soon. You'll go home and live in the park.'

'You can come and see me. There's lots of rooms. You can play with all my toys and my friends.'

'No,' Shona says, 'I don't want to go. I'm going to stay here for ever. And then I'm going to live in a house for the blind people, so that no one will be nasty to me ever again.'

I can offer no comfort. My thoughts are drowned by the sound of Danny Kaye, as Hans Christian Andersen, singing 'There once was an ugly duckling' to a boy with no

390

hair. I have never felt so conscious of the inadequacy of fairy tales.

As we drive to Arundel on a visit that is overdue by over a year, Pagan tells me that Shona has already run away from two foster-homes. She then asks tentatively if she might come to live with us. I scotch the idea before there is time for it to become an issue. 'They wouldn't let me unless I were married; and I couldn't find a wife that soon. Besides, you'll be more than enough of a handful on your own.'

'No, I won't. I won't even be a fingerful . . . a thumbful.'

'Don't contradict; it's rude.'

'No, it's not.'

I cannot help laughing. I am glad that she has made a friend and glad too that she has widened her social circle; although I regret that it has been accompanied by a coarsening of her speech. When she tells me that the home is 'fulking awful', I am as shocked as if I were wearing mutton-chop whiskers and a morning coat. And yet I refuse to tell her that it is a bad word; in my book, bad language is ill used not immoral. I say, instead, that it is the wrong word, adding that fucking is a way in which grown-ups show that they love one another and that it is a good thing; it only becomes bad when it is done crudely or cruelly . . . or to a child.

Later, as we sit taking tea in the castle café, she extends her vocabulary further. 'What's a poof?' she asks. 'Are you a poof?' The questions are less distressing than the timing. I have always known that one day I would have to answer them. And yet I feel bitter that, thanks to your parents, she must face the truth so soon.

'Who told you that? Was it someone in the home?' I recall Ronald's insult.

'No, it was . . . it was . . .' The pause leaves no room for doubt.

'Was it Grandpa?'

'He's not my grandpa. My mummy didn't have a daddy. She was adopted.' Resisting the temptation to take the escape-route of adoption, I return to the subject of grown-up love. I attempt a simple illustration of the connections and differences between the sexes, using her Kit-Kats and my scones. She watches rapt; and yet I wonder how much she retains. I go on to say that the reason that people have tried to take her away from me is 'because I liked other Kit-Kats'. She laughs and bites my head off . . . metaphorically.

'Do you mind about that?'

'Of course not. I think all bottoms are horrid.'

'That's because you're a little girl. You won't when you're older. But you're already too old to call everything bottoms. There's a difference. A boy has a penis and a girl a vagina.'

'That's me.'

'Yes.' I lower my voice in response to suspicious looks from the neighbouring table. 'You'll find that people call them all sorts of names . . . silly names, naughty names, nasty names. But there's no need. Use the proper names so that they sound no different from any other part of the body . . . your elbow, your shoulder or your knee. Does what I'm saying make sense?'

'I think so. Can I have another Kit-Kat?'

'Don't you think you've had enough?'

We buy a Mary Queen of Scots doll and a tin of traditional butterscotch for Shona and then head back to Brighton. In the car, Pagan frets that she will never be allowed home; and I dispense promises like Monopoly money. We return to find the house in chaos. After his fight with Ronald, Eugene has slit his wrist with a Swiss mountain knife, succeeding, for the first time, in hitting an artery. He has been patched up in hospital and will be sent straight from there to a secure unit. Meanwhile, the recreation room is off-limits, until the staff have had time to scrub down the walls.

I am sickened by the thought of such self-destruction at the age of twelve. I blame his parents for stigmatising his skin as vilely as yours did your blood. I picture a scenario in which their hunger for a family blinded them to their prejudice. They convinced themselves of their ability to love a child from any background and yet, as the years went by, increasingly resented being stuck with what they saw as second-best. So they gave him back as though he had been sent on approval. . . . Well, God may not have cursed them, but I do. I fill with fury at a fatherless universe. And, while assuring Pagan that I will be here to

392

take her out again on Tuesday, I have never felt a more pressing need to take her away for good.

The opportunity occurs five weeks later, when my application is finally heard in the family court. It is not contested . . . not by the Welfare Officer, who makes a forceful plea that Pagan be returned to me, regretting her previous misjudgement and supplying a full account of my acquittal . . . not by the Manager of the Children's Home, who praises my devotion and the effect of my visits on Pagan's morale . . . not by your parents who, in a letter from their solicitor to Max, admit that they are no longer able to look after a child, citing ill-health (your mother is suffering from glaucoma) and the stress of your father's forthcoming trial . . . not even by the Judge (His Honour Judge Curtis), who, after reading the affidavits and my transcription of Mrs Justice Campbell's summing up, dispenses with my appearance in the witness box.

He grants me residence, albeit with reluctance, repeatedly emphasising that his sole concern is with the best interests of the child. He is determined that she should be removed from the home as a matter of urgency and can see no more suitable placement. Adoption is a possibility (I blanch); and yet, in view of the family history, it is not one which he intends to pursue. Even as he makes the ruling, he cannot resist chiding me for my breach of the Contact Order . . . as though my prime responsibility were not to protect Pagan but to observe the letter of the law. He ends by recommending that she be given some form of counselling; which I agree to arrange.

As we leave court, I decline Max's offer of lunch; I have arranged to spend the time until Pagan's return from school with William. I drive to Worthing and then follow his directions to the old-fashioned Watch and Clock Repairers where he works. I negotiate the complex insecurity system (so named by William, who claims that it is worth more than the entire stock) and enter the shop to which he has devoted the best part of fifteen years.

'My finest worker,' his boss says as we are introduced.

'Your only worker, Mr Hill,' William corrects.

'Now yes; but in the old days. . . . I wouldn't know what to do if he went.' The edge to his voice betrays further insecurity.

'No danger of that,' William says with a shrug. 'What else could I do? "Doesn't he have delicate hands?" a customer said last week, as though it was compensation, like a blind piano-tuner or fat men who are light on their feet.'

'People trust you. They come from miles around.'

'A dinosaur in a digital world.'

'There'll always be a call for a craftsman.'

'That's not how my parents saw it. I think they equated working with my hands with manual labour. Whenever my mother spoke of it, she made it sound like a hobby that they were indulging . . . that I was earning pocket money to supplement an allowance.'

'My finest worker,' Mr Hill repeats; 'I don't run a charity.'

'I don't suppose it looks much,' William declares defensively, 'but I know nothing more beautiful than the insides of a clock. Such grace and precision, such history. When I'm at my bench, I feel in control . . . and not just of the clock but what it signifies. In my own small way, I feel I'm the master of time.'

'William's the chairman of the South East committee of the British Horological Institute.'

'It used to be the standing committee till I joined.' I am not sure whether I am expected to laugh. 'Still, political correctness has even reached our antiquated world. So, I'm known, to everyone's embarrassment, as the chair.'

With that, he takes his leave of Mr Hill and leads me to the car. I am glad to see him again, although I find his mordant humour disconcerting. And yet, if you roll through life at 'armpit level', as he puts it, it may be the only way to survive.

'If you're ever on the run again, Leo, get yourself a wheelchair,' he says, as he drives me to the restaurant; 'it's the perfect hiding-place. No one ever thinks of looking inside. Two things happened to me last week that brought it home. The first was when I was waiting outside a shop with narrow aisles and a woman tossed 50p into my lap. She immediately assumed that I was begging. She didn't say a word; she just dropped the coin as if I were a collection box.'

'She must have been trying to assuage her guilt.'

'That makes me feel much better! The other was when I went to a party given by a collector I've done a lot of work for. "It's so good of you to come," she said, shaking my hand as limply as if she were the Queen. "There's someone else here in a wheelchair I'm longing for you to meet." '

'I'm sorry.'

'What makes it worse is that she's a genuinely well-meaning woman. You'd think that, after thirty-six years, I'd be immune . . . but no.' He pulls up. 'Still, here we are. Door to door service.' He pats his permit. 'Lose your legs; and all your parking problems will be solved for life.'

We enter the restaurant, which William declares to be his favourite, although he warns that his criterion is as much ease of access as quality of food. We order and chatter. He is heartened by my account of the morning's proceedings and intrigued by your parents' submission. It is only when I am halfway through a piece of under-ripe melon that I am struck by a discrepancy.

'You said thirty-six years.'

'Yes.'

'But I thought that you were thirty-nine.'

'I am.'

'I also thought – forgive me if I'm wrong – that you'd been . . . that you'd never been able to walk.'

'So did I. That's the story of my life, at least the authorised version . . . that my birth mother rejected me when she found I was crippled but I was rescued by my new parents. They took me in out of compassion, as though I were the runt of the litter who would otherwise be put down. However hard I tried – if I fetched them their newspapers and slippers for the next forty years – there was no way I could repay the debt. But it was an illusion.'

'How . . . when did you find out? Candida never said.'

'Candida never knew. I didn't share her lifelong obsession with discovering her parents . . . if I had, I might have learnt sooner; although it was her attitude, more than anything, which put me off. As a kid, I was deeply offended by the way that she talked about our parents. She portrayed them as thieves – no, racketeers – who'd profited from other women's mistakes. I couldn't bear the ingratitude. For their part, they made it clear that they would regard any search for our birth parents as a betrayal . . . now

395

I understand why. So I told myself that there was nothing to be gained from knowing; it would simply cause everyone pain. Ironically, it was Candida's death that prompted my change of heart. Even though we'd lost touch, I'd believed that we'd always be there for each other; I suddenly felt so alone. I became curious . . . less about my mother than about any brothers or sisters. So I applied for my birth certificate and finally tracked my mother down. It's a gruelling process.'

'I know; I lived through it with Candida.'

'My first surprise was that my mother welcomed me. Ever since the change in the law, she'd longed for me to make the application. I wrote to her and she rang me the following day. We agreed to exchange photographs. I sent her a close-up of my head and shoulders; I didn't want to remind her of my chair. I didn't even mention it; it seemed like rubbing her rejection in her face. We arranged to meet. I saw at first glance that she had no idea. She tried to disguise her reaction; but I didn't want her to. And I learnt that the reason she'd had me adopted was simply that she wasn't married. I was a perfectly healthy baby. She could never have given me up if I'd had any sort of disability. It would have made the guilt a hundred times worse.'

'So when . . . how did it happen?'

'That's what I wanted to know. I went to see my doctor . . . my new doctor. The old one was a friend of my father's. Rotary . . . the nineteenth hole. I explained that I needed to consult my medical history for a talk I was giving to a local youth group on surviving an accident. It was a shot in the dark . . . it was a bull's eye. He detailed the treatments I'd undergone, not for a birth defect but for breaking my spine in a fall at the age of three. And I suddenly remembered – no, relived – what had happened; it was happening again, as if the clock had stopped . . . only, this time, I wasn't in control. I was three years old. I could see my father hurting my sister. She was crying, but he wasn't smacking her. I tried to pull him off, and he grabbed me and lifted me onto the top of a wardrobe. Then he took her away into another room. I could hear her scream. I put my hands to my ears to shut out the noise and crashed down onto the floor.'

His memory permeates my vision. I see him lying lifeless on the ground, while you are assaulted by your father. But there is one face missing. 'Where was your mother?'

'I've no idea. Most likely out on her St John's work or one of the other good causes which she always found so "satisfying".'

'So how did he explain what'd happened?'

'How do I know? I was three years old. I've protected myself from the truth for thirty years. I don't know what she knows about him. I suspect . . . I suspect she suspects; but I don't know. But, whatever else, she lied about my always being like this. She lied about their compassion. She lied about my mother's rejection.'

'So she may have lied about Candida?'

'She may. I think that Candida tried to tell her; but she refused to listen. Which is why she came to hate her even more than she did my father. She seemed to assume that what he'd done to her was what men did; after all, my mother repeatedly told us that men were animals. I thought that she meant "the rats and snails and puppy dogs' tails" left over from childhood . . . how could I have been so naive? While Candida felt that the one person who should have protected her hadn't. Whether it was blindness or complicity, I leave to you.'

'God knows, I've little love for your mother; but I can't believe that she would connive at the abuse of her own daughter.'

'Not just her daughter.'

'What?'

'Not just her daughter.' The waiter interrupts. I wave him away, but William appears to welcome the respite and asks him to return first with black pepper and then with more wine. The delay does not make the revelations any easier to absorb.

'You too?'

'Oh yes. It must have been several years later; although I can't say when exactly . . . memory's not as precise as time. He turned his attention to me. And he carried on for years. Years! I couldn't run like Candida. And I didn't scream. Why didn't I scream? Because boys don't, I suppose. And why did I never tell anyone? Like I said: because I was a boy. And such things didn't happen to

397

boys; they couldn't happen to boys; they destroyed everything that I believed boys were. And, day after day, night after night, he raped me. He'd say to me "This can't hurt you; you can't feel anything; they've told us, you have no feeling." But I had feelings. Didn't I have feelings? And I knew that he was inside me . . . pounding me, polluting me.' He thrusts his plate away. I reach across the table, smearing my sleeve, to place a hand on his arm. 'Don't do that!' He flinches. 'Sorry. Force of habit. I can never bear to be touched by a man.'

'And a woman?' I keep my tone as detached as possible.

'I've only been touched – as you put it – by one woman in my life. And guess who that was. . . . You say nothing, Leo; are you shocked?'

'I can't tell where one shock ends and the next begins.'

'It wasn't incest; after all, we weren't related. When we were kids – we were never kids – she regularly announced that, when we grew up, we'd marry each other. If there was one thing calculated to make my mother mad, it was that. "I should hope that William can do a good deal better for himself than you," she'd say. Oh yes? Then Candida discovered that, when they framed the law, they deliberately left adopted brothers and sisters free to marry. She was triumphant. What clearer proof could she have that we were a non-family . . . that the only thing that counted was blood? And yet she was inconsistent. For her, the attraction of seducing me was breaking a taboo. For me, it was more complex. I didn't want to sleep with her; she was my sister, the person I felt closest to in all the world. "This will make us closer," she said . . . she lied. But I wanted desperately to sleep with someone. "William's paralysed from the waist down," my mother would say, as though she were reading a label on a cage. But it wasn't true. There was one part whose activity made up for all the rest: one part that obsessed and shamed me. And it was the part that Candida aroused. For over twenty years, I've looked back on that night with a tangle of emotions: pain for the circumstance, pleasure for the sensation. It's my only sexual experience and so it's had to stand in for all the others. Twenty years of soiled sheets and soggy tissues. How could anyone call it a life?'

'It doesn't have to be like this. You're a very handsome man. I'm sure that a lot of women find you attractive.'

'Oh yes? Do you think they could find a friend for my friend?' He taps his chair. 'No, you're right. I expect my disability would suit someone's requirements. I remember reading about the offers of marriage in *The Times* during the First World War from women whose fiancés had been killed at the Front. They were open to anyone – that is any officer – who'd been gassed or blinded or shell-shocked or wounded or preferably all four. Well, I'm sorry; they can reach for sainthood on someone else's shoulders.'

'It wouldn't be like that.'

'Come on, Leo. Shall I tell you about my toilet arrangements? . . . No, I thought not. For years, I believed the solution might lie with prostitutes. Are you disgusted?'

'Do you never read the newspapers?'

'Of course; I forgot. Once, when I was in London for the Institute's AGM, I went as far as looking round Soho. I negotiated the narrow streets and the crowds and the rubbish, and read the peeling notices in doorways: "New Young Model, first floor. Come on up". . . . "French Lessons, second floor. Come on up". . . . "Busty brunette, third floor. Up, up, up!" ' He rams his chair into the table.

I am finding the heat of the restaurant oppressive. I long for a walk by the sea to clear my head. But William wants a dessert. 'This is an event for me. It's not every day I'm taken to lunch by a celebrity.'

'It's not a meal I'll forget in a hurry. I'm trying to understand your father. Your adoption makes his behaviour somehow worse. It seems like a double abuse.'

'I don't want to understand him. If I did, I might start to forgive him. And I don't want to forgive him. Forgiveness is for people with legs. So what if he regretted leaving the Army? So what if he felt an outsider twice over as a bursar in a public school? Does that excuse what he did to me?'

'You shouldn't be so sensitive. I said "understand", not "excuse". I need to believe . . . I do believe that human beings are rational . . . that even the most bestial act has an explanation.'

'You mean "Hello, Herr Hitler, sorry we were rude about your paintings"? I'm afraid it's not that easy. My father was a mass of contradictions. To the world, he put on this dapper, chipper front; and yet, at home, he was moody, morose, depressed . . . no, I'm falling into the trap of your way of thinking, giving him a good and a bad side when they were one and the same. He'd sit for hours in his chair without speaking; the only sign of life would be the vein vibrating under his eye. How I dreaded that vein; I knew what it meant. Then, the next day, he'd be all affability. He'd buy me presents and my mother would complain that he was spoiling me; so she became the shrew and he the open wallet. Of course, I realise now that he was buying my silence; but, at the time, all I saw were the toys. How can anyone grow up with a shred of self-respect when, as a boy, he's so easily bribed?'

'Was he affectionate to your mother?'

'Do I spy another rational explanation? Should I see myself as a mother-substitute? You're as bad as Candida. She spent her life speculating as to why they hadn't had children. Was he impotent? Was she infertile? Or was it that they never had sex? She told me about tubes and sperm-counts long before I had any idea of their significance. She laughed at my revulsion . . . "You call yourself a scientist; you're supposed to be an objective observer." I didn't call myself a scientist; I simply studied the sciences because I didn't trust the arts. But in answer to your question – you did ask a question? – no, he was never affectionate to her. He kissed her on the forehead on special occasions. And she pecked him on the cheek.'

I picture a hen-pecked husband. She has always seemed the senior partner, making decisions, speaking on his behalf. Which came first: her shrillness or his indifference, her dominance or his guilt?

'What angers me most is that we both let him get away with it. Not just then, but ever since. No wonder he thought he could try again with Pagan. I blame myself. Why did I bury the truth? How could I have let my memory become as useless as my legs? I've made up for it at last. I've been to the Special Inquiry Unit. I've given a statement to Derek Bridges . . . he goes drinking with one of my friends. I'm not going to let the only charge against him be Pagan's. Isn't my pain worth something too?'

I assure him that it is. I pay the bill and we leave the restaurant. He drives me back to the shop. He tells me that he has not seen either of your parents since the trial. When she learnt that he had testified against your father, your mother sent him a venomous letter in which she accused him of being warped by his disability and of taking his revenge on the only people who had ever loved him. 'She ended by saying that she never wanted to set eyes on me again. I felt like replying that, in that case, she'd better not attend the Court; but I held back. Oh, there is one good thing to have come out of all this. Now that I no longer have my meals on wheels, I've started to cook for myself. I go to a class one evening a week. Why did no one ever tell me it was such fun?'

When we reach the shop, he asks me not to go in with him. 'I couldn't bear any more of the "good and faithful servant" routine. I know he means well; but he also suspects something's up . . . and he's right. I'm thinking of moving away. I've been to visit my mother – my real mother . . . birth mother . . . soon I won't have to make these distinctions – several times. She lives with her husband outside Ipswich. They want me to join them. So do my three brothers. They've all kept within twenty miles of each other . . . that's a good sign, wouldn't you say? Two of them are married, with kids who already call me Uncle William. . . . They're all three such strong, able-bodied men. And, believe it or not, they all look like me.'

'I hope you won't lose touch with the other side of the family. I know that there's no blood, but there are affinities . . . and memories: such complex, confusing memories. Pagan needs to be given some sense of where she's from. I have to be both father and mother to her; I can't be an uncle as well.'

'You're on,' he says and wheels himself into the shop. I drive back to Kemp Town and arrive at the home just as Pagan is clambering out of the minibus. She is surprised to see me and excitedly recounts how, for homework, she has to write a poem about butterflies. . . . 'Will you think of a word that rhymes with wings?'

'For once, you needn't worry about homework,' I say, 'you're coming home.' She stares at me as though she suspects a trick. 'It's true. If you don't believe me, ask Mr Skipton; he was in court.' She is taking no chances and runs to my car, demanding to leave at once, before the

Judge changes his mind. It is only after much persuasion that she agrees to go indoors to collect her things.

The Manager is waiting for us in his office. He congratulates Pagan and reminds her of how he always promised that she would be sent home. Jess gives her a hug and urges me to look after her, in a tone that implies doubt. She then goes upstairs to pack the cases, while Pagan and I take our leave of her friends. I urge her not to flaunt her good fortune; but, far from resenting her departure, the others seem to see it as a sign of hope. The one exception is Shona, whom we find hiding in the linen room, squashed between two of the shelves and wrapped in a pile of towels. She refuses to turn to us and shrugs off Pagan's embrace as though it were an adult's. As we make our exit, she calls in muffled defiance, 'I'm going to have plastic on my face like a packet; I'm going to look like a doll.'

We drive home. Pagan veers between elation and apprehension. She needs constant reassurance that she is not going to be snatched away the moment that we arrive. As we turn into the avenue, she insists that the houses have all been painted. I promise her that, as far as I know, they are exactly the same as last year.

'I've looked at them over and over in my head; but I've still got them wrong. Why?'

'Everyone finds things hard to remember.'

'But not important things. Or how can we be safe?'

I unlock the door. Trouble lurks in the hall. I will him, just for once, to rouse himself and greet her with a show of enthusiasm equal to her own. He does not disappoint. She carries him to her bedroom; and I see that her eyes are full of tears. She sniffles an explanation: 'I thought it was only grown-ups who cried when they were happy; but now children do as well.'

We set about re-establishing our lives. She returns to school with as little fuss as I return to work. June is full of new possibilities: a nanny for her, a housekeeper for us . . . and a man for me. I can scarcely believe it. I have put my sexuality on ice for so long that it feels less like passion than cryonics. I am almost afraid to speak his name in case he vanishes; so I shall murmur it under my breath: Benedict . . . Benedict Menzies. He is an independent television producer, who has just been commissioned to make a documentary on the Nazis' treatment of homosexuals for Channel Four. He phones me the morning after we are introduced at David Sunning's to ask me to read the commentary. I assume that he is only interested in my voice, until he invites me to dinner the next weekend.

We date, as though sex were still a mystery. He claims that he wants to know everything about me. I reply that he must know more than enough already; I feel as exposed as a newspaper headline. He says that he would rather have my words than theirs. I introduce him to Pagan. She takes to him as fast as if the last two years had never happened and strangers were as benign as friends. One Thursday afternoon, we collect her from school and go boating on the Serpentine. He describes how he rowed for the regiment . . . he was an army officer until dishonourably discharged for being gay. I sit back, letting the fantasies waft over me and watching his muscles catch the sun. Then, at tea, he entertains Pagan by pulling coins out of his ears.

'Show me how it's done,' she clamours, more intrigued by the mechanics than the magic.

'It's magic.' He insists against the odds.

'Phooey! Show me!'

'I assure you it's magic. Doubt everything else, if you like; but you must always believe in magic. Even grown-ups believe in magic.' He talks to her and smiles at me.

That night, we sleep together . . . which is an even emptier phrase than usual, since all chance of sleep is dispelled by his Olympic-sized water-bed.

'Why didn't you warn me?'

'I didn't think it was important. It's hardly like "my playroom's in the cellar" or "my boyfriend's asleep next door".'

The mattress matches our mood and mirrors our every movement, as what starts as a gentle ripple swells to a tidal wave. It is as wet above as below . . . no, I am not being crude; I am hit by a flood of emotion that flows out as tears. It is an age since I felt the bristly kiss of a man rather than the sticky lips of a child; and I feel it in such unexpected places.

'Did the earth move for you?' I mock myself with a

million clichés. 'No, but the waters parted, and I reached the promised land!'

In the morning, I watch him shave in a bathroom that smells of cedar. He uses his father's razor, which, for some reason, I find more moving than all the Standish traditions combined. He wants to meet again in the evening, but I invent a prior engagement and put him off for a day, partly from policy, partly from fear.

'We mustn't go too fast,' I say, reading from an official rule-book.

'Why not? So long as you have a steady hand and a clear road.'

'And an ancient motor?'

'It's vintage,' he says, making light of our twelve-year age-gap. 'They don't make them like this any more.' He slips his fingers beneath my shirt, and I agree to break every engagement and meet him in Holland Park at eight.

I find that I believe in magic as fervently as the most spell-bound child.

It may be the start of something new, but, first, we have to settle the old; and, in July, I drive Pagan to Lewes Crown Court. The indictment against your father has been amended to include the abuse of William, who is waiting for us in the witness room, as spruce as for a wedding. He and Pagan both give their evidence on the opening day, while I am not called until the second morning. I feel remarkably relaxed in the witness box and only falter once, when I reply to a question about the changes in Pagan's behaviour with a reference to your father's abuse of you. This provokes an immediate response from the Defence Counsel, who leaps to his feet, declaring my remark to be hearsay and irrelevant. Nevertheless, and in spite of the Judge's rebuke, I do not regret having made it. I firmly believe that your past should also be acknowledged, if only by your father, who gazes steadfastly at the floor.

The next morning, I return to watch the proceedings from the gallery, much to the annoyance of Pagan, who has been excluded on account of her age. I promise to report back to her as soon as I know the verdict, which comes shortly before lunch on the fifth day. The jury is unanimous: guilty on all counts. The sentence is heavy: five years. The Judge declares that he has taken your father's

404

age into consideration, nevertheless 'since he was not too old to commit the crimes, he is not too old to pay for them'. Your father shows no reaction. I gaze down at his liver-spotted head, sunken eyes and sallow skin, and wonder if he will ever emerge from jail; and yet I cannot allow myself to take his part. Now that the ordeal is ended, I hope – I truly hope – that there are others who will; but I have to focus on healing the life that he has maimed.

I am startled by a deep groan from the far corner of the gallery. It is so long and hollow that I take it for one of the pipes, until I see your mother, clutching her head and rocking. She has sat in the same seat each day, staring at your father and studiously avoiding every stray glance. Today, she is wearing her St John Ambulance uniform, as though for security . . . I worry that it may cause confusion should she faint. 'No!' she cries and is comforted by a woman on her left. I hurry away to join William, who has been watching from the body of the Court. He shakes my hand. His eyes are filmed with tears. 'I don't expect you to understand, but, at last, I feel like a man. I can stand up for myself.'

First, he has to dispel the final spectre of childhood, as your mother runs forward and throws herself at his chair. 'How can you abuse us like this? Have you no gratitude? It's not too late. We can appeal. You can say you lied. We'll forgive you. You can tell them he led you on.' She points at me.

'Mother, you know it's true. You've always known it's true. Face up to the truth while you still have the chance.'

'He loved me. We should never have had children. It was him who wanted them – you – not me. And now he's paying for it. We were happy the two of us; we had a good life. Then we had you and everything changed.'

Her companion leads her away. William and I adjourn to a nearby pub, where he informs me that he has definitely decided to make the move to Ipswich . . . he may not be able to escape the past, but he can put it at a distance. We eat a celebration snack. Then, after eliciting his promise to come up to town for our party, I drive home in time to collect Pagan from her therapy. I tell her the verdict. Her relief is mingled with fear, as she demands my most solemn pledge ('cross your heart and hope to die') that your father will never be able to break out of prison and harm her. I give it to her gladly.

'What about *her*?'

'She won't either.' And I realise that, although not charged, your mother is serving her own life sentence, from which there is neither remission nor release.

My vehemence heartens Pagan, who asks if I want to hear a joke.

'I'd love to. Were you told it today at school?'

'What's pink and wrinkled and belongs to Grandpa?'

My heart skips a beat, and I almost lose control of the wheel. I want to turn round, drive straight back to Dr Lister and demand that she exorcise the demons. Pagan addresses me impatiently.

'You're spoiling it. You should say "What's pink and wrinkled and belongs to Grandpa?"'

'I'm sorry. What is it?' I play my part with reluctance.

'What's what?'

'What's pink and wrinkled and belongs to Grandpa?'

'Granny.'

Granny . . . I laugh way beyond the merits of the joke.

'It's funny, isn't it? Sophie told me at lunch.'

Granny. . . . I laugh, and I know that all will be well.

# 2

'Why are gay men so sentimental about weddings?' you ask, as we make our way to Tristan's and Deborah's. 'It's as bad as liberal Jews and Christmas.'

'I don't know. Perhaps it reflects a deep desire for assimilation. We don't burn babies . . . we don't want to convert you. Or perhaps it's the thought of returning to a world from which we're so often excluded. On the other hand, it may simply be that we'll grab any excuse for a party.'

I reflect on the question, as I sit dewy-eyed in the small village church, watching Susan walk down the aisle. Far from shocking her mother-in-law, she wears a dress that would pass muster in St Paul's. I am so proud of your daughter who carries the train, along with two of the bride's cousins and the groom's niece, to the manner born. Apart from one minor accident when the guiding loops on the train tear off and Susan appears to sashay down the aisle and one major affront when the cameraman asks the vicar to repeat the vows on account of a technical hitch, everything runs smoothly. Geoffrey's fellow officers form a guard of honour up to the porch; and even his stiffest relatives allow themselves to unbend.

The vicar is an embarrassment at the reception, accosting me over the buffet and making several coded references to the London of his youth and the evenings he spent watching 'Judy' at the Palladium, which I affect not to comprehend. I am relieved when his wife, a florid woman called Pansy (did he marry her for her name?), hauls him off to meet Geoffrey's episcopal uncle. I meander through the marquee, an intruder in an alien world of people who tut and vote Tory. Exploring the garden, I come across Pagan arguing with a page-boy about why a meal in the middle of the afternoon is called breakfast. They appeal for adult arbitration, but I am saved by the summons to watch the bride and groom drive away. Pagan catches the bouquet.

Susan and Geoffrey may be otherwise engaged ('they're not engaged; they're married,' says Pagan), but, considering the time of year, there have been remarkably few refusals to our party. It is the first that I have given without you, and it is to be a dual celebration of Pagan's birthday (of particular note after last year's separation) and my rehabilitation. Jessica's catering company is in charge of the food (Imogen warns me that she has recently become a fruitarian), while my mother, Una and Juliet are helping in the house.

Pagan's return to Thomas's is marked by the reappearance of so many old friends. Even Stephanie has come with Stephen and Delia; and, if they have any misgivings regarding their last visit, they are too discreet to say so. Pagan's particular welcome is reserved for Minnie Mouse, alias Shona, whom I have invited along with her new foster-parents. 'I told you you'd come to see me,' she says, linking arms and taking her up to the playroom, where she talks to her to the exclusion of all others and protects her from anyone who tries to remove her mask.

William arrives in a wheelchair festooned with balloons and scores an immediate hit with the children, which I suspect has a lot to do with his height. I watch one small boy leap around him in a weird mixture of a war dance and a pirouette, before asking ingenuously, 'Can you do that?' I wait with alarm for William's reaction, which is unusually relaxed.

'No, but can you do this?' He crosses his eyes and wiggles his ears.

'No,' the boy says, 'that's great.' He spends the rest of the afternoon gazing into mirrors and squinting.

William gives Pagan a Victorian clock which he has restored himself. Two friends carry it into the hall. 'You lucky girl,' Juliet says. 'What a beautiful grandfather clock.' I look in dismay from Pagan to William and pray that the present will not be tainted by the phrase.

'It's not a grandfather,' William says, 'its proper name is a longcase clock. If anything, it's a grandmother, since it's under five foot.' I fear that this may be no improvement.

'I shall call it an uncle clock,' Pagan says; 'since it's made by you.'

None of her other presents is so impressive, although the competition is strong. My own favourite is an exquisite Edwardian edition of *David Copperfield* from Benedict. 'Do you know who Charles Dickens was?' he asks her.

'Oh yes,' Pagan replies with conviction. 'He wrote *The Muppet Christmas Carol*.'

I blush.

My biggest headache has been the entertainment, much to the annoyance of my mother, who makes a characteristic *ex-cathedra* (or, rather, ex-chapel) pronouncement that 'children don't need entertainment; why did God give them imaginations if not to entertain themselves?' I reply that, far from trying to destroy their imaginations, I am seeking to nourish them. To which end, I have hired a semi-educational presentation from a Nature Conservation group, which combines clowns and comedy with lectures and animal displays.

The two clowns, Marmaduke and Coco, are a huge hit, holding the attention of thirty-five children for an hour and a half . . . well, actually, thirty-four, since I am forced to evict Rory, whose running commentary threatens to destroy the magic. As I thrust him protesting into a world of adults, he waves his credentials like a half-price ticket. I remind him that he is thirteen while the others are eight.

The remaining children sit engrossed in the tricks, but it is the animals which enthrall them. They are all invited to participate, with the largest part falling to Pagan. At one point, Marmaduke dispatches an owl across the room to land on her shoulder; at another, he pulls a tarantula out of her ear (prompting Juliet to take flight). Then, after by-play with a lizard, a rabbit and a fruit bat, he passes round a meerkat, which allows itself to be universally pawed but takes a genuine fancy to Shona. Twice, it escapes from the circuit and jumps back into her arms. She is overwhelmed by this mark of distinction; her Minnie Mouse grin glows.

The final exhibit is a twelve-foot python. It takes all of my strength of mind not to bolt. The children, however, sit in a state of rapt revulsion, apart from Pagan, who runs tremulously to me.

'It's a snake; it's horrid.'

'No, it's not. It won't hurt you. It's more frightened of you than you are of it.'

'It can't be.'

'What's this? It's your house; you're the birthday girl, and you're the one who's making all the fuss.'

I appeal to her sense of propriety. With extreme reluctance, she returns to her friends, as they split into groups of five, link arms and pretend to be trees, allowing the python to be draped around their shoulders. The room fills with shrieks and giggles, but no tears (I wish that I had had a similar opportunity at eight; it might have cured me of my lifelong phobia. Instead, I was left to my own imagination and the dusty imagery of Genesis . . . ). The benefits are revealed a few minutes later when Coco makes the children lie on the floor with their stomachs bare and slides the snake over them. I am on the verge of vomiting, but the participants scream with delight. Pagan appears to have conquered all her fears, shouting 'More, more,' and running to the back of the line for a second turn.

'I felt its muscles move on me,' she says, 'it tickled.'

'It likes the warmth of your tummy,' Marmaduke says.

'Leo, you know when you asked me what I want for my birthday . . . ?'

'Don't say it; don't even think of it; just enjoy it while you can.' It may sound naive, but I believe that I have reconciled her to far more than a snake.

After the birthday tea, in which, to judge from the cake, Rapunzel's tower has been relocated to Pisa, most of the children and their parents leave. It is my six o'clock nine o'clock watershed, and I feel free to turn my attention to the adults. It is so cheering to see so many of my old friends, although I wish that they were as well behaved and as easily pleased as Pagan's ('She's my best friend and I hate her' is no joke when the pair are married). I fear a confrontation between Edward and Melissa. My invitation crossed with the news of their split, and, much to my dismay, both have insisted on coming . . . Melissa to show

410

off her boyfriend, Edward to plead his cause. In the event, he seems too stunned to do anything but moan. 'Why now?' he asks, 'she's forty-one. I admit I've not always been faithful . . . at least not in practice. But she knows she's the only one I've ever cared about. Perhaps I should have been more furtive. But to lie seemed such an insult to her intelligence.' His little-boy-lost act is wearing as thin as his hair. She, on the other hand, looks rejuvenated, strolling like a schoolgirl with Ronald, hand in hand.

'What can she see in him?' Edward asks, shredding a pile of napkins. 'He's fifty-five, overweight and writes books on management consultancy.'

'Security?'

'She has three sons who need her. Hasn't she thought about them?' I bite back my reply.

'They're almost grown up.'

'Rory's thirteen . . . at a critical stage in his development. He'll probably turn out queer. Oh, no offence, old man.'

'None taken.' I bridle. 'Still, if he does, at least you'll be able to blame it on her.'

'That's true.' He is deaf to all irony but his own.

I leave him for more congenial company, moving to the pond, where Imogen, voluminous in a silver wrap and black turban, is making great play for Griffin Lennox, proving yet again that, should there ever be a lost cause, she will find it.

'Would you like to hear my motto?' she asks him. 'I stole it off an advert for deodorant: "I smell nice, use me." ' As she sways towards him, all I can smell is the Pimm's on her breath. 'What do you say to that?'

'My nose is stuffed.'

She looks at him, first in bafflement and then in lust. 'You're a very attractive man. Leo, darling, wherever did you find such an attractive man?'

'He's David Sunning's Boyfriend,' I say in capital letters. 'You remember David?'

'In other words, I'm queer.' A shadow crosses her face.

'Not to worry, I can accommodate that.'

'I'm not sure that I can.'

'Don't you like these?' To my horror, she resorts to the old breast-baring act, which has not improved with age.

'You'll catch cold, Imogen,' I say, trying to rewrap her.

'No, Leo,' she says, brushing me off, 'I asked him a question. Aren't you going to reply?' She juts out her bust; he ponders for a moment.

'Well,' he replies, 'since you ask. I quite like that one.' He points to the left. 'But I can't say I think too much of the other.' She looks at him in silence and then laughs. I am relieved, especially as it licenses my own guffaw. Then, just as I am letting rip, she bursts into tears and runs into the house.

'Why's Aunt Imogen showing you her bosoms?' I swing round to find Pagan.

'She ate too much and her buttons burst. So let that be a lesson. Now I think it's time for bed. All the children have gone home. Run on up. I'll come and see you later.'

'You promise?'

'Of course.' She trots off, her lack of protest attesting to her exhaustion.

'Do you turn everything into a cautionary tale?' Griffin asks.

'No, of course not. But it wasn't bad for the spur of the moment.'

'I thought I did quite well myself.'

'You were cruel.'

'You laughed.'

'Nevertheless . . . being oversexed, overweight and over forty is not a recipe for happiness.'

'Don't expect sympathy from me. How would she have felt if it'd been the other way round and I'd been the flasher?' I refrain from saying that she would probably have been thrilled.

I go off in search of Benedict, whom I find charming my mother with carefully edited stories of military life. I wince as I watch the two sides of my life connect – or, at least, make contact – but then anything is better than the self-defeating struggle to keep them apart. Besides, he is very much 'meet the family' material . . . I wish that he could meet you. I feel sure that you would approve. We would spend long, lazy evenings when three would be company, but never a crowd. You would ask me if I loved him. The short answer is that I don't know, but I do know that the question is no longer the only one that counts.

412

I circulate. The party is a great success, although there are a few exceptions to the general geniality. At ten o'clock, I come across Imogen looking glum and William looking lost. I have an irresistible urge to play Cupid and then instantly regret having succumbed. I need not have worried. At eleven thirty, she pulls me aside to ask why I never told her that you had such a dishy brother. At one, he tells me that he has drunk far too much to drive home and is taking up Imogen's offer of a bed in her flat.

'You can stay here,' my mother says . . . an instinctive, if inadvertent, killjoy.

'I don't want to put you to any trouble.'

'It's no trouble. We can make up the downstairs sofa.'

'No. We can't, Mother; it has woodworm. Besides, we don't have any sheets.'

She stares at me open-mouthed. I order a taxi before anyone else intervenes.

'Killing two birds with one stone?' Griffin asks as he sees my look of triumph.

'Or setting them free with one key.'

Benedict is the last to leave. I want him to stay more than ever, but I apply my 'no men after midnight' rule as rigorously as a Girton porter. In any case, Pagan is no longer the sole consideration, as my mother catches our doorstep kiss and corners me in the hall.

'Is Benedict a homosexual?'

'Yes.'

'But he was in the Army.'

'Was is the word.'

'And he seemed such a nice man. I liked him.'

'He is such a nice man. And you can still like him.'

'Don't be hard on me, Lenny. I'm trying.'

'I know you are.' And I know how confusing it must be for her to have a son who is not a child of the chapel. At least now she is prepared to accept what she does not understand, whereas before she refused to understand what she did not accept.

I take her arm and lead her up the stairs, thanking her for everything that she has done to make the day a success.

'I couldn't leave you to do it all on your own.'

'I don't just mean with the arrangements. The effort you made to get on with everyone.'

413

'Your friends have some very odd habits, Lenny,' she says cryptically. 'I'll leave it at that.'

Work continues to progress. I return to the screen like a character in an American soap who discovers that his death was just a dream. I float through Television Centre on a tide of goodwill . . . I only hope that Susan is enjoying as happy a honeymoon. Kaye Blake calls me in to say how much it means to her 'personally' to see me back. She relives the battles that she fought on my behalf like George IV regaling Wellington with descriptions of how he led the troops at Waterloo. When she claims to have come close to resignation, I can barely keep from laughing. On leaving her office, I instinctively wipe the soles of my shoes . . . it would take a second Hercules to clean out her 'bullshit-free zone'.

One result of my rehabilitation is that I am no longer deemed a minority interest. My show has been promoted to BBC1. But the popular channel need not lead to a gentler style. On the contrary, I am less inclined to tolerate any evasions now that I have abandoned my own. The opening programme is a statement of intent. My first guest is Franklin Polero, an American evangelist of the smarmiest 'hot line to Heaven' variety, who hangs himself with each scrap of rope that I throw him and yet refuses to play dead. 'Kick him, kick him!' Vicky hisses down my ear-piece during his non-stop monologue, which I duly do, but to no avail. I repeat the kicks with increasing ferocity, to the delight of the studio audience and, no doubt, the bafflement of the viewers at home. I come to the conclusion that his flesh is as unfeeling as his church. It is only after his next anecdote, with its reference to a wartime accident, that I realise that he has a wooden leg.

Making a mental note to murder the researchers, I finally manage to introduce my next guest . . . in whom you have a personal interest. 'Best known as Fred Docherty in ITV's *South of the River*, he's about to tackle one of the most demanding roles in the dramatic repertoire: the Captain in August Strindberg's *The Father*. He is, of course, Lewis Kelly.'

The audience applauds loudly as he saunters down the stairs. My own response is more subdued. It will be our first encounter since the family court eighteen months ago. I have always vetoed his appearances in the past, but, this time, I allowed myself to be swayed . . . although less by Vicky's assurances of his good value than by my own fantasies of revenge. To which end, I deliberately refrained from my customary pre-show chat. Far from wishing to put him at his ease, I am determined to make him sweat. And, as he walks across and shakes my hand, I find that I have succeeded.

I assure him that I am not going to waste time by talking about Fred Docherty, as he must be sick to death of him after all these years.

'Hang on. I'm very fond of old Fred; there's a good deal of me in him. A real rough diamond.'

'Surely more of a rough rhinestone . . . ? I refer to Fred, of course, not you.'

'I'm glad to hear it.' He fakes a laugh.

'So what's made you break away? Boredom?'

'Not at all. There's a lot of mileage left in Fred, you can take it from me.'

'Then there's no truth to the rumours that the producers are planning to kill him off?'

'Absolutely and categorically none. I'd like to get my hands on the person who started them.' The audience is chilled by his change of tone. 'As Fred would say.' He laughs quickly. 'No, but seriously, folks. I'm an actor; I need new characters . . . fresh challenges.'

'And yet your last attempt to throw off the Docherty image, McMurphy in *One Flew over the Cuckoo's Nest*, was a legendary flop. How long did it run in the West End? A week?'

'Thanks for mentioning that, Leo; you're a pal. No, but seriously, there were special factors. The recession . . . British Rail.'

'Your own reviews can't have helped much either.'

'I never read reviews.'

'I'm sure you're very wise.'

'If the critics don't like me, well, there are two "l"'s in bollocks.'

'Is that so? It's not a word I have much occasion to spell. Let's turn to *The Father*: was it the part or the play that attracted you?'

'I shan't deny that it's one of the great parts, but the

415

whole play is the most brilliant portrait of the power-games in a marriage. The tension never lets up.'

'But what about the subject? Surely the Captain's obsessive agonising over his daughter's legitimacy must strike an audience today as self-indulgent?'

'You're making it sound a real barrel of laughs. Much more of this and we won't have an audience at all! No, but seriously, folks, it is a comedy. It's not that different from a soap.' He retreats onto familiar ground. 'At least the American type, where characters are constantly discovering that either they or their parents are not who they thought they were.'

'So what you're saying is that it's a metaphor for our shifting identities?'

'I am?' He acts dumb and raises a laugh.

'I'm giving you the benefit of the doubt.' I act cool and raise a bigger one. 'But, to return to the central issue of fatherhood: isn't the play's portrayal of it dangerously simplistic? The Captain has a daughter whom he claims to love, and yet, as soon as he suspects that he may not be her father, he tries to shoot her. It's as if she only existed to perpetuate his genes. How can anything so conditional be described as love?'

'That's all very easy for you to say.'

'Is it?'

'Well, it's no secret that you're not – how shall I put it? – a prime candidate for fatherhood. So, for you, the issue is academic.'

'On the contrary, as you well know, I'm the guardian of an eight-year-old girl.'

'Ah yes, guardian,' he smiles smugly. 'Guardian's very different from father. Guardian's a signature on a dotted line; father's in your blood, in your guts, in your history.'

'And, above all, in your pride. Can't we make a distinction – I'll make one anyway – between fatherhood and paternity? Paternity is possession and property; fatherhood is love.'

'Thank you. I'll try to bring it out in my performance.'

'But it's fundamental . . . and not just to Strindberg. When love is based on blood, society turns inward. The family is isolated and so feels under threat, putting up

416

walls instead of building bridges. Those inside live in a permanent state of siege and those outside in exile.'

'How fascinating. You must come and lead an after-show discussion.' He is growing nettled. 'Meanwhile, I'm sure there's plenty more we could talk about.'

'Oh, I'm sorry. I was under the impression that you were here to plug the play.'

'Right now, I'd rather plug you.' He cocks his finger like a gun and shoots. His grin deceives no one.

'Well, it wouldn't be the first time. Still, I don't want to open old wounds, especially when they proved to be fatal.'

'What the . . . ?' He censors himself just in time. Vicky is urging me to change the subject.

'Well then, let's return to the subject of families; it is, after all, the Year of the Family.' (Even Brian Derwent cannot claim the credit for a United Nations designation.) 'You're not married, are you?'

'There's nothing bent about me.'

'Did I say?' I swivel round and appeal to the audience. 'Did anyone say . . . ? But that's interesting. I obviously hit a nerve.'

'That's nothing to what I'll hit if you don't drop it.' There is a discernible hiss from the audience.

'I'll take the risk. So could you never conceive – I'm talking purely hypothetically – of having a gay relationship?'

'Why?' He minces his delivery, though not his words. 'Are you offering?'

'I'm afraid not. Don't forget, we had a mutual friend. I've seen you at close quarters.'

'And that's as close as you're going to get.'

'I wonder if the reason that you find the idea so repellent is that the relationship is too equal. There isn't a clear enough delineation of power.'

'Not every relationship's a relationship of equals. I believe in celebrating the differences between men and women.'

'And in denying the similarities between men?'

'Was that a question?' he asks, after a neatly timed pause.

'It was. But don't worry, I've plenty more. What intrigues me is that you've spent most of your adult life in

worlds where homosexuality is commonplace: prison and
the theatre.' He clenches his fist. 'I'm sorry, am I embarrassing you?'

'Not at all. My life is an open book.'

'And I'm sure that it makes a compulsive read. But what
I want to know is in all those years you were in prison . . .
how many was it now?'

'Twelve.'

'Twelve. Do you mean to say that, in all that time, the
thought – just the thought, of course, the tiniest thought –
of sex with a man never crossed your mind?'

'What the hell is this? I've come here today, September
17th 1994, to talk about a play.'

'But I understood that you didn't want to talk about it.
You told me to change the subject. And you were the one
who brought up being – sorry, not being – "bent".'

'It'll take someone a damn sight cleverer than you to get
the better of Lewis Kelly.'

'Then perhaps you'll answer the question.'

'No, I bloody well won't.' Vicky instructs me to wind
things up before he loses control.

'I see. So, even an open book contains some expurgated
chapters. Thank you very much, Lewis Kelly; I'm afraid
that's all we have time for, except to wish you good luck
with the play. It should prove to be a fascinating collision
of actor and role.' I start to move across the stage. Lewis
stands up behind me.

'Is that it?' he asks. 'It's a fucking frame-up. You planned
this.' He makes to lunge at me but is tackled by two
technicians and dragged cursing off the set. The camera
remains fixed on me.

'I should explain, for the benefit of viewers at home, that
any unidentified noises come from Lewis Kelly rehearsing
his role as the mentally unstable Captain.' The studio
audience applauds. 'Now I'm delighted to introduce The
Bretts, an exciting new band from Sunderland, about
whom I predict we'll be hearing a good deal more in the
months to come.'

I end the show in a state of euphoria. I am the seven-
stone weakling who built up his muscles and broke the
school bully's nose. It is only when my adrenalin level
drops that I realise what I have done. None the less, I do not

regret it. Nor, to judge by the applause as I enter the hospitality room, do the production team. I look round nervously for Lewis (my Charles Atlas punch is strictly metaphorical), but the studio manager assures me that he has stormed out of the building . . . I still request an escort to the car. Vicky is more concerned about the press response. She need not be. It may be that they wish to make amends for last year's malice or it may simply be that it is Lewis's turn to take a fall, but even the reports in the *Nation* and *Sentinel* are favourable. The *Daily Mail* insists that I am worth every penny of my new contract. The *Guardian* declares that I am back where I belong.

Autumn passes with no notable incident apart from Pagan's joining the Brownies. Her conversation is so full of Brown Owl, Tawny Owl, elves and pixies, that we might be back in the woods at Crierley. Then, quite unexpectedly, I am transported there in earnest, when Duncan Treflis rings with the news that Eleanor Standish has died of a heart attack. Unknown to me, she had a long history of angina, which made it even more imprudent that she should have chosen to live in a caravan. And yet it was the only way that she could stay close to the house. She seemed to believe that her presence was as crucial to its preservation as the ravens to the Tower of London. To protect Robin's patrimony she would endure any amount of pain.

I drive to Crierley for her requiem mass, refusing Treflis's invitation to 'share my chauffeur' . . . he would insert an innuendo into the Second Coming. I arrive early and stroll around the ancient churchyard, exploring the tumbledown tombs with their mouldering epitaphs. As I pause to take stock by a gnarled yew tree, I am hailed by an unctuous voice.

'Fertile soil,' Treflis calls with macabre relish.

'Have you seen this withered trunk? It's charming.'

'Oh, withered trunks can have their charm. May I borrow your shoulder?'

'On condition that it's only a temporary loan.'

I help him into the church, which is better attended than I expected. I identify villagers, neighbours and members of the family. I am forced to share a pew with Duncan who grabs three kneelers.

'Stiff joints?'

'Stage management. One has to be seen.'

I contemplate the church, which has barely changed since our previous visit. I gaze across the transept at the Standish memorials and recall Robin's reluctance to take us on a tour. . . . 'You've no idea how much I loathe coming here. It's so depressing. Like one great family tomb. I remember the first time that my mother showed me round all these cold old faces and told me who was who and how we were related. I felt as if we were no longer a family of flesh and blood but of bones and marble. I think it must have put me off church for life.'

'You exaggerate.'

'And families.'

'You were a child.'

Now there will be another inscription for him to avoid. The realist in me says that he may be dead himself; the sentimentalist refuses to believe it. The latter takes such a hold that I am seized by an overwhelming urge to stand and light a candle. Much to Duncan's annoyance, I move to do so in front of a statue of the Virgin. Warmed by the flames, I light two more: one for Lady Standish and another for you. I return to the pew, where Duncan informs me, quite untruthfully, that I almost collided with the coffin. He has a perverse need to make the whole of life seem like a narrow escape. I silence him as the service begins. It is short, dignified and strangely moving. All the sprinkling, censing and chanting, however alien to my tradition, appeal to my love of ritual: religion justified by art.

We process into the churchyard. The heavy, heady scent of the incense is replaced by the dank-leaf smell of autumn. After the novelty of the requiem, I am surprised by the familiar phrase 'Earth to earth, ashes to ashes, dust to dust,' at the burial, but then there is nowhere as ecumenical as the grave. In a bid to escape morbidity, I examine my fellow mourners. Lydia is the only one to look truly distressed; there again, she has the most reason. Moreover, according to Duncan, her grief has been compounded by the legacy of her mother's last words: an accusing shriek of 'You'll be the death of me', which has left her at once a ten-year-old orphan and a thirty-six-year-old matricide.

420

I would like to offer her my condolences, but I feel constrained by the presence of Jenny Knatchpole, who has made her distaste for me abundantly clear. Her husband, however, does not seem to share it, shaking my hand as warmly as if I were a prospective voter or, even, a contributor to party funds. My speculations over what will become of Lydia are resolved by his news that she is going to live in the country with Jenny. 'What choice do we have? She has no one else, and she is my cousin. Besides, it'll be company for Jen; she's on her own far too much. I'm kept so busy at the Treasury that I rarely have a chance to get down.' Pity silts up my mind as I picture the two women growing old and incoherent together. 'Anyhow,' he adds, 'I'm sure that she'll prove a natural with the dogs.'

Duncan invites the family and friends (but not the villagers) to lunch at Buckstone. Any suggestion of stiff joints is banished, as he scurries back and forth like a man half his age. I observe him talking to a tall, veiled woman in a black pillbox hat, who has intrigued me throughout the service. Her elegance and sophistication catch the eye in a world where wealth is characterised by dowdiness. As we walk away from the grave, I carefully slacken my pace until we are side by side.

'Leo Young,' I introduce myself.

'I know,' she says and walks on. She is evidently a viewer and a far from gracious one. I try again.

'Did you know Lady Standish well?'

'We were related. By marriage. And you?'

'I'm . . . I was a friend of her son.'

'I don't think I saw him here, did I?'

'No. No, you didn't. He disappeared several years ago.'

Our lack of intimacy leads me to change the subject. I ask if she is going with Duncan or travelling to London and find that she is doing neither but attending to business near by. Then she tells me that she will be in London for twenty-four hours tomorrow, before flying abroad, and would welcome a chance to talk. Full of curiosity, I invite her to lunch.

'Do you live alone?'

'I have a little girl. That is, I'm her guardian. Her mother was my closest friend.'

'Will she be there?'

421

'She'll be at school. I collect her at three thirty.'

'Thank you. I'd be delighted to accept.'

As I drive back to London, I replay our conversation in my mind, growing increasingly convinced that the mystery woman is Robin's wife. This would explain the 'related by marriage', the knowing no one and the patently false question about her husband. They live abroad; and I speculate on the reason that Robin could not return to England himself. Is he in danger of arrest . . . or already in prison? Does he deal in drugs? Is he being targeted by MI5? My theories become more and more fantastical. As I pass a sleepless night, I realise how much I have missed him or, rather, how well I have concealed it. The morning creeps by like a Christmas Day sermon. At half-past twelve, I wait in the hall trying to look casual. The doorbell rings at a quarter to one, and I see at once that all my theories are wrong.

She stands at the door, unveiled and bearing an uncanny resemblance to Robin. I account for it by recalling his narcissism; he has married his female image.

'May I come in?'

'Of course.' I try to make my words make sense. 'You didn't give me your name, yesterday.'

'Robin,' she says. 'Robyn with a y.'

I totter. He grabs my arm and holds me up. I cannot tell if it is my legs or my world that has collapsed.

'I'm sorry, Leo; I've shocked you. I shouldn't have come, at least not like this. But any other way seemed like an apology, and I have nothing to apologise for. People must be allowed to grow . . . to change.'

'This isn't change, it's mutation!' I shrug off his hand. 'How could you do it?'

'To myself or to you? It's a crucial distinction. Until yesterday, my past belonged to someone else. I gave myself a new identity, like a police informer or a refugee. Then I saw you, and I was suddenly a boy again. You carry the memory of my youth on your face.'

'And what about my memories? Do they count for nothing? You were the most beautiful man I've ever seen.'

'What is it that's hurting you: that I'm a woman or that I'm middle-aged?' The question takes me by surprise, obliging me to examine my own motives as well as his. I ask him upstairs. We switch into social mode. He – that is, she – tells me that it is the first time that she has visited England for seven years. 'It was so odd to see all those people and have none of them recognise me; I felt like the Invisible Man.' I look at her quizzically; she shakes her head. 'That was a literary allusion, not a Freudian slip.'

I allow the small talk to sustain me until we have time to return to the main issue, which we do over lunch.

'You're not doing justice to this excellent crab, Leo.'

'I still feel a bit bruised. You must tell me if it's none of my business, but it would help me so much to have some idea of why you did it.'

'I'm happy to try, although it's not the easiest thing to remember. It's as if it happened in a previous lifetime.'

'You sound like one of those people we used to laugh at who claim to have been Bonnie Prince Charlie or Cleopatra.'

'It's not all that different. The man I was may not be buried but he is dead. I told you I'd changed; you said that I'd mutated.'

'Spur-of-the moment words, I'm sorry.'

'Most words are. In fact, I feel that this has always been me . . . the face I see in the mirror now, not the one in the school cricket team or the freshers' photograph. I hated being the boy that I was. People were constantly telling me that I'd grow up to be like my father, which was the very last thing that I wanted. And yet I felt that I had no choice; physically, I was becoming more like him every day. It got worse as I reached puberty. At school, we used to call our penises our weapons. Which, in my father's case, seemed all too true. From my earliest childhood, I watched him drink and lash out at my mother and then drink to drown the guilt. And then Lydia was born, like a permanent reproach. And he drank and lashed out even more. And, when he couldn't lash out any longer, he drowned himself in the lake. But, although I lived in fear and hatred of him, I felt no affection for my mother. I learnt young that a shared pain may breed pity but never love.'

'But, when I met you, you seemed so sure of yourself. I was struggling to accept my sexuality, while you seemed to embrace yours with open arms.'

'Sex was as much of an escape for me as alcohol for my

father. I felt that, if I had enough of it, I could shake off the demons. I was never gay.'

'What?'

'No, hear me out. I was sexual, yes, and I knew that I could never be heterosexual (I could never do to any woman what my father had done to my mother). So, in the Manichaean universe I'd created, I assumed that I must be gay. I had so many men, but they never moved me. I was always playing a part.'

'Always?' I feel the poles of my past melting.

'Not you, Leo, and I say that to be truthful not kind. You were the only one I felt not just close to but part of. With you, it might have been different . . . no, what's the good of a might-have-been with a man who never was? But, if I remember – and I do . . . and I have – we were neither of us all that comfortable with the sex.'

'I never knew where I was with you. On the one hand, you were always urging me to sleep with you, and, on the other, you kept so aloof. You never let me touch you, at least not your penis. You wouldn't even touch it yourself. You just rubbed yourself up and down on the sheet like a fish flapping its fins on the shore.'

'Thanks,' he . . . she laughs. 'I'm sorry if I confused you: I confused myself. While I found the idea of intimacy appealing, the mechanics filled me with disgust. Sex became a compromise . . . as though I were wearing my skin back to front.'

'I struggled so hard to understand. I thought that there must be something wrong with me. I used to discuss it with Candida. She began by saying that you were hung up about your body and blamed it on Treflis. Later, she took a broader view and attributed it to religion, claiming that Catholic guilt was about sex just as Protestant guilt was about money.'

'Candida managed to find explanations for everything. And some of them were true. And some of them simply sounded as if they were. At first, I believed that she would prove to be the answer to all my problems. If I live to be a hundred, nothing will ever give me as much status as being the boyfriend of the only girl in the school. I use the word "boyfriend" loosely; I always did. But she didn't object. On the contrary, she was more than happy to provide the screen behind which I could pursue my genuine – what I supposed were my genuine – interests. That was when I came to realise that the idea of me was far more attractive to her than the fact.'

'She wanted to marry you more than anything in the world.'

'Yes. She told me not long after we met that it was her destiny. I laughed . . . out of embarrassment, not mockery. No one our age used words like that. A couple of the religious boys talked about vocations, and there was someone in my house who wanted to be a vet. But we were at school; we'd barely started life. What terrified her most was the prospect of losing me. I'm convinced that she only applied to Cambridge because she knew it was a family – my family – tradition. She even went on the course in Venice to be with me. Somehow she managed to persuade her father to pay; which was amazing because it was way beyond his means (your old friend Duncan Treflis subsidised me). She implied that she had some sort of hold over him . . . I think she may have discovered him with a mistress.'

'Really?' I picture an old man locked in a lonely cell, with nothing to mark the days but misery and masturbation.

'It was then that she started making herself indispensable to me in other ways. It was as if, since we couldn't make love ourselves, the next best thing was to find me the men who would.'

'I remember her introducing us in San Marco.'

'Oh, I'd seen you before that. I was the one who noticed you looking round the church. I can still hear myself saying "I want some of that" and her saying "nothing easier", and so it proved.'

'You mean that her picking me up was all a sham?'

'What difference does it make now? It was more than twenty years ago.'

'It makes a difference to me! My mother was right; I wish I'd never gone to Venice.'

'I shouldn't have mentioned it.'

'No, I'm glad. How you must both have laughed at me: hooked like an old boot from a lake.'

'Don't rewrite the past, Leo. Memory's confusing

425

enough without the complication of hindsight. We both loved you ... far more than we did each other. Candida was determined that you and I should stay together, so much so that she contrived to do the very thing that pushed us apart.'

'What do you mean?'

'She told my mother that we were spending the night in the Temple of Love.'

'What?'

'I'd told her of the plans afoot for me and Jenny, and she was scared. She had no objections to sharing me with a man – quite the reverse – but she knew that it wouldn't be the same with a woman. She felt that she could head off the challenge by showing my mother how, given my true nature, I would be better off with someone who understood it, who'd give me children but make no other demands, who'd be the perfect daughter-in-law if only a token wife. I think she genuinely believed that my mother would fall on her neck and thank her. She had a very strange view of family life.'

I try to assimilate his revelation. Is this the betrayal that you so often intimated? Is this what Lady Standish meant when she said that you were no friend of mine? The naked nineteen-year-old abandoned in the wood condemns you, but his thirty-nine-year-old counterpart is more circumspect.

'The irony is that, a year or so later, my mother would have welcomed you with open arms. I became the despair of my family. Duncan offered me the job at the bank, which I refused as easily as I did the wife who went with it (I couldn't believe how old Jenny looked yesterday). My Uncle Lennox said that, if I were determined to do something artistic, he'd buy me into a Duke Street gallery. They even tried the traditional last resort of a black-sheep farm in Australia. Can you imagine? What they wouldn't understand was that they had no hold on me. I was a free agent.'

'I also worried. Whenever we met, I felt that you'd lost direction.'

'On the contrary, I'd found my true destination. And, although she never realised it, it was Candida who set me off on the road. I used to visit her when she was working in

426

Soho. I began to hang out with some of the other women, in particular the transsexuals. I owe them more than I can say. They took charge of me. They encouraged me to put on a dress, and – don't laugh – but it changed my life. Before that, I'd had to make it a game . . . dressing up at Crierley or play-acting at school, but this was like stepping into a second skin. It was as if all my other clothes had been pinching and cramping and chafing, and, at last, I'd discovered the perfect fit.'

'Is that when you had the operation . . . you have had the operation?'

'Oh yes. What you see is the genuine article . . . or at least a serviceable copy.' Her face suddenly looks strained. 'Though, for years, my identity was the product of the make-up bag and the wardrobe; I didn't have the op till much later. Not that I didn't have the chance. Whatever the horror stories of waiting for it on the NHS, for two thousand quid, anyone could go to a private clinic. You didn't have to have so much as a half an hour's counselling. You paid your money and you were admitted the next day. It fills me with rage when I remember all the kids who did it without thinking . . . because it was a new experience or "it seemed like a good idea at the time" or they were making good money as male whores so they'd be bound to make more as the real thing.' Her eyes water. 'It was appallingly easy. It doesn't take long to make two thousand quid in Soho if you're young and compliant.'

'Surely all that's changed with AIDS?'

'The only thing that's changed is the risk. . . . I saw the after-effects of those operations. The haemorrhages. The colostomies. The infections. The vaginas that slipped out as easily as handkerchieves that they'd stuffed up their knickers. And worse, I saw what it did to their heads. Not just the drugs that they took for the pain . . . the drugs that became their only pleasure, but the sense of mutilation . . . for which they had no one to blame but themselves. Their motives led me to suspect my own; their experiences made me afraid.'

'Did you know no ordinary . . .' I cannot finish the sentence; the phrase sounds like a contradiction in terms.

'Ordinary transsexuals? No. I'm sure there are some. I expect they're all playing bridge and sipping tea with Jan

Morris. The problem – at least for so many of us – is that we go through so much to assert our real selves . . . to enter the space in which we are ordinary, only to find that we're forced to live as freaks.'

'You could be anything. When I saw you in the church, I thought: a banker? a writer? a diplomat's wife?'

'I'm flattered, but you're way off the mark . . . why are you looking at my feet? Is there something on my shoes?'

'Oh it's nothing,' I blush. 'I was remembering a remark of Candida's.' I fix my gaze across the table. 'You were saying?'

'Just that I decided to take a course of female hormones. None of the threatened side-effects occurred, which I was sure must be an omen. I felt so happy. My whole being – not only my body – seemed to be glowing. Are you happy, Leo?'

'How can I answer . . . most of my adult life has been spent evolving strategies to avoid the question; until last year when they all broke down.'

'And since then?'

'I'm working on it. I've come to see that the key to happiness is not to accept anyone's definition but your own.'

'That sounds like a fair start. . . . As for me, I was just, as you might say, becoming who I am, when I met Candida for the first time in years. The joke is that it was she who recognised me. She presumed I was dressed in drag. I didn't intend to disabuse her; I was determined that mine shouldn't be a before-and-after story, but a begin-again-halfway-through. Then she invited me here for a meal (we sat in this room . . . if I remember rightly, you were abroad filming). We drank a couple of bottles of wine, smoked some dope, and I told her that I'd begun to take the pills. I think she was quite moved . . . and not a little frightened. I let her feel the bumps on my chest, which were barely perceptible, except to me. And, before we knew it, we were in bed.'

'What?'

'She went into this big routine about it being my last chance to sleep with a woman . . . little did either of us know. And it may have been because I was high, but, although the thought seemed absurd, it was funny ha-ha

428

rather than funny yuck-yuck. I found the whole process extremely pleasant and surprisingly passionate . . . I suppose because I felt free to make love to her as a person and not as a man. The next morning we went our separate ways. I gave her my new number, more for old time's sake than anything else; then, six weeks later, she rang it and told me that she was pregnant.'

'What?'

'At first I thought that it was another of her stupid jokes.'

'How long ago would this have been?'

'About eight and a half years.' Connections explode in my brain. 'I told her she'd have to do better than that. How could it be me? She'd felt my breasts.'

'You're Pagan's father?'

'I can't be anyone's father, I said, and, least of all, a child of yours. The list of candidates must be extensive. But she insisted – preposterously – that I was the only man she'd slept with in over a year.'

'No, that was true. She had an abortion, followed by a miscarriage, which turned her totally off sex.'

'She was prepared to take any test, but the only one I wanted was my doctor's. Then, when I explained to him that I'd come – more than once – although I couldn't believe it'd had any potency, he told me that fertile sperm could be stored in the testicles for up to a month.'

'You're Pagan's father?'

'As soon as I saw Candida, I knew that she'd told me the truth. "I know what it is to be no one," she said; "the last thing I would ever lie about is my child's father." I told her that she'd have to get rid of it; I can still see the way that she moved to shield herself, as though I were trying to tear the child from her womb. What choice did I have? How could I be a father? I wanted to be a father even less than a man. But she made it clear that she'd make no demands on me; she never even wanted to see me again. I'd played my part; you were to do the rest.'

'You mean that she'd planned it?'

'That's what she said. She described it as having the best of both worlds.'

'You're Pagan's father!' The shock suddenly shifts to apprehension. 'If you've come to take her away, I warn you, I'll fight. I'll spend the rest of my life in the courts.'

'Leo please, relax! I haven't the least intention . . . or the least interest. When I had the operation, they cut away more than my genitals. As my body became softer, my heart became hard. I couldn't see anyone from the past, for fear of being hurt; I wouldn't allow my new self to be undermined by images of the old. Do you think it's been easy knowing that I could never contact my mother or my sister? I didn't even dare to speak to Lydia yesterday. So I've done away with the desire. I'm strong and self-contained.' She speaks gruffly, as though to herself. 'I run a guest-house.' I think of Gleneagles. 'Like your mother. Although we cater to a rather different clientele. In Copenhagen.'

'What on earth are you doing there?'

'Running a guest-house.' She smiles.

'No, but . . .'

'No, I know. It's a long story . . . several chapters of accidents and a happy ending. My partner, Brita's, Danish.'

'Are you trying to tell me something?'

'Yes. Ironic, isn't it, that I should go through all that to find myself with a woman? No.' Her expression hardens. 'That's not true. I didn't do it to make my sexuality respectable but to make it natural. And my nature changed along with my body. This is what's natural to me now; this is who I am.'

'I see.'

'Your turn now: do you have anyone?' Her interest is purely formal.

'I have memories.' She smiles. 'Otherwise, no. I thought that I'd found someone this summer. Benedict Menzies: a man as beautiful as his name. We were right for each other in so many ways, but not quite enough. In spite of all my assurances, he felt that he'd always come a poor second to Pagan. But, at least, he proved that the potential still exists.'

'Did you doubt it?'

'Every day of my life.'

We sit in silence. I burst out laughing. 'Please don't be offended; I'm not laughing at you. I've remembered something truly ironic. Candida's parents tried to have Pagan taken away from me . . . that's a whole other story. The Judge declared that all our problems would be solved if only he knew the identity of her father. The God-given, my-father's-bigger-than-your-father, wait-until-your-fath-er-gets-home order would be re-established. They've spent so much time trying to prove that fatherhood is located between the legs, when her actual father, her natural father, is a woman . . . and not just a woman but a lesbian.'

'You're right. They find it hard enough to stomach a lesbian mother; but a father . . . they'd probably shoot me on sight for crimes against my sex. Which is another reason why no one must ever be told.'

She gives me a gentle wink but a genuine warning. And, for a moment, the craziest logic fills my head. I loved him then; I could love her now. Man and woman could be father and mother. We would be the perfect family for Pagan. But I dismiss this parody of parenthood; I am determined to be a father on my own terms.

The meal . . . the ordeal is over. The clock strikes three, and I tell Robin (the 'y' will take practice) that, in a quarter of an hour, I must set out to fetch Pagan. I ask if she would like to come with me or wait for us here.

'I don't think I could bear either. Not the emotions,' she adds quickly, 'but the complications.' She then picks up one of the photographs that she has studiously ignored since her arrival.

'Is this recent?'

'This summer.'

'You see; I feel nothing.' Her knuckles are white. 'She looks a lot like Candida.'

'I think she looks like you. Would you like to keep it?'

'No. It's kind of you, but no. My flat's full . . . my life's full. I'd have nowhere to put it. Now I should go.'

'Will I see you again?'

'I fly first thing tomorrow morning. This evening, I have to attend to some legal matters apropos of Crierley.'

'You've been in touch with your solicitor?'

'He's always had my address. How else do you think I knew of my mother's death? It turns out that, for the past six months, he's been trying to persuade her to rent the house to an American yoghurt company that wants to use it for its English base. I've instructed him to offer it to them for sale.'

'You used to say that Crierley was in your blood.'

431

'Too much has been spilt since then. I'll never go back, nor will Lydia. Do you want it for Pagan?'

'She didn't have much joy on her last visit.'

'Then we'll get rid of it. New blood . . . or, at any rate, yoghurt.' She laughs and moves into the hall. 'Goodbye, Leo. This may sound presumptuous, but I can't think of anyone I'd rather have caring for my child.'

'I can't think of anyone's child I'd rather care for. It's mad; I've spent so long speculating on the identity of Pagan's father. I've virtually combed the London phone book. Yours is the one name I've never considered.'

'I suppose I'm what you might call ex-directory.'

'I finally see why Candida never told me. Knowing my feelings for you, she must have thought that, one day, I'd be bound to tell Pagan. She remembered the trauma of finding her own father and was desperate to prevent there being more of the same. Nevertheless, I wish that she could have trusted me.'

'But she did. You were the one man she ever did trust, with herself and her daughter. I was a father for a few stoned minutes; you've been a father for life.' She moves to the door. 'You're going to be late.'

'You will keep in touch?'

'Believe me, Leo, it would be a mistake. We have nothing in common but memories. And, if we talked for much longer, I'm afraid we'd find that we didn't even have those.'

She opens the door. I clasp her shoulders and try to hold him in my arms again. But the hug is hollow; the intimacy is tenuous; I feel nothing but her shape.

She leaves and I doubt that I will ever see her again, but the shock of her visit makes me all the more determined to pursue my adoption plans and to have my position protected by law. I discuss my decision with Max, who is surprisingly supportive, while insisting that, to fulfil the regulations, I must wait until she has been back with me for at least a year. So, on May 12th, he writes to both the Court and the local authority. Six weeks later, I am allocated a social worker: Charlotte Walsh, an effusive woman in her mid-forties, who tells me that she special- ises in adoption since she finds general social work too harrowing . . . 'I think of it as the difference between being a midwife and a nurse.'

That may be why she finds it so difficult dealing with a single father. She subjects me to a series of interviews. She wants to be sure that Pagan will have adequate female role models and that my friends are not all gay. She is anxious to learn how I will cope when she starts seeing boyfriends and how she copes when I introduce my boyfriends to her. Puberty features high on her list of pitfalls. I insist that my gender need not put me at a disadvantage . . . after all, your mother left you to face your first period totally unprepared. She seems impressed by my conviction and eager to demonstrate that she is no prude. Indeed, my admission that, since the split with Benedict, I have neither current nor prospective attachments elicits a look of such sympathy that I suspect that she may be about to supply me with a list of eligible men.

By her third visit, I sense that she is on my side. She apologises if the questions seem tortuous, explaining that, unlike some of her colleagues, she believes in preparing the fullest possible report, since, as well as constituting the basis of my application, it will provide Pagan with the only official record of her natural parents. Assuring her that I am happy to do anything to assist the process, I talk extensively about you and Robin, faltering only over the details of his death. I hate having to lie to someone so sincere; nevertheless, Pagan's peace of mind outweighs my scruples. As Robyn herself said, the man she was is dead. Far better that he should be laid to rest at Crierley than return from beyond the grave.

The report is submitted, the recommendations accepted, and, on the 3rd of August, the local authority approves the adoption. The rest is up to the Court. The hearing is fixed for the 28th September at 9.45 a.m., so Max takes the train to Brighton the evening before. Pagan's aversion to the town means that we decide to drive down on the day. My mother rings as we are setting off to tell me that she is praying for us, while David sends a card to say that he and Griffin have been chanting. Now all we need is for Imogen to prepare a Druidical sacrifice, and we will have propitiated all the gods.

'You promised that we'd never ever come to Brighton

again,' Pagan reminds me, as we pass the Handcross Happy Eater.

'It's worth it, isn't it? Just this once. If we can be together from now on.'

'I hate going to court.'

'It's not my favourite occupation either. But remember, this time, we're here for us.'

The courtroom is the same as for the first residence hearing. It seems larger now that there are only five of us: Max, the adoption officer, the guardian ad litem, myself and Pagan, who looks so pretty in her new coat, with her hair cut short and her face puzzled by the import of Mrs Walsh's 'dressed up to the nines'.

'Does that mean that, last year, I was dressed to the eights and, the year before, I was dressed to the sevens?'

'No, it's always to the nines.'

'Even when I'm ten?'

'Even when you're forty like me.'

'I'll never be forty.'

'No?'

'I'll stay twenty-nine for ever, like I heard Aunt Imogen telling Uncle William.'

'Well, at least you'll be consistent.'

'Then he said that she'd put all his plans at sixes and sevens –'

Any further revelations are forestalled by the arrival of the clerk, who summons us to the Judge's room. On entering, I see, to my horror, that it is occupied by Judge Flower. The coincidence is as chilling as a black cat, the Queen of Spades and a single magpie crossing my path, my palm and the sky all at once. I am steeling myself for defeat, when, to my amazement, he stands and shakes my hand as though all our previous encounters had been at the Athenaeum and smiles at Pagan as though she were his favourite niece. He leads her to the chair next to his and asks for her views on the adoption, which she gives as unequivocally as ever.

'I'm very pleased to have the chance to meet you at last, young lady. What with one thing and another, I've heard quite a lot about you over the past three years. No child of your age – or, indeed, of any age – should have to go through what you have. But I'm delighted to see that you've been able to put it behind you so successfully. You've been very fortunate in having had Leo to fight for you . . . more fortunate than you may realise, certainly more fortunate than I realised. I was at fault, and I trust that he'll forgive me.' I nod furiously; I am prepared to forgive anything for such a change of heart. 'I've read all the papers, the Schedule Two and the Guardian's report, and I'm struck by the force of their recommendations; although I note that Pagan's grandmother expresses objections to the proposed adoption –'

'That's not fair,' Pagan blurts out. I calm her.

'I say only that I note it, as I am obliged to do. I see also that there is no parent from whom I have to obtain consent. Since I am satisfied that the adoption is in Pagan's best interests, I am happy to make the Order as asked. May I be the first to congratulate you both?'

I hold Pagan tight to my chest. Her heart thumps against mine. I dare not allow myself to cry, in case the Judge should revoke the Order on the grounds of effeminacy. Mrs Walsh feels no such constraints. The Judge tells Pagan that an adopted child is special, since she has two days to celebrate: her birthday and her adoption day; and, as a token of the occasion, he presents her with a box of Brighton rock. He then removes his wig from a battered tin and offers her the chance to wear it. She is initially reluctant but, after some coaxing, puts it on. He lifts it out of her eyes and leads her on a judicial progress around the room, which the clerk interrupts with a reminder that he is due in court.

'Oh well. I fear that the rest of my day is unlikely to be so pleasant.' He frowns, and I catch a glimpse of the familiar Judge Flower.

'Aren't you going to give us a piece of paper?' Pagan asks.

'That'll come later, darling,' I assure her.

'But it won't be proper if it's not on paper.' Her lower lip quivers. 'I said I'd take it to school to show my friends.' The Judge ponders.

'Well, I can't give you an official document here and now, but I may be able to manage something.' He takes out a sheet of headed paper and writes in a hand that resembles my mother's: 'This is to say that Pagan Mulliner was today formally adopted by Leonard Peter Young. By order of His

435

Honour Judge Flower at the Brighton County Court.' He gives it to her. 'There, will that do?' She reads it carefully and replies very quietly.

'Thank you.'

We leave the room and return through the Court to the foyer, which is now packed with people. I stride through all the divorces, injunctions and maintenance claims, feeling nothing but my own elation . . . the black cat has vanished; a second magpie is hovering; the Queen of Spades is part of a royal flush. I look at my watch. Unlike the weeks that I have spent in courtrooms over the past few years, the hearing took a mere fifteen minutes. We stroll out into the salty September air. Max is heading straight back to London, but Pagan and I decide to spend the morning in Brighton, to which she is suddenly reconciled. She asks me to take her to the pier.

I hold her hand as we stare into the sea. 'Isn't it wonderful,' I say, 'to think that all these people, all these buildings, all this life, came from out of here?'

'From the sea?'

'Yes.'

'Like mermaids?'

'Like tadpoles. Like the tiniest tadpoles. Like tadpoles we can't even see.'

'And that made me?'

'Yes. Though it didn't happen overnight. It's taken over three hundred million years to create something as perfect as you.'

'I wish I could live for three hundred million years.'

'If you're perfect enough, perhaps you will.'

We walk along the pier and into the amusement arcade, where some of the faces on display point to a less rosy theory of evolution. We do not linger and return past the poster shop, palmist and handwriting analyst. Pagan pauses by a booth that offers 'surnames traced by computer'.

'Can I have a go?' she asks. 'I didn't last time.'

'If you like,' I say and listen to her give the name Mulliner.

'No, that's wrong,' I alert the assistant. 'Your name isn't Mulliner any more; it's Young.'

'Of course.' She claps her hands. 'Like yours.'

'That's right.'

'Does it mean I'm going to have new name-tapes?'

'I suppose it does.'

'Will Juliet sew them on for me?'

'If you ask her politely.'

'And will I have to rewrite my name in all my books at school?'

'Whatever you want. It's up to you.'

'And does it mean I'm allowed to call you Daddy?'

'Would you like to?' I savour the new-found legitimacy.

'More than anything in the world . . . in the galaxy . . . in the universe.'

'Then you shall.'